Words of Wisdo

Stuart Michaels

1

Acknowledgements:-

Bryan Moffat for designing the book cover

Ed, Roger, Diane and Michaela reading the novel before publishing

Words of Wisdom is the sequel to Saw You Leaving

Chapter one

Friday 22 August 2003

Stepping outside onto my patio, drinking a mug of coffee on a less than convivial late summer morning, I have escaped the chaos and mayhem of my own home. I am slowly coming to terms with the dramatic changes in my life style. A month on from both Jack and Sam becoming a permanent part of my life we have settled in well. Being the responsible member of a family isn't totally new to me and although coping with the situation, I still need my moments of peace and quiet to think.

Out of plaster Jack has embarked on the long road to recovery. Painful physiotherapy sessions once a week at the local hospital, Jack also has three supervised hydrotherapy sessions a week at home in the indoor swimming pool. Lucy is always there with him, watching and as every session begins, young Sam complains over why he isn't allowed to join in. Despite the fact he's told every time he asks that it's too risky for him to be in the pool at the same time, he still persists.

Richard's mother, Jan, spends four hours every weekday at the house cleaning and tidying up after us. Since the end of July I have become very protective over what I now have as a family and Jan being here regularly, does allow me the freedom to come and go during that time.

I still have business commitments and make frequent visits to the office for meetings and updates. Unofficially retired I am having trouble letting go, but I'm no longer out in the field earning my keep. As the major shareholder there is no reason to be an active member, but I'm the first to admit I miss the excitement of the daily challenge. I also understand I now have other priorities which are key to my future plans, and theirs.

Clock watching I'm waiting for Jan to arrive at 10am. As far as I'm aware I have a meeting with business partner Graham at 10-30 and I want to be fully up to speed before I sit down and discuss the matter with him. Unfortunately, Jan has a habit of being late and although pre-warned, she will always have a plausible excuse for her late arrival. Her timing isn't critical because Jack and Lucy are both sixteen and legally competent to look after Sam, but I'm against placing that responsibility on their shoulders so soon.

Lighting a cigarette I step out onto the lawn and look across the bay in the direction of the village. This morning the murky weather obscures the village from view. It's the August bank holiday weekend and the prospects for local businesses making this final summer's weekend a good one, doesn't bode well. Thirty years ago I would have worried about how that would affect Jan's shop business. Turning to return to the covered area of the patio I see Jan standing, looking at me from inside the house. Glancing at my phone I note she's ten minutes early. Do I say anything or not? Putting out my cigarette I step inside and close the door.

'You should give that up.' Jan offers.

'What? The smoking, or believing you're early?'

'I see. Going to be one of those mornings is it?' Jan adds, as I follow her into the kitchen. 'Where are you off too this morning?'

'Meeting at the office with Graham, I think. Shouldn't be too long.'

Watching Jan place her shoulder bag on the work surface, I note she has brought the post in with her and its protruding out of her mobile workshop. Removing the letters from her bag I see one from the NHS. Seeing what I have seen Jan offers her thoughts.

'More appointments?' Not responding I open the letter in front of her and proceed to read the contents. 'More overtime for me I hope,' she adds.
'Sorry to disappoint you. There's nothing here for you to get excited about. It's about Sam. They say that following his recent tests and scan at the hospital they have finally given him the all clear.'

'Well that is good news.'

'Of course it is. Sam has waited a long time for this news, but he'll want to start playing football again and you know what that means? Even more driving for me.'

'You'd best go and tell him the good news. I know how much that will mean to him. He loves his football.'

'I'm aware of that, but I'm not sure he's ready.'

4

'Nick, love, I think it's you who's not ready. You cannot go on smothering him, wrapping him up in cotton wool. He wants to play football and up until now he's been very patient. Let him move on and progress, and encourage him to fulfil his dream.'

'You're right. I will.' Placing the letter back inside the envelope I set it down on the work surface and open the rest of my mail.

'Is Lucy here?' Jan asks, setting about the pile of dishes in the sink waiting to be loaded into the dishwasher.

'As if you need to ask.'

'She might as well move in.'

'No!'

'That was a very positive answer.'

'There is a huge amount to discuss before that ever happens. Lucy will always be welcome here, but until their futures are clearly defined I won't have her moving in here. They're only sixteen, how do any of us know their relationship will last?'

'I take your point, Nick, love but that baby will need a good home and looking after.'

'Lucy has parents and they have a say in the matter. We need to work together, not against each other. I'm not going to make decisions or suggestions without their consent.'

'Do you know if they are all here for lunch?' Jan continues, changing the subject.

'I suggest you ask them.'

Finding a letter from my solicitor I hesitate to open it. I have a feeling I know what this is about. Reluctantly I became involved in my old friend Tom's business affairs at the farm. After giving him twenty thousand to pay off his existing debts, to reduce his overheads I then insisted he sold off the milking herd to hold off the banks foreclosure, but the farm is still in trouble.

I knew at the time I was throwing good money away when I took the decision to help but I couldn't stand by and let my friend be thrown out of his

5

home onto the streets. It is wasted capital and I'm not prepared to repeat the potentially damaging financial gamble. Technically I have become a creditor, which my solicitor advised me to do, I know I'm unlikely to recover even a small part of that debt at any time in the future. Hence the letter because legally I'm kept up to date with the current proceedings. It's a catch twenty-two situation, because helping my friend has already cost me but to sit back and do nothing, will cost me far more…friendship.

Separated by a river, my own, managed farm is next door to Tom's and his land could possibly be an asset to me in the future. Valued I understand at over two hundred thousand pound, buying Tom's place is a bridge to far for me at the moment.

My letter from the solicitor doesn't make good reading. What I dislike the most, because I have been lied to, Tom's debts are far greater than he declared to me. That really does annoy me immensely. Reading between the lines it appears, Tom hasn't paid the mortgage on his other guest house property for some considerable time. Even if Tom could achieve the estimated sale values of both properties my return would be minimal, to the likes of three pence in the pound. Quick mental maths equates to a loss of nineteen thousand four hundred pound. I need to deal with this, one way or the other, very quickly.

'I'll talk to Sam later, once I've had this damn meeting. You can show him the letter when he appears, if you wish.'

'I think you should go and give him the good news now. It will be far better coming from you. Once you get back from your meeting you can sit down with him and find out what he wants to do…and that part is important because he must be the one making the decision.'

Letter in my hand I leave Jan to crack on and head off to the swimming pool. Reaching the door it opens in front of me. Holding the door open, Lucy helps Jack back in to the main house after his hydrotherapy session. Following Jack, Sam pushes past the hydro therapist and walks towards me.

'Don't run off, Sam, I want to talk to you once I've spoken to the hydro therapist.'

'What have I done wrong?'

6

'Nothing. I have some news for you that's all. Go and get yourself a drink and I'll be with you in a minute. How's Jack doing?' I ask the hydro therapist.

'Jack's doing well but I think three sessions a week are too much for him at the moment. I recommend we cut the sessions in the pool down to twice a week. Tuesday and Friday morning's at ten. We can up it again in a month or so when he's a little stronger.'

'As long as Jack's happy with that, I don't see a problem.'

'I'm fine with it, dad. I am finding it very tiring.'

Seeing the hydro therapist out I return to a very crowded kitchen to collect my car keys. Placing the letter down in front of Sam, who's sat at the breakfast bar stuffing his face, I pick up my keys and wait for him to respond.

'Does this mean I can play football again?'

'It does, Sam. When I get home we'll sit down and talk about where you want to play.'

'Anywhere!' Sam says excitedly.

'I understand your enthusiasm to start playing again, but the level locally may not be what you need.'

'I don't care. I just want to play.'

'Second chance, Sam, remember what I promised you.'

'How long will you be?'

'Not long. Is there anything anybody wants or needs while I'm out?'

'I need my prescription taken into the chemists,' Jack offers.

'Where is it?'

'You put it in the draw over there,' he adds, pointing across the kitchen.

I've got my dates wrong, our meeting is on Tuesday. I really must buy myself a diary. With time on my hands I've driven over to Tom's place. This needs to be sorted. Standing beside my car I light a cigarette and have a smoke for a few moments before entering the lion's den. With no livestock there's an eerie silence surrounding me. When I first came here over thirty years ago this farm and guesthouse was a thriving, profit making business. Where has it all gone wrong I ask myself? My simple thought says I cannot be everywhere at the same time looking over everyone's shoulders.

I've always classed Tom's place as my second home, a place I have many fond memories of, but I know sentiment cannot rule the head. I'm not sure how much more I can do for Tom, or in fact, whether I should. Quietly absorbing the silence I finish my cigarette and head for the side door. Knocking first I let myself in. Inside the kitchen mother stands watching the kettle boil. Tom is fast asleep in his chair by the range cooker. Not an altogether uncommon scene but the lack of urgency immediately hits home. Closing the inner door I notice that the kitchen table is littered with paperwork.

'He's a broken man, Nick love,' mother says softly, gesturing at her sleeping husband. 'There is no way out of this and to cap it all, we had this in the post this morning.' Crossing the room to the table mother picks up a letter and offers it to me. 'Read it for yourself, we have nothing to hide from you.' Mother picks up on my reluctance to read their private mail and continues. 'Because we haven't been paying our repayment plan arranged with the bank they have given us twenty-one days to pay fifty-seven thousand pound or they will take us to court. We need to file for bankruptcy. Nick, love, we haven't got fifty-seven pound to our names, let alone the thousands they want.'

Turning my back to the window I read the letter in the relative light from outside. Mother is not wrong, they do only have twenty-one days to sort their finances out. Even if they did have that sort of cash at their disposal, with no income, what happens after that? Both in their eighties, starting a new life to support themselves is, in all honesty, beyond them.

'What happened to the money from the sale of the cattle?'

'That was a direct bank transfer. That's the way they like doing it. We didn't see a penny of that money.'

Folding up the letter I place in down on the table. Staying silent for the few moments to clear my thoughts, I rest back against the windowsill. 'Have you any idea of what your total debt is?'

'Does that matter now? Other than our state pensions we have no other income, so how on earth can we pay what we owe, and the next round of bills when they arrive. It's hopeless, Nick, love.'

'You have assets. Why haven't you realised those?'

'Because boy,' Tom chips in. The old bastard is awake. 'The other guesthouse isn't a viable business anymore. Outdated, it needs thousands spending on the place to bring it into line with current legislation and market needs. Money we don't have and with this no longer being a working farm to support that, we're going nowhere quickly. Look around you, all we have here is an old run down house in a couple of hundred acres. That, boy, with no business model, devalues both properties by a big margin.'

'Then sell one to save the other.'

'Don't you think we've tried? We were offered seventy-five thousand for the other guesthouse which I must add, is less than half of what it's worth, without spending huge sums of money doing it up.'

'Sorry, Tom, but I don't see the logic behind that. Why didn't you accept the offer on the guesthouse, because it's a drain on resources and from where I'm standing, you wouldn't be going through all this shit now if you had?'

'Seventy-five thousand wasn't enough to pay off the mortgage on the property.'

'Stubborn that's his problem,' mother adds. 'I told him we should cut our losses but would he listen…no!'

'Think what you like. We paid one hundred and twenty-five thousand for that place years ago and it's not going for anything less. Anyway, boy, this isn't your problem.'

'I wish I thought differently and you both know why I don't. Tom, as things stand you'll lose everything you've ever worked for without a penny in return. It's time you started thinking about your families future, not what you once had. Take this from someone who learnt a lot from you and put your foolish pride behind you, get off your backside and at least try to salvage what you can before it is too late.'

9

'It is too late.'

'Well, if that's your defeatist attitude then nobody can help you…not even me.'

Standing down by the railway line which borders Tom's land, I find myself leaning against the livestock crossing gate, staring at a white painted house on the side of a hill across the other side. It's where Linda grew up with her two brother's.

Over thirty years ago I had stood in this very same spot wondering what I was going to do next after I discovered the love of my life already had a steady boyfriend. I was devastated back then, like I am now.

Tom and mother helped and supported me during that difficult time and have done ever since. They are good friends. My own conscience won't let me walk away from their situation, simply because of my loyalty to them, particularly Tom as he gave Jan and I five hundred pound to restock her post office and general store business after her tragedy. Had Tom not been so generous back then, God knows where I'd be now or what I would be doing. When I take the time to think about what I do have today, and that has become very special to me, Tom's influence and guidance when I was a spotty teenager gave me the courage and opportunity to move my life forward and become successful.

Walking back to the house, crossing the empty yard, I head for the milking shed. At first I have no idea why I'm doing this, but opening the small door I step inside to a desolate place, which was once the hub of Tom's life…his office. Lying on the floor, to my left, are several bales of hay. It was in that very place all those years ago that Tom and I had sat down for a smoke and he told me the truth about Linda. What he said that day shattered my life and after a sleepless night worrying about my future I walked away, never expecting to return.

Twenty-four hours later, hungry and cold, I found myself in the village where quite by accident, or luck, I met Jan and Richard. At the time I knew I should have gone home to face the music but I had made a huge mistake and felt I couldn't, because I wasn't ready too. A few days later, after talking to my parents and Linda, Tom turned up at Jan's run down shop. What Tom did that day changed both Jan's and my life and I haven't looked back since.

Feeling very emotional I step outside and light a cigarette. Staring across the yard at the old farmhouse I can see how right Tom is. The place desperately needs renovating. Somehow, I need to resolve this situation…and quickly.

Late home I half expect to find an invoice from Jan for her extra hours on the kitchen work surface. Only joking, but I'm sure at some point we will have a conversation on the topic. Introducing myself to the waifs and strays I find Sam up in his room on the play station. Asking him to join me downstairs for a chat about his football, he tells me he'll be down when he's completed the level he's on. Technology hey! So much for the keen footballer?

Watching Jan put her coat on and leave I settle down in front of the television to watch the lunchtime local news. My concentration level is low because I cannot release my thoughts and worries about Tom's situation. Even the breaking news about a large kitchen fire at a hostel near Manorbier, close to Fenby, doesn't spark my enthusiasm. Perhaps I don't care anymore.

I'm woken when I hear Sam say he's given up while throwing himself onto the settee. Looking up at the wall mounted clock I've lost half an hour.

'You wanted to talk to me about football.'

'Actually, Sam, I thought you wanted to talk to me about playing football.'

'I do!'

'So talk to me and tell me what you want.'

'I don't know any teams here.'

'What level would you like to play? For instance, a lot of the local clubs may not be up to the standard you want. Having said that, there are some good clubs around but do you want to be pushed to gain a regular place at this stage. What I don't wish to do is become involved and push you too hard to soon, and I don't want to become that pushy parent trying to relive their own frustrated footballing careers. Sam, you must decide where you would like to play. I do know a few people at Haverfordwest County football club who might be in a position to help. Their first team play at a reasonable level, so if you are interested, I'll talk to them and see what they think. What age group are you?'

11

'Under 11's.'

'Would you like me to inquire on your behalf? And, Sam, I will also talk to them about your situation so they understand, so don't worry. It may take a few days, so please be patient with me.'

'Is it far from here?'

'No, not too far. About twenty to thirty minutes in the car, but that can depend on the time of year. It's up to you. Your choice, Sam, and if you'd prefer to play with some of your friends at school, then its fine with me. Perhaps you'd like to ask them? The one problem with this area is the weather. During the winter months, a lot of games are called off because of water logged pitches which unfortunately, on council run facilities affects many of the lower leagues more than most. The season can be a little disjointed at times. As I said, it's up to you.'

Leaving Sam to think over his choices I decide to go and make a coffee. As I stand my front door bell rings. I've forgotten to close the gate because someone has reached my front door and not used the intercom on the edge of my property. Walking through the house I also remember that I've forgotten to contact Sam's head teacher about him going back this coming term. She was informed of the prospect when then social services reversed their decision, but I've not followed that up to confirm his place. I most certainly do need a diary.

Opening my front door DI Wallace invites himself in. As he steps inside I ask him if it's business or pleasure. Both he informs me, sort of he adds. Returning to the lounge I can see that Sam looks a little worried when he sees DI Wallace.

'When does Sam go back to school?' Wallace asks.

'Why?'

'We'd like to talk to him officially about Barry Mullins. We're making progress with our inquiries but there are some grey areas which we hope Sam could help us with. The reason I'd like to know when Sam goes back to school is because we'd like to do this before he does. I need to arrange this as quickly as possible because I want to include Mary Robinson in the interview and I'd need to sort some dates out with her.'

12

'And me of course.' I hasten to add.

'Most certainly.'

'Why Mary?' Sam asks.

'I'm not going to tell you it's a legal requirement for Mary to be present, but you may say something in front of her that may trigger her memory, and if she can confirm your statement, Sam, it may help us in getting a conviction.'

'Barry Mullins is dead,' I suggest.

'He is, but someone like Barry Mullins doesn't work alone and we know for certain he wasn't working alone when the jewellers was held up.'

'Are you alright with this, Sam?' I ask, sitting down next to him.

'Not really.'

'Why?'

'Because it scares me.'

'Why does it scare you?'

'I don't want anyone else coming after me.'

'That's the whole point of this, Sam,' DI Wallace adds. 'If we act quickly that won't happen. And, Sam, that sentence alone suggests you do know something. I need your help to conclude this, can you do that for me?'

'I suppose so.'

'I'll find out when Sam goes back to school and let you know. What else did you want to talk to me about?'

'Can we talk privately?'

'No,' I reply and smile at Sam.

'Please yourself, but can we at least do it over a cup of coffee?'

'Go and put the kettle on for me, Sam?' Without hesitation he's on his feet and doing as I asked, leaving DI Wallace little choice.

13

'So what is it you want to talk to me about?'

Looking at Sam first, DI Wallace responds. 'I need your help on a little matter. Its work related and not about you or Sam.'

'Not interested, Reg. You know that.'

'It's not field work, more office related.'

'My answer is still no, whatever you say it might be. I have my own responsibilities to worry about and bending over backwards to help you isn't one of them. I don't have the time or the inclination, however important you want to make it sound.'

'I just want you to check through your records for some information. That's all it is.'

'Not as easy as it sounds. We're currently in the process of transferring and updating all our paper records onto the new computer system. It's a bit of a mess at the moment and I for one are not going to spend hours looking through both for information for you. And, Reg, I am not going to pay any of my staff to do that for me. I hope I'm making myself clear?'

'We're looking for a lady by the name of Hanna Green. She skipped bail and didn't turn up in court for sentencing on two counts of arson. You may have already heard this but there was a large fire in a hostel near Manorbier earlier today, which has her trade mark written all over it. I simply want to know if you have any information on her, things like known associates and previous addresses that could help us. She's a dangerous piece of work, capable of just about anything and we must find her quickly.'

'You don't give up easily, do you?'

'Nick. Luckily for everyone concerned no one was hurt this time because the staff reacted very quickly to the situation, but that hasn't worried her in the past. Can you help me with this?'

'Do you take sugar, Reg?' Sam asks, rather too confidently for my liking. Staring at him, Sam looks at me and decides to continue. 'I could go crabbing while you're in the office.'

'Sam!'

'Why not?'

'Because, that's why not.'

'Jan told me you didn't trust me. She said you want to keep me wrapped up in cotton wool. Please can I go crabbing on my own?'

'Go and find the tide time table if you can in your untidy room and, Sam, so you know, for a very good reason, I am finding it difficult.'

Chapter two

Saturday 23rd August

Sam caught a few small crabs yesterday while I was sifting through the office files looking for the information Reg had asked for. To be honest it was a token effort just to get him off my back. Fishing within the harbour, where I could keep an eye on him, Sam seemed quite content with his efforts and the trust I had bestowed upon him. I'm not going to say Sam is precious to me but from this day on, I will always be cautious where he's concerned. Through my own stupidity I could so easily have ended his life. I wasn't given a second chance with Simon and that will always haunt me.

I didn't find anything relevant for Reg to work with and passed that information on as soon as I could. It wasn't conclusive due to our upgrading and the completion of that exercise is futuristic. Something may turn up in the future but that's of little help to Reg.

Outside the front of my house I'm loading the car. After a monotonous day yesterday I asked the guys last night if they'd like a day out. Their response was unanimous, but going shopping in Swansea wasn't what I had in mind. I know Sam has his eye on a new play station game and bless him, Jack does need some new clothes. This day out is going to cost me.

Finishing my pre-shopping trip preparations' I become aware of a lady standing watching me from the other side of the electric gates. I've never seen her before but she's quite obviously lost, or unsure of her bearings.

'Excuse me sir. Are you Mr Thompson?' She finally inquires.

'I am. How can I help you?'

'My name is Sue White. I'm the manager of an exchange program in South Wales for foreign students. Have you a few minutes to spare me? I'd like to talk to you if it's convenient.'

'Sure.' I respond. 'I'll open the gate.' Turning to go back into the house I see Jack operating the small control panel in the hallway which controls the gate. He's obviously overheard our conversation.

'This is very kind of you,' the Sue adds.

'How can I be of assistance to you?'

'I'm having a bad morning. I have a group of twelve students arriving on Wednesday morning and last night the hostel they were due to stay in had a big fire. I'm looking for alternatives,' Sue adds as we reach the front door. Jack hasn't moved by the time we go to step inside the house and Sam has joined him.

'Oh my God! Jack and Sam. What good looking son's you have.'

'You have me at a disadvantage here Sue. How come you know so much about me?'

'Using the word desperate sounds so wrong but events have overtaken me slightly, and I am. I have twelve Austrian students arriving on Wednesday, staying here for a month on a work place related scheme and I need to find places for them to stay. Making numerous phone calls this morning I was put in touch with Mary Robinson, and she gave me your name.'

OK guys,' I say to both Sam and Jack. 'Ten minutes. Thankfully it may save me a few quid.'

'Don't hold your breath, Dad.' Jack adds.

'Would you like me to put the kettle on?' Sam asks. 'And I think we have some chocolate digestives in the cupboard.'

'Sam! Where has this chat suddenly come from?'

'You!' He replies before heading off.

We were late leaving home for our shopping trip. Sue spent more than half an hour explaining the situation while she drank coffee and ate chocolate digestives. In the end I agreed in principle to her request. I have a spare room with en-suite facilities, although Jack thinks its Lucy's room, so it isn't a problem.

I was informed by Sue that the students are on a part work related and educational trip. She assured me that it's well organised, where the students will be picked up and dropped off every day. All timed she claimed to within half an hour of their stated itinerary times. The one down side is, they have a number of recreational days within their month stay. Days off to do what they like. If this goes ahead, which is in doubt unless Sue finds enough places, I hope whoever turns up here can speak reasonably good English, because I don't have a second language.

If Sue finds enough places for her students I will sit down with Jack and Sam before the student arrives and read them the riot act. However they feel about the situation, they will be civil and polite at all times. Jack will be fine, I know, but Sam's recent verbal out-bursts are a concern to me. More recently he has become a little too confident for his own good. There could be a lot of reasons for the change in his behaviour and that may be as simple as being told he can play football again. I don't know.

I've given up. I couldn't keep up with the guys and their excitable shopping trip, racing between clothing and shoe outlets. Even Jack in his wheelchair, which he hates, wasn't going to miss out. Exhausted and quite frankly, very bored, I told them to stick together, decide what they want and when they're ready, I'll flash the credit card in front of the shop assistants. Mistake? Probably, but my patience has worn rather thin.

Grabbing another cup of coffee I make my way back to the castle and perch myself on the nearest available bench seat to relax. That's where I told them they'd find me. Strange affair Swansea castle. With very little left of the old Norman castle there isn't much to see. In the middle of the city centre the castle is surrounded by shops and modern buildings. Still, I'm not the one to blame for passing the planning applications, so why should I care? Odd though, because it took months for the planning permission on my extension to be passed and many changes were forced upon me, because the original plans weren't in keeping with the local area.

Stretching out and lighting a cigarette I notice Jack coming down the slight gradient towards me in his wheelchair. On his own, this should be interesting to see if he manages to stop in time. Fortunately Jack is in control. Oh ye of little faith. Coming to the most perfect stop right in front of me, Jack whacks on the break, hauls himself out of his chariot and plonks himself down on the bench next to me.

'We're ready.' He informs me. 'Lucy and Sam are waiting in HMV for us.'

'Oh I see, so I've got to push you back up the hill to the shops?'

'I'll walk if it makes the old man happy.'

18

'Thanks for that. I'll manage, you'll see.'

'So why complain?'

'I wasn't complaining, merely stating facts. I assume from what you've just said that Sam has found the game he wants? Let me guess, it's a football game?'

'FIFA 2003.'

'Tell me something, Jack, before I struggle up the hill. Have you noticed a change in Sam recently?'

'Why do you ask?'

'Well, he seems to be a lot more vocal than usual.'

'Goby, you mean.'

'I was being polite. Yes, goby if you like.'

'Do you want me to be honest with you?'

'Most certainly.'

'It's you.'

'That's what he said. How come it's my fault?'

'You talk a lot and sometimes, like just now, you say the most ridiculous things. He's obviously watched you and latched onto the things you say. It could be attention seeking.'

'So you think I do it because I'm attention seeking?'

'I didn't say that. Sam probably thinks it's funny and copies you. Give him some space, Dad. Like me he's finding his feet in new surroundings and perhaps for the first time in his life, mine too for that matter, we feel free to express our feelings in the open. We should go. Save your breath, because you'll need it by the time we reach the HMV shop.'

I got my own way in the end. Two hours of shopping in Swansea and paying the bills I took the guys to The Worm's Head Hotel in Rhossili for a late lunch. I love it there and as they tucked in to a wonderful lunch, chatting and

19

laughing I mentally worked out how much today has roughly cost me. A lot as it happens, but seeing their smiling faces is more than enough in return.

Promises were made about returning one day soon, when Jack is fit enough to climb, well not exactly climb, more a tough hike up onto Rhossili down. I'm going to hold them to that because the view from up there is stunning.

Before we left Rhosilli I phoned Tom. There's something I want him to do for me. I've invited us for supper, but I did ask if there was anything they needed for the extra people at their table. Mother's list was longer than my own shopping list. I think that will see them through the next few days…at least.

When the guys realised what I had done Sam complained bitterly…over and over again. Using the excuse that he'd been there and didn't want to go again, he kept on saying he wanted to go home. In a way that was rather sweet, because he sees my home as his. FIFA 2003 will have to wait, but I'll guarantee he'll be up all night on the play station and I won't see him tomorrow. Timers, that's what I need to spoil his late night entertainment, especially on school nights. Jack was right, Sam is finding his feet and he's showing me he has a strong character. I like that.

Unloading the groceries from inside the car, I had to squeeze them inside as the boot was full, Lucy and I bring the last few bags inside the house. Seeing Sam standing next to mother stirring a large pot of stew, which she's loading as fast as she can unpack the shopping, I notice he has his football game in his left hand. If he's trying to explain the merits of the game to her, he really is wasting his time and effort. Mother could describe the entire anatomy of a cow to him in great detail, but I bet she doesn't know what shape a football is.

'Found a few special bottles left, boy.' Tom says to me. Seeing him pouring two small glasses of homebrew beer I immediately say no because I'm driving. 'You'll do as you're told,' he adds. 'Stay the night like you've always done. You can all stay.'

Seeing Sam's jaw drop and his squinting, beady eyes staring at me, I quickly get the message. Sam has the look about him that says, 'I've had a lovely day, don't spoil it.'

'This isn't the last supper, Tom.'

'Then why are you here?'

'Because I want to talk to you.'

'Another bloody bollocking I shouldn't wonder.'

'If you see it that way then its fine, but if you want my help then you will listen.'

Picking up his tobacco pouch even I can see it's empty. When he realises and tells me he'd meant to go out and get some, I hold out one of my cigarettes for him to smoke. Taking it from me he insists he never smokes tailor made brands.

'Not in front of the kids,' he mumbles before shuffling across the room to the yard door.

Outside we light up and take a couple of drags in silence. Something we've always done. 'So?'

'So firstly, Tom, you never swore in front of your own kids, so please don't do it in front of mine.'

'Yours, boy?'

'Yes mine and don't you ever forget that. More importantly to you, I'm going to give you seven days to work out and tell me what your total debt is.'

'Why? What is the point?'

'The point is, and you will do as I ask, if we know the exact figure Graham and I will look at ways to help you. But so you know, if we can find a solution, things around here will change dramatically.'

'You're no better than they are. You're going to throw me out, aren't you?'

'That depends on how much you want to stay and how much you value your families future. Work with me, Tom, and things might work for you. Now, I'll have one small beer with you while we eat and I promise you, we'll finish off the bottles another time.' Holding out my hand, Tom grasps it tightly and we shake hands in agreement. 'Seven days, Tom.'

Sunday 24th August

With nothing to do I've sat myself down in the office at home and decided to undertake a little research on my personal computer for DI Wallace. In his wisdom Reg had emailed me a photograph of Hanna Green and printing the picture off, I'm trawling through my own files for a match. My files are not as comprehensive as the office, but I've always logged and stored my own case files.

Jack went off about an hour ago to spend the day with Lucy and her parents. Something I need to encourage him to do more often because they are an important part of his life too. Certainly at the moment, anyway.

At nearly eleven-thirty I haven't seen Sam yet. I'm sure the lazy tyke is still asleep after staying up half the night playing on his play station. It's a safe bet really, because the first thing he does when he wakes is ask what's for breakfast. I have checked on him a couple of times to pacify my worries and hearing him snoring his head off the last time I poked my head around his door, has settled my concerns.

I haven't found anything on my computer of interest to Reg. I didn't think I would but for some reason the name Hanna Green means something to me. If she's a local girl or perhaps I've seen her picture in one of the local newspapers, then that knowledge would make sense. In my line of business though unsolved mysteries need answers and its not until every avenue is explored and exhausted, that one can put it down and say "maybe I was wrong". Nagging doubt is a terrible thing, trust me I know and those thoughts can play awful mind games.

There's a chance I may know Hanna Green under a different name but the more research I do, the less convinced I've become. We work privately for clients and although I don't remember all of them, I have no recollection of her in that scenario. A private thought I have makes me sit back in my chair. Contemplating its validity I notice my office door slowly open. A very weary looking Sam appears. About time too I think. Before he has the chance to say anything I tell him to shower and dress because we're going out. I've made up my mind, I'm going to try something that hasn't worked in a long time.

The rear of the hostel has extensive fire damage. We cannot get too close because the emergency services have cordoned off the area. To achieve what I hoped might happen I need to be up close and personal. Without DI Wallace here and Sam in tow, I'm not likely to get any closer than I am. Trying everything I know, I wander around the perimeter with a very quiet Sam scuffing his shoes walking behind me. I'm concentrating, hoping one of my bizarre visions manifests itself. Something isn't hanging well with me over this fire and the only thing for sure at the moment is, I've been in this very same situation before. Coming to terms with my failure, I also know this exercise was just another avenue to explore. It hasn't worked and I should have known that. In the past, trying to force the issue has always failed. Telling Sam I'm done I stride off towards my car. I have more work to do on this before I satisfy my curiosity. Reaching the car I ask Sam if there's anything he'd like to do. Expecting him to say he wants to go home his response is a little surprising, but very current.

'Can we go shopping? I need some new football boots, and some new trainers.'

'Why didn't you ask me when we were in Swansea yesterday?'

'I didn't want too in front of Jack and Lucy.'

'Why ever not?'

'Because Jack's your favourite.'

'Wow, Sam! That's not true and you know it. I'm trying my best to treat you both equally. As far as I'm concerned, you're both my sons'. Is that why you've been vocal latterly, because you think you're being left out?'

'I don't know.'

'Sam, it will be pleasure to buy you some new football boots...and some new trainers. Just don't make it too expensive.' The look he gives me tells its own story. 'Only kidding. You can have what you want and just maybe, in thirty years from now, you'll take them out of a cupboard, dust them off and remember the day your dad brought you your first pair of professional boots.'

Sometimes things happen for a reason. Driving home Sam asked if we could take the scenic route along the coast. Passing through Threeman Bridge the road winds down into Hooper's Hill Cove, where my attention is immediately drawn to the number of emergency services vehicles parked close the beach. It's obvious something serious has happened. Curious, I turn into the car park and pull up as close as I can to the police exclusion tape. Turning off the engine I tell Sam to stay where he is and exit my car.

Making my way along the cordoned off area, in the distance I can see DI Wallace talking to a group of fellow police officers, three of which, by wearing white coveralls, are forensic officers. Conscious of the fact that I shouldn't leave Sam on his own for long, I turn to leave the very second DI Wallace spins around to face me. Calling out my name he stops me in my tracks. Walking towards me his pace is hurried. Reaching me, slightly out of breath, he opens our conversation.

'A local person walking their dog discovered a body amongst the rocks. We think its Hanna Green. Forensics are doing their initial checks. I'm told there are no obvious signs of cause of death so I've arranged a post mortem examination to be carried out once we're given the all clear to remove the body. Would you like to take a look?'

'I can't. Sam's in the car and I don't want to leave him alone for too long. By the way, I checked my own case files on my home computer and there's nothing there regarding Hanna Green. I also went over to the hostel earlier to take a look at the fire damage.'

'Why?'

'I was hoping it might trigger one of my episodes. Remember them? Nothing happened I should add, then again I didn't really expect it too. I've put it down to not getting close enough.'

'Do you want too?'

'No, not really. I had to try though because Hanna's name, for whatever reason, rings alarm bells. Will you let me know the findings of the post mortem?'

Agreeing to my request I leave Reg to his job and head back to my car. From my earlier search I know Hanna Green wasn't a client, but that doesn't rule her out from any other case I've investigated over the years. I have a little more in depth reading to do.

Sam hasn't taken his new football boots off since we arrived home. The number of times he's said thank you is uncountable. He questioned me briefly over what was going on at Hooper's Hall Cove but, so as to not worry him, I simply told him there had been an incident. He doesn't need to know all the ins and outs of my job and for the time being, he's accepted my vague response.

Still only about 5pm I can't settle. I want to sit in front of my computer, open up my case files and search in greater depth for any information I may have stored on Hanna Green. That would take me away from Sam and leaving him in isolation isn't fair. This is where I must be careful. My work has always consumed me. Knowing I need to find the answers takes over and nothing else matters. In the past no one cared and neither did I. My circumstances and responsibilities have changed and they must come first. I am seriously beginning to struggle with retiring.

'What time is Jack coming home?' Sam asks.

'I'm not sure. Why?'

'Can we go out somewhere?'

'Where would you like to go?'

'I don't mind.'

'We could go for a drink and something to eat around in the village, if you like.' On a pleasant late August evening my idea is a good one. I could phone Jan and invite her to join us. 'I'll phone Jack, see what he's up to. Why don't you go and put your new trainers on?'

Going for a stroll along the beach first we cross the promenade and grab the one vacant table outside in the front of the Temple Bar public house. Telling Sam to stay put I head inside to get us a drink.

Jan told me she had a visitor and they will both join us around 6-30pm. I'm intrigued. Jan rarely has visitors and while we spoke on the phone she seemed very vague and reluctant to tell me who her visitor is. I find it odd because our circle of friends, if I exclude her WI friends, is very similar.

Back outside in the pub garden sat with Sam at the table I see Jan walking along the seafront towards us. I stare at her so-called visitor. At first I don't recognise her friend, but the penny soon drops. Linda. It's at least twenty-five years since I've seen her and at least the same amount of time since she's stepped foot in the village. My cynical mind wonders why she's here and what she wants. As they approach I try to decide on whether I should remain seated or stand when they reach us. In front of Sam I should conduct myself in the correct manner. He is blissfully unaware of the situation Jan is placing me in. I'm far from impressed. Jan could have told me over the phone who her visitor is. When Sam stands he leaves me with little choice.

Standing, after a very reserved hello, Linda and I shake hands. That's as close as she gets. After such a long period of time I have no feelings at all for her. As Sam offers them a seat I inquire what they'd like to drink and beat a hasty retreat inside to the bar. Boring as it is to me, I'd rather be at home watching Sam playing his FIFA 2003 football game.

Returning with their drinks, Sam has sat himself down on Jan's lap. Taking up the opportunity, placing their drinks on the table in front of them, I sit down where Sam has been sat. As far away from Linda as possible.

'So, how are you, Nick?' Linda leads with.

'I'm very well thank you. How are you?'

'Not too bad, considering.'

'Good, good.' I reply, not wishing to know what she eluded too by saying…considering.

'Jan has told me all about what has happened.'

Has she now I think and when. If that is why she's here, then she has an even less chance of getting back into my life than she had before, and that was rated as zero.

'Where's Jack tonight?' Jan asks.

'Spending the day with Lucy and her parents.'

'That's a shame. I was hoping he'd be here as well so Linda could meet you all. Linda's staying with me for a few days so perhaps we can organise a little get together another day before she goes home.'

'Maybe,' I respond. 'Busy life, Jan, as you know. We'll see.'

'Dad bought me a new pair of football boots today,' Sam pipes up. As he speaks I become aware of Linda staring at me. I feel sure she wants to question his use of the word...dad. 'They're the best boots I've ever had. And he's going to get me a trial at Haverfordwest.'

'You're a lucky boy, Sam.' Jan answers.

'I know, and so is Jack.'

'Are you hungry, Sam?' I ask, because the sooner we eat, the sooner we're out of here. Nodding at me I ask him to find us a menu. With Sam out of ear shot I'm ready to speak my mind. 'Right! I don't know what's going on here ladies, but this is not a good time for a reunion.'

'Lighten up, Nick,' Jan snaps. 'I know you've had a tough time recently but you're not the only one. Linda is going through an acrimonious divorce and she needs a little support. I invited her down to stay for a few nights so she could get away for a while. She doesn't need you snapping at her ankles.'

'I'm sorry to hear that, Linda, I truly am and Jan's probably the right person to be with right now. Fortunately for me, I don't tell her everything and there is far more going on in my life than she knows about. For her to sit there and tell me to lighten up is misguided. I apologise for saying this in front of you, but I'm dealing with my problems, which are numerous and I don't need any further complications. Sorry, but the way it is at the moment.'

'That's ok. I thought that by coming back here would help me relax. Meet old friends and relive the good old days. Perhaps I was wrong.'

'You're not wrong,' I quickly respond before Jan interrupts. 'I never did go back after coming here but I understand for some people, returning to their roots helps them appreciate what they once had.'

'Do you miss what you once had?'

'Not at all. I have more here than I've ever had. I wouldn't change a thing.'

'The man says if we want to eat. We've got half an hour,' Sam informs me. Coming to stand right beside me he continues. 'Can I have a burger and chips?'

'You can have what you like. Shall we go and order?' Making sure the ladies are fine I follow Sam inside to place our order.

'Who is that other lady?' Sam asks.

'Her name is Linda. To cut a very long story short, she was the reason I came back here many, many years ago.'

'Was she your girlfriend?'

'Sort of. You know that book I suggested you read, well it's all about me, Linda, Jan and old Tom. I can dig it out for you to read if you like. You'll understand better if you do.'

'Is she coming to live with us?'

'Honest answer, Sam…no.'

'Are you going to have a get together so she can meet Jack?'

'What do you think we should do?'

'I don't mind.'

Having ordered our food we return outside to sit with the ladies. On the way, as I've had my say and I'd bet they've been talking about me in my absence, I've decided to take a softer approach. More for Sam's sake than any other reason. Sitting down where he first sat I have no other option than to sit opposite Linda.

'Linda, Jan, you're welcome to join us for a BBQ tomorrow. Jack will be at home and if you like I'll phone the others to see what they're doing.'

'That would be nice, thank you.' Linda responds.

'Shall we say about 2 o'clock? I'll go shopping first thing in the morning.'

Monday 25th August

Up early the first thing on my mind is to clean the BBQ and check the gas cylinder. It's a little chilly this morning but the forecast is reasonable. My thoughts though suggest it may be a wise move to invest in a couple of chimaeras, just in case the met office have got it wrong. The weather in this part of the country is unpredictable at best and I'm against standing in the kitchen slaving over a hot oven. Graham's great with BBQ's and loves cooking for the masses. When the door intercom goes into overdrive I stop what I'm doing and amble through the house to the front door to find out who is in a panic at this early hour.

Opening the door I first see DI Wallace peering through the railings. Standing next to him is Sue White. I have things to do and wanted a quiet morning to get on…oh well. Pressing the button the gate slowly draws across to let them both in. Reg can make his own coffee while I talk to Sue. Reaching me Sue immediately informs me that she has placed all her students and she'd like to see the facilities I have. Giving her a quick guided tour we return to the kitchen where Reg has made himself at home. Satisfied with what I have to offer I proceed to ask Sue what the arrangements are.

'We'll be here around midday on Wednesday. My idea is to place a young lady by the name of Michaela with you. I understand she speaks good English so there shouldn't be a problem with a language barrier. If you're comfortable with the arrangements, I'll see you on Wednesday?'

After seeing her on her busy way I re-join Reg, where he immediately asks me about Sue and what is going on. Giving him a quick explanation I turn the conversation around and question him about why he's here.

'Hanna Green,' he begins. 'She didn't drown. Her lungs weren't full of liquid so she was dead before she went into the water. Someone put her there. The post mortem found large quantities of amphetamines in her system and at this point we believe the dose may have been enough to kill her.

'That's not all we've found. We were called out in the early hours of this morning to a shared house in Fenby were a body of a man in his late thirties had been discovered. Early tests show he died of an amphetamine overdose. His time of death has been recorded at a time before Hanna Green's. We think the suspicious deaths are linked but he could not have been responsible for disposing Hanna's body in the sea.'

'Did they know each other?'

'We don't know at this stage but we are continuing with our inquiries as we speak. What we have established, is he worked as a kitchen porter at the hostel, which of course raises suspicions.

'How do you feel about taking a trip over there with me this morning?'

'Sorry, Reg, I can't help you.'

'It's important.'

'I have a houseful of people coming around later for a BBQ. I must go shopping. Reg, I'm not leaving the boys on their own.'

'It won't take long and providing the building has been made safe, I'll take you into the kitchen.' Shaking my head and repeating myself, Reg continues. 'Something special going on?'

'No, but if you must know, Jan has a visitor and after being rude in front of her yesterday, I invited them and a bunch of other people around for a BBQ.'

'This female visitor, do I know her?'

'To stop you asking more personal questions, it's Linda and no, there's no ulterior motive. As far as I'm concerned the sooner she goes home to face her own problems, the happier I'll be.'

'Just be careful where she's concerned.'

'Oh I will be. Have no fear.'

'Are you sure you haven't got a few minutes to spare? I'd really like your help on this Hanna Green thing?'

'Sorry, Reg, I have far too much to do.'

Reg is a persistent man when he needs to be. After several further attempts to talk me into meeting him at the hostel I finally agreed to be there at eleven. Manobier isn't far from Fenby and I need to go there for the shopping I must do. The hardest part for me was getting the boys up and ready. The trick was, promising them they could choose their own food for the BBQ.

Slipping on a pair of wellies I'd placed in the car boot I join Reg. I've told Jack and Sam to stay near the car and not to wander off. They're not happy, but I'm sure they'll get over it.

A colleague of Reg's hands me a high Vis jacket and hard hat to wear when we're onsite and instructs me not to touch anything as forensics are not finished. I don't really want to go inside because there's nothing to be gained. If one of my episodes does manifest, I simply need to be close.

It's certainly a mess inside. Much of the stainless steel kitchen ware is blackened and twisted. The ceiling has collapsed and some of the wall tiles have fallen away because of the intense heat, which was probably fuelled by the cooking fats. The walk-in chiller is a shadow of its former self. Reg explains they think it's where the fire started and it could have been an electrical fault, but that is yet to be established. Asking him to give me a few minutes I realise that my so-called episodes depicted death and as no one actually died here, being here isn't likely to trigger anything. I decide not to pass that information onto Reg, because he'll drag me back to Hooper's Hall Cove and probably the shared house in Fenby. I'll leave his forensic team to their job.

Many years ago my dearly departed friend Beth Rhys, who was a white witch and herbalist, tried to introduce me to her friend Henry Sinclair. Henry was a druid, an arch deacon and because of my weird visions, had chosen me as successor. We never held that conversation simply because I didn't want too and declaring that I was the powerful one was a bridge to far. After his death, before his funeral, I found a rather bulky A4 sized sealed brown envelope under suspicious circumstances. It sits in my safe unopened. Beth later told me I should. She claimed at the time it was my future, my path to greatness. In a way, through the way Beth had explained the situation, my visions, my episodes made sense but I'm not a believer in the afterlife and I don't want to believe. What would happen though if I now choose to open Henry's letter? Helping Reg out isn't a good enough reason.

Stepping outside, away from the choking smell, I shake my head and apologise to Reg for my failure. Removing my hard hat and high Vis jacket, giving them back to his colleague, I let him know I'm off.

Taking the boys clothes shopping in Swansea was challenging. Going food shopping with them for the first time was definitely an experience never to be forgotten. Considering we only went food shopping for the BBQ, by the time we reached the checkout, the trolley was overflowing. Well over one hundred quid later I loaded the car by myself. Sam however did offer to take the trolley back. I will ask him for the pound back for the trolley release at some point.

In the small garden centre at the super-store I did find a couple of terracotta chimaera and along with two large bags of chopped wood, I purchased them. They weren't particularly cheap so on the surface, the food shop wasn't so extravagant. What really did annoy me was the boys telling me several times that I smelt like a bonfire. Needless to say, I showered and changed the moment we got home.

When I invited Graham and his family he immediately offered to do the BBQ. He loves cooking so naturally I accepted his offer. Jan has offered to help which means she and Linda will be here a little earlier than planned. She said she'd do the rest, like the salads and things, so that leaves me very little to do other than to be the perfect host and have a few beers. That too will be controlled and kept to a minimum because since I donated one of my kidneys to Jack, I've cut right down. Checking for the second or third time that I've got everything, my home phone rings. My first thoughts are that someone can't make it today. Who the caller is catches me a little off guard

'Nick, its Jason Foggety from the Weston Telegraph. I'm in the process of proofing tomorrows' edition and I've come across an interesting planning application I thought you should know about.'

'Can't see how a planning application would involve me, Jason.'

'This might. You know Tom Morgan from Penrice Farm, well there's a forward planning application submitted on his land to build twenty holiday chalets.'

'There's what?'

'Twenty holiday chalets and there's a few other things as well.'

'Like what?'

'A caravan and camping site and an application to turn the old farm house into a shop, bar and restaurant.'

'Who has submitted the application?'

'Summerbee holiday homes.'

'It's a little premature.'

'That's what they do. They are a very aggressive company and if they can pick up the land for a song, gain planning permission, the sell on price can double or triple. It's good business for them.'

'Thanks for letting me know. I'll look into this tomorrow.'

'Is Tom Morgan selling? I thought you'd be interested in the land as it's so close to your place.'

'Between you and me, Jason, Tom has gone bankrupt. I'm in the process of sorting out his finances to see if we can salvage anything. From what you're telling me, I'd better get a move on.'

'I'll keep in touch, Nick, let you know if I hear any more, but I suggest you put one of your guys onto this.'

'I have just the person in mind.'

I should race over to Tom's and sort this out. Tom has the reputation of being very vocal and if the local community have got to hear of his predicament, word will quickly spread. If he has spoken to anyone then I need to know who. Now isn't a great time though. My guests are due to arrive soon and if I'm not here when they do, it won't go down too well.

Going outside for a smoke my mind is focussed on Tom's situation. Sam is in the garden kicking a football around and although I'm watching him my thoughts are elsewhere. It takes me few moments to realise I've been joined by Jack.

'Are you all right? I don't like it when you're quiet. Is something the matter?'

'I'm fine, Jack, thank you. Too much going on at once, that's all.'

'Is it me and Sam?'

'Jack. You and Sam are not the problem. I've waited a long time for you, my son, to be a permanent part of my life. You probably don't really realise just how much this means to me. It is taking me time to adjust and if I'm getting things wrong, you must tell me.'

34

'You're not getting anything wrong. It's just, when you are quiet it worries me. We had a conversation like this the other day in Swansea.'

'I know we did. Jack, I have far too much going on and I shouldn't burden you with my problems, but you've been over to Tom's farm and I can imagine that you are more than aware of his situation. I had a phone call a few minutes ago from someone I know at the local paper, saying he's discovered there's a planning application submitted on Tom's land. The farm isn't on the market as yet and that bothers me. Tom is an old friend of mine and a good man. I feel it's my duty to help him but it appears someone is one step ahead of what I'm trying to do for him and that grates. I need to sort this out quickly and that may disrupt our lives. It's that important to me.'

'Let me help.'

'I'll think about that.'

'Why?'

'Because, Jack, you have a child on the way, you're not a hundred percent fit and this can be a dangerous business to be in. You of all people should understand that. I'm going to ask James to look into this while I sort out Tom's finances. I'll introduce you to him when he arrives. You'll find James a very flamboyant character but he's good at what he does. I think you'll like him. If it's ok with you, we'll take things from there but, Jack, I'd rather you didn't get involved in my line of business. That's something we need to sit down and talk about. Your future plans.'

'I'd really like to help.'

'Believe me, Jack, you already are.'

'How?'

'Because you're here. Because for the first time in my life there's a structure to what I do. Unfortunately I have unfinished business to attend to which cannot be pushed to one side. I could do without having this BBQ today but if cures a certain persons' curiosity, then its one monkey off my back.'

'What's Jan's friend like?'

'I'll leave you to gauge that.'

After disposing of the pleasantries and introductions I left Jan, with the help of Sam, to show Linda around. I used the excuse for the lack of a personal touch, saying I wanted to be free to welcome my guests. When they're done, the ladies will retire to the kitchen to prepare the salads, rolls, cheeses, all that side of a BBQ for what promises to be a feast.

I know I'm going to be caught by Linda at some point, which I'm prepared for, but there's the old adage of there's safety in numbers and the longer I can postpone the inevitable, the better.

Losing myself outside, I light the BBQ in readiness for Graham's culinary skills. When Sam appears I know the house tour is over. Sam is fascinated by the BBQ. When I pause to think why I conclude, because of his mother's lifestyle, today could be the first time he's seen one, or at least in action…sad really. Having a BBQ in these modern times is something most of us take for granted. Asking him not to touch he asks me about his football. One way or the other, let's say I had forgotten, I haven't been in touch with Haverfordwest FC. Turning the heat down on the BBQ I close the lid and ask him to follow me. Sitting Sam down in my office chair I find the number and pick up the receiver to make the call.

'Sam, if I can speak to the right person are you ok about talking to him? You know more about your football than I do and it will be a lot easier.'

'I don't mind,' he responds, lazing back in my leather chair.

Speaking to the club secretary first, a man I know, I'm given the youth team managers mobile number and proceed to phone him. A man called Matt Wilson soon answers.

'Hello, Mr Wilson. My name is Nick Thompson. I'm told you might be able to help me. I have a young man by the name of Sam Cornish living with me and he's keen to get back into playing football.'

'Mr Thompson, it's a pleasure to speak to you. I've read all about what's happen in the papers. How can I help?'

'Well, it would be better coming from Sam. He can tell you more about where he's played and what position.'

'That's fine. How old is Sam?'

'Ten. I'll pass the phone to him.'

'Please do.' He responds as Sam sits forward in the chair. Passing him the phone I listen carefully to Sam's story. I'm impressed. He explains himself well in an articulate manner. He does mention the fact he was due to go for a trial with Bristol Rovers but skirts around why he didn't. I will take care of that issue when the time comes. Looking up at me Sam takes the phone away from his ear.

'Can you take me training on Thursday at 7pm?' He asks.

'Of course. Where do we need to go?'

'Dad says,' he continues, speaking into the phone. 'Where does he need to take me?' Listening for a few moments he looks at me again. 'Can we be at the ground by 6-30?' I nod my head. 'Dad says yes. Thank you, Mr Wilson. I'll see you on Thursday.'

'Well done, Sam. You handled that very well.'

Leaving the office I go to lock-up. Before closing the door I pause for a moment staring at the safe. Henry's letter is in there and as each hour passes, the temptation to open it increases. My will power is strong enough at the moment to say…don't. What stops me is the unknown. The contents of Henry's letter may contain things I don't wish to know about and may give me one more issue to deal with. That could be one too many.

I have a problem now. Tomorrow I have a meeting with Graham and Jack has a hydrotherapy session at home in the morning which means Jan will need to be here earlier and the likelihood is, she will bring Linda with her. I don't want her thinking its fine with me, her being here on what could be a regular basis. Brad was right when he said some weeks ago I complicate my life. I do, I know that, but in trying to lessen the burden by retiring, life around me is spiralling out of control.

I must speak with Tom tomorrow and while thinking about his predicament, I should also speak to my accountant. My thoughts at this time are to look at ways of borrowing the money to buy Tom's farm against the business of New Barn Farm, as part of an expansion program. It is a gamble but Tom has some good pasture land, which would allow a greater flexibility for stock grazing. I'm not going to discuss my thoughts with Tom until I know more about the planning application.

Chapter Three

Tuesday 26th August

Behind the farmhouse Tom's land rises steeply away. In contrast, the land falls away down towards the railway line at the front. I've always known this place as a working farm but viewing it now with a different perspective, I can see the appeal of turning this farm into a holiday camp with all the modern facilities. From the top of the hill, down the valley towards Whitland, the view is picturesque. The woodland fenced off behind me is my land. I'm not allowed to use the land for farming as there is a conservation order in place to protect various rare wildlife species and plants. We are currently in conversation with the council over creating a nature trail for educational purposes. So far the talks have been encouraging.

Sam is with me. He didn't want to stay at home with Jack, Jan and possibly Linda. On the way over we stopped off to buy him a pair of Wellington boots. He wanted a green pair like mine, but he insisted on a pair with a fur lining. I refrained from making any sort of comment. Standing in silence, with Sam at my side, I'm beginning to warm to the idea of a holiday camp on site. It does have potential and if the facilities are comprehensive, the remoteness of the area wouldn't matter. The cost of such a project could be huge. Even before a brick or slab of concrete is laid the installation of services would be crippling. For now though, the meadow land below us is an asset to New Barn and if Tom can afford to pay his own bills, he can stay put in the old farmhouse for the time being. Leaving our boots outside by the yard door we step into the warm kitchen.

'You said seven days, boy!' Tom snaps.

'I know I did. Something else has come up and I need to ask you and mother a few questions.'

'I'll make us a nice cup of tea,' mother suggests as she gets up from sitting at the table. 'I'm making good progress with the figures but I will need a bit more time.' She adds, passing me.

'Mother, it's fine as long as I have them by the end of the week.'

'What do want to talk to us about then?' Tom asks, barely moving in his chair parked in front of the range.

'Ok. You both need to think very carefully about what I'm going to ask you, and I want honest answers or any deal or solution we may come up with is off. I hope I'm making myself very clear?'

'Have either of you, or Ceri, spoken to anyone outside of these four walls about your financial situation and pending bankruptcy?'

'Why?' Mother asks.

'I just need answers for now. I'm going for a smoke to give you time to think about my question.' Stepping outside I slip into my wellies and light a cigarette. I'm soon joined by Sam...not for a smoke thank heavens. 'You're very quiet. Is there something wrong?'

'No.'

'Come on. You've been very vocal of late so your silence is noticeable. Is it your football?'

'No. I'm really looking forward to Thursday.'

'Then what is it?'

'I don't like the lady with Jan.'

'Linda. Why not?'

'Because she kept on asking me questions.'

'What sort of questions?'

'About you. She asked me how long I was staying and lots of things about my mum. I didn't like it.'

'When was this?'

'Yesterday.'

'So why didn't you say something to me? We've had lots of conversations about talking to each other and you know you can at any time. I'll talk to her when we get home. I don't want you getting upset over something I can deal with.' Putting my arm around his shoulders Sam leans into me. 'We're a team and teams win by working together.'

39

'I showed her my new football boots and she said you're spoiling me. I didn't like her for that.'

'Ok. I'll deal with Linda, so don't you go worrying yourself over what she has to say. It's none of her business in the first place. And, Sam, I'm not spoiling you. You needed a new pair of football boots and they are as important to me as they are to you. Same goes for Jack and you know that. Are you really looking forward to Thursday evening?'

'I can't wait.'

'Good. So no more keeping things to yourself. There's a saying, Sam. A problem shared is a problem halved, which basically means a person doesn't have to deal with a situation on their own. My job is to help and support both you and Jack, and I will do that to the best of my ability.'

Choosing to have another cigarette Sam and I stroll across the empty yard and rest on the gate, looking out across Tom's meadows. So many memories for me. Tom and I have done the very same thing many times over the years. Am I standing with to the next generation, who in fifty years from now will reminisce with the following generation?

Returning to the house Tom hasn't moved. Pointing at our mugs of well brewed tea mother invites us to sit down. Joining her at the table she speaks first.

'The only person I've spoken to about our problem is my younger brother, David. He has his own farm in the valleys. I spoke to him hoping he could help but even he's struggling at the moment. I've not told anyone else.'

'Nodding my head I look across the room at Tom. Eyes closed I know he's not asleep. 'Well, Tom?'

'I told a few of the old boys in the pub a few weeks ago. Said we were struggling and thinking of selling up.'

'Names, Tom. Names.'

'Why?'

'Because there's something going on behind your back and I want to know who is behind this. It's an aggressive action which could affect others.' Seeing a note pad and pen on the table in front of mother I pick them up and make my way across the room to where Tom is sat. 'Names, Tom, please. All

40

of them, however insignificant you may think this is and if you know their addresses, write them down too. They could save me a lot of time.'

Taking the pad and pen from me Tom begins complaining about the arthritis in his fingers even before he starts writing. He's really frustrating me with his negative attitude, so I walk away and leave him to his moaning. Seeing mother re-boiling the kettle I join her. Apparently Sam told her his mug of tea was cold.

'Tom's lost his fighting spirit,' mother whispers. 'Please don't be too hard on him. He needs help, not shouting at.'

'What do you think I'm trying to do? But to help him and you, I need help first.'

'I'll talk to him, Nick, love. Can you tell me what this is about?'

Looking over my shoulder at Tom, who is attempting to write something down, I respond to mother's request. 'Let's give Tom a little more time.'

'Can I help? Sam asks. Looking at him first I look at mother who shrugs her shoulders. Why not she says. We both watch as Sam joins Tom, crouching down beside him. Looking at what he's writing Sam asks him a question. 'Is that Welsh writing?'

'It is. Can't spell very well though. Do you speak Welsh?'

'No, but you could teach me.'

'I'd like that young, Sam. Here,' Tom adds, offering him the pad and pen. 'I'll tell you what to write.'

Taking the note pad and pen from Tom, Sam sits himself down on the floor right in front of him. 'We can spell it wrong together.'

'That we can young, Sam.'

'He's a good kid,' mother whispers in my ear. 'You're doing a good job for him.'

'I'm going outside for another smoke while I take in what I've just witnessed.'

Not bothering with my Wellingtons I step outside in my socks and stand on the cold concrete. I've just witnessed something quite incredible. I think there's a side to Sam we're yet to see the best of. He's had a blip where Linda is concerned, then who hasn't, but yesterday he spoke to youth team coach Matt Wilson very confidently and he's now talking to Tom as if they've known each other for years. The latter is not something easily done. Although Tom has been good to me over the years, it takes someone special to break down his barriers. What Sam is doing, as I stand outside putting another nail in my coffin, could work in my favour. If Tom opens up and talks to him, as he did with me all those years ago, the end product could prove beneficial to us all. Pre-occupied with my own thoughts I don't hear the yard door open and see Sam come to a stand beside me. Waving the note pad in front of my eyes he speaks.

'Tom says he can't think of anyone else.'

'Thank you, Sam.' Taking the pad from him I cast my eyes over the names.

'Is it what you wanted?'

'I don't know what to say to you. It's perfect. Thank you for helping me out. Tom's a difficult man to deal with at the best of times and when he's on the defensive, he can be very stubborn.'

'I wanted to help you. Like you said to me, a problem shared is a problem halved.'

Holding out my hand, Sam takes hold and we shake hands. 'Let neither of us forget that.'

Thanking Tom for his cooperation I lean back against the old and worn work surface and quickly run through in my own mind how I should handle this next stage. I don't want to be too heavy with them and make it sound final, but I need answers to move forward.

'What I've discovered isn't something that has happened recently, so I'd like you both to cast your minds back and try to remember anything or anyone acting suspiciously in or around the farm. We could be talking up to, let's say, three months since.'

'We've had a lot of people knocking on our door more recently.' Mother informs me. 'I don't remember all of them.'

'Fair comment. Has there been anyone asking you about the land? Perhaps you've seen someone taking photographs?'

'I did have some fella ask me if he could go down into the bottom field and take photographs of trains. Wasn't doing any harm so I said yes.' Tom tells me.

'When was that?'

'Ages ago.'

'Did you know him?'

'Never seen him before, or since. Found it strange that he was up on the hill when I went out later to help with the milking. Takes all sorts.'

'Any idea why he was up on the hill?'

'I wasn't about to walk up there in my condition to ask him.'

'Do you remember what sort of camera he had?'

'All I remember is it had a long zoom lens attached. Nothing else.'

'What about his dress code?'

'Smart. Not typical of a train spotter.'

'Can you expand on that?' As I finish my sentence I become aware of Sam staring at me. He appears to be studying me.

'Good pair of walking boots. Jeans and denim jacket over a polo neck jumper. A rich kid by the looks of him.'

'Kid. What sort of age would you say?'

'Late teens or early twenties.'

'And you didn't know him?'

'No.'

'Thank you, Tom. So if I now tell you that I have discovered that a planning application has been submitted on your land to build twenty holiday chalets, camping and caravan site, what would you say?'

43

'Not happening, I say.' Tom snaps.

'So neither of you have sat down with someone to look over the plans, or been offered money up front for a quick sale?'

'Certainly not!' Mother snaps back.

'Good. Had to ask, because someone is well onto your problem. This is what I want you to do. As soon as I can arrange an appointment with my solicitor, I'd like you to give me the power of attorney. If you're not sure what I mean by that, it will give me control of your financial affairs and no deals or transactions can take place without my consent. I may have to put up a bond or become a guarantor to hold off your bankruptcy, but I'm prepared to do that. If you're both in agreement, I'll set this up ASAP and I want you to understand that, from that point, it becomes my problem. Any mail for instance regarding the farm or your debts, go through me and my solicitor. What do you say to my proposal, or would you like time to think it over?'

'We don't need time to think about it, Nick, love.' Mother says softly as she walks over to me and throws her arms around me. 'Just tell us when and where.'

I'm feeling sorry for Sam. When we left the farm I called in at my solicitors in Haverfordwest and set the wheels in motion for the power of attorney. Sam says he's fine but I'm sure he's bored of being dragged around the countryside. I pacified him a little by buying him a triple scoop ice cream which was melting quicker than he could eat it. Calling in at the office before finally going home, I'm sure, didn't go down that well. Fortunately, his crabbing gear was in the boot of the car and after buying him some bait, he seemed quite content.

Finding James in his office I tell him I haven't got long and he's to be brief. He doesn't know this, but I want to spend some time with Sam watching him fish.

'Jason Foggety wasn't wrong,' he tells me. 'A girl friend of mine works for the council and she confirmed the planning application does in fact apply to Tom Morgan's farm. After a little persuasion she showed me the drawings.

'They're quite comprehensive. The artists impression makes it look the bees' knees. They were submitted by Summerbee holiday homes. There is no name connecting them to the plan other than the companies, but the architect

44

was Guy Hamilton, an independent freelance surveyor and architect. He's not responding to my calls but I'm in the process of finding another way in.'

'Could he be a silent partner in Summerbee holiday homes?'

'I don't know that…yet.'

Handing James the piece of paper Sam had given me I explain. 'This maybe something or nothing. Between them Tom and Sam made a list of people Tom told about his problems. Sam's handwriting is good but Tom's interpretation of surname spellings is something to behold. Keep it. Check the names on the list against anything you come up with. There's also the mystery of a train spotter Tom allowed onto to his land to take photographs. A young guy by all accounts who Tom claims was well dressed. Tom wasn't sure when this was. He just said, ages ago. At the moment my money is on him. Look into the possibility of him working for Guy Hamilton.'

I spent an hour or so watching Sam fish. Our chat was easy, everyday stuff. What pleased me the most was how he spoke to some of the other kids fishing, many of whom were local. He's settling in well. He was reluctant to go home and I understood. Once again, I reassured him that I would deal with Linda if she is up at the house. He in turn reminded me that the exchange student is arriving at lunchtime tomorrow. I hadn't forgotten but with everything else going on, I had put it to the back of my mind. I did leave Jan a reminder to blitz the room and I hope she's taken care of carrying out my instruction.

Seeing Linda sunning herself out on the raised decking makes my blood boil. I need to calm down before I confront her. The last thing I want is for Jack and Sam to see me angry, and I am angered by what I see.

Dumping my stuff in the kitchen a hot and sweaty Jan, huffing and puffing, joins me. In one hand is her cleaning gear and in the other, a portable vacuum cleaner.

'That spare room was a mess,' she grumbles.

'Don't blame me, you're the cleaner. Anyway, Jan, why is Linda here?'

'She asked if it was alright to come over with me and I didn't see a problem,' she informs me, dumping her stuff of the floor.

'It's not on. I know she's got personal problems to sort out, but not at my expense. She upset Sam yesterday and I'm not having it. I've bored him shitless today, dragging him around with me but he clearly didn't want to stay here. This is his home and I've worked hard to make him welcome. No one is going to spoil that. When I've calmed down, she and I are going to have words. She might be your friend and I'm sorry to say this to you, but she's not welcome here.'

'What did she do?'

'It's more what she said. Linda never has had the capacity to keep her thoughts to herself and this time she really has over stepped the mark.'

'I've finished, so if you want to check the spare room I'll take her home.'

'I'll go and do that. Where's Jack?'

'He and Lucy went into Fenby. I think they said they were meeting some old school friends.'

'Right. I'll grab Sam, gave Jack a call and disappear. Don't disturb Linda until we've gone.'

Chapter Four

The boys were up early this morning. They haven't said as much but I think they are excited over our guest arriving today. I sat down with both of them last night and spoke about their behaviour and manners while she's staying in our house. They have both promised me they will be perfect gentlemen.

Sam's headmistress returned my phone call and he goes back to school next Wednesday. He tells me he's looking forward to going. That means there's another shopping trip on the horizon. I've decided not to push this interview Reg wants to conduct with Sam and as he's a little preoccupied with the hostel fire and Hanna Green, he may not have the time himself. I certainly haven't and although the case bothers me, I'm trying my hardest not to get involved.

Chilling out on the raised decking while we wait for our guest to arrive I'm joined by Jan. She's a little early for a change but she appears to be alone. After exchanging good mornings she sits down opposite me.

'Linda sends her sincere apologises'. She didn't mean to upset Sam. Her own children aren't talking to her at the moment which she's finding hard to deal with. Reading between the lines, I think she's a little jealous.'

'Perhaps now you'll understand why I snapped at you both at the pub. I of all people know what she is capable of and she has proved me right. She hasn't changed and I very much doubt she ever will. In hindsight, it was a mistake inviting her to the BBQ.

'You know how hard the boys and I are working to make this work, and that includes the support we're getting from you and everyone else. There is no room for a disruptive influence and Linda has always been that in my life. I can't and won't deal with her on top of everything else.'

'I'm sorry, Nick. I will be far more vigilant where she's concerned. I went shopping on the way here this morning and I have something for Sam in the form of an apology. It's from me and if it's ok with you, I'd like him to have it?'

'It's fine, but please explain why to him.'

'What time is this young lady due?'

'Midday. I'm beginning to think saying yes to this was also a mistake. If nothing else, it too will be disruptive. Through no fault of my own, I have a busy few days ahead of me and if I'm side tracked, I may just take my finger off the pulse. We both know what happened the last time.'

'Now you've made me aware, I'll make sure nothing goes wrong.'

'Thank you.'

With Jan pottering around in the house, when I hear the front door open and close it can be only one person...Brad. Standing by the open patio doors I watch as he enters the lounge and walk over to me. Its 11-30, not good timing.

'I thought you were away?' I open with.

'Hi, Jack, Sam,' he responds, walking past them while they're watching the TV. 'Arrived home in the early hours.'

'And you couldn't wait to pay us a visit. By the look on your face this isn't a social call.'

'Can we talk in private?'

'This has got to wait. I have a guest arriving in about half an hour and it's important for me to be ready and waiting?'

'Not really. I have a number of things to discuss with you. More importantly, I need your help on a little matter.'

'Jesus! Not you as well. Seems everyone wants a piece of me at the moment. Now isn't a good time. I'll call you in the morning.'

'See that you do. I'll see myself out.'

As Brad leaves I find myself standing, staring into space, wondering what on earth he wants from me and who will be the next person knocking on my door making demands. Whatever he wants, I'm not gallivanting off around the globe and he knows that. Once he left I opened the gate to ease my guests' passage to my front door.

A few minutes after midday my front door bell rings. The boys are out of their seats straight away but I quickly insist on them staying put while I go to the door. I do ask them to switch off the TV as I pass. Opening the door the young lady is standing in front of Sue.

'My name is Michaela.' She says, holding out her hand.

'I'm Nick.' I answer, shaking her hand. 'Welcome to Saundersby. Please come in.'

'This is so good of you, Nick.' Sue adds. 'Michaela is a lovely young lady and I'm sure she'll fit in well with you guys.'

Taking Michaela's suitcase I ask them to follow me. Entering the lounge Jack is stood behind Sam with his hands resting on Sam's shoulders.

'These are my two boys. Sam is the youngest and Jack the eldest. Jan, my housekeeper, is the lady hovering in the kitchen doorway. Say hello to Michaela guys.'

Cautiously following Sam both boys meet Michaela halfway. Shaking hands with her I notice that Jack appears reserved. Sam though is full on and offers to carry her suitcase upstairs and show her around. Sue though insists she and I do the honours.

'Your room is ready and if there's anything you need, please don't hesitate to ask. Please follow me. Once we leave you to settle in I'll pop the kettle on and make us a hot drink. What do you prefer, tea or coffee?'

'I'm fine at the moment. Thank you. Perhaps later.'

Micaela stands about five foot five or six. Has long dark hair and a pretty face. She's seventeen, about a year older than Jack. Perhaps that's why he's being a little cautious. Her English seems good, which is an advantage to all of us in this household.

Watching her as we first show her the room, then around the house, I get the impression Michaela is a little taken aback by the house. I have spent a lot of money on the place over the years and until recently, I have rattled around inside very much on my own. A lot of that time I was away on business so the general wear and tear on the infrastructure has been minimal. Let's wait and see if the quality I was guaranteed holds up to the task. To be

49

fair on the boys they are playing their part, but familiarity does breed contempt.

Sam has taken Michaela out into the garden and up onto the decking. They are chatting continuously and Sam, by his animated arm movements, is giving her a visual tour. Jack is sat outside in one of the relaxing garden chairs, so I sit down with him.

'Are you alright?' I ask, because from what I've witnessed, he's been the more reserved and the quiet one since our visitor arrived.

'This is going to take a bit of getting use too.'

'In what way? Does Michaela being here make you feel uncomfortable?'

'I've told Lucy about her coming but I'm worried about what she will think. I don't want her thinking I'm getting to close or there's something going on between us.'

'Then don't give Lucy any reason to think those things. Be nice and pleasant to Michaela but be mindful of what you say. Keep her at arms-length and you'll be fine. If you have any issues talk to me, don't hide them.

'This may not be the best time to bring this up, but Sam goes back to school on Wednesday so we should discuss what you'd like to do. Your mobility is much better and if you'd like to go on to college there are certain things we need to do before it's too late.'

'I'm not bothered about going to college.'

'Ok. So the other day you suggested that you'd like to help me and I gave you my thoughts on that particular subject. Jack, you need to do something so if you feel at this time that you would like to earn some money, then I'll talk to the guys in the office. It will also give you time to think about your future. It will be desk bound job in the office.'

'I'd like that.'

'Let me see what I can do. If we say three days or three mornings a week to fit in around your hydrotherapy and physio sessions, how would that suit you?'

'That would be good. I won't let you down.'

'Jack, I already know you have a good work ethic from helping me with the boat and I know you won't. What are your typing skills like?'

'Not too bad. I'm not that fast, but I can improve.'

'It won't earn you a fortune, but it will give you some money to support Lucy. And I won't be asking you for any housekeeping money.'

When Jack goes back into the house, leaving me alone, I have time to think through our conversation. It has pleased me that he felt comfortable enough to talk openly about a potential problem. I need to check Michaela's itinerary. Tomorrow evening I'm taking Sam football training which potentially could leave Jack and Michaela alone in the house. I could take Jack with us but leaving Michaela alone in the house would be unfair on her. The alternative is to take her along as well but I have promised Sam I would watch him and talk to the coach. That in turn would leave Jack in the company of Michaela and he clearly doesn't want that to happen. In the grand scheme of things it's a minor problem, but one I should avoid for Jack's sake.

Thursday 28th August

Michaela was a little late being picked up. I sincerely hope that isn't a sign of things to come because with Sam going back to school next week, we have deadlines to meet. I phoned Brad the moment she left and we've agreed to meet at the mansion at 11pm. I'm taking the boys with me and we're picking up Lucy on the way. Sam has stayed at the house and knows the setup, but this will be a first for Jack. I made sure Brad was happy with the situation before asking the boys.

Jack's reaction when he first lays eyes on the house says it all. It's one of total disbelief. I park in front of the house so he and Lucy get the whole picture. Once out of the car they stand side by side quite speechless. Sam, in what appears to be something he likes doing and fairly good at, gives them the lowdown. Listening to him deliver his talk, his descriptive narration is virtually word perfect and very confident.

'Is this really your house?' Jack asks.

'I co-own it with Brad. We're equal partners.'

'It must be worth millions.'

'It's only worth what someone is prepared to pay for it. If we ever decide to sell up, with the land, we'd market the place at around three and a half million to perhaps realise three.'

'Can I show Jack and Lucy around?' Sam inquires.

'You can, just remember where the alarmed private areas are. And guys, remember what I've told you, you've seen the house but you can't remember where it was.'

'Why are there alarmed private areas'?' Jack responds.

'Let me just say there's more to this place than meets the eye. There are things about this place you don't need to know, and things its best you don't know. We should leave it there. Shall we go inside and wait for Brad to arrive?'

'I can't wait,' Lucy suggests.

While Sam gives Jack and Lucy the guided tour I settle myself in the large kitchen and make a coffee. I did a bit of shopping on the way over for a few basics, like milk and bread. With no one in permanent residence, perishables need replenishing on a frequent bases.

Brad doesn't keep me waiting too long. Once we've dispensed with the niceties we retire to the office adjacent to the computer room. The boys are under strict instructions not to disturb us.

'So what's this all about?' I ask, sitting down behind my desk. 'You know it's impossible for me to walk away from my commitments at this time.'

'That's one of the items we need to discuss, but on this occasion I need to talk to you about something a little more important.

'I have been over in Eire for three weeks fishing. That was the pretence anyway. What I was there for was to gather intelligence on a large drug smuggling operation. We're trying to find the source and until we're certain, that chain continues to operate. To date we know they vary their routes and our immediate concern is to stop the drugs reaching our shores. It's almost certain that some of those drug runs come ashore in Pembrokeshire, and various other destinations. All from the County Cork area. We have identified a number of fishing trawlers that don't stack up and plans to intercept them are in place.

'This is serious stuff coming ashore and I can inform you, there is a contaminated batch on our ground. That's where I need your help. I gather you already know about Hanna Green and David Griffiths. Well, we believe they were supplied amphetamines from that source and we need to find the supplier…quickly.'

'DI Wallace has already approached me. I've done a couple of bits for him but to be honest, my heart isn't in it. I've told him I'm not interested.'

'I need you to be. Whatever your feelings are where this is concerned, lives are at risk so it's important. I want to know if there is a connection between what I have information on and what Wallace is investigating.'

Sitting back in my chair I let out a huge sigh. For many reasons I don't want to become involved, but it looks like I'm not being given the chance to say no. When Brad makes demands I usually step into line. That's the way it's always worked.

'So what do you want me to do?'

'There's a theory that the fire at the hostel was started deliberately to cover someone's tracks. So far we understand, DI Wallace's forensic team haven't found anything positive to work with. I want you to look into the hostels suppliers. He's probably already doing that so I want you to keep anything you do come across to yourself. The most obvious starting point will be fish products, but just about anything or anyone could be involved.'

'I'm going to have to do this around the boys. They come first…over everything.'

'I understand that. Are you in?'

'If I must.'

'I wouldn't ask if it wasn't so important, and you do have an advantage. People will naturally assume you're working for Wallace…not the department. There's another thing. Has Jack heard from his mother?'

'I don't think so. I'm sure he'd tell me if he had. Why?'

'While I was in Cork I did a little snooping around. I found out where she is and who she's living with. Would you like her address?'

'Certainly not!'

'What about Jack?'

'That's not for me to decide and I'm not going to ask him. When he's ready to face her I'm sure he'll talk to me. I suggest you keep it to yourself and if the need arises, I'll ask you for it.'

'Ok. One final thing. The commander wants to see you. His proposal is to drive down and meet you here, or at your place if you prefer. I recommend you take up his offer. All you need to do is throw a couple of dates in my direction and I'll sort it. Got to be soon though, Nick.'

My problem with Jack and this Michaela situation has been sorted. I'm dropping him at Lucy's on the way out with Sam and a very gracious Jan has offered to wait for Michaela to arrive home and take her over to Richard's for dinner. In an unusual mood Jan offered to do it for nothing. Then I gather, she was already going to Richard's for dinner anyway and her drive virtually passes my front door. I'm grateful to her for her offer as it avoids a potential situation and frees me up to be with Sam when he goes training.

Arriving at Haverfordwest ground a few minutes early, Matt Wilson is there waiting for us. Sam is wearing his new Bluebirds football shirt, which he hasn't taken off all day. Jan bought Sam the shirt in the way of an apology for Linda's behaviour. It was a nice thought and I know they're not cheap.

Sam is hesitant getting out of the car. I can understand that and reassure him that I'm not going anywhere. He'll be fine once he starts training and I know once he does, he'll enjoy himself. By the time we both get out of the car Matt has joined us.

'Nick. It's pleasure to meet you.' Matt enthuses as we shake hands. 'And you must be Sam who I spoke to on the phone.' He adds, shaking Sam's hand. 'Welcome to Bluebirds junior football club, Sam. The training ground is a five or six minute walk from here, or a two minute car drive,'

'I'll drive.'

'Follow me. Just to let you know, my assistant Will Jones will be taking the training session so we'll have plenty of time for a chat, Nick.'

Watching Sam go off with Will Jones and join the other boys his own age is a little challenging for me, but it's what he wants and I must give him the opportunity.

'Nick, when I spoke to Sam on the phone, as you are aware, he told me all about his football. Afterwards I was tempted to do some phoning around to get a little more background knowledge on him but thought better of it. I know there's a lot going on for him personally and decided to give him a fresh chance to impress. The only thing that worries me, after everything he's physically gone through, is he fit enough to play?'

'In my car, Matt, I have a letter from the hospital giving Sam the all clear. Sam went through a number of tests and a MRI scan to confirm all was fine. You are welcome to read the letter if you wish and trust me, I wouldn't be here with him now if I hadn't had that confirmation.

'As you can imagine, Sam is a little nervous and quiet right now but I can confidently say, once he's settled in you'll have trouble stopping him talking. At home I'm learning things about him on a daily basis. Sam is a complex character but an intelligent young man not frightened to speak his mind. Under the circumstances that's a good thing and I openly encourage him to continue.

'He may come across as being over confident at times, but if that brings with it success, whether playing football or intellectually, I'm not going to pull him up. He is learning to channel his enthusiasm in the right direction, which is something he and I are working on.

'All that said, he has had a very difficult upbringing and a fresh start in life is doing him good. Sam wants to forget the past, which at the moment, because this is likely to drag on well into next year, remains a constant reminder to him. With new friends and new places to visit he can at least put the bad times behind him for a while. My job is to make sure that continues.

'For legal reasons I cannot discuss this in any form of detail with you, and neither will Sam. Some of your students may know something about Sam and if a difficult situation should arise, I won't hesitate taking him away. Where the other boys are concerned, he's just moved into the area. Your decision to judge him on merit is a good one. I haven't seen him play so like you, I'm interested to see how he gets on. I have seen him juggling and kicking the ball around in the garden and he does have a good level of ball control. Apart from that, he's a normal kid who wants to play football. In this environment he's just another young boy enjoying himself so please, don't treat him with kid gloves.'

I'm impressed. The training session only lasted an hour and from a layman's point of view, it was very professional. Starting with a series of stretching exercises, they are then split into teams to play ball related games. Team building devised I imagine. The final half an hour was spent playing football. A roll on roll off system I gather to mix and match the players. I, quite naturally, watched Sam throughout and although every parent is biased, he was head and shoulders above most of his potential team mates. When they finish, after a quick team chat, Sam races across to join me holding a piece paper in his hand.

'Matt wants me to sign on.' He declares. 'And can I play in a friendly on Sunday?'

'If that's what, Sam, wants, then let's sign you on now.'

'I really want too.'

'There's a pen in the car.' Handing him the keys I continue. 'You'll find it in the glove box.'

'Where's that?'

'In front of where you sit. Just press the button.'

As he runs off I notice Matt Wilson walking towards me. 'I guess Sam has told you I'd like him to sign on?'

'He's gone to the car to get a pen. If you can hold on I'll do it now for him. He's keen to play, Matt.'

I wait for Matt to give his reason. I am biased and could say a lot, but I want him to talk about Sam without hearing my opinion. Oddly, he waits until Sam re-joins us. Taking the pen from Sam, Matt hands me the clip board he's been carrying around.

'Can I drive home? I know the way.' Sam asks, shaking my keys in my face.

'We left your seat at home.' Finishing my sentence I look at Matt and shrug my shoulders. 'I took it out to fit your ego in.'

'And yours,' he responds.

'True, but mines the more intelligent.'

'No it's not.'

'That's for you to prove.'

'I will,' he continues, placing his arm around me. 'Are you going to sign the form?'

'Is this what you want?'

'Before you answer that, Sam,' Matt interrupts. 'I'd like to say something. Your dad told me that you have a lot to say for yourself at times and listening then to you both, I could see that for myself. It clearly works for you both and, Sam, it was working for you out on the pitch.

'You have a rare talent. While you're with us, we'll nurture that, talk about it and move forward positively. Watching you, I noticed how quickly you identified a problem and talked it through with the other players. They all appeared to listen and slowly saw the sense in what you were saying about positioning and options.

'Sam, I'd like to put you to the test, if it's alright with you and your dad. On Sunday I'd like to make you captain, but to start with it would mean playing in midfield. How do you feel about that?'

'They might not like me.'

'Sam, I'm trying to play this down to stop your ego growing. They saw and heard what I did and it was so basically simple, it was brilliant. You work hard, you're good on the ball and your vision is superb. You were talking to them as a friend, not a frustrated coach. Sam, you need to be playing to improve on what you already know you can do. You are good and you have potential. See, I've already declared my hand. If you're willing to work hard on improving your game, who knows where that could take you. That's why I'd like to test you. Are you up to the challenge?'

'What do you think, Dad?'

While Matt was talking I filled in the form and signed it. Handing the form to Sam I tell him it's his decision.

'Why me?'

'Because, Sam, when decision making is down to you, you are the one it affects the most and you must feel comfortable with what you decide...right or wrong.'

We're the first home. By the time I enter the kitchen Sam is foraging in the refrigerator. He gave Matt his signing on form and we're to be at the ground by 9-30am on Sunday. I can't help myself but sitting down I find myself watching him as he stuffs his face with sausage rolls, cocktail sausages and cheese strings.

I'm giving Sam the chance to better himself and he's meeting the challenge head on. Everywhere he goes and everything he does he can't help to impress. He had a glowing report from school at the end of last term. The social services were impressed by his determination and today Matt Wilson was singing his praises. At times it's hard to believe he's still only ten. If we can get through the next few months without a drama or major setback, I'm sure he'll go from strength to strength. He really is quite a unique character. When he's had his fill he grabs a can of coke and closes the fridge door. Turning to face me he rests by his elbows on the work surface.

'Is it all right if I go to bed and watch TV for a while?' He asks.

'Sam, its fine. Make sure you have a shower first. I do have a favour to ask you. Will you try on your school uniform to make sure it still fits? You don't need to do it tonight. Tomorrow morning will do and if it doesn't, we'll need to go shopping. Also tomorrow, after Jack's hydrotherapy I'm taking him down to the office.'

'Why?'

'Jack's going to start working for me in the office a few hours a week doing some typing. I'm not sure what the weathers going to be like tomorrow but you can go crabbing if you like. I have a few things to do myself while I'm there so we'll be a while. Is that ok with you?'

'Can I phone my friend Jamie and see what he's doing?'

'Is that the boy you were talking to the other day?'

'Yes. He likes going crabbing as well.'

'Of course, and lunch is on me.'

Standing up straight Sam looks me in the eye. 'Did I really play well today?'

'Does it bother you?'

'I know I can play better.'

'When was the last time you played a match? And don't forget, you've had major surgery recently and that can take its toll. Sam, I only played at a low level, a low standard, but I'd have you in my team anytime.'

'Thank you. I will get better, you'll see.'

Friday 29th August

We finally make the office at around 11-30. My first priority is to get Jack settled. His job is to put the information in the paper files onto the new computer system. He says he's looking forward to it but I'm sure he'll become bored very quickly. My office manager, Sue, who Jack knows well, will spend time with him, showing him the ropes.

I'm sitting with him while Sue runs through the process. A lot of the documents can be copied and pasted, apparently and that's where they lose me. I've always been a hands on person and although I have my own setup at home, it's very basic.

The pile of files Sue had placed on his desk in readiness is rather daunting and if I was in Jack's shoes, with the task being set, I think I would have handed my notice in by now. Sue's instructions are very precise and she has prepared a check list for him, one of which, is when he's finished the transfer of information he must double check all the information is correct and electronically recorded. Privately, I wish him luck. Setting up his password, one of his own choice, Sue reminds him that the information on the files is confidential.

Jack knows his way around the office so when he's ready to start I suggest he makes himself a cup of tea or coffee and join me in the office for a quick chat. It's a twofold reason. I want Jack to keep an eye out for the information I've been searching for and Sam's friend Jamie couldn't make it today so I left him in the company of James, who I share an office with. Reaching the office I pause in the doorway. Sam is sat next to James starring at the computer screen. They are both totally engrossed. I hope they're not playing computer games.

'Are you guys all right?' I ask.

'James is showing me the pictures of Tom's farm. Is that what you are going to do?'

'Not if I can help it,' I add, joining them.

'Why not? It looks brilliant. I'd love to go on the aerial slide.'

'Where did you get the pictures from, James?'

'It's just come up on Summerbee's website, and so has the CEO's name. I think I'll pay them a visit.'

Leaning over Sam I take a good look for myself. What I see is impressive and futuristic. Over the top in my opinion. What they are proposing will take a huge investment. Basically it's a residential theme park. An updated version of a holiday camp. I'm not convinced it's right for this area.

'I've made you a coffee too, Dad.'

'Put it on my desk, Jack. I'll be right with you. Not just yet, James. I'm in the process of getting the power of attorney from Tom, so I don't want to raise their suspicions. I would like to know who in the council is responsible for this, so put it on your to do list until I'm ready.'

'That's going to cost you.'

'I'm working on that.' Pulling up a chair at my desk I ask Jack to sit down. 'So what do you think? Will you cope with the task?'

'There's a lot to remember.'

'There's no time limit, so take your time and double check everything you do. If you're not sure about something...ask. We're here to help, not make your life difficult.'

'I know that and I will ask.'

'Good. So there's something I'd like you to do for me.' Writing down the names Hanna Green and David Griffiths on my note pad I tear the page out and hand it to Jack. 'Your first piece of detective work. As you work your way through the files, if you come across either of those two names, let me know.'

'Is this something to do with the fire at the hostel?'

'It is. DI Wallace is pestering me for help and now Brad thinks he could be working on something connected to the fire. I didn't want to become involved for obvious reasons so the quicker I find some answers, the better it will be for all of us.'

'You lead a complicated life, Dad.'

61

'I do and I'm supposed to be retired.'

'I hope I find something for you.'

'Thank you. It's a bit of a long shot but I need to be thorough.'

Before Jack returns to his desk I tell him we'll take a break in an hour for lunch. Sitting back in my chair I switch on my computer terminal and wait for it to boot up. I have some ground work to do before I return to my roots…out in the field investigating. I'm still not sure how this going to work for me because of the time element. It's Sam I need to worry about and I'm not going to drag him around with me into what could be a potentially dangerous situation.

For an hour I surfed the internet for information on the hostel and possible suppliers, local or otherwise. Naturally there is nothing incriminating but what I have come across has given me a starting point. In this modern day and age businesses will be tied into deals with suppliers, but they are not always responsible for deliveries. Satisfied I have all the information I need to get started and with that in mind, Sam and I walk down the office to Jack's desk.

'Nothing yet.' Jack informs me.

'I don't want to disillusion you, but there's plenty of time to find what I'm looking for. In the store room there's probably several hundred yet to do.'

'Really!'

'If you don't want to do it, just say so. I wouldn't blame you but, Jack, my plan is to get you involved in other ways, so give it a go and see how you get on. Right, let's have lunch and I'll leave it up to you whether you want to come back for couple of hours.' Standing he tells me he does.

I've arranged to pick Jack up at 4pm. Dropping Sam home Jan was happy to look after him until I return. She's also agreed to be flexible with her hours while Michaela is staying with us. That's going to be a big help.

Driving into Fenby my plan is to walk the streets looking for the known addicts and drop outs. Most of them won't give me the time of day but at a push, one or two will talk to me. They have their favourite hang outs, places to congregate or sit begging. If they're out and about they shouldn't be hard to find.

Parking down in the harbour, where I have an unwritten agreement with the harbour master, I head back up the hill to the old castle area. While undertaking this task I notice a degree of hostility towards me from some of the local fishermen preparing their boats for their next trip. In the past the majority of them have acknowledged me, but not today. I also have the feeling I'm being watched.

Reaching the top of Pier Hill, where the slipway drops down to castle beach I stop to look around. On occasions one or two of the unfortunate ply their begging trade in this area. It can be a busy area of town and in the peak season, they're good at targeting the foreign visitors who want to off load any loose change they might have. Unfortunately for me there's no sign of them. With that in mind I decide to walk around castle hill, then I'll walk up through the town past their favourite haunts.

I'm looking for two characters in particular. One who calls himself Jonny and the other claims his name is Ossie. Who am I to question them, but its common knowledge that someone wishing to lose themselves and forget the past have a tendency to change their identity. So far my search isn't going well. To be honest they're conspicuous by their absence, and that's a little concerning. These guys are very streetwise at a level most of us know little about or choose to ignore. When trouble comes to town the truly homeless move on at the drop of a hat. That's the way they live.

Exhausting the possibilities of finding anyone hanging out on Castle Hill I walk up through the town. I'm going to make my way up to the train station. Not my favourite place. It's where I last saw Jenny, not that I have any feelings for her, because she was the one who walked out on our son…Jack. In the end she did the right thing, but I had so many questions to ask her. I'm trying to let go of the bitterness and contempt I hold for her for what she did to both of us. That will take time. My real fear is, when life goes wrong for her again, will she come knocking at my door one day.

These days Fenby is basically an unmanned train station because of the sparse footfall. I understand it suffers from regular vandalism and graffiti artists visits, and is frequented by the down and outs. Not a great environment to be in late at night. It's the last port of call for me today and once again I draw a blank. The station is deserted. My gut feeling is, if the homeless guys

63

are still in the area they'll keep a low profile until the trouble blows over. This exercise would be better carried out later in the day when the sun has gone down. I'll not be doing that on my own.

Back down in the harbour I pause for a moment or two watching the goings on while I have a leisurely smoke. I don't think my earlier concerns are correct. These boy's fish in our inshore waters and any transfer of contraband could be easily monitored from the shoreline. I can't rule out the possibility but with the main catch being shellfish and what takes place out there in the dead of the night, without suspicion, is any bodies guess. As I stand mulling that over a strange thought crosses my mind. I've stood here on many an occasion and I've never seen or recorded who collects their catch. However large or small, it must go somewhere. Most likely to the nearest fish market, or maybe direct to a wholesaler. My immediate thought challenges me. Who do I trust enough to ask?

Returning home with Jack he tells me he's tired and wants a lie down before we eat. Telling him its fine I go on through the house. Michaela is home. She's sat watching TV with Sam. Saying hello to both of them I'm asked by Sam what we're doing tomorrow because Michaela's at home. The fact that its Saturday tomorrow had slipped my mind.

'I'll give it some thought,' I tell him.

'Tom phoned. He asked me to tell you the accounts are finished.' Jan informs me. 'And your solicitor phoned. He said the papers you wanted drawn up are ready for you to look over. He'll be in the office until five thirty tonight, or nine on Monday morning if you can't make it tonight.'

'Anything else?'

'Not that I can think of.'

'Good. A cup of coffee would be nice.'

'Have you sat down with Michaela and had a chat yet?' Jan continues as I sit down on one of the breakfast bar stools.

'No.'

'Don't you think you should?'

'Probably.'

64

'If you don't mind me saying, you look tired. You're doing too much, Nick. You go on at the boys about taking things easy and yet you're not looking after yourself. You should be taking it easy too after major surgery. I'm worried about you.'

'I have things to do that can't wait. I'll take a holiday when this is all over.'

'Look around you, Nick. What would happen to Jack and Sam if you had a heart attack?'

'Don't be such a drama queen. I'm fine, just a little tired that's all.'

'Go and sit down with Sam and Michaela for a chat. Put your feet up and relax. I'll bring your coffee over to you.'

Taking her advice I amble through to the lounge and flop down in an armchair facing Sam and Michaela. I am tired but I'm not going to give in.

'I must apologise to you, Michaela. I've been a little busy since you arrived and it's rude of me not to have had a good chat.'

'That's OK.'

'How's your room?'

'It's lovely, thank you and the bed is very comfortable. I sleep well. I love your decking too, the view is beautiful.'

'Not a bad idea of mine, was it? So, are you working yet?'

'I start on Monday. I'm working as waitress in a café three days a week.'

'Where's that?'

'I think its Narberth. Is that right?'

'Narberth is correct. It's a lovely little town not too far from here and full of history. Is that what you do at home?'

'No, I make chocolates. I have an apprenticeship. They've given me time off to come here and learn more about Britain.'

'How do you like West Wales?'

65

'It's nice. You drive on the wrong side of the road. That's a little scary.'

'You wait until dad's driving somewhere in a hurry. That's really scary,' Sam pipes up.

'Thanks for that, Sam. I'll have you know, some years ago now I must admit, I did an advance driving course with the police and I did well.'

'That sounds interesting.' Michaela adds.

'I did, or do a lot of work for the police and they suggested it would be beneficial. Tell me, where's home for you?'

'A place called Linz. It's in the north of Austria, not far from the Czechoslovakia border. Linz is where my family live.'

'Do you have a big family?'

'Not really. I have two sisters and we live with our mother. My Grandpa lives close.'

When Jan brings my coffee over our conversation ends. I at least know a little more about Michaela and I'm sure we'll talk again.

'What are you doing for dinner?' Jan asks. 'Are you going out or would you like me to cook you something?' Shrugging my shoulders I look across at Sam and Michaela.

'I'd prefer not to go out. What would you guys like to do?' Asking the question I get no response.

'Where's Jack?' Jan continues.

'Upstairs having a rest.'

'I hope you haven't been working him too hard.'

'Of course I haven't. Three hours sitting in front of a computer isn't that difficult, but it was enough for his first day. I have no intention of pushing him too hard, if that's what you're thinking. The hours he works are up to him.'

'See that you don't.'

'Jan, I don't really want him working for me, but a bit of office work to earn some money isn't going to do him any harm. And what he does earn can go towards helping Lucy and their expected child. That's all I'm doing this for.'

'Are you going over to the solicitors?'

'No, that can wait until Monday.'

'So what am I doing about dinner?'

'You go home, Jan. I want to give Jack an hour or so. If the worst comes to the worst, I'll order us a takeaway.'

Saturday 30th August

When Jack surfaced last night we all went down into town and had fish and chips…well not all of us. Sitting out in the harbour eating our takeaway was very pleasant…but a little chilly. After discussing the merits of buying a new boat with Jack, we took a stroll along Saundersby beach. I will buy myself another boat, but that won't be until the New Year.

Although Jack is Saundersby born and bred his local knowledge is surprisingly limited. With that in mind and Michaela in tow, I've decided to take them all out for the day on a guided tour. Jack insisted at the time that he would like Lucy to come along and I accommodated his wishes. Setting out for Freshwater Bay the three of them pile into the back of my car while Michaela sits up front with me.

I have never been to Freshwater Bay but I understand it's good for surfing, especially if you're a novice or beginner. I want the boys to see what's on offer to them locally because a hobby or passion for water sport could be a great outlet for them. We're in luck. On a dry but cloudy day there's a stiff onshore breeze. In the surf there a number of body boarders and wind surfers. The boys are immediately drawn to what they see. While the four of them head off down the beach to the waters' edge I find myself a comfortable place to sit and watch their progress.

Last night, in front of Michaela, I deliberately mentioned Lucy's pregnancy and the fact that Jack was working for me to support her. It's too early to say if my statement has sunk in and although they are walking together, Jack is holding Lucy's hand and Sam is walking beside Michaela. Sam isn't getting all his own way in their conversation but with what is fast becoming the norm, he's doing his fair share. I'm totally relaxed sat where I am and that is probably because they are.

Over a drink and sticky bun later the conversation naturally turns to surfing. Both Jack and Sam would like to give it a try. I've told them I'll look into the possibility but suggested, because of the cost, that a few lessons first would be a good idea. They both agreed with me and there's no rush. With the right equipment and experience, surfing or body boarding can be an all year round sport.

Leaving Freshwater Bay I drove through Fishguard, out across the Preseli hills, down into New Quay. Beautiful, beautiful countryside. They loved the drive but Jack surprised me when he said, "he didn't know these places existed". I'm opening his and Sam's eyes to what they have on their doorstep. The reality is, in two years-time Jack could be driving himself and perhaps, he Lucy and their yet unborn child, could take Sam with them.

What I've shown them is for them to embrace and it was a worthwhile exercise, but I have an ulterior motive, something I must do on the way home. Leaving New Quay I turn left off the main road into a narrow country lane. Just beyond a small cottage on our left, about a mile along the lane, I pull into an entrance to a farm field and switch off the engine. Telling the guys I have something I must do and they can get out of the car if they wish, I inform them I want to be left alone for a while. Walking back along the lane I stop in front of the cottage, under the pretty, thatched gateway. Starring at the lovely, neat white painted cottage, it's changed a lot since I was last here…thirty years ago. I know why I'm here but the boys will find it strange that I've stopped to look at a random cottage in the middle of nowhere. This was where Henry Sinclair once lived. It's where I found him hanging by the neck in the orchard at the bottom of the garden. I was later told he had been dead for at least a week. I struggled with that information because I know he knocked on my apartment door, Beth's old place four days before I found him. Stranger still and I'm not a believer in ghosts or the afterlife, when I was told I could leave the scene and take a very upset Beth home, Henry was sat on the bonnet of my car. I knew that wasn't possible but he spoke to me and I looked away, when I looked back he had gone. Beth, despite being relatively sober, didn't see him at all. Logic alone cannot explain that.

'Are you alright, Dad?' Jack asks. Turning to face him, looking over his shoulder, Lucy has stopped some five or six metres away behind him.

'I'll be fine.'

'Something terrible happened here, didn't it?' He adds.

'Can I ask you a serious question? What has made you say that? Is there something I'm doing, or was there something you sensed?'

'I don't know the answer to that, but Sam wouldn't walk over here with me.'

'Why?'

'He said something scarred him.'

69

'We should go.'

Walking back towards the car we collect Lucy on the way.
Continuing on our way something lying in the road stops me in my tracks.
Aware that Jack and Lucy are staring at me I turn around to face the cottage.
Lying in the lane behind us, over ground we've just traversed, is a piece of
crumpled up paper.

'Do you see that piece of paper, Jack?'

'Yes,' he whispers.

'Would you pick it up for me?'

'What's going on?'

'Please pick up the piece of paper.' Reluctantly, Jack does as I ask.
'Is there anything written on the paper?' Opening it he replies…yes. 'Read it
out too me.'

'It says, words of wisdom.'

'Nothing else?'

'No.'

Holding out my hand I take the note from Jack. To confirm what he
has said, I read the note for myself. Turning away from Jack, the grass I had
seen strewn all over the road, which stopped me in my tracks, has gone.
Walking on, deep in thought, Sam runs up to me and throws his arms around
me. Crouching down in front of him I ask what had scared him.

'I thought I saw something strange.' Giving him a hug I reassure him
that he didn't and it was probably his imagination, or maybe a light reflection.
Making sure Sam is alright first, I ask them all to wait in the car. Henry's
here, whether I believe it or not.

Leaning on the gate, clutching the note in my hand, I speak out loudly.
'Not Sam, Henry. He's too young and fragile to understand.'

Home, sat outside on the decking I'm drained, mentally exhausted. I've
succeeded to do something I thought wasn't possible. That was the reason
behind asking Jack to read the note first, because if he could, it's real, not a
figment of my imagination. The mere fact that the hand written text on the

brown envelope locked in my safe reads the same, "words of wisdom", makes it so real for me. The fact Sam said he thought he saw something really bothers me. It makes me wonder, because of my denial, is Henry trying to move on, find his successor elsewhere?

I'm destroying myself with stupid, crazy thoughts. Thoughts like, when Colleen phoned me, was it really my decision to help and meet Sam? What were Austin, Abby's and Simon's part in this? Jenny and her decision to admit that Jack is my son. Going to the cottage with Jack, Sam, Lucy and Michaela when I should have taken them straight home. None of which makes any sense to me at the moment. Could be its Sam. He is an intelligent, unique character and I do believe there's a lot more to learn about him. His communication skills are good and his dislike of certain characters, well judged.

I sat down with them all when we got home and briefly told them about Henry. I had to get that off my chest. They listened without saying very much. I also told them about my visions but did not expand, just that they happened.

'Come back inside, Dad. You must be freezing.' Jack prompts.

Starring at Jack before replying, if this is Henry's doing then I'm a lucky man, having my son by my side. 'I will. You guys must be hungry.'

'All taken care of. We raided the freezer and Michaela cooked us dinner.'

'Did she?' I question, standing up.

'She's a good cook.'

Chapter Five

Sunday 31st August

Following a restless night, searching, questioning myself for reasons and answers, I'm downstairs early. To my surprise, Sam is sat in front of the TV watching God knows what. For a brief moment, don't know why, I expect him to challenge me over what he believes he saw yesterday. Thankfully he doesn't, but he's dressed and ready to go off to football. Wouldn't it be nice if life for me was as simple as that?

Lucy stayed the night…with Jack. Before anyone doubts my reasoning and decision making, it's a little late too question me. It's wrong of me to suggest the damage is already done and to the purist it probably is, but it's not going to be a regular thing in my house. A one off perhaps and last night it was convenient. For this to work for Jack and Lucy, they must learn to live with each other in everyday situations. Harsh as it sounds, the day in day out drudgery of life is monotonous. If a person can cope with that tedious existence, then they are halfway there. Jack and Lucy are on a huge learning curve and that will escalate to massive proportions early next year when they become proud parents and me, a proud grandfather. I know they are excited by the prospect of becoming parents. I have no idea how I will feel when they do.

'Is Michaela coming to watch me play?'

'I can't leave her here on her own can I? Why?'

'I don't really want any of them to watch.'

'Why ever not?'

'Because I might have a shit game and they'll laugh at me.'

'Sam! I'd rather you didn't talk to me like that.'

'Sorry, but I just know I will if they're watching me.' Pointing at the breakfast bar stools I gesture to him that he sits down. 'You're going to tell me off, aren't you?'

'I should, shouldn't I, but I'm not going too. Sam, I don't like you using language like that in front of me. That's all I have to say on the matter.

What you should know is, on Thursday night at training you only looked over at me twice, because once you had your boots on and the football at your feet, nothing else mattered. You'll be absolutely fine…you'll see. So!' I ask, standing up. 'What would you like for breakfast?'

'I'm not hungry.'

'But you will eat before we go?'

'I'll have some cereals in a minute.'

'What about after the game?'

'How do you mean?'

'Do I need to take some snacks for you?'

'I'll do it. I'll find my lunch box. I think it's under my bed. Will it be OK if I take some crisps and chocolate bars?'

'Whatever you like, and take a bottle of water with you.'

I sent Sam upstairs at eight o'clock to wake the others and tell them they have one hour to get ready because we're off to football at nine. Michaela appeared first and asked if she could go into Fenby to meet up with some of her friends. I had no problem with that but phoned Sue to make sure it was fine with her. Michaela gave me a few names of the people she was meeting, which I conveyed to Sue and she was happy for her to go. Saying she wanted to go at ten o'clock wasn't great timing but as luck would have it, Jan turned up soon after I made the phone call and said she would drop Michaela off. I gave Michaela my mobile phone number and told her, as long as it was after midday, I would pick her up.

Sam's game is in Milford Haven. Following Matt Wilson we have no problem finding the ground. Sam didn't say too much on the way over. I could see he was nervous so I talked about going back to school and fishing. Before we left the house I asked both Jack and Lucy to wish him luck and not to be vocal while he's playing. Jack retorted at the time that I should do as I preach. I accepted his comment…because I know I shouldn't.

Kicking off at ten thirty, Sam's age group only play twenty-five minutes each half. To be fair the first half isn't great. I can see Sam is becoming frustrated as the half goes on. That's not a good sign, but when he walks out for the second half he gives me the thumbs up. I take that as a sign of, "dad, I've sorted it". There are two changes that I can see. They were 1-0 up at halftime, so let's see what happens.

The two changes Matt Wilson makes change the game. Sam's attitude has changed and as the half progresses he slowly starts bossing the game. When he scores the fourth goal for the Bluebirds I want to run onto the pitch and celebrate with him, but turn and give Jack a hug instead. That's how the game finishes, 4-0 to the Bluebirds. While Sam disappears into the clubhouse we walk over to wait outside for him. We're soon joined by Matt Wilson.

'What did you think?' He asks.

'The two changes you made worked well.'

'Sam and I had a little chat at halftime and I asked him what he wanted. I wasn't going to play the other two lads that came on because one only got back off holiday yesterday and the other broke his arm about ten weeks ago and I wasn't confident he was ready. Playing them was a risk but I could see Sam needed help out there. He told me he couldn't do it all on his own and he needed more time on the ball, not chasing shadows. I agreed with him so I made the changes. I think we all saw the difference in the second half and I now know what my starting midfield will be in the future. Sam did well for me today and that was a sweet goal he scored. Nick, good players need good players around them and today proved the point.' Pulling me to one side Matt continues. 'Sam worked his socks off for the team today and without his first half input, the final score may have been very different. At halftime I could see he was frustrated and upset so I sat him down in the clubhouse away from the other boys and we had our little chat. I don't want to lose him, but Sam should be playing at a higher level. I can assure you, once the season is a few weeks old and the word gets out, he'll have scouts from the professional clubs watching him. In my view, that's where he should be if he's ambitious.'

'Matt, thank you for saying that. Sam is ambitious and wants to play professionally, but at this time it wouldn't be good for him. I've told you that he has some tough times ahead of him and I have personally seen how that affects him. He goes into himself and won't talk to anyone. The social service described him as an introvert and I know how that affects him. I'm not going to stand here and say the changes in him are all my doing, but if you had met him four months ago you would have seen a very different young man. I talk to him all the time and he talks to me, you've seen that for yourself and that growing level of confidence may just help him through the days ahead. I don't want to hold him back but in the same breath, I don't want to push him into a situation he's not ready for.

'That's where I am with Sam and if anything changes I will sit down and talk it through with him…and you. I would prefer Sam to have at least one season with you. Take small manageable steps forward and see where that takes him.'

'Here he comes.' Matt offers. As I turn to face the clubhouse Sam is standing close to us and I watch as Jack gives him a brotherly hug. That says so much. Joining us Sam has a big smile on his face, but he looks exhausted. Matt speaks first.

'How do you think it went, Sam?'

Dropping his football bag on the ground Sam removes his lunchbox and takes out a bag of crisps. 'Liam and Brody are good players,' he respond, opening his crisp bag. 'I hope they start the next game.'

'I have arranged a friendly against Narberth at home next Sunday and the league starts the following weekend. I will start Liam and Brody alongside you next Sunday. It's not such a big test as Milford Haven so it will give you guys a chance to sort mid-field out. Not that I'm saying it needs sorting out in that way but the more you play together, the more you'll get to know each-others' strengths and weaknesses.'

'I think they should swop over. Brody can use his left foot, Liam can't.'

'Ok, Sam, we'll give that a try. How do you feel after todays' game? Happy or not?'

'Happy,' Sam splutters, stuffing a handful of crisps in his mouth. 'Because I got to do what I like doing.'

'That's good to hear. So, shall we talk about your diet now, or leave it until Thursday?'

Monday 1st September

I've left Sam in the capable hands of Jan. He seemed tired after yesterdays' exercise and was quite happy to spend the day lazing around. I won't be out long and after dropping Jack at the office I'm heading over to the hostel for a meeting with the manageress. A lady by the name of Gwyn Roberts, she has obtained limited, escorted access to the building and I've asked her if I can look through her list of suppliers.

Pulling into the car park my first observations surprise me. Apart from the fact that DI Wallace's company car is in the car park, there is now a small porta cabin outside the main entrance, where a BT engineer appears to be installing a phone cable. Guessing that's where I will find Gwyn Roberts I head in the direction of the porta cabin. Reaching the open door there is a lady sat at a desk inside.

'Gwyn?'

'Yes,' she replies. Stepping inside I introduce myself.

'Nick Thompson. We spoke on the phone Saturday.'

'Do come in. Sorry the place is in a mess. DI Wallace only gave me a short time to gather together what I needed. I have lots to sort out as you can imagine. With the students going back to school this week we have a number of bookings to re-arrange. I have had a quick look at what you asked to see and I think it's all there.' Sitting down at her desk Gwyn places some paperwork down in front of me. 'Can I ask what you're looking for?'

'You are aware that the fire is being treated as a suspected case of arson?'

'Yes.'

'Right, so DI Wallace has tasked me to look into the reasons regarding that possibility. While I'm here, I would like to see a list of your employees.'

'I can do that for you.'

'As we're working along the lines that this could be arson, do you have any concerns or worries about any of your staff, past or present?'

'I'll need to give that a little thought. I've lost one anyway…sadly.'

76

'What was David Griffiths like?'

'A man of few words, but he did his job and never let me down.'

'What were his responsibilities?'

'Pot wash mainly, and he also made sure he was here to put the deliveries away. I should say here that I had no idea he had a drug problem. He never gave me any reason to be worried.'

'Was he a person you could trust?'

'With what I asked him to do…yes.'

'So let's go through your suppliers.'

'Technically we have four suppliers. Our deliveries consist of frozen foods, fresh foods and one for consumables. All different companies. The fourth I do myself. Once a week I go over to the local wholesalers to buy the hot and cold drink products and sometimes items we're running low on. Things like milk. You have in front of you all the latest invoices and receipts, going back three months.'

'What about laundry?'

'Well yes of course we do but they're not kitchen items.'

'So who does the kitchen laundry items?'

'The kitchen staff are responsible for their own uniforms, like the front of house staff and there are washing facilities on site for those who cannot do it at home.'

'And items like tea towels are done on site?'

'Yes they are. One of the morning cleaners do it first thing.'

'What's your stock control like?'

'Indifferent at times, but generally its fine. We're no different to any other business. Someone will always look to take an advantage.'

'Is theft an issue to you?'

'Petty theft walks hand in hand with life in general, Mr Thompson, but we've never had a serious problem and cash on site is very limited because our bookings are pre-paid. We do accept walk-ins but the company policy is card payments only.'

'What about maintenance work? Things like gas services, refrigeration and general maintenance.'

'One company called, Marstons, do all that sort of thing. Not particularly reliable but we get by.'

'Could I have their details as well, please? I want to look into every aspect.'

'You'll need to give me a little time to find their details. I might need to speak to DI Wallace to see if he'll let me go back to the main office.'

'I'll go and see him while I'm here. I have other business to discuss with him. I won't be too long.'

Holding court outside at the rear of the building DI Wallace isn't difficult to locate. Not wanting to interrupt I wait until he finishes. I'm not interested in their company politics, only in what they may have found. Any information I can gleam from them could help my cause.

Fuck Henry Sinclair! Waiting for DI Wallace I have a dizzy spell. Leaning back against a bollard to steady myself I see a name, in graffiti style, painted on the side of the hostel building. Gathering my senses the image slowly disappears as my dizzy spell subsides. Fortunately it's not as severe as previous episodes. They left me feeling nauseous and quite drained. As normal though, what I've witnessed means nothing to me, but there has always been a connection. I simply need to find the answer.

'Got anything for me?' Reg asks as he approaches.

'Give me a chance. This is the first time I've had any real free time to give you.'

'Why are you here? I thought you would be better off in your office going through your files.'

'I've got Jack doing that. I was hoping you may have discovered how the fire started.'

'Jack's working for you now?'

'In the office. He's transferring the information in the paper files onto the new computer system. So, have you found the cause?'

'We think it may have been an electrical fault. I'm getting a specialist in that field to look at what we've found and to confirm whether it was deliberate or otherwise. He's due tomorrow so I should know by the end of the day.' Pausing for a moment he looks straight at me. 'Why are you really here? You didn't know I would be here so you're up to something. What's MI5's interests in this?'

'This is where this conversation ends. Even if I was working for the department, which I'm not, I'm under no obligation to discuss any matter with you. You asked me for help and I've found the time to do that. If you don't want me to bother then please say so because I have other pressing matters to attend too.'

'Nick. I have a right to know if you're otherwise involved. In the long run it would be to both of our benefits.'

'Right! Let's have this conversation in front of your superior.'

'That won't be necessary. But, Nick, we need to be working together on this.'

'Fine. If you believe I am working for the department, use the correct channels to set up a joint investigation. I am not, or ever have been in a position to make that decision. To reiterate, I am not working for the department. I'm going. If I do come across any relevant information, I'll be in touch.'

Sat in my car I wait for DI Wallace to leave before returning to see Gwyn Roberts. While I was waiting I phoned home to make sure Sam was OK and the office to speak to Jack. I gave him some money this morning so he could buy himself some lunch and told him I'll pick him up at 4pm.

Gwyn has put together all the information I need. During our short conversation I promised to return the documents at some point tomorrow. She believes I'm going to read through them for relevant information. I'm going to photocopy the documents later at the office when I pick Jack up. Not strictly legal I know but I rather fancy she has more pressing matters to worry about than what I'm intending to do.

On the way to my solicitors I picked Sam up from home. I did tell him where I was going and he'd probably get bored, but he told me he was bored and wanted to do something. Hardly an exciting afternoon for him but he's company for me and I'm not officially working.

Sam is sat next to me in the solicitors. Didn't really want that but I couldn't leave him on his own. Once we're settled Paul Davis, my solicitor, opens the conversation.

'Power of attorney, Nick. Under the circumstances a lasting Power of Attorney, which covers property and financial affairs of someone in need of help is more appropriate if all parties are in agreement. However, this can take between 6-8 weeks to finalise. Once everyone one is happy with the arrangement, I can witness the signatures and submit the document to the office of public guardian.

'My question here is simple. How much time does Tom Morgan have before the banks file for bankruptcy?'

'Not sure exactly. They were given twenty-one days to pay £53,000 for defaulting on a payment plan they arranged with the bank. They don't have that money and their bank accounts have been frozen.'

'Ok. If their bank does file for bankruptcy then the receivers will be called in. Those guys will sell the assets to pay off, in part or full, their debts. Technically that could make them homeless and in this situation I think that is highly likely. You know what I'm going to say next?'

'Buy the farm. How long would that take?'

'With my contacts, between 1-3 weeks but, Nick, as they are a failing business you will become liable for their debts, because you would be buying their business. I would suggest, if that is your preferred action, you get a full and detailed set of their accounts and total debt owed.'

'Once I'm finished here I'm going over there to do just that. They tell me they have the figures ready. I'll naturally have my accountant scrutinise the figures before I make any sort of decision. If I do go down that route I'd like you to work alongside my accountant to sort this out quickly. What do you think I should offer them?'

'I'll make it a priority. What you offer is entirely up to you and I would suggest, dependant on their debt value. Another factor will depend on what your plans are for the farm in the future.'

Driving over to Tom's my head is full of thoughts regarding the farm and Tom's family's future. If they agree to sell me the farm, unconditionally, then I will make them an offer. I will need to support them while I work out what I'm going to do. Any money given to them will be dependent on their total debt. The one stumbling block for me is the other guesthouse. As it stands, it is a worthless piece of real estate which sits in no more than half an acre of freehold land. What it may achieve at auction, which is the way I'll sell it, the guesthouse has no other value or interest for me.

Totally absorbed by my meandering thoughts I have ignored Sam. He was privy to what my solicitor had to say and perhaps, through his own silence, understands where I'm am with this. That is pure conjecture on my behalf. His young mind probably doesn't understand the significance of what I'm thinking of doing for Tom and Mother.

Clearing my mind I come up with two figures. The most difficult one is the business debt. Knowing my own financial situation I've set a limit of £250,000, with a small contingency plan. My initial thoughts were to raise the money against New Barn Farm but I see that as too much of a risk. I do not want to over extend my own farm's business assets and plunge that into debt.

'Sorry, Sam. I have lots to think about and I'm ignoring you. We shouldn't be too long at Toms.'

'That's alright. I could see you were thinking.'

'Thank you. You know what, Sam, making decisions for someone else isn't easy. When I think about it, what I'm trying to do for Tom isn't so very different to what I did for you. When it matters, I can't sit still and do nothing. It's a case of, if I can do something to help, then I should.'

'How much does Tom owe?'

'We're about to find out.'

Having a crafty cigarette before stepping inside the farmhouse I stub it out and open the door to let Sam inside first. Before I say anything to them I want to go over the figures first. Making that obvious mother points at the table before putting the kettle on. Sitting down I take my time studying their accounts. I don't time myself because it's irrelevant. Once I've seen all I need to see at this point I put the paperwork down and look over at Tom.

'As far as you're both aware, there's nothing you've missed or forgotten? If there is, now would be a very good time to tell me.'

'That's it boy.' Tom answers.

'And this figure includes the other guesthouse?' As this conversation evolves I become aware of Sam standing at my side.

'It does.' Tom replies.

'My first move will be to have my own accountant verify your figures and on my behalf, he will look for county court judgements and any pending litigation. Once again, at this point, is there anything else I should know about?' With their silence and half-hearted head shaking, I choose to continue. 'I will take these papers with me. If you would like a copy to keep, I will ask Jack to do that later when I return to the office. Have either of you anything you wish to ask me?' Silence once again prevails. I'm getting the impression they're embarrassed by their total debt. 'I'm not going to question you, or make you feel uncomfortable but, £174,468 and a few pence is an extraordinary high amount of money to owe. I will, at a later date, look into how this was allowed to happen. However, we need to address this situation without delay and I have a proposal to put forward. Once I've had a cigarette and there's a cup of tea in front of me, I'll talk you through it.'

Sam follows me outside and watches me light a cigarette. 'Are you going to help them?' He asks.

'I'm very cross with them. I'm also angry with the financial institutions involved for allowing this to happen. This situation could have been avoided had they exercised a duty of care. I shouldn't be talking to you about this but I was the one who dragged you along and exposed you to this very traumatic time for them. You know more than most about this because of me and I must ask you not to speak to anyone about what you've heard. Not even Jack. I will tell him when the time is right. To answer your question, yes I am and you probably know what my proposal is going to be?'

'You're going to buy the farm like your solicitor suggested.'

'That's my intention. It's up to Tom and Mother to agree to the terms. I suggest you listen, because one day this could be yours and Jack's problem.'

Sitting back down at the table I wait until Sam has settled himself, sat on the floor in front of Tom.

'I spoke to my solicitor before coming over here. He says a lasting power of attorney is an option open to us. That however takes time, about 6-8 weeks. Time we probably haven't got if the bank does file for bankruptcy in twenty-one days and the receivers are called in. Once that happens it's over for you and the farm. The quickest way to resolve this is for you to sell the farm, the guesthouse and their debts. I'm told by my solicitor that can be achieved within 1-3 weeks if both parties are in agreement. I am prepared to take your debt on but there will be conditions to meet, and agree. If there is an initial agreement I will instruct my solicitor to start the ball rolling and he will work alongside my accountant, once he's verified your debt total, to resolve this problem as soon as possible. This means I will buy your land and both of the properties. Do you wish me to continue?'

'Yes,' Sam says and I stare at him. Shaking my head I put a finger to my lips suggesting he keeps quiet. He quickly gets the message.

'Please.' Mother adds.

'Let's look at the facts. You have no income or money to pay your debts, just your land and properties. Assuming your predicted debt is, and I'll round it up to £175,000, on top of which you already owe me £20,000, that makes the known debt £195,000. Then I have my solicitor and accountants fees to legalise the sale transaction at a cost of something between £4–6,000, making the total in the region of £200,000. That money and a contingency can be in my account by Friday. Once the figures are finalised and we have agreed a settlement, I will instruct my solicitor to write to all your creditors and inform them they will be paid within five working days to hold off bankruptcy being filed.

'I'm going to inform you here that once we sign a contract of sale, every square inch of what you currently own will become mine. I don't want the other guesthouse, so that will go on the market ASAP. The land here I will incorporate and use as an extension to New Barn Farm. That just leaves the house and out-buildings. Is there anything you wish to ask me at this point?' Seeing them both shake their heads I continue. 'I have no immediate plans for the house or the out-buildings but the latter maybe useful for storage. So this is where you both need to listen. I'm not going to throw you out, nor do I have any current plans to spend money on the house. You can stay put for the foreseeable future but you must become responsible for your own household bills. At some stage we will need to discuss your rent and at this point I feel I should make you aware that that will happen, but I'm not going push point. This next statement concerns Ceri and Fabian mostly. There are no current vacancies at New Barn Farm which means I cannot offer any of you a job. However, if Ceri would like to speak to Marcus at a future date there might be an opening. That will be her choice.

'Lastly, more as a favour to you, I will give you £5,000 to see you through the next few months while you sort yourselves out.'

'We don't have an active bank account.' Mother offers.

'That can be rectified easily once we're in agreement, but that amount will be final. It may not seem a great deal where you're concerned, but it's a better than what's currently on the table. It's a lot to take in I know but think about my proposal.' Standing, picking up my cup of tea I inform them I'm going outside for a cigarette.

It isn't long before my shadow follows me outside, only this time he walks past me. As I watch him walk across the yard and lean against the gate on the far side I'm already questioning myself over whether I'm doing the right thing. This going to cost me in the region of £200,000. That sum takes away any chance of me buying a new boat next year. It's all about priorities and whether this will work for me and New Barn Farm. If I can raise at least £75,000 from the sale of the other guesthouse, that end figure won't seem so bad.

Walking back towards me I notice that Sam is looking around at the house and out-buildings. I know he liked the idea of an adventure park when James showed him Summerbee Homes' futuristic plans. Perhaps he thinks it's a good idea.

'Where is the other guesthouse?' He asks, which comes as a surprise.

84

'In a place called Ludchurch. It's on the way home from here.'

'Why don't you sell it to Sue?'

'That's an interesting thought. What makes you ask that?'

'She needs somewhere doesn't she?'

'Not her personally, but it's an interesting idea. Why don't we go and take a look on the way home?'

Confronting Tom and Mother again I have one more question to ask. 'Do you need more time to think about my proposal?'

'Yes, boy.' Tom grunts.

'That's fine. I'll give you until this time tomorrow. Please remember that you are running out of time.'

'I want Ceri to run this farm. It's her rite of passage.'

'And let her inherit your debt. Be realistic, Tom. Where and how is Ceri going to raise the funds to pay off the farms debts? There is no actual collateral to bargain with and she probably doesn't have a credit rating, certainly not good enough to cover the £200,000 you owe anyway.

'We'll deal with that.'

'I'm going to go, Tom. This time tomorrow or I will pull out and if I do, you are on your own.'

Opening the inner door I gesture to Sam to go first. As he reaches me he turns to face Tom and Mother. 'Goodbye,' he says emotionally. When he looks at me I can see he's upset. Ushering him outside I close the door behind us and in silence we walk back to the car. 'Will this be the last time we come here?' He asks as he opens the front nearside door.

'I'm not sure. I told you Tom is a stubborn man. Too proud of his own heritage to see beyond his nose. I can't do or say any more than I have already done. It's up to them now.'

'Why don't you let Ceri run the farm?'

'Two reasons why not. To start with there is no farm to run. To pay the wages and bills you need an income and that is something they don't have. Secondly, Ceri has been running this farm for nearly four years and look where that has got them. Sorry to say this in front of you, but she hasn't got the managerial skills to do that. Plus, if she was really concerned about the farm and her future, she should have joined us. Come on let's go and don't let this upset you. On the way home I'm going to drop these figures in at my accountants first, then I'll show you the other guesthouse.'

'Why?'

'Just in case, Sam.'

Resting against the boot of my car, drawing on a cigarette, I'm starring at Penrice House. From the outside it doesn't look too bad but I'm well aware of the internal issues. None of the six bedrooms, two of which are family rooms, have en-suite facilities. Served by two bathrooms, todays guests want private facilities. That's just the tip of the iceberg and after at least three years of lying empty, I feel sure the inside will be suffering from damp issues. I don't have a key to let myself in to take a look. Like Tom's farm, it is very isolated. The nearest big town from here is Narberth, some three to four miles away. Staying here a car is a necessary convenience.

Sam has wandered off to take a look around. At the moment he's out of sight around the back of the house. I'll be interested to hear his thoughts on what he sees. Whether it's my influence or not, he does appear to be taking an interest. I believe that's a good thing because any distraction from what is going on in the background for him, can only be positive.

Penrice House – a spin off from the farmhouse - I've never understood why they didn't come up with a more original name – is "L" shaped. On the rear of the building is an annex which doubles up as staff quarters. Someone had to remain onsite twenty-four hours a day to deal with problems and emergencies. While Tom was running this as a business that same person was responsible for preparing and cooking breakfast. Quite a solitary existence, in the middle of nowhere. You certainly had to like your own company. That very same isolation did create staffing problems for Tom.

Finishing my cigarette I head towards the back corner of the building to find Sam. It's getting late and I have a few things to attend to at the office before taking Jack home. Reaching the corner of the building Sam appears in front of me.

'Seen enough, because we need to make tracks?' I ask.

'It's a big house, Dad. A bit quiet but I think Sue would like it.'

'I don't want it, Sam, that's for certain, but I need to sell it, not give it away to a charity.' I respond as we turn to walk back to the car. 'If Tom and Mother agree to sell, and for your ears only I'm not going to phone them tomorrow, this place will go on the market straight away.'

'Why not?'

'Because I've put my cards on the table and there's no negotiating. They know the situation they're in, so the outcome is down to them.'

Reaching the car I pause for a moment in thought. Un-wittingly Sam has put a thought into my head. Not one about this place because that's decided upon, but an idea regarding the farm. Quite bizarre really, because there's no connection to what he said? What if this nature trail I'm in discussion with the local authorities about, through my land, ended up at Tom's place? It would need a lot of thought, but I could turn the farm into an educational centre. Equipped with perhaps a small shop come café, with a large picnic area for the students to rest and eat their packed lunches, before walking back to New Barn Farm. An enterprise like that would be looked upon favourably by the authorities, and it would need staffing. It was Marcus, my manager at New Barn, who came up with the idea of the nature trail. He's well into the educational side of farming and he's very concerned by the lack of young people coming into the industry. I'll run the idea past him once I know where I'm going with this situation. My quandary is, do I use my idea as leverage to persuade Tom to sell, or do I leave the decision up to him?

Quickly showing Sam how to do the photocopying I leave him down in reception and head upstairs to Jack's desk. He's not there and his computer terminal is switched off. Puzzled, I find Sue to ask her where he is.

'He went out with Richard about an hour ago,' she tells me. 'Richard said he'd drop Jack home when they've finished, and he wants to talk to you.'

'Where have they gone?' I ask with some concern.

'Not sure exactly. He had a big delivery arrive after lunch and he needed a hand to get it onsite, quickly as he put it, so he asked Jack to go with him.'

'Why didn't he, or someone at least, phone me?'

'They tried I understand, but you didn't answer your mobile.'

Pulling my phone out of my pocket I see that I have three missed calls and my phone is on silent. 'Any idea why Richard wants to talk to me?'

'I'm not a mind reader, Nick.'

Walking back down to reception I have no idea what this could be about. Hopefully, business related. Sam is nearly finished when I re-join him. Once he explains what he's done I tell him he's doing a good job. The originals he's placed on a brown A4 sized envelope and marked accordingly and the copies likewise. Watching him finish he slides the relevant paperwork inside their envelopes and hands them to me. I wish he was as tidy as this at home.

When Jack finally gets home I'm sat watching TV with Sam and Michaela. He looks very tired but very buoyant…talkative.

'Dad, Richard has come up with an idea. He'd like me to work for him and see if he can get me an electrical apprenticeship. I like the idea because I could earn a lot of money once I'm qualified. If I do like a day release course, I can work with him and learn the trade hands on.'

Standing, I become aware of myself tilting my head to one side while I digest the information.

'What do you think?' Jack adds.

'Nick.' Richard joins in. 'Some of the contractors I use are becoming unreliable and I also believe a few of them are under cutting our prices. I want to bring the whole operation in-house so I can control it better. I'm in the process of quoting for a couple of large local authority contracts for service and repair work and it makes sense to do that. I feel this is the ideal situation for Jack to progress. You've frequently said you don't want him to follow in your footsteps because it's too dangerous and he has responsibilities, so I see this as the perfect solution for him. And quite honestly, I need someone I can trust.'

Staying silent I let Jack continue. 'Please, Dad. You know I won't let you down. I'd really like to do this, if it's OK with you?'

'I think it's a very good idea. I'll leave you guys to sort out the details. It will be hard work, Jack, with lots of homework, but if you want this then you have my blessing.'

Shaking their hands I offer Richard a coffee before he goes and wish them luck. Before I have a chance to move Sam passes behind me and disappears into the kitchen. When I join him he's already switched the kettle on and getting the mugs ready.

'There aren't any chocolate digestives, Sam, so don't bother offering.'

'Yes there are! I asked Jan to get some.'

'Really?'

'Yes, really.' Pausing for a moment he continues. 'Now that Jack is working for Richard, can I have his job in the office?'

'You're doing enough already and don't forget, you're going back to school on Wednesday.'

'I haven't tried my old uniform yet.'

'Make sure you do that tonight, because we only have tomorrow to go shopping if you need anything.'

'I could give up school and work for you.'

'You'd have to give up your football as well because work always comes first.'

'Can we forget about what I said?'

'And the chocolate digestives.'

'Never!'

Chapter Six

Tuesday 2nd September

I have made a rod for my own back. Once Jack has his hydrotherapy session we're all going our separate ways. I don't know if Tom has my mobile number and I'm not going to be at home if he does change his mind and phone me. My own deadline was sort of a threat, trying to make him see sense and understand the seriousness of his own situation. A few hours won't make a difference, but I can be awkward towards things at times. One thing is for certain, I'm not going out of my way to phone him after what he said.

Sat alone in the kitchen I'm going through the paperwork Gwyn gave me, making notes as I go. I have a window of opportunity today to follow this up. Jack is working at the office and Sam is going out for the day with Jan. He needs some new school shoes so I'll leave some cash in an envelope for her to take him shopping while they're out. Where Jack is concerned, I'm not sure he'll be working for me today or sorting out a possible apprenticeship with Richard. The latter would be my guess as there isn't time to waste setting that up. Aware someone has joined me I look up from my work. Michaela is standing in the doorway holding a pile of clothing in her arms.

'I need to do some washing.'

'Of course you can,' I reply, standing up. 'Over here.' I add, opening the washing machine door. 'I'm not sure where Jan keeps the stuff but I'm sure we'll find it somewhere.' While Michaela loads the machine I open a number of cupboards and locate what she needs. 'I'm not sure how many of these liquid tabs you'll need so help yourself.'

'One is enough, and some softener.'

Softener I think. Is that what this bottle of comfort is I wonder? Passing it to her she says thank you. While she completes the task and switches on the machine I do the simple thing…switch on the kettle.

'How's the job going?' I ask.

'It's going good. We have some lovely customers and they ask me lots of questions about Austria.'

'Have you phoned home since you've been here?'

'I text my sister the day I arrive.'

'You are more than welcome to use the home phone. I'm sure your sister would like to hear your voice.'

'That's very kind of you. Maybe later.'

'Are you working today?'

'Yes. Until four o'clock I think. I'm not tomorrow, we're all going out on an educational trip.'

'Somewhere nice?'

'I think we go to St David's cathedral first then Pembroke castle. Have you ever been?'

'Er. I'm ashamed to say, no, but I'm told they're well worth a visit if you like history.'

'I like history very much. I'm keen to learn more about your British history. Can I ask you something?'

'Sure.'

'Sam told me you have a farm and thinking about buying another one. Can you take me there before I go home?'

Michaela's question makes me a little cross. I asked Sam to keep quiet about Tom's place. He may not have said too much but anything at this time, is too much. I will remind him of that. 'Have you any plans for the weekend?'

'No. Not that I'm aware of.'

'Ok. Let's see what happens.'

'You're very good with Jack and Sam. You listen well and that's a good thing to do.'

'I'm trying too. It's a massive change in lifestyle for me, but I think I'm coping.'

'They both seem happy and that's what matters. Were you really a private investigator?'

'For my sins, I still am. I'm desperately trying to retire but there's always something around the next corner for me to deal with.'

Placing our coffees on the breakfast bar I elect to sit down. I have a long day ahead of me. I'm working, so my plan is to leave Sam with Jan and she can take him shopping later for some new school shoes. Once I've dropped Jack at the office I'm going to follow up the on information Gwyn has provided.

'Why don't you tell everyone you're retiring?' Michaela adds, as she joins me.

'If only it was as simple as that. It's my life's work and my colleagues are like a family to me and you cannot turn your back on that and simply walk away. They are my friends, my family…particularly Richard. He's like a younger brother to me. I've known Richard and Jan since the day I arrived here over thirty years ago. I also have commitments outside of my company to fulfil. I will work my way through this and I can assure you, the boys are my main priority.'

'That's good.' As Michaela finishes talking Sam appears in the kitchen doorway. With his dressing gown over his shoulders he's still in his pyjamas. He looks terrible. We have an unwritten agreement that he should always be dressed when he comes downstairs, so something is wrong.

'Are you all right, Sam?' I ask and he bursts into tears. Virtually running over to where I'm sat he throws his arms around my shoulders. 'What is it, Sam?' Still crying he tells me tearfully that he's had a bad dream. Looking over at Michaela she nods her head and leaves us alone. Trying to pacify him I repeatedly tell him everything is fine and he's safe. Slowly he calms down and I wait for him to open up. This isn't the first time he's had a nightmare, but it's the first for a number of weeks.

'They were chasing me.' He eventually tells me.

'Who was, Sam?'

'Larry's friends.'

'Larry's friends? Why would they want to do that?'

'They always punched and kicked me.'

'Why, Sam?'

'Because Larry was cheating them.'

'And they punched and kicked you for that. How was Larry cheating them?'

'He used to add things to the coke to get more hits. They told me the stuff was shit and hit me so I would tell Larry. He didn't care and laughed when I told him. Even the stuff he gave mum was crap, sorry, but she didn't know the difference in the end. They were chasing me to get their money back. I'm frightened they might find me here.'

'Sam. In my opinion they'd be pretty stupid to turn up here and they don't know where you live.'

'Can I change my name so they don't?' He asks out of the blue.

'You'll be fine. There's no need to do that.'

'You don't understand.'

'I'm trying too.'

'I heard what Matt Wilson said to you about people coming to watch me once I've played a few games and I don't like that. Someone might see or hear my name. Even Larry knew I was going for a football trial and he might have told people. Can I change my name to Sam Thompson?' He concludes, standing looking at me.

Once again he's put his case and fears across well and I do understand. He does have a new life here but he does carry an awful lot of baggage. In the long term, changing his name isn't the solution, concluding matters of involvement is.

'How about we talk to Reg first? If you know these people he can do something about it.'

'I don't know their names. Larry called them things like, "A, J, D." That's all I knew about them.'

'When you delivered the stuff, did you take it to their houses?'

'Sometimes, but not often. I usually went to the local park or shopping centre car park to meet them. Don't you want me to change my name to Sam Thompson?'

'If that is what you would really like to do then I'll make inquiries, but I don't think it's as straight forward as that. What about your mum? If you do achieve great things in life, don't you want her to proud of you? You are Sam Cornish, do that in her memory.'

'She won't know will she?'

'But you will, and by fulfilling your dream, by working hard for what you want, sends out a very positive message to anyone in a similar situation.'

'Please let me, Dad.'

Leaning forward I take hold of Sam's hands. 'Sam, there may be a way around this. If this is something you really want I'll speak with Mary Robinson and DI Wallace. Because of your age there is a media ban on using your name in the press and we may be allowed to change your name on those grounds. Leave it with me and I'll see what I can do, but we must speak to DI Wallace. Can I phone him?'

'I don't mind.'

I've changed my plans for the day. Sam's state of mind is a concern and as his guardian it is my responsibility to deal with the situation. I have already contacted DI Wallace and he's due here at 10am. Mary Robinson is proving a little more difficult to contact directly so I've left several messages on her mobile phone. I have an idea that might just work for Sam in the short term but it needs authorising. Fact is, Barry Mullins managed to track him down so, his fears are justified.

Now dressed Sam is sat quietly watching TV. For the time being, unless we can resolve this, I'm not going to let him out of my sight. Mobile phone in hand I sit down on the settee with him. I must cover all the bases for his sake and speaking to Matt Wilson has become a priority.

'Sam, I'm going to do my utmost to resolve this today, but there is something you might need to think about. If we can change your name, we should change it completely. My gut feeling tells me we should change your

Christian name too because anyone with an ounce of sense will put two and two together.'

'I don't want to. I like my name Sam.'

'I do understand that. So this is what we can do. I want you to think of a Christian name you hate. It can be any name you like. Peter, John for instance and then, for argument sake, call you Peter Samuel Thompson. Then you can tell you friends you don't like your first name and that's why you like being called, Sam.'

'I don't like the name Larry.'

'Perhaps a little too obvious under the circumstances.'

'There was a boy called Frederick at my last school I didn't like. He was a bully and picked on me all the time.'

'Perfect. What about, Frederick Samuel Thompson?'

'I don't like the name…Frederick.'

'That's the whole point. Sam, I fully understand your fears and it's important we act quickly to keep you out of trouble. The sooner we agree on a name the better. We also need to get Matt Wilson up to speed on our intentions. You have training on Thursday and a friendly on Sunday and if this situation affects you in any way, I may be forced to stop you playing. It's that important, Sam. I am not knowingly going to put you at risk and playing is a risk. I'll give you a few minutes to think about what I've said, but one way or the other.' I add, holding the phone out in front of him. 'I will be phoning Matt very soon.' Standing, I step outside for a cigarette.

I don't like or want to be heavy handed with Sam, but he has raised a serious concern to his wellbeing and I must try to guide him into making the right decision, or I may be forced to make it for him. It's not long before he joins me outside.

'I knew a boy called George and his friends called him Georgie. That's a girl's name…isn't it?'

'It's more a nick name but I agree with you, it is a bit girlie. Is that what you'd prefer…George?'

95

'Yes.'

'Shall we agree on, George Samuel Thompson then?'

'Yes, but can I go back to Sam Thompson when this shit is over?'

Realising he's used the word shit again in front of me he immediately apologises. Acknowledging his apology I offer my hand and we shake on the deal.

Sam and I are sat waiting for DI Wallace to arrive. My understanding is, he's being accompanied by special officer trained in child phycology. I want to get this interview out of the way first before I discuss the matter in any detail with Matt Wilson. A self-employed heating engineer he's agreed to call in here on his way home. I asked him to for Sam's sake because this should be kept confidential. Particularly if any problems or issues arise at a later date.

Luckily, because I didn't want her here when DI Wallace arrived, Lucy hasn't turned up for Jack's hydrotherapy session, which is a blessing in disguise. According to Jack she has a hospital appointment. Nothing serious he told me, just a routine check-up. I also phoned Jan and told her not to bother until later on. I'll take Sam shopping for shoes later. I feel sure the fresh air will do us both good after this.

Not long after the hydro therapist has left and Jack has disappeared upstairs to get ready for work my door bell rings. The worried look on Sam's face concerns me. I've always maintained, knowing about Sam's background, that there's more to come from the young man. I have tried to avoid this interview, probably for that reason, for as long as I could but the consequences of delaying it any longer could be costly…for Sam.

Opening the front door DI Wallace has a female officer accompanying him. Not in uniform, she looks very young. Leading them through the house to the lounge, Sam has already switched off the TV. Making themselves comfortable I sit down next to Sam. DI Wallace opens the conversation.

'Nick, Sam, this is WPC Heather Grover. Heather is an expert in child phycology. If it's ok with you and to help us understand what is going on for Sam, we'd like to record this interview?'

I'm not happy with this and look at Sam to see his reaction. Nodding his head DI Wallace produces a tape record from inside his brief case. Setting it down on the coffee table he presses the record button. With it now running he looks at me.

'When we spoke earlier, Nick, you stated this was rather urgent. Would you like to explain that?'

'Sure. One of Sam's wishes was to start playing football again. Once he was given the all clear medically, I spoke to a guy by the name of Matt Wilson who is the youth team manager of the Bluebird juniors in Haverfordwest. Sam went training last Thursday and played for the under elevens last Sunday. After the game Matt suggested that Sam should be playing at a higher level because it was obvious to everyone he has potential. Matt's own words have scarred Sam. Matt told me that once Sam has played a few games and word got out, scouts from other clubs will be watching him, in particular, scouts working for professional football clubs.'

'Why should that be a problem?' WPC Grover asks. 'I've taken the time to read Sam's case notes and a hobby or sport would be great distraction for him.'

'Forgive me for saying this, but if you have read Sam's notes you would know that he already has connections with a professional football club in Bristol. His name is known within that community and anyone looking for him will make that connection.'

'What are you asking us to do, Nick?' DI Wallace adds.

'Something perhaps you, me, should have done weeks ago. Sam may have information stored away that's vital to you and as a key witness to, two ongoing investigations, you, me need to protect him.'

'I assume here that you are talking about the witness protection scheme. We can sanction that but there could be consequences in doing that for both you and Sam.'

'Like what?'

'Placing Sam in a safe house under 24/7 protection. In a place where he's not known and changing his name. Nick, we agreed to place Sam with you because it was deemed, considered a safe environment for him but if the situation has changed, then I must take the appropriate action. You are also right when you said Sam is a key witness in our enquiries.'

'Sam,' WPC Grover butts in. 'As DI Wallace stated, you testimony is very important to us. Therefore we have a duty to protect you and that can be achieved, but we also want you to progress and stay safe. Contrary to Mr Thompson's suggestion, I have read your case notes and you appear happy here. Is that the case, Sam?'

Nodding his head first, Sam verbally responds. 'I am happy here. Dad talks to me all the time and if I do something wrong, we sit down and talk about it. We do lots together and he likes watching me play football.'

'Dad, Sam?' WPC Grover responds.

'Why not? Dad has done more for me than anyone ever has. I want to change my name so those people can't find me.' While Sam continues I notice DI Wallace and WPC Grover look at each other. 'Dad and me talked about a name and we came up with, George Samuel Thompson. I don't like the name George, that's why I like people calling me Sam. Dad says I can go back to my old name if I want when this is all over. He says I should in memory of my mum, to make her proud of me.' I become more than aware that the two of them are staring at me. Sam is doing exactly what I hoped he'd do. To be positive, confident and talk openly about his own thoughts and concerns. He's listened to my advice and ideas, taken them on board and made up his own mind. 'People say I've got potential and I want to play football to see if I can prove them right.'

'Is playing football the only problem you have?' WPC Grover asks.

'Yes!' Sam answers her positively.

'Am I to assume here that you have already signed on for the Bluebirds in the name of Sam Cornish?' DI Wallace adds.

Time for me to take over. 'That is correct. I've asked his manager to call in to see us this evening and talk it through with him. I made it later today because I wanted to discuss this with you first. I have no wish to over complicate matters for Sam because he's adapted well and really moving forward. If we can change his name without too much difficulty he can continue to move on and do the things he wants to do without worrying about it.'

'Ok.' DI Wallace responds. 'Leave this with me. If WPC Grover is happy, I'll talk to the super when I return to the office. I'll be in touch as soon as I have and as far as Sam's football manager is concerned, find out if there are any complications. I'm sure you'll know what to say to him so I won't lecture you on the dos and don'ts.'

'I'm very happy,' WPC Grover adds as she stands. 'It's in our interest too, Sam, so we'll take care of this. Carry on doing what you're doing however, we will need to talk to again soon.'

Switching off the recorder DI Wallace stands and informs us he'll be in touch soon. Opening the front door for them my attention is immediately drawn to two smartly dressed men walking across my forecourt. Attired in suits, the one in the pinstripe I know. Sir Anthony Fothergill...my boss. Reaching me he holds out hand and I reciprocate.

'Nick. Good to see you. I must profoundly apologise for dropping in unannounced. I have business in the area later and thought I'd kill two birds with one stone.'

'Sir Anthony. Good to see you, Sir.'

'Agent Harvey confirmed you were at home but I see you have company.'

'Not a problem, Sir. This is...' I go to add, looking at DI Wallace when Sir Anthony cuts in.

'Detective Inspector Wallace. I do hope there isn't a problem, Nick?'

'Nothing I can't handle.'

'That's what I like to hear. DI Wallace, as you're here I'd like you to join us. I won't detain you long. Your colleague can wait for you in the car.'

'WPC Grover is here on official business with me...Sir. I'd like her to stay.'

'Be a good chap and do as I request. Your super is aware of this and what I must discuss with you both is not for the lower ranks to know about.'

'You don't mind if I check that?'

'I'd be worried if you didn't. Be quick, I don't have the time to be held to ransom.'

'I'll leave the door open.' I add churlishly.

Entering the lounge the look of horror on Sam's face when he sees the two suited gentlemen following me is clear for all to see. I quickly explain.

'Relax, Sam. These are the good guys.' Reacting quickly Sam comes and stands next to me. 'This is mine and Brad's boss...Sir Anthony Fothergill.'

Working for the home office, Sir Anthony is a tough but fair man. He's been very patient and tolerant where I'm concerned and my position within the department. Homeland security is a minefield. It's a team built on trust and knowledge who deal with extraordinary circumstances endeavouring to maintain our sovereignty. Saying he's tough probably doesn't do him justice. Top of his tree, the buck stops with him. That's a huge responsibility. I wouldn't want his job.

'Sam.' Sir Anthony says, coming to a stop in front of us. 'It's a pleasure to meet you at last. Agent Harvey has kept me up to date with your progress and he tells me you are doing well.'

'I am...Sir.' Sam answers as they shake hands.

'Come. Sit down with me for a moment.'

Watching with interest they sit down either end of the settee, facing each other. I instinctively know this isn't the time for me to say anything...to speak for Sam.

'DI Wallace is going to join us very soon. When he does I have private business to discuss with Nick and him. For many reasons you shouldn't know about our business so I'd like you to go up to your room for a while. Are you ok with that?' I watch as Sam gently nods his head. 'Good! I'll see that Nick makes the time up to you. Tell me, Sam, is DI Wallace here to see you?'

'Yes.' Sam answers quietly.

'I imagine he has many questions to ask you. Was he asking you questions about Sir Richard Moor and Barry Mullins?'

'No.' He again replies softly.

'I see. So what did he want to know?'

'I want to change my name.'

'I see! Are you on a witness protection scheme?' He adds, looking at me.

'An oversight by all parties…Sir.' I inform him. 'May I continue…Sir?'

'By all means.'

Sitting myself down on the arm of the settee next to Sam I prepare myself for a negative response. Mistakes are not tolerated in Sir Anthony's world, because mistakes cost lives in our business. I wish I had a pound for every time I've heard that said.

'This is an unusual situation. We have collectively done everything by the book to keep Sam safe. Sam though must lead a normal life as far as possible and his one wish from the start was to play football again. After weeks of hospital appointments and treatment Sam was finally given the all clear to follow his dream.

'We sat down together and spoke about where he'd like to play and as I have connections with Haverfordwest FC, I rang them and they suggested I spoke to the Bluebird junior's manager Matt Wilson. An ex semi pro himself, he's a good guy.

'I took Sam training last Thursday and spoke to Matt about Sam's position. Without giving too much away I explained his situation to him. Sam impressed Matt and once training had finished Sam signed on. He then played in a friendly on Sunday, which they won and Sam had a very good game. Sir, Sam has real potential, everyone could see that last Sunday and that's where the problem has arisen. After the game Matt told me that Sam should be playing at a higher level and once he's played a few games word would filter through the leagues and there would be a good chance that professional club's would show an interest in him. Sam overheard our conversation and it's worrying him. Sam has brought this to my attention, Sir, because when he lived in the Bristol area he had connections with a professional club there. His name is known within that community and anyone with an ounce of sense could put two and two together and come looking for him. Sam wants to change his name to stop that happening and I agree with him.'

'May I ask, what is DI Wallace doing about this? Is he going to help because in my opinion, this should have been taken care of from the beginning?'

'He hasn't disagreed with Sam's request and told us that he'd talk to his superintendent ASAP. To be fair on all parties concerned, the only person to see this coming was Sam. The minute he expressed his concerns to me, which was this morning, we've all reacted swiftly. It's being dealt with and I hope, without too much upheaval in Sam's life.'

'I hope not too. I'm on your side here and I will and make it happen.'

'Thank you,' Sam whispers.

My attention is immediately drawn to Jack appearing in the hall doorway. He stops in his tracks when he sees two strangers in the lounge.

'What's going on, Dad?' He asks.

'Jack.' I reply, taking a few steps towards him. 'This is my boss, Sir Anthony Fothergill and an associate of his. We have some business to discuss so can you phone Richard and ask him to pick you up.'

'I already have. I saw Wallace arriving,' he adds with distain. 'And didn't want to hang around.'

'I gather you're not a fan of DI Wallace.' Sir Anthony asks as he stands.

'That's a polite way of saying it.'

'Do you have a problem with authority, Jack?'

'The man's a prick.'

'Jack!' I shout at him.

'Let him finish.' Sir Anthony responds. 'Why do you think he's a prick, Jack?'

'Because he's relied on my dad for information over the years but treats him like shit. Sorry, Dad, but it's true.' Finishing Jack looks straight at me. Glancing at me briefly, Sir Anthony continues engaging with Jack.

'Forgive me for asking you this, but how do you know that?'

'Everyone knows. Ask anyone in the office and they'll tell you the same thing.'

'Have you spoken to your father about this?'

'No, Sir, but I have seen it for myself too. It's one way traffic with him because he never gives in return. Sam's a great kid, Sir, but had Wallace got his own way he wouldn't be sat with us now. I know Brad got involved at some point and that's when things changed. I have no idea what was said then but you need to know Dad's doing a great job for Sam and me and he should be taking the credit, not some arrogant prick.' Finishing his rant Jack walks over to me and puts his arms around my shoulders. 'Sorry, Dad, but someone had to speak up on your behalf. Sam and me know you're going through a tough time too and no one else seems to care that much, or ask how you are feeling. You know we do and we will help you with anything you need.'

'Thank you, Jack. I do know that and I appreciate you telling me.'

'I do hope that wasn't for my benefit?' Before I have the chance to respond to Sir Anthony's jibe, Jack jumps in feet first.

'How dare you, Sir! Dad works hard for Sam and me, supporting us, driving us here and there, talking to us when we need him to and I also know he has a lot of other things on his mind right now. I would not have said those things if I didn't mean them and you should know that.'

'That's enough, Jack. I think Sir Anthony has got the message. What time is Richard picking you up?'

'Now!' He tells me, looking at his wrist watch. 'He's taking me over to Haverfordwest so I can enrol on an electrical and electronic course.'

'That's great news! Have a good day and I'll see you late.'

'Will you be alright?'

'I'm good. Don't keep Richard waiting.' Giving him some money for lunch I watch him push past DI Wallace on his way out. Despite what he's said in my defence, I don't like hearing that sort of thing from him.

'Detective Inspector Wallace. How nice of you too join us, and you are alone.' Sir Anthony offers.

'My super has instructed me to give you my full cooperation, Sir.'

'Good, good. Just as I had expected.'

Looking at Sam he knows it's time he disappeared. As he passes me I inform him that once I'm finished we'll go shopping for school shoes.

'Ok gentlemen, shall we get down to business. Please take a seat.' Once we're comfortable, Sir Anthony continues. 'There is one thing I must make very clear to you both first. This is a joint operation between departments and information sharing is a mandatory requirement. I hope I'm making myself very clear on that point? Something Detective Inspector I understand you're not very good at…information sharing.'

I become aware of Reg staring at me so I shrug my shoulders. Jack was right, Reg has never given me any information unless it was worth his while.

'Let's move on. In this instance Detective Inspector, Agent Thompson is working for the department, not himself so to allay any confusion, he is your equal on this assignment. This is very important simply because we 'must' conclude this business quickly.

'This is the point where I stress upon you, Nick, that I need your time and dedication and as always, working alongside Agent Harvey. Your boys gave a good account of themselves today and I feel sure they will understand. The thing I liked most, they're not afraid to speak up for themselves and I respect that.

'Detective Inspector. Get this business with young Sam sorted quickly. You would if he was one of your own so see to it. I will be speaking to your super in the morning and I will ask him for an update on the progress.'

'Consider it done, Sir.'

'Excellent. Right gentlemen…drugs. I'm reliably informed that you are both aware of the current problem locally and this is serious enough in its own right. However, gentlemen, recent information received has highlighted a far more serious issue and it's possible this situation is deliberate action to tie up already stretched resources. I'll let Agent Mitchell take it from here.'

Stepping forward, standing in front of my fireplace facing us, Agent Mitchell places his hands behind his back. 'Thank you, Sir. Gentlemen, as of 8am this morning the national security level was raised to amber. Ports and airports have increased their security levels accordingly but as we know, freedom of travel within the European community makes that task a little more complicated. Agent Harvey has done a lot of groundwork recently and we are currently following up on his findings. The national security level was increased because we intercepted coded messages which lead us to believe a terrorist campaign is imminent. The target is unknown so we need to stay alert.

'In 1995 similar distraction methods to those we are witnessing here in South West Wales tied up vital resources and it was only by pure luck that we prevented a potential catastrophe. We are not going to rely on luck this time gentlemen, so your diligence and hard work is required to thwart any attempt to smuggle in arms or explosives. I don't need to tell you that it doesn't take a great deal of explosive material to create havoc and mayhem, so we are looking for a needle in a haystack until we gather more information. We also appear to be targeting fishing vessels but please be aware that we have numerous other shipping movements, such as the leisure industry at this time of year. Harbour Masters have been made aware of the situation and will work alongside you guys, so routinely check in with them and double check all regular and unusual movements. You are not alone in this operation, however, it is your responsibility to check all comings and goings in this area. Needless to say, any information gathered must be shared and passed on up the chain of command immediately. Leave no stone unturned gentlemen. Any questions?'

Silence prevails before Sir Anthony takes over. 'Thank you, Agent Mitchell. Detective Inspector Wallace. Your orders will come directly from your Super who is putting a team of experienced officers together to work with you. Nick, you liaise with Agent Harvey as normal. Gentlemen, if you are clear about where we need to go with this I'll leave you to carry on.' Standing, Sir Anthony turns to face me. 'Nick. I am fully aware of your situation and having met your boys, I fully understand the pressure you're under to make their lives better. Nick, you are good at what you do and I value your input, so I really do need your help on this one. I'll make the lost time up to you when we're done, that's a promise. Can I rely on you?'

'Yes, Sir, you can.'

'Good man. How does a trip to Lapland or Disney World for you and the boys later in the year sound to you?'

'I don't expect you to do that for us, Sir.'

'Look after me and I'll look after you.'

Closing the front door behind them my mood turns to anger. Committed, I have no choice in the matter. I fully understand the urgency attached, but I'm not ready to give them my time. Christ! I'm only a couple of months down the road after my major surgery and the physiological affect that has. Turning to walk back through the house Sam is standing at the bottom of the stairs. Shoes, I think. Heading off to collect my car keys the home phone rings.

Chapter Seven

Sam selected the most expensive pair of black shoes in the shop. Under the circumstances I refrained from making any sort of comment. The last thing I want right now is to place the pressure I'm under onto his or Jack's shoulders. Once that task was completed I phoned my accountant on the cars hands free set while driving over to Tom's. Sam of course heard every word, which wasn't ideal, but at least he may begin to understand the pressure I'm under.

Tom phoned me just as Reg and Sir Anthony left. I have an incoming number display on the home phone and I didn't recognise the callers' number. When I was asked by the telephonist if would accept the charges and heard Tom's voice, alarm bells started to sound. Hopefully, being cut off from the outside world will bring the seriousness of the situation home. I may need to buy him a cheap pay-as-you-go mobile.

On the way over Sam criticised my driving…again. Normally it's because I drive too fast. Today he said I was driving like an old man…to slowly. My response was very simple, I told him that I was in no hurry to get to Tom's because the last time I was there he was rather sharp with me and I don't care for that much. I put a great offer on the table for them to consider and all he cared about was Ceri's future. In a way I do understand his feelings because blood is thicker than water, but there is no future for the farm if Tom plays out his own hand.

Pulling up outside the farmhouse, with the instruction not to say anything, I suggest to Sam that he goes on inside ahead of me. Where they are concerned, I don't discuss their business privately with him. I need a few moments to digest what my accountant said and think over the possible consequences of moving forward with the purchase if they agree to my offer. When Tom phoned he didn't say very much, other than he needed to talk, which bothers me. Smoking a cigarette I decide to phone my solicitor to brush up on the latest. He was undertaking a land registry search on Tom's land and knowing the outcome before stepping inside could save me a lot of time and trouble.

Sat in his chair Tom doesn't move or look at me when I step into the kitchen. Sam I note is sat with mother at the table. Empty tea mugs in front of them suggest I've missed out on a brew. Electing to join them I sit down opposite Sam who informs me I've been a long time. Staring at mother I wait for them to speak first.

'We have decided not to sell the farm to you.' She eventually offers.

'Fine! That's your decision and if you've had a better offer...good luck. Let me just say one thing before I leave. There is a covenant on the land which you may or may not know about. That covenant could change things drastically for any prospective buyer.'

'That's nonsense boy!' Tom growls at me.

'I beg to differ, Tom.' I reply standing up. 'Your Great, Great Grandfather, Alfred Morgan, signed an agreement in 1883 with the district council, stating that no buildings can be erected on your land, other than on the footprint you have now. I've seen Summerbee's futuristic plans for your land and because of the covenant, they have very little chance of gaining planning permission. To add insult to injury where you are concerned, your figures don't add up to the tune of thirty grand...more. Sam, we should go. Matt Wilson is calling into see us later and I want to be ready.' Reaching the outside door Sam joins me. I have one last thing to say. 'I've done my homework and laid my last card on the table, so I'm done. I have to get on with my own life and that's complicated enough without this shit. When I walk out of this door, it will be for the last time.'

Closing the outer door behind me I pause for a moment and take a last look around me. Thirty three years of coming to the farm, spending time with Tom and his family has come to an end without fight or a goodbye. I didn't want it to be like this and that saddens me.

'Are you really not coming back?' Sam asks as we head back to the car.

'Sam, I made them a great offer. Told them they could stay in the house and you heard what mother said, they didn't want to sell the farm to me. There is nothing else I can do. Plus, I have bigger priorities, like you and Jack and unfortunately, going back to work. Trust me, Sam, it's not an easy decision for me to make and it hurts deep down.

'Can I talk to them?'

108

'That's very sweet of you, but I don't think it will do much good.'

'Please! Let me try.'

'Why?'

'I want to do something for you.'

After a moments' thought I respond to Sam's generous offer. 'Thank you, Sam. If you're sure you want to do this for me, then I'll wait.'

Aware that I'm clock watching, I know Sam has been gone at least ten minutes. Either he has had a lot to say for himself or they are still in denial. In that time I've wandered up the lane towards the main road. The dirt track is in a sorry state of repair. Fixing that alone will cost a lot of money, but why am I worrying? Pausing, I can hear Sam calling me. Approaching the house he's stood waiting beside the car. His demeanour doesn't look great. Then I'm not surprised.

'So?' I ask, reaching him. When he takes his time answering, it bothers me.

'Tom said they signed some papers one day last week.'

Taken aback I answer him quite sharply. 'Get into the car, Sam. Let's go.' When he doesn't move I repeat myself.

'Don't you want to know who with?'

'Well it wasn't me, so it's none of my business.'

'What was that thing you told them about? You know, about building.'

'A covenant. An agreement. Why?'

'He says you're lying. Making it up to scare him.'

'Really?' Opening the car door I order Sam to get in. I've heard quite enough and knowing they've gone behind my back…grates.

Matt Wilson arrived at the house a little before 6pm. What I had to say didn't take very long and he fully understood Sam's concerns. Confident the FA will understand, he promised to phone the league secretary tonight and explain the situation. There may be nothing either of us can do until DI Wallace sorts his end out. I understand that, but it may result in Sam missing the game on Sunday morning. He wasn't best pleased when he heard that. Sitting down with him after Matt left I tried the best I could to make him understand, with the promise that I would take care of the problem. Sam though lives to play football and reasoning with him where his football is concerned, takes a lot of patience. I like to think I made some progress but Sam is a very driven young man, in most of the things he tackles. Naively, at times it must be said, he carries the attitude that life revolves around him and it's all about what Sam wants.

In the chaos of what was this morning I overlooked the post. Taking a few minutes to myself, which are becoming rarer by the day and finding myself already mentally planning my movements tomorrow, I pick up the small pile of letters and flick through them. Tucked in the middle a white envelope addressed to Jack stands out from the rest. It's painfully obvious to me, from the hand writing on the envelope, who the sender is. I cannot, not give Jack the letter, but I'm certain a letter from his mother will unsettle him at this time. Starring at the letter for a moment I set it down on the kitchen work surface where I know he will find it. Situations such as this must be left for him to decide upon, without my interference. Recent developments have given Jack a direction in life and a pleading, miss you so much letter cold be detrimental to his progress.

Wednesday 3rd September

Getting Sam ready for school, making sure he had everything he would need occupied my time this morning. I did however notice that the letter I left on the side for Jack to find had gone. Curious, I did check the waste bin in the kitchen and I couldn't see it. He must know I know but in our rush to get ready, nothing was said or discussed. My opinion is, if he wants to talk about the letter it should be on his terms. My own thoughts and feelings towards her are possessive and not those that Jack may share or agree with. Jenny walked out seven weeks ago without a care or thought for him and a lot of water has passed under the bridge in that time. Getting on for two months ago that's a long time. My concern is as always, she's finding that life on the other side isn't always greener.

I have been set a monumental task. Brad emailed me a list of harbour masters in Pembrokeshire this morning. Long enough in itself, he also suggested I should check all the inlets and sheltered coves along the coastline where mooring is allowed in agreement with the local harbour master. That is a huge task to undertake, especially when the River Cleddua is navigable for miles inland and has numerous tributaries.

I know I am the foot soldier in this arrangement, doing the groundwork, but I doubt they know my overall knowledge of the local area is very limited. I am ashamed to admit that because my work has taken me far and wide and unless I've had the need to be somewhere locally for work purposes, my life here has otherwise been cocooned. The sad truth is, I've probably seen more of Pembrokeshire in the past few months with the boys, than I have over the last thirty-years. That is shameful but it's time to explore and educated myself.

My feelings about todays' foray are that I'm wasting my time. If the harbour masters are doing their jobs, and I've no reason to think otherwise, they will pick up anything unusual or mooring requests that have become suspiciously regular. I believe I will be of more use following up on the information Gwyn Roberts supplied me with. There's an answer there somewhere. Against my better judgement I'm carrying out this thankless task because if I don't, questions will be asked of me. Brad probably, or perhaps Sir Anthony will double check that their orders are being carried out to the letter.

Jan is on standby to collect Sam later in the day just in case I lose track of the time. He seemed happy enough when I dropped him off at the school gates and drove off to start my own incredible journey. As I live in Saundersby and my office overlooks the harbour I stay up to date on the goings on, so I'll start my day at Fenby.

Parking on the quay close to the harbour masters office, I place my unofficial parking permit on the dash board and exit my car, pausing for a moment or two looking down at the boats in the harbour. I've done this countless times and nothing looks out of place. The harbour master, Euan Price, is a relatively new face in this old harbour. A forthright man, he's already ruffled a few feathers in his short time here. Far be it for me to say but some of the older characters using the harbour needed to know who the boss really is. Euan is responsible for the harbours activities and safety and anyone I understand, business or otherwise, who steps out of line is very quickly told to sort it, or move on.

Stepping inside the office Euan doesn't look up from his computer screen. His assistant, a much younger man, nods his head in acknowledgement. I've not had a lot of dealings with him and know little about him.

'Take a seat, Nick. I'll be right with you.' Euan pipes up. Taking up his offer he looks up at me. 'I was expecting a visit this morning but I didn't think it would be you. I assume this is on official business?'

'You've had the communication then?'

'Yes. Came through yesterday evening just before I went home. Not very helpful if I must say, because it's not specific. What exactly are we looking for? Is it drugs? Illegals? You tell me.'

'You know as much as I do. We're looking for anything we consider unusual or suspicious and report our findings if we do.'

'I'm struggling with that, Nick, because if you are working for DI Wallace you'd be better informed. You said this was official, so come on.'

'No. You assumed I was here on official business.'

'Aren't you then?'

112

'I am, but I'm not working directly for DI Wallace. Can't say any more than that, so take it or leave it.'

'I think we should take a little walk.' Euan suggests, looking hard at me. Nodding my head I stand and make my way back outside. Euan soon joins me.

'Nick. Rumours have been circulating for some time that you are working for the government in some capacity. Is that true?'

Taking my time to respond I head in the direction of the breakwater with Euan at my side. 'You shouldn't believe everything you hear. Even if there was some truth in the rumour you know I'm not at liberty to confirm your thoughts. I strongly suggest we leave it there. So! Are your records computerised and if they are, do you have access to other harbour masters' information?'

'That's an admission if I ever heard one. For your information, I log my movements every morning and yes, we do share information but that information is classified.'

'It may be sensitive information, but it's not classified. I want access to that information by linking it to my business computer.'

'You know I can't do that.'

'I should make you aware that I can and will force you to comply and will take it to the top if required. I have a copy of the email you received yesterday and I know it states, that you are to assist the authorities in any way you can. It is vital that we get on top of this situation quickly, so please don't obstruct my investigation. I am aware that your files contain personal details but I will guaranty those details will not be shared, unless we have reason to believe otherwise. I stress upon you that your cooperation is vital.'

'Nick! I am in charge of this harbour and until you prove to me that you have the authority, I will not comply too your ridiculous demands. I will not be helping you today. You are a private investigator who occasionally works alongside the police...nothing else.'

Stopping in my tracks I pull my mobile phone out of my pocket and phone DI Wallace in front of Euan. Informing Wallace that I'm being obstructed in my line of duty by Euan Price and he needs to sort this out, he tells me he'll be about ten minutes.

'DI Wallace is on his way. I hope he fucking cautions you.'

I elected to wait outside while Wallace discussed the problem with Euan. I hope he's been professional in his approach and not given sensitive information away in exchange for Euan's cooperation. Twenty minutes down the road Wallace steps out of the harbour masters office and joins me.

'Sorry, Reg. I'm not ready for the intensity of this. I became very frustrated by his negativity because I want this shit over and done with.'

'It's fine. I've sorted it. Euan made a couple of phone calls in front of me and he's been told to cooperate. I've given him your email address, and mine for that matter because I want to be in the loop. All we need to do is open the email, click on the link and we'll have that information. Don't be too concerned by what has happened, just try and be a little more tactful. Unfortunately, although his information gives us names and addresses, it's also flawed.'

'Of course it is. Like now, we have a near high tide in the middle of the morning, which means the next high tide will be in the early hours of tomorrow. Who is taking notes then?'

'The bad news doesn't end there…does it? Along this wonderful coastline of ours we have numerous inlets and coves, many of which are secluded. A good mariner with local knowledge, charts, tide-times and up to date weather conditions, could sneak in and out undetected. It's a ridiculous situation to put us in. That guy with Sir Anthony at your place said he didn't want to rely on luck this time, but that is exactly what it will be if we do find something illegal going on. I'm heading back to the factory to speak with the super, which reminds me, to request we have off shore support in our search. It isn't going happen otherwise. Meet me there, Nick. The super has some news for you and I think you should hear it first-hand.'

After thirty odd years of working alongside DI Wallace and walking through the inner sanctum of the factory to his office on many an occasion, I should be at home here. I'm not and it still makes me feel uneasy. This morning though we're heading for his super's office. Entering his office, Super Intendant Lewis is sat behind his desk in full uniform.

114

'Ah, Nick. Please take a seat. I have some news for you.'

'Good news I hope?' I respond as we sit down.

'Can you be here at 3pm tomorrow? I ask you this because Mary Robinson and a colleague of hers will be here at that time to sort this business with young Sam out once and for all. Sam will need to come with you as Mary has requested to talk to him personally.'

'Sam is back at school, sir.'

'I have spoken to his head mistress and she's fine with that. In fact she has requested to attend and I have agreed.'

'May I ask, sir, can this meeting take place at my place?'

'Absolutely! I did suggest that when we spoke. Like you I image, meeting at your house will be more comfortable for young Sam. I'll make those calls when we've finished.'

'Thank you, sir.'

'I have also spoken to Sir Anthony Fothergill on your behalf. I personally feel that asking you to monitor all the ports and harbours is too much. You cannot be everywhere at once. If it is acceptable to you I would like you to work with us on the arson attack at the hostel. Led by DI Wallace, his team will monitor the ports and harbours. How do you feel about this change, Nick?'

'Is Sir Anthony fine with this, sir?'

'Yes. Sir Anthony trusts my judgement.'

'Then I won't let you down.'

'Good. DI Wallace, I would like you to spend time bringing Nick up to date with the investigation so far and introduce him to DS Thomas and PC Hughes.'

'Yes, Sir.'

'When you're done, you and I will brief the team.'

Having spent nearly an hour with DI Wallace it's a relief to be back out on the street, making my way down to the harbour. I have some reading to do before I meet DS Thomas and his team at the hostel. He's a man very much in the same mould of DI Wallace. Black and white and always looking for an edge, he has no personality. This should be fun.

Reg gave me a copy of the pathology reports on the death of Hanna Green and David Griffiths and the latest forensic report on the cause of the fire. I'd like to talk to both of those authors to gauge for myself the level of investigative effort that went into those reports. That is never going to happen it saddens me to admit. Being bottom of the food chain you spend your life looking over your shoulder, not the other way around. Left with just the paperwork to digest I need to sit myself down somewhere quiet and read between the lines, in the hope I might find something that could be considered…ambiguous.

Dropping by the house to pick up Gwyn's paperwork and having a quick chat with Jan, who informed me that Tom phoned, I head down to the office. Parking in my space I question why I'm here. If I go into the office I'll not have the peace and quiet I seek. Locking my car I walk down the harbour wall towards the breakwater. Halfway down, with the sun on my back, I sit on one of the many bench seats dotted around the harbour.

I've chosen this particular bench to rest on because it's right in front of my mooring berth. Three months ago, almost, I could have sat on the sun deck to relax. Its demise was my doing, my decision and I'm still arguing with the insurance company over the claim I submitted. It was hardly accidental and I do see their point in refusing to pay out, but the policy I had with them was comprehensive and included a clause for using the boat on work related business. Sketchy I know, so I've left it in the hands of my solicitor.

I know why I'm here. Yesterday, the decision to buy Tom's farm was taken out of my hands. I was extremely angry with them at the time for being so deceitful. I don't want the farm but I wanted to help them and they turned their backs on me. Once I had calmed down, with the knowledge of having the money available in the back of my mind, I began thinking about what I could do with the cash. Buying another boat was high on that list. If I go with that, the decision to go ahead will probably be based on what the boys think, not what I think. I rarely used my boat last year and viewed its purchase as a waste of money. From what Jan told me, regarding Tom's call, the situation may yet change.

Looking at my phone for the time I have around thirty minutes to drive over to the hostel, which in reality should only take ten minutes. Deciding to read one more paragraph before I tidy up and leave, someone speaking to me disturbs my concentration.

'Penny for them?'

'Where do I start?' I reply, looking up to see Ed Morgan, the shipwright who rents the ground floor space underneath my office.

'May I?' Ed asks, gesturing at the bench.

'Sure'

'Thinking about getting another boat, Nick?'

'I'm considering it. The way forward isn't to clear or certain at the moment, so I'm not sure.'

'Things around here certainly haven't been the same since you and young Sam were shot.'

'Tell me about it.'

'Can't put my finger on why, but folks don't seem to want to stop and pass the time of day anymore.'

'I'm sorry if this has affected your business, Ed, but I can assure you I didn't plan what happened.'

'I'm not blaming you. What happened that day has affected a lot of people in town and I'm thinking they're being over cautious. Life is very fragile and it only takes one idiot to change peoples' lives.'

'Are you suggesting that because my office is still here, people are assuming it could happen again?'

'I'm only saying.'

'It was a one off and you know that and let me remind you, no one deserves to be stabbed or shot at…right or wrong. I'm telling you once and for all, this shit stops here and now and if it impacts in any way on Sam, I will have something to say about it. Am I making myself quite clear? Are people blaming me for the stabbing in Milford Road last year, too?'

'No! We all know that was drug related. That kid was a wrong-un and had it coming to him.'

'You don't know that?'

'I'm just saying, Nick. Anyway, you won't hear it from me. I'm calling it a day…moving on as they say. I can't compete with the new generation of mobile workshops in their flashy vans, loaded up with top of the range tools, test gear and equipment. I'm going to live with my sister on the edge of Dartmoor, across the water there in Devon. She has a small holding and needs a little help these days.' Standing he continues. 'I'm in the process of clearing my workshop. I reckon it'll take me about two weeks, so kindly let me know how much rent I owe.'

Finishing, Ed storms off but my mind is already thinking about the teenager stabbed last year. I wasn't involved at any stage but I understand, no one was ever charged for his murder. I'd like to see the file.

My enlightening conversation with Ed has delayed my progress. Parking near Gwyn's temporary office I set off for the rear of the hostel when my phone rings.

'Yes, Jan?' I snap, answering her call.

'Tom phoned again. He said it was very important he spoke to you.'

'I'm very busy, Jan, and I haven't got the time.'

'You're not going to speak to him…are you?'

'For your ears only…no. He knows what the deal is and if he's got anything more to say, give him my solicitor's number and tell him to talk to him. I have wasted more than enough time talking to them and I'm done with it.'

'Are you alright?'

'No I'm bloody not and Tom's not helping. Don't forget to pick Sam up later.' Ending the call I'm really angry. With what Ed had eluded to about the folks in town, suggesting I was the one at fault for their mood, it now sounds like Tom has discovered the truth concerning his land and may have changed his mind…again. I can't be doing with all this shit.

'Problem?' DS Thomas asks as I approach.

'My housekeeper is sticking her nose in where it's not wanted. Nothing I can't deal with.'

'Where do you know Linda Jefferies from?' He asks out of the blue.

'I don't know a Linda Jefferies.'

'A long time then. I believe her maiden name was Griffiths.'

Stopping in my tracks I stare at him. 'How do you know that?'

'I know her estranged husband Paul. He's head of the forensic department at Cardiff University now. I got to know him before he made his career move, during the period when he did a lot of good work for us. In my opinion, he is a very clever man.'

'How? Work wise or getting shot of Linda?'

'Now, now. My wife and I use to socialise with Paul and Linda back then. Admittedly, she could be hard work at times, with her controversial views.'

'So it's not just me she bitches at?'

'You do know her then?'

'I have known Linda a very long time, but until the other day I hadn't seen her for at least twenty-five years. And quite honestly, I hope it's another twenty-five years until I see her again.'

'That's probably when I saw you together. I had been playing with the kids on the beach one Sunday afternoon. When we decided to go home we walked along the promenade and you and Linda were sat outside the Temple Bar with two other people. I must assume the young lad with you was Sam, the elder person I didn't know.'

'That would have been my housekeeper, Jan. Linda is staying with her for a few days.'

119

'Can I advise you not to get involve?'

'There's no fear of that. The woman's poison, but thanks for the warning. Shall we get on with what we came here for?'

Spending half an hour in the company of DS Thomas talking about the cause of the fire, I've learnt nothing new. DI Wallace had given me the lowdown a few days ago and they've said pretty much the same thing, which is echoed in the forensic report. His report concluded that sparks from a loose terminal on the freezer, in which he stated the large flat bottomed screw was 1.8mm above the coinciding base, was probably the root cause. Adding in a following statement, the insulation surrounding the freezer was not of a fire retardant manufacture. DS Thomas did air his views on that point, because he has his doubts. I nearly suggested he phoned Paul Jefferies for a second opinion, but thought better of it. I do however tend to agree with DS Thomas, purely because the report suggested, due to the tarnishing found on the underside of the screw that the screw in question had been in that position for three to four weeks, possibly longer. The uneducated side of me questions the reliability of the freezer in that period. I agree it was unusual, but the loose screw could simply be down to bad maintenance procedures. In my mind, the freezer would either have worked, or failed, not spewed out sparks every time it ran. The report is way too flimsy for my liking. Which could be the reason why they didn't find anything incriminating.

Going via my car to collect Gwyn's paperwork I step inside her temporary office. She's talking to someone on the phone. Waiting for her to finish I cast my eyes around her new office. She's well organised and has a number of home comforts surrounding her. On her desk I notice a rather ornate silver picture frame which contains a photograph of an elder gentleman standing next to three children in front of a steam locomotive.

'My husband Alf, and three of my grandchildren.' She offers, noticing me looking at the picture. 'The boys love steam engines so we took them up to Porthmadog for a trip on the Ffestiniog railway last May bank holiday. Beautiful it was and the grandchildren loved it.'

'Your paperwork, Gwyn, as promised.' I respond, placing the pile on her desk in front of her.

'Thank you. Any use to you?'

'Could be. I'm still working on that. Does your husband work here with you?'

'No. He's a self-employed gardener and odd job man. He does alright for himself, but the winter months can be slow.'

'I imagine they can. I should think he gets under your feet in the depths of winter?'

'Not really. The winter storms we get here can generate quite a bit of work for him. Repairing garden fences, sheds, summer houses and the like. He loves his woodworking and often builds summer houses and garden sheds from scratch for clients. His basic knowledge of electrics comes in handy too.'

'I'm sure it does. Thanks, Gwyn, I'll be in touch if anything comes up.'

'Before you go. Do you know how soon it will be before we can get the builders in?'

'I don't, but I'll make a few enquiries for you.'

I'm sat outside 72 Milford Road in my car. A quick phone call to the office before I left the hostel confirmed the address I wanted. This is where murdered teenager Owain Parry lived with his parents.

I'm hesitant. Knocking on the door could open up nasty and challenging memories for the family. My persistent knocking is eventually answered by whom I believe to be Mrs Parry. Of average height, her long black hair and thick rimmed glasses obscure her facial features.

'Mrs Parry. I'm...'

'I know who you are. What do you want Mr Thompson?'

'I'd like to ask you a few questions about your son Owain, if it's ok with you?'

'Are you working for DI Wallace?'

'With him and his team, yes. I'd like to ask you about Owain's last movements and a little about his background. Can I come in?'

121

Opening the door fully Mrs Parry invites me in. Following her through the house to the kitchen at the rear, she pulls out a stool and asks me to sit.

'We went through all this with the police. Owain was a good son, Mr Thompson. How they think he was involved with drugs is beyond us. I assume that is why you're here? He never gave us any reason to think he was an addict and they didn't find any drugs, needles and the like in his room, or the house. The police later told us that he was clean when they found him, but they did find traces of heroin in one of his coat pockets. In our mind, that wasn't proof enough of him being a dealer.'

'Did he have money problems?'

'No! Owain started working in a warehouse a week after leaving school. He earned reasonable money and always paid his house keeping on time. When he passed his driving test, the company asked him if he'd like go out on deliveries. He always told us he loved his job and we have no reason to doubt him. Driving gave him the freedom he liked.'

'What about his friends. Do you know if they were into drugs?'

'I don't know the answer to that, but one or two of his friends couldn't be trusted and Owain knew that.'

'Could they have influenced him?'

'They are boys he grew up with. Peer pressure and wanting to be part of the crowd can play tricks on the mind. Yes Owain did have his problems as a young teenager, don't they all, but he turned into a loving, caring young man and he's missed by everyone he knew. Owain was a happy young man, Mr Thompson, I would do anything to get justice for him.'

'I'll do my best for you, Mrs Parry. Tell me something, where did Owain work?'

'He worked for a company called Forrest's, in Haverfordwest.'

Stepping outside through the open front doorway Mrs Parry grabs my arm. 'There is one thing I've just remembered. Soon after Owain started driving for them, he told me that Friday's were always manic during the summer months, so he asked his boss if he could have some help on that day.

They apparently paired him with an old bloke who Owain immediately took a dislike to. He said he only put up with him because he finished his round on time.'

'Does this old bloke have a name?'

'I believe Owain called him Alf. Don't know a surname.'

'Did you tell the investigating officer this at the time?'

'I'm fairly sure I didn't. It just came to me then as we spoke. Could it be important?'

'It could be. Thank you, Mrs Parry, I'll let you know. One last thing. Did Owain ever say why he didn't like Alf?'

'I don't remember. Hang on! It could have been something to do with extra drops Alf wanted to make. I'm not sure.'

Driving the short distance down to the office I'm questioning whether I should pass the information on as instructed. Protocol demands I must but I have a problem with that. I'm connecting two quite independent sources of information with Alf without solid evidence. The common denominator in both cases is drugs but I cannot prove that connection...yet.

Parking my car Jack and Richard are unloading their tools from the back of Richard's 4x4. A Toyota Tacoma SR5, the demands of his work secured its purchase earlier in the year. Sadly, rural crime is on the increase and many farmers are turning to modern technology to enhance their security. Cameras and powerful flood lighting seem to be the way forward at this time. This increase in his work load is keeping Richard busy and the need to have a reliable, all-terrain vehicle for those awkward jobs, fast became a necessity.

'Jack, Richard. Finished for the day?'

'Where's Sam?' Jack asks.

'I'm working so I asked Jan to pick him up from school. I hope she did anyway.'

'I don't like you working, Dad.'

'I'm not too pleased myself, but I have little choice in the matter right now.'

'I need a lock-up, Nick. This loading and unloading, taking the tools up and downstairs to and from my office every day, is a painful exercise.'

'Hold that thought.'

'What do you mean?'

'Ed informed me this morning he's calling it a day. Says he needs a couple of weeks to clear his crap away, then he'll be gone. Ideal place for you to set up I shouldn't wonder.'

'It would be perfect. Two weeks you say?'

'That's what he told me.'

'Won't you miss the income?' Jack adds.

'We won't miss the amount Ed managed to pay us over the years. I'd like a fiver for every time we've threatened him with legal action for non-payment of his rent. We won't miss the money, Jack, because we've never had it.'

'I'll go and speak to Ed when we've finished. See if I can hurry him along.'

'I'd rather you didn't. If Ed thinks for one minute that we've plans for the workshop, he'll go out of his way to obstruct us. Let's give him a week or so to make sure he's on the level.' Seeing Jack pick up a couple of tool boxes I stop him from leaving. 'Jack. Did you know a lad called Owain Parry at school?'

'I knew of him. He was three years older than me.'

'Did you know any of his mates?'

'Not really. Couple of them were losers so we ignored them.'

'Do you remember any of their names?'

'Why?'

'Has this got something to do with the deaths in Fenby?' Richard inquires.

124

'I don't know yet, but whoever murdered Owain Parry is still out there somewhere and his death was linked to drugs, so who knows. Jack, if you do remember anything, please let me know. Right! I'm going to pop into the office and speak to Graham. I'll be about ten minutes if you want a lift home, Jack?'

Graham is standing in the kitchenette off the main office making himself a coffee when I arrive upstairs. 'Hello stranger. What brings you to the office this late in the day?'

'I need your expertise.'

'I'm listening.'

'How easy would it be to trace someone's business credentials?'

'Local?'

'Yeah. A self-employed gardener by the name of Alf, or Alf Roberts.'

'Let's take a look. It'll take me a few minutes, so make yourself a coffee and join me.'

Leaving me to make my own coffee I top the kettle up, switch it on and stand waiting for it to boil. I'm told that doesn't make it any quicker. Annoyingly my mobile rings. It's my solicitor, Paul Davis.

'Paul. How are you?'

'Good thanks. Nick, Tom Morgan phoned me this afternoon. He wants to go ahead and sell the farm to you. I can't do the necessary over the phone so I have arranged to meet them at the farm tomorrow at three.'

'Let me stop you there. I can't make three o'clock tomorrow. I have a very important meeting at the same time so can you change the time?'

'Not really. Can you alter the time of your meeting?'

'Not a chance. It's to do with Sam and it's very, very important.'

'I see. I'm flicking through my diary to see what I have available. How about five?'

'I'll do my best, but Sam comes first. I'll let you know if there's a problem by four-thirty at the latest.'

'That's fine. Hopefully see you there at five.'

'Has Tom told you that he signed some papers last week with someone else?'

'He did. He told me there's a cooling off period of fourteen days before it becomes legally binding and I have double checked that.'

'As long as you know, because I didn't until yesterday.'

'It appears to be the case. I'll check again in the morning.'

Armed with a mug of coffee I join Graham in his office. Sat behind his desk he's starring at his computer screen.

'You did say the surname was Roberts, didn't you?'

'I did, but that is an assumption. Gwyn Roberts called him her husband so I assumed they are married.'

'Well there's nothing showing here under that name. Do you have an address for him?'

'No I don't. Again I assumed it would be local. Have you looked underneath things like, Alf's garden services, Alf's landscaping? I was told his forte was garden fencing and shed erecting. It could be along those lines.'

'How soon do you need this information? I have a pile of paperwork to get through before I go home and I'd like to finish it tonight. Is tomorrow good with you?'

'Of course, and I'll see if I can dig out a little more information in the meantime.'

Jack is stood beside the car waiting for me. He gives me the impression he wishes to talk. Seeing the way he is I ask him if he's alright.

'The letter was from mum. She's asked me to go over to see her in Ireland. What do I say to her, Dad?'

Unlocking the car first I walk around the car to where Jack is standing. 'Tell her the truth.'

'What! Tell her I don't want to see her.'

'No, Jack. Let her know that you've started an apprenticeship and when you're not working, you are looking after Lucy. Tell her that's important to you and you haven't the time at the moment. Plus, you are still undergoing physio and you can't miss any sessions. She'll understand.'

'I think I should tell her to get lost. I don't want to see her or her boyfriend. She can go to hell for all I care.'

'Jack! We both knew she would write to you sooner or later. She is your mother don't forget and deep down under that thick skin of hers, she probably does care about you. If you do write to her be nice and don't burn down the bridges.'

'What do you mean by that? Burn down the bridges?'

'Once they're gone, they're gone for good. You know my feelings about her and they will never change, but you're young and yours might. Please don't spend the rest of your life thinking…if only. I spent fifteen years thinking like that but in a twist of fate, my life changed for the better.'

'That was different. You knew and despite all the obstacles you faced, you never gave up. Mum doesn't care about me. She walked out without a thought or care for anyone else and now she wants me to support her decision and say everything is fine. Not happening, Dad. You think I'm wrong…don't you?'

'No. I want you to make your own decisions in life, but please make them for the right reasons. So you know, I will support you whatever you decide.'

'Why aren't you angry with her?'

'I haven't said I'm not, but my anger towards her is not yours. And you were wrong when you said she walked out without a thought for anyone else.'

'How do you work that out?'

'Ask yourself exactly why we're standing here having this conversation?' Turning away from me Jack puts his arms on the roof of the car and rests his head on his hands. 'Jack. I could spend several hours telling you why I'm angry with Jenny and list the things I missed over the years. That's not going to help us now and I feel sure you have your own list. We need to move on, which I believe we're doing very well at. We are who we are today because of the past. It's made us stronger people and we should never forget that.'

Turning to face me I can see is eyes are heavy. He's not crying, but he clearly is in an emotional state. 'I'm sorry.' He whispers.

'There's no need to feel sorry.'

'But I am. You knowingly missed lots of things, me growing up. We both did. I am still coming to terms with that. Can I ask you something?'

'Sure.'

'What did you miss the most?'

One situation comes straight to mind. It's something I experienced several weeks ago, although there have been many similar experiences since Jack moved in. This one brought out the emotions in me. As his father it encapsulates everything I should have been and done for Jack. I'm struggling to tell him.

'Don't worry, Dad. I can see it hurts you. You don't have to tell me.'

'It's such a silly thing, Jack.' I stumble to say. Reaching for my cigarettes I continue. 'The first time I stood at the school gates waiting for Sam it dawned on me that I should have been there waiting for you. Carrying your school bag home, listening to you telling me about the day you've had. Asking you what you'd like for dinner and what you wanted to do after school. I wasn't that person and I hate myself for that.'

'That wasn't your fault.' Jack assures me while throwing his arms around my shoulders. 'And it's not silly. It means so much to me and shows me you care.'

'The simple things in life are often the hardest to deal with, Jack. Don't write to your mother in anger, write to her as a friend.'

128

'I will. I promise.'

Home I have two important issues to deal with. Talking to Jan is not one of them but she has other ideas.

'What is going on with Tom?' She barks at me, as if it was her problem. 'He sounded desperate on the phone and you won't talk to him.'

'Not now, Jan.' I respond, raising my voice.

'What do you mean, not now? That man has been good to you over the years and you're ignoring his pleas for help. I suggest you get yourself over there.'

'I said not now and I meant it.'

'I'm not going anywhere until you tell me what is going on.'

'Then may I suggest you take a seat.'

Leaving her to stew I head out into the garden where I'd seen Sam kicking a football around. Stopping on the patio I light a cigarette and watch him for a few moments.

'Brushing up on your skills?' I ask.

'I'm trying to work out a few new moves. The manager of Viking juniors encouraged me to work on my skills because a good player could soon sus me out. That's why I taught myself to kick with both feet.'

'How was your first day back at school?'

'It was alright.' Flicking the ball into the air he catches it and turns to face me. 'Why is Mrs Martin coming tomorrow?'

Fiona Martin is Sam's headmistress. Superintendent Lewis informed me she asked to attend but never actually said why she had.

'Just alright, Sam? You're not filling me with confidence.'

'You didn't answer my question,' he continues, walking towards me with the ball in his hands. 'Is she going to stop me playing football?'

'School, Sam?'

'It was fine, Dad. I found it difficult going back after a fantastic summer holiday, that's all.'

'It was a good summer…wasn't it?'

'Anything's better than hanging around car parks waiting for Larry's punters to turn up.'

'That's all behind you now.'

'Is it? What if Mrs Martin tries to stop me playing football.'

'It's none of her business. I have no idea why she's asked to come to the meeting, but you playing football isn't something she should concern herself with. Sam, your end of term report was brilliant and I'd like to think Mrs Martin wants to reiterate your good progress in the time you were in her school, not be obstructive. You have some good people on your side who want the best for you. She'll be shot down in flames if she goes against their efforts and hopes for you. I wouldn't worry about Mrs Martin.'

'I can't help worrying about things.'

'I know and most of the time it's justified. You have been through a lot and I'd worry if you weren't worried. We're here to support you and do what is right for you. Playing football is something you want to do and we're not going to stop you. We simply must get it right and safe for you to do so. Let's see what tomorrow brings. I'm sure it will be fine.'

'Mrs Martin says she'll bring me home. Is that alright with you?'

'Is it alright with you?'

'Doesn't bother me.'

'Then it's good with me.'

'Are you taking me training tomorrow?'

'Yes, but I need to talk to you about that.'

'Why? You said everything would be fine.'

'And it is, but this isn't about your training. I have another meeting after yours at five and you'll have to come with me. It shouldn't take too long so you won't get bored.'

'Is it with your solicitor?'

'Sort of. I'm meeting him at the farm.'

The penny soon drops and his glum facial look soon changes to one of delight. 'Has Tom changed his mind?' He says excitedly.

'It appears so. I can see it pleases you. Providing there are no last minute hick ups, the farm should be mine very soon.'

'Was it because of the covenant thingy?'

'I don't know the reason behind his change of mind, but I'm sure it has something to do with the covenant.'

Behind me someone opens the patio door. Looking past me Sam's excitement gets the better of him. Jack already knows about the farm. I told him while we drove home from the office. If it is Jan standing behind me, I'll let Sam tell her. That's how it should be.

'Dad's buying Tom's farm tomorrow.' He blurts out in sheer delight.

With a dead pan face I turn to face her. 'Don't ever, ever doubt me.'

'Why didn't you tell me?'

'Very simple really. There are other people in my life who should be told before you. It's not a done deal yet. I'm meeting my solicitor at Tom's tomorrow evening and if we all sign the agreement, the farm will become mine in a week or so.'

'Does Jack know?' She asks.

'He does. I told him as we drove home.'

'Where is Jack?' Sam asks.

'Doing what I'm going to ask you to do. We're going out for a meal, Sam. Why don't you shower and change while I make a phone call. You're invited too, Jan, and Richard if he's not otherwise engaged.'

131

Chapter Eight

Thursday 4th September

My plans for this morning were put on hold last night by Brad. He refused to talk business over the phone and knowing my commitments later, he agreed to meet me at home. My intention was to pay Forrests a visit, but Brad recommended we spoke first. That alone has raised my suspicions. Stuck at home I let Jan know she wasn't needed today. She likes to be in the know and what Brad and I have to discuss, isn't something she needs to know about.

I was informed this morning Chief Superintendent Lewis will attend the meeting this afternoon. They all want to talk to Sam before I join them. I fear for the young man. A team of four highly intelligent adults bombarding him with questions will be daunting for him. His outwardly strong character will be severely tested. I guess that's the intention, but hardly what I'd call fair on a ten-year-old.

In the downtime before Brad arrived I set up my private home office for their meeting. In the privacy they can discuss what they like without compromise. Kept under lock and key I'm not comfortable letting them use my private space. In taking that decision I've cleared my desk and locked all the cupboards and draws to keep them fully focussed on the task in hand. I have a private phone line in the office too, so I unplugged the phone and locked it away. I've done the same with the laptop. There's nothing incriminating for them to find, they just don't need to know my business.

Tucking the file DI Wallace supplied me with under my arm I pick up two mugs of instant coffee and make my way outside. Brad arrived on time and elected to sit outside on the patio for our talk. It's an indifferent day weather wise but that is of little consequence. Joining him I put the mugs down on the table and drop the file in front of him.

'Before we start I have a couple of things I want to get off my chest. You are aware Superintendent Lewis changed my job role?'

'I am. Does it bother you?'

Shaking my head I continue. 'Why did you stop me from going to Forrests this morning? Is there something I should know? Something you've forgotten to tell me?'

'I'm not doubting your ability, but why Forrests?'

'You were the one who asked me to look into delivery companies. I'm doing what you asked me to do.'

'Yes, but why Forrests?'

'Because they make deliveries to the hostel. Frozen products which includes fish and all manner of fresh products. I had to start somewhere. Why not?'

'Why not? Walking into a male dominated workforce of over forty people alone, asking questions about drugs, isn't a recommendation I'd make. You should know better. Surveillance first, never walk in blindly.'

'It wasn't just about drugs.'

'I'd guessed that much.'

Standing, I light a cigarette and pace up and down the patio. 'Yesterday I went to see a lady by the name of Mrs Parry. It was an odd connection, but her son was stabbed to death at the top of Milford Road last October. Almost a year ago. Police believe it was drug related. Mrs Parry was adamant their assumption that he was dealing is nonsense. She told me, after a thorough search of their house they found nothing to suggest he was and there were no drugs present. She went on to say that they based their findings on a trace of heroin found in one of Owain's jacket pockets. Very flimsy if you ask me and there could be a million reasons as to how it got there. Sketchy I know, but when you take into consideration Owain worked for Forrests as a driver, you begin to wonder.

'Then, as I was leaving, Mrs Parry told me her son had help on a Friday because it was busy delivery day. His assistant was always the same person, an old guy by all accounts by the name Alf. She told me Owain didn't like him because Alf forced him to make extra deliveries which delayed them. The reason I became interested in this is because Gwyn Roberts, the manageress of the hostel, husband's name is also Alf. Coincidence maybe, but I need to know if there is a connection. My gut feeling tells me, if Alf turns out to be one of the same, Owain may have been about to spill the beans. Was the heroin found in his pocket a set up, or was someone trying to pay him off to keep his mouth shut.

133

'Gwyn Roberts told me her husband is a successful self-employed gardener who does alright for himself. I've asked Graham to look into Alf Roberts' business affairs and so far, he's found nothing connecting the two. I know you're sceptical about my visions and so am I at times and I hadn't had one of my episodes in a long time, but I did when I met Reg out at the hostel for the first time. During my short trip into the unknown I saw a name painted on the wall of the hostel. That name was Alf and in the past, whether I worked it out or not, I have never been wrong.'

Pausing for a sip of coffee my mobile rings. Looking at the screen it's Graham. Telling Brad I need to take the call I suggest he reads the forensic report covering the file.

'Yes, Graham?'

'It wasn't easy but I've found the information you wanted. Alf Roberts was trading under the name of West's Garden Services.'

'Was?'

'Yes, was. He ceased trading in March 2002. Filed for bankruptcy, owing the taxman a lot of money. His business was registered to an address in Pembroke and there were three named directors. Alf Roberts. Gwyn Roberts and Paul Linnette. Anything else you need to know?'

'Yes. Any idea why he called the company, West's Garden Services?'

'No, but as I have business commitments I've asked James to follow it up for you. Anything else?'

'Email the details over to me as soon as you can and ask James to see what he can find out on the third name you mentioned. I want to know all there is about him, Graham. Please tell James there is to be no direct contact with any of them.' Ending the call I face Brad. 'Gwyn Roberts lied to me. Alf's company went bust in March 2002 and as a named director, she would have known that. Now I know why she's in a hurry to get the builders in.'

'What makes you say that?'

134

'Because that forensic report is full of holes. They've missed something and she knows that. I want that place boarded up and an independent forensic team in there to do a proper job.'

'That will take some convincing. I tend to agree with you though. It's certainly not the best and most detailed I've ever seen. Leave that with me.'

'For what it's worth, neither did DS Thomas.'

Sam and Fiona Martin are the last to arrive. The look on Sam's face says it all and when he hugs me in front of our guests, the tension of the moment is felt. Mary Robinson is keen to make a start. Wasting little time in obliging her request I take them through to the office. Making sure the space is enough for them to hold their meeting, I tell Sam everything will be fine. Closing the door behind me, leaving him alone to deal with their questions is one of the hardest things I have mentally had to do.

Mary's associate, Kate Noble, is an advocate. Uncertain of exactly what her title means, I was told she is a professional in law. Her roll here is to listen, to support and recommend cause or policy. In this situation she's here to help Sam, to put his case forward on his behalf. I'm not sure that's a good or bad thing.

In reversal of this mornings' decision I phoned Jan and asked her to be here. This is tough on me too and I needed some support and not just personally. When she needs to be Jan is a great hostess and keeping my guests happy is, in my mind, part of the battle. They have water and glasses on the desk in the office and if they need anything else, they only have to ask. At this stage there's not a lot else I can do.

Sat in the kitchen drinking coffee after coffee while Jan potters around, I'm finding it difficult to concentrate on anything particular. Talking to her about my plans for the farm does pass a few minutes but with that technically still in the air, isn't doing me any favours. I'm finding it difficult to understand why such a simple request to change his name so he can play football, has created a high level of debate and discussion. Knowing what he's gone through and witnessed, Sam should be on a witness protection scheme…end of. No debate or discussion about it.

Agitated and restless I've stepped outside and made my way up onto the raised decking. Starring out across the bay at the village I first lived in when I turned up here in South Wales, my mind drifts into thoughts of the good times I shared with my friends back then. There were some bad times along the way too and the support and care of those friends, helped me through them. Jan is one of those people I consider a friend. Tom and Mother too, but for some unexplainable reason, when the boot is on the other foot, it appears I'm not capable of reciprocating. When Jan calls me, saying they are ready for me, my heart sinks. I've been in this situation before and it's not a great place to be. Passing the kitchen I notice the time on the wall clock. I have been outside for over half an hour.

Mary Robinson is waiting in the open doorway. Her facial expression gives nothing away. Chief Superintendent Lewis is sat in my chair behind the desk. His position leads me to believe he's chairing the meeting. Unbiasedly is my wish. Asked to take a seat I sit down next to Fiona Martin. Sam is sat opposite me between Mary and Kate Noble. All very formal. I hate this shit.

'Fiona. Would you swop seats with Sam?' Kate asks. Surprised by her decision I watch Sam stand and cross the room. He appears quite relaxed. I notice he has crossed his fingers. 'Mr Thompson, or may I call you, Nick?'

'Please do.'

'I'd like to ask you a couple of questions before we declare our decision, just to clarify a few things for us. Nick, where do you see yourself in five years from now?'

'In what respect? Work or family life?'

'Both would be an advantage. We know Sam's thoughts on this. Why don't you start with family life?'

'Well, as you know this is all new to me. I'm learning every day and trying very hard to do right by Sam and Jack. We talk, we listen and we make decisions together. Jack for instance is now working for my company. He's going to be working alongside Richard installing and maintaining security systems. I fully endorse Jack's wishes and he is in the process of enrolling in an electrical and electronics apprenticeship, which is something he wanted to do. He has my full support and I will help him in any way I can. The same goes for Sam.

136

'Sam is bright young man and I feel sure Fiona will agree, his school work and ethic is exemplary. In five years from now I hope Sam is ready and confident enough to sit his GCSE's, with the view of going on to sit A levels. Perhaps even go to university. That is in the future for Sam and I will discuss those possibilities with him when the time is right. Sam also loves his football. I have watched him play and he does have the potential. If that works out for him in the future, I will support and encourage him in exactly the same way if he decides to take football up as a career. I will never push either of the boys into something they don't want to be or do. However, and I think Sam understands this, his education is important and you can combine the two disciplines. Especially if you have someone like me behind you.' Out of the corner of my eye I notice Sam turn and look at me. Facing him I gently nod my head. Seeing him smile back is reassuring. 'Like my son Jack, Sam needs the security I, we, can give him. That's why we're here…isn't it? Changing his name is a must and should have been dealt with long ago. How we go about that is your responsibility.'

'That is why we are here, Nick.' Kate responds. 'What about work? What are your plans there?'

'I'm not sure how much I can tell you. It's a delicate situation at the moment.' Looking at Chief Superintendent Lewis for support he nods his head as if to say go ahead, then decides to offer his own thoughts.

'Nick has done some very important work for us in his capacity as a private investigator. We're currently working together on something sensitive and I'm not at liberty to discuss the matter further. Take it from me, it's very important. However ladies, and this must stay in this room, Nick is also working for the government on the same investigation. Nick has a lot of pressure on him at the moment, from both sides and I'm sure once this is concluded he will fulfil his dream and retire. When you take into consideration what has happened more recently and how that has affected him and the two boys, I think Nick is doing a damn good job. Before I finish I'd like to ask Sam a question. Sam, has Nick, or Dad as you like call him, ever let you down?'

'No, Sir.' Sam replies softly

'Is there anything you'd like to add, Nick?' Kate asks.

'Not really, except to thank Chief Superintendent Lewis.'

137

'My pleasure, Nick.'

'You might like to know, apart from taking good care of the boys in retirement, I have or I am in the process of buying another farm. It's a project for the future, that's for sure and it's going to keep us busy. Perhaps, Sam, as you're excited about the farm, you'd like to tell them about our plans.'

'Can I?'

'You know as much about the farm as I do. Go ahead.'

'Dad is going to buy Tom's farm. Tom has run out of money and the bank is going to take it away from him. Dad is going to let them stay in the house while he decides what he's going to do. I like it at the farm and I can help Dad.'

'You're well informed, Sam. Does Nick encourage you to be?' Mary suggests.

'Yes. Dad says that I should know because one day the farm could be mine and Jack's to look after.'

'Ok. So what would Sam like to see happen with the farm?'

'I liked the idea of a theme park. It's cool. Dad found out there's a covenant on the land which means he can't build houses or chalets for people to stay in. It doesn't matter though. We're going to buy animals instead. Pigs, goats, sheep, ducks and chickens. Whatever we can afford to buy and turn it into an educational centre. I'm really looking forward feeding them, looking after them and telling people about them. Never done anything like that before. It should be really cool.'

'Thank you, Sam. I will make a point of coming to visit you when you are up and running. Nick, I have just given our decision away. Sam is staying with you. I'd like to check one thing with you first. The name you both agreed upon is, George Samuel Thompson?'

Both Sam and I say yes at the same time. Handing the document to Sam we both take a good look. Passing me the adoption document Sam stands. I watch as he first shakes Fiona's hand and says thank you. Moving on he repeats the hand shaking and thank you's with Kate and Chief

138

Superintendent Lewis. Reaching Mary, she stands and gives him a big hug. I hear him say thank you to her.

'You deserve it, Sam. It's up to you to make sure we don't regret it.'

'I won't. I promise.'

Letting go of Sam, Mary crosses the room to where I'm now stood. We shake hands as I say thank you.

'That is a legally binding document, Nick. Enough for Sam's football manager to do what he needs to do. We will have to take this to court for verification which should take a couple of weeks. It's a formality so don't worry. Once I'm in possession of the final document I will send it registered post to you. Good luck, Nick, and I hope setting up the educational centre goes to plan.'

'With Sam looking over my shoulder I'm sure it will.'

Keen to finish the meeting I see my guests to the door. As Fiona and Kate step outside I hear Mary ask Sam to walk her the car. I guess she has a few final words of wisdom to pass onto him. Watching them cross my driveway I'm joined by Chief Superintendent Lewis.

'Good result, Nick.'

'Yes, Sir, it is. Heaven knows where Sam would be now had we not intervened. He has choices now, so the futures up to him.'

'Have we time for a chat?'

'Sir. I have a farm to buy. I'm meeting my solicitor as soon as I can get away to finalise the deal. Can this wait until tomorrow?'

'Nine o'clock. My office?'

'That's fine, Sir. Gives me time to drop Sam at school first. Can I ask what this is about?'

'I understand you're not happy with the forensic report.'

'I'm not, Sir. Neither is DS Thomas.'

'We'll discuss that in the morning.'

139

After a very emotional few moments together once they'd all gone, I asked Sam what Mary had said to him. Tearfully, he told me she asked him not to mess things up. Clutching the adoption document firmly in his hand, he promised me he wouldn't. With the promise of a take away after training we raided the fridge for a quick snack on the run first before Sam went upstairs to change into his football kit. I spent those few minutes putting my office back into some sort of order thinking about what Sam meant when he said, not messing things up.

Driving over to Tom's it becomes obvious Sam is on a massive high. I don't blame him but his excitable chat is rather draining. I think, behind the façade of being given the go ahead to play his beloved football, the security of adoption is a huge relief to him. Turning into the lane leading up to the farm I stop the car. I have some words of wisdom for Sam…too.

'Sam. I'm as pleased as you are about todays' meeting and what that means to us both. I want you to understand here that what I'm about to do is equally important to us, so while I'm talking business I'd like you to calm down. Give me the time and space to deal with this first. Can I rely on you to do that?'

'Yes, Dad, you can rely on me. Can I tell them my good news afterwards? I can really call you, Dad, now…can't I?'

'Yes, son, you can.'

Paul Davis is leaning against his car smoking a cigarette when we pull up outside the house. Sam gives me a funny look when we join him. Treading on his roll up to put it out, Paul offers his hand and we shake.

'I've left them reading through the paperwork to refresh their memory. Tom has already asked if the extra costs will affect the amount they will personally receive. I took it upon myself to say it wouldn't. They should be done by now. Shall we join them?'

Following Paul's lead Sam tugs at my sleeve. 'He's smoking weed. Is he allowed to?' He whispers.

My immediate reaction is to ask Sam how he knows that but of course, growing up in an environment where smoking and taking drugs was considered the norm, he would know.

'Lots of people smoke weed. As long as it doesn't affect what I'm here to do, we'll turn a blind eye. How do you feel about that?'

'I don't like it.'

'Right answer.'

'Have you ever smoked weed?'

'To the best of my knowledge, no.'

'But you might have done?' He suggests, stopping right in front of me. Giving me a stare.

'Remember the day we stopped outside old Henry Sinclair's cottage and something frightened you.'

'I didn't like that place. It gave me the creeps.'

'I know it did. Do you remember, when we got home I sat you down with Jack and Michaela and explained briefly who Henry was. I'm sure at the time I told you about Henry's friend Beth. She was a white witch and herbalist.'

'I didn't like the sound of her either.'

'Well, I got to know Beth very well over the years. She worked in Jan's shop for a while, selling her potions. Beth was a strange person but she had a fantastic character. Something which is sadly being bred out of us. Anyway, she lived to smoke weed and tried for years to get me onto the stuff. I believe I avoided her incessant challenges but I was never really sure. Beth was a great baker too and her fairy cakes were often laced with whatever she could get her hands on at the time. I soon learnt to avoid the ones coated with pink icing and always made sure I singled out the white coated ones. They were ok, but the pink ones were something else. She caught a few people out in her time.'

'You liked Beth didn't you? I can tell.'

'I did and I miss her. Beth was a dangerous person to know, with her odd ideas on life, but she was funny and a very knowledgeable old lady. I have a lot of stories I could tell you about her antics.'

Paul has left the door open for us. I let Sam go ahead of me and following him inside, two things immediately strike me because they're different. Tom and Mother are sat side by side at the dinner table. Paul is sat opposite them with his back to the window. On the table between them sit three sets of documents with pens resting next to them. On the side, beyond the drainer are four plates covered by clean tea towels, hiding what looks to be prepared food. As I pause taking in what I've seen, Sam cheekily sits himself down in Toms' old fireside chair. He too has noticed the food.

'Please take a seat next to me, Nick.' Paul offers. Settling myself in I observe both Tom and Mother's demeanour. Mother is staring straight ahead. Probably looking out of the window. Tom's head is bowed. More likely he's looking down at his hands resting on his lap.

'Nick.' Tom says, looking up at me. 'I have something I'd like to say before we sign the documents.' Resting his arms on the table he picks up one of the pens. 'We have an apology to make to you. Mother and me are sorry for causing you so much stress and trouble. Young Sam there, when he came back inside the last time you were here, told us that by saying no to your generous offer was killing you and there was nothing else you could do. He said you were very angry with us for not accepting your help. That lovely young man didn't stop talking or trying to change our minds all the time he was here. When he came back into the house and told us he wanted to help you, it rekindled so many wonderful memories for mother and me. We sat talking for hours that night, because we saw what you were doing for young Sam and it reminded us of the things we did to support you. I'd like you to accept our apology…please.'

Left quite speechless I look away. I notice that Sam is looking at the food and not us. I now understand why he got so excited when I told him the news. In a short space of time, he achieved something I couldn't. Still looking over at Sam I respond to Tom's question.

'Of course I will. It goes without saying. That's what friends are for.'

'Shall we conclude our business?' Paul suggests.

'Certainly!' Tom replies, removing the top from one of the pens.

'Before we do, Sam has something he wishes to say.' Facing me at last I can see he's choked up with emotion. 'Why don't you join me, Sam?'

142

In his reluctance to do this now, he delays the moment by his own laboured progress. Shuffling across the room he comes to a stand next to me.

'What is it, Sam?' Mother asks with concern. 'I hope it's not bad news.'

Gathering his composure he answers her question. 'They've let Dad adopted me. We got the papers this afternoon.'

'That's wonderful news.' Mother continues. 'Does that mean you are now Samuel Thompson?'

'George Samuel Thompson. Dad and me came up with the name for other reasons. I don't like the name George, that's why I like people calling me Sam.'

'Oh that's so lovely. Come and give me a hug.'

'It's a long story. One for another time,' I add.

Walking around the table to join Mother, Sam shakes Tom's hand as he passes behind him. I hear Tom wish him luck.

'Shall we continue gentlemen?' Paul asks.

In total silence. Tom, Mother and I sign all three documents. Competed, Paul adds his signature as the witness. I'm relieve we've finally reached a conclusion, but there's much to do now to make this work.

'I'll get the ball rolling first thing in the morning. My first task will be informing all the creditors they will be paid in full within five working days from completion. Nick, you will need to transfer the funds into the agreed account by Monday at the latest.' Tidying away the paperwork he slips it back into his brief case and asks if there's anything else.

'I need to open a new bank account.' Tom tells us.

'Are you sure you won't stay for some refreshments, Paul?' Mother asks. 'We should celebrate Nick's generosity.' Standing, she and Sam walk over to the drainer and remove the tea towels from the plates.

'I believe, Tom, Nick has that in hand,' Paul adds.

'I put it on hold. If I pick you up on Monday, Tom, we'll drive into Narberth and sort the account out. In the meantime…' I'm distracted by Mother and Sam placing plates of sandwiches, sausage rolls, crisps and cakes onto the table in front of us.

'It's not much, but please help yourselves.' Mother offers.

'It's lovely, Mrs Morgan. Thank you.' Paul responds, helping himself.

'I was about to ask if you needed any cash to tide you over, but it appears you're coping.'

'Nick, love, funny you should mention that. I went up to your farm shop to buy a few things for today. We couldn't celebrate the moment without offering you all something. I hope you don't mind, I put this on your account.'

Leaning over the table in front of me, grabbing a handful of crisps, Sam's beaming smile distracts me. He's seen the funny side, I guess I should too.

'Its fine, Mother. It's a lovely thought. Thank you.' Looking at Sam I smile back. 'We should celebrate properly. How does Saturday afternoon sound?'

'That would be very nice.' Mother tells me.

'Ok. If I bring the gang over, with some refreshments, can you organise the food? Go back to the farm shop, get what you think you'll need and put it on my account.'

'They don't sell tobacco, boy.' Tom grunts.

Taking my wallet from my back pocket I open it and slap two, twenty pound notes down on the table.

'Can we have some fireworks?' Sam asks, turning his back on me. I know he's laughing. The little shit.

'I know a man who makes great fireworks, boy.' Tom suggests.

'I don't doubt that, Tom. Having just bought the farm, I really don't want to see it go up in smoke.'

144

Friday 5th September

I'm early. Left waiting by the front desk for Chief Superintendent Lewis I have time to reflect on yesterday. The day of extreme pressure ended well. When Sam and I left Tom and Mother's I took him training. His football manager wanted to keep the adoption form for a couple of days for proof of identity, but Sam was having none of it. Using some blue tack he found in a kitchen draw, it now takes pride of place on his bedroom wall. In the end, Matt settled for second best. Taking the information he thought he would need from the document Matt agreed it should suffice.

I was concerned for Jack in the event of Sam running around with the adoption papers in his hand. Although he appeared to be happy for Sam, he gave the impression that his nose had been put out of joint. Jack has every right to change his surname. Before she walked out on him, his mother Jenny admitted I was Jack's paternal father, my flesh and blood and gave him the legally binding evidence. I already knew that through the blood tests I received while in hospital. They also carried out, unbeknown to me, DNA tests to confirm what I had always believed was true, but Jack and I have never sat down and spoken about his right. We had a lot going on at the time and just maybe, I should have taken the initiative. I held back because I didn't want to pressure him. My belief is, it's his decision and I believe it should be. Talking it over now wouldn't be good timing, but it is my responsibility.

Waiting isn't one of my better traits. Meeting and talking to a member of the hierarchy is another one. Twenty minutes isn't a long time but when you have things to do and people to see, it seems like a lifetime. Finally taken up to Chief Superintendent Lewis's office he asks me to take a seat. Reading, he has a file open on his desk.

'How did the farm buying go?' He asks.

'Well, Sir. Thank you.'

'Good to hear. How about young Sam? How's he doing?'

'He's like a kid with a new toy. Very buoyant as you can imagine.'

'We talked over a number of issues before we asked you to join us. I must commend you for your efforts. From what I heard and was told, you have turned his life around. Keep up the good work, Nick.'

'It's not all my doing. Sam must take some of the credit here.'

'Shall we begin?' Nodding my head he continues. 'I have in front of me DS Thomas's initial report on his view of the fire at the hostel. Like you have expressed, he has doubts over the cause. I'd like you to give me your reasons for believing the original report was inaccurate.'

'By all means, Sir. I don't profess to be an expert in the field of electrical matters so I undertook some research and sought advice on the subject. I'm told that when electricity jumps from surface to surface heat is generated. Those temperatures can be very high. The heat generated under those circumstances would cause scorching or pitting marks on the mating surfaces. The report suggests the terminals had been loose for three to four weeks which had caused a certain amount of tarnishing to the mating surfaces, not damaging them. In this instance, with a low domestic voltage and current value, arcing of any magnitude is unlikely. Certainly not enough to travel across the gap and ignite a flammable surface…anyway.

'Secondly, Sir. If that terminal had been loose for that period of time the likelihood is, the freezer would have failed under those conditions or at best, worked intermittently. I have looked through the call out list for repairs on the freezer and there is no documented evidence of Marston's, the sub-contractor, being contacted to attend. It's not the cause of the fire and if that terminal was tampered with three or four weeks ago, and somehow did manage to cause a fire several weeks later, I would suggest we should be looking at circumstances of why, back then. I don't have the answers yet, Sir, but I'm making progress.'

'I understand you have requested another forensic investigation is conducted?'

'I have, through my contact Agent Harvey. I'd would like the building secured until that is carried out. We may be too late, Sir. Anyone could have walked in and out of there the way things were left. May I ask, what has DS Thomas had to say?'

'He agrees with you but his report is not as detailed as what you have told me. I have agreed to conduct another forensic investigation. That will take place within the next few days. Is there anything else you have for me?'

'No, Sir. I have a few lines if inquiry open but nothing concrete to work with.'

'Keep me up to date with your progress.'

Knocking on the door of 72 Milford Road I'm hoping I'll catch Mrs Parry at home. I'm in luck. Opening the door she speaks first.

'Have you caught someone?'

'No not yet. I'm sorry. There is something else I'd like to ask you, something I omitted to ask the last time I was here. Was Owain on his way out, or was he on his way home from work?'

'Is that important?'

'Regular working practices, Mrs Parry, makes us people of habit and if someone knew the time Owain passed the place where he was attacked, they could have been waiting for him.'

'He was on his way out, Mr Thompson. He told us he was going to see his girlfriend Ellie and wouldn't be too late.'

'Do you know if the police spoke to her at the time?'

'I think so. Can't say for sure.'

'What is Ellie's surname?'

'Simpson. Ellie Simpson. You don't think she has something to do with my son's murder?'

'Anything is possible. I'm looking at the wider picture and part of that process is eliminating people from my enquiries. Is it likely they agreed to meet there?'

'I have no idea. You're putting doubt in my mind, Mr Thompson, and I'm not sure I like it.'

'The doubt is already there. My job is finding the truth…and I will.'

I need to find out more about Hanna Green and her connection with David Griffiths. Last time I tried to find Ossie or Jonny begging in their prime squats, I made a mistake. It was an afterthought after having harsh words with

147

the harbour master. Ossie and Jonny avoid any type of conflict and seeing me drive down to the harbour may have spooked them. All the local beggars, homeless, however they class themselves, have one thing in common…drugs. In a small town like Fenby it's a fair bet the supplier is one person.

Parking my car on the outskirts of town I walk the mile or so to Ossie's favourite patch by the harbour. I'm in luck this time. With his head bowed and his eyes closed, he doesn't see me approaching. Placing a coffee and sandwich down the ground next to him, he opens his eyes.

'What do you want?' He slurs.

'May I join you?'

'No!' He replies, attempting to stand up.

'Stay put, Ossie, or I will arrest you.'

'You ain't got the authority.'

'I think you'll find I have.' I inform him. Sitting down next to him I grab his arm, preventing him from making an escape.

'I said go away. I have nothing to say so fuck off and leave me alone.'

'Ossie. I could make life very difficult for you. We either do this here or somewhere a little more quiet. I don't think you'll like that.'

'You ain't good for business sat here.'

'I'll sort you out, if you tell me what I want to know.'

'They all say that. You aint no different.'

Taking a twenty pound note out of my pocket I hold it in my hand where he can see it. 'Try me.'

'I'll think about it.' Holding out his hand I shake my head.

'That's not the way it works. Was Hanna Green your supplier? You had a thing about Hanna…didn't you?'

'Wrong on both counts. Hanna was a friend…nothing more.'

148

'If it wasn't Hanna, who was it? David Griffiths?' His silence speaks volumes. 'Ossie, this is important. Was David Griffiths your supplier?'

'I hated that excuse of a man. Can't say I'm sorry he's dead.'

'Why?'

'Cos I owed him money. Lots of money and so did a lot of the other boys. He'd turn up here and take all the money I had. That aint right. How am I going to eat without money?'

'Or buy drugs.'

'Taking drugs is how I get through the day. It lessons' the pain'.

'Did Hanna get her gear from David?'

'They were pretty close. I guess so.'

'Ossie. With David Griffiths off the scene, where do you get your gear from now?'

'There's a new kid, and he is a kid. Turned up a couple of days after we heard Griffiths was death. He gets us anything we want. I aint complaining.'

'Does this kid have a name?'

'Seb. I only know him as Seb.'

'Seb didn't waste any time muscling in on David's patch. How old would you say he was?'

'Nineteen, twenty. Maybe older.'

'Do you think Seb has anything to do with David's death?'

'As long as I get my gear, what do I care?'

'But you cared about Hanna. Doesn't that bother you?'

'Of course it does. Despite what you may think, Hanna was a nice person. She didn't deserve to die like that.'

'How did Hanna get into the water, Ossie?'

149

Bowing his head and closing his eyes, I know I've hit a raw nerve. He knows something and I need to push him for answers. 'Come on, Ossie. You're doing good.'

'I saw her that night. It was getting dark and cold so I decided to call it a day. Hanna walked past me. She was out of her head. She didn't see me or recognise me and she could barely stand up on her own. When I saw her go down onto the breakwater I picked up my stuff and went after her.

'Hanna could hardly speak and what she did say didn't make sense. I didn't know what she had in mind so I encouraged her to stop and sit down. Eventually she just dropped to the floor and I put my arm around her. Hanna gave me her phone and managed to ask me to phone David. I didn't want to but she wanted to know if he was alright. I tried a couple of times but there was no answer.

'I'd had a couple of hits myself and crashed out. Don't know how long for but it was very dark when I came to. Hanna was lying across my legs. I knew she was dead and panicked. I didn't know what to do. I did know if someone found me with her I would get the blame. I didn't kill her, Mr Thompson. I swear I didn't.

'I have some knowledge of first aid and checked her pulse to see if she was breathing. She wasn't and her body was cold. Stupidly I decided to push her over the edge into the sea. I didn't see I had a choice because I knew I would get the blame. I did say a prayer for her before I got myself out of there. I promise, I didn't kill Hanna.'

'I know you didn't, but you could have got some help.'

'I know I should. I was scared, Mr Thompson. Who's going to believe a druggy?'

'Thank you, Ossie. You have answered a number of questions for me. I can see this has been difficult for you, but you know I must report this.' Taking another twenty from my pocket I hand him the two notes. 'It would be better coming from you.'

'I can't. What I did makes me an accessory to murder.'

'We can't say for sure it was murder. If it helps, Hanna died from a massive overdose of amphetamines. She didn't drown.' Hauling my frame

150

off the ground I stand and face him. 'I'll leave it for a few hours so it's up to you what you do and where you go.'

'You might want this?' Ossie suggests, holding a mobile phone out. 'It's Hanna's. There might be something of interest on there.'

Taking the phone I wish him luck and leave him in peace. I don't endorse it, but a few cans of cider or special brew might see him through the next few hours and days.

I struggle keeping up with modern technology. I couldn't work out how to operate Hanna's phone. I need too because there's a good chance any information found on her phone, could prove vital in solving this case. I need I nerd, more importantly, James may have some information for me.

Pulling up outside the office my first observation concerns the two skips outside Ed's workshop. It appears he was telling me the truth. Time will tell. Not wishing to involve myself in his progress, I chose not to intrude. For his sake, I do hope he has acquired a licence from the council. They are strict on things like that. Here though, that could be the responsibility of the harbour master, I'm not sure. Either way, he needs permission to have skips in public areas.

James is in reception. First glance suggests he's on his way out. 'Glad I caught you, James. I need your help.'

'I'm on the way out to meet a client, Boss.'

'Two minutes.' I suggest, handing him the phone. 'I need you to unlock this phone so I can see what's on it.'

'Whose phone is this?'

'You know better than to ask me that?' Holding out his hand to take the phone I snatch it away from him.

'I can't unlock it unless you give it to me.'

'I don't want your finger prints all over the phone. Have you some surgical gloves?'

'In my office.'

'Your office now…is it?'

151

'You're hardly ever here these days. Do you want me to unlock the phone or not?'

'I wouldn't normally stop you going about your business but this is important.'

Following James up to our office he heads directly for his desk. Opening one of the bottom draws he takes out a box. Placing it on his desk he pulls a couple of gloves out and puts them on his hands.

'Happy?' He groans. Passing the phone to him, James takes a good look first. 'It's quite an old model. What are you hoping to find on this? Models like this one don't have a lot of storage space so information will be limited.'

'Phone numbers, messages, that sort of thing.'

'Would you like me to download the information onto my laptop? It shouldn't take long. I can send it to you once it's complete.'

'That would be useful. Can you send it to my home computer?'

'No problem. Why the secrecy?'

'Because it's evidence and I've got to hand the phone in.'

'You like living dangerously don't you?'

'Comes with the territory. I'm old enough and wise enough to know that once I've handed the phone over, I'll never know what information there is on there. Information that could be useful to me.'

'Explains why you didn't want my prints on the phone. Yours will be.'

Taking an interest in what James is doing, trying to comprehend the ins and outs of transferring the information, I stand looking over his shoulder.

'Mine don't matter. Someone gave the phone to me to hand in. How's the progress with the other matter?'

'Not good. I've hit a brick wall. I must admit I haven't given it my full attention. I'm busy on official business and that comes first.'

152

'What's the brick wall you've hit?'

'Well, I thought I would start by looking into his family's history. Using the Ancestry. Com site I started with what I knew. Alf and Gwyn were married in July 1968. Her family tree goes back several generations, his don't. His in fact start and finish on the day they were married. Could be a number of reasons for that, like no one has ever bothered for instances. Stumped, I took a look at the census register for clues. Alf Roberts appears on the 1971 census, but not on the 1961. Gwyn is very much a local lass, homely would be the expression and Alf not appearing on the 1961 is odd, because how did they meet? I need to dig deeper to find what you're looking for.'

'He's changed his name.'

'Quite possible, but from what?'

'His own garden business was called, West's, which would make sense if he has changed his name.'

'Later please.' James adds, handing me the phone. 'All done. I'll email the information across to you now, then I must make tracks. I have a client waiting.'

I think I know of Ellie Simpson, Owain's girlfriend. I'm sure I've seen that name tag on a young lady working in the local convenience store across the road from the office. Catching a person off guard often pays dividends. I'll give it a try.

Entering the store is nothing unusual. I often use the shop. Traversing a couple of isles, pretending to shop, I decide to buy the boys something while I'm here. Turning down the third isle the young lady I see ahead of me tidying shelves fits the bill. Facing me as I walk towards her I can see her name tag on the company shirt she's wearing.

'Hi, Ellie. Can I have a few words with you?'

'I made a statement to the police after Owain was stabbed. If that's what you want?'

'Sounds like you've been talking to Mrs Parry.'

'She told me you'd been asking about me. I told the police all I know. I've got nothing more to say.'

153

'I don't believe that to be true. You see, I know you live further down the road from Owain's house, closer to the seafront. If Owain was on his way to your house, why was he going in totally the wrong direction?'

'Go away or I'll get my manager.'

'Go ahead, then we'll do this down at the police station. Your choice.'

Thinking for a moment she chooses to answer. 'I don't know why he was going that way. Maybe he was on his way home from work.'

'We both know that's isn't true. Was he meeting someone else first? Ellie, was Owain selling drugs?'

'No! He wasn't like that.'

'Was he getting something for you?'

'Certainly not! I don't do that sort of stuff.'

'Fine. So you wouldn't object to having a blood test done?'

'You can't do that.'

'Not personally, but my colleagues in Fenby can. And you do know, if a blood test proves positive, you'll have a criminal record…for life.'

'Ok. Ok. I'm waiting for an operation on my back. It hurts like hell at times and smoking cannabis helps, especially doing this job. Yes, Owain was going to get me some but I swear, I don't know who from. Don't you think I wouldn't have told someone if I knew? I was in love with Owain and I miss him like hell.'

'Did he buy stuff for anyone else?'

'Sometimes he got some for my brother.'

'Heroin, by any chance?'

'Yes.'

'Why didn't you tell the police this?'

'Because I didn't want to get Owain, or my brother into trouble.'

154

'You do know the police think Owain was dealing? I want some names from you, Ellie. If you genuinely loved Owain, then help me find the person who killed him. If it's any consolation, I'm beginning to think he was lured to his death. Right now, anything you know about him and his movements, could be useful. You've got to trust me, Ellie, so please give it some thought. Does Mrs Parry know about this?'

'Of course not. Please don't tell her.'

Escorted up to their inner sanctum by DC Hughes for a meeting with DS Thomas, I go over my story. The timing of my conversation with Ossie is crucial. That was about an hour and a half ago and he'll no doubt want to know why it's taken me so long to hand in the phone. I'll need a solid explanation for the delay and remember word for word, what I do come up with.

DS Thomas is sat with DI Wallace in the latter's office. I'm not looking forward to this, but in my own right I'm officially involved and I find myself in a unique position. I'm their equal here.

'Take a seat, Nick. DC Hughes, will you organise some coffee for us all, then join us.' Wallace begins. As DC Hughes disappears I sit myself down. 'We all have work to do so let's make this as brief as we can. For my part, with the assistance of the Glamorgan police in Cardiff, I have turned my attention to container shipping and distribution thereof. The port authority aren't too impressed with our presence because it slows down their production levels. We are paying particular attention to containers arriving from known hot spots around the globe. I'm afraid to say it's not an exact science. We simply cannot stop and search hundreds of containers through the course of one day. What we are focussing on is the where, i.e., containers coming directly into this area and warehouses shipping the goods on to here. This is where you guys become important. We haven't the manpower to stop and search every consignment. Tracing the line of distribution is very important. I'm talking here about the dealer, who supplies them and so on.

'We aren't ignoring our local ports. The harbour masters' are all up to speed and keeping us well informed. For the time being, they have drafted in extra manpower to carry out patrols and we are supporting them. I'm pretty much up to date with DS Thomas, Nick, so over to you.'

Taking the opportunity I produce Hanna's phone and place it on the desk in front of DI Wallace. Both he, DS Thomas and PC Hughes, who has returned with the coffee, stare at it.

'Whose is that?' Wallace asks.

'Hanna Green's.'

'How do you know that?'

'Someone told me.'

'You're being evasive, Nick. I know what you're like. Spill the beans.'

'Over the years I've got to know a number of our regular homeless characters. For a few quid they can be useful. One of them, Ossie, saw Hanna the evening she died. He told me she walked passed him out of her head. Fearing for her safety he followed her down onto the breakwater. Later that night she died in his arms but not before she asked him to phone David Griffiths on her phone. He told me he couldn't get through.'

'Why David Griffiths?' Wallace asks me.

'Because he and Hanna were close, according to Ossie and she wanted to know if he was alright. Ossie said he panicked and convinced himself he'd take the blame for Hanna's death, so he pushed her body into the water.'

'And you believe him?'

'Ossie and Hanna were good friends. So yes, I do believe him.'

'Where will we find Ossie?'

'He could still be in town, but I doubt he hung around after I left.'

'I suggest we go and take a look.'

'There's more.' I suggest, watching DS Thomas pick up Hanna's old phone. 'The batteries dead. So no, I don't know what's on there.'

'What else do you know?' Wallace continues.

'I know Ossie didn't like Griffiths. He told me he owed him money, lots of money were his words, and so did a lot of other people.'

156

'You saying, Griffiths was the dealer, which when you take the fire into consideration, begins to make sense. What do you know about him?'

'Nothing at the moment, but I don't think he was responsible for the fire.'

'What makes you think that? He worked there and had the opportunity.'

'He did, but why? Gwyn Roberts told me he saw in the deliveries, which fits nicely into what you're doing, so why destroy what appears to be a link in the chain.'

'Because he had been rumbled?'

'That's a possibility. It's also possible someone found out what he was doing and wanted to take over. I don't think Gwyn is telling us the truth, that's why I want another forensic team in there, to make her sweat a little. I don't know if she is involved, or turned a blind eye to what he was up to but if she did know, putting pressure on her may just push her over the edge.'

'I agree.' DC Thomas adds. 'Like you, I don't think the fire was caused by a faulty freezer. We missed something in that kitchen, so obvious we all missed it.'

'I have one last thing for you. Ossie told me a new kid turned up a couple of days after Griffiths died. Told him he could get him anything he wanted. A young lad by all accounts by the name of Seb. That's all Ossie knew about him. It suggests to me, Seb was waiting and ready in the background for Griffiths to be dealt with.'

'You're suggesting, Griffiths and Hanna Green were murdered. Was she part of the set up?'

'Ossie said not. They were close allegedly and she may have been selling favours...who knows?'

'I'm going to say something here that must stay with us. When we searched Griffiths bedsit we found absolutely no proof of him dealing. No drugs, no physical evidence, not even on him. If he was dealing, his gear must be somewhere else which is odd, because all dealers keep a record of who

157

owes what. We need to pull the hostel apart. DS Thomas, no one goes in or out until we've torn that place apart.'

'And you let Gwyn Roberts remove items from her office.' My observation takes DI Wallace by surprise. That is exactly what he did. Starring at me he responds.

'We'll pull her in for questioning.'

'If it was my decision, I'd let her stew for a while. She'll lead us to what we want to know. Gwyn asked me the other day, to ask you, how soon she could get the builders in. From a business point of view that's perfectly understandable but I have to ask myself, is there something in there she needs to deal with before it's found? Let her do the worrying. She'll make a mistake. With no evidence to support our views, we have no case against her. Why don't we monitor her movements for the time being, see who comes and goes, even monitor her phone calls if we can and while we do that, lead her to believe it's the David Griffiths connection to the fire we're investigating.'

'And what will you be doing, Nick?' DS Thomas requests.

Looking at Wallace I respond. 'Does DS Thomas know the full story here?'

'What full story…Sir?'

'No.' Wallace replies to me. 'DS Thomas, if and when it's appropriate, I may be in a position to confide in you, until then, I want you to assemble a team and search that hostel from top to bottom. Starting now.'

'Yes, Sir.'

'And DS Thomas. Gwyn Roberts is to be left alone…for now.'

Once DS Thomas has left the room, Wallace leans across the desk. His tone is much softer now. 'You're onto something…aren't you? You needed to tell us this crap to keep DS Thomas off your back.'

'Ossie, that phone and his story are genuine. It is my belief this Seb, probably Sebastian, is part of the root cause in this investigation. I have a problem there. Agent Harvey stopped me from continuing with this. I have my own ideas but he suggested it was an extremely dangerous path for me to take, so I reluctantly backed off. I'm going back to basics, see if I can find another option. I'll keep you up to date with my progress.'

Once I'd picked Sam up from school my priorities changed. It has been a long day and it's time to switch off. Before I collected him I went over to the bank and transferred the money for Paul Davis to conclude the business.

My day has not finished though. I have a party to organise and with Paul Davis confirming the deal is going through, tomorrow could be a good one. Tom suggested we arrive around two o'clock. He doesn't want a late one. Making phone calls first to see who can make it, I'm going to offer taxis for them all so they can have a drink or two without worrying. I hope Jack, Lucy and Michaela are free to tag along. I have something to show them first and I have employed the services of Marcus to explain.

Starring out of the kitchen window, looking out into the garden, I'm miles away thinking about who I should invite. Leaning on the work surface waiting for the kettle to boil, Sam disturbs my thoughts when he places a letter down on the side next to me.

'Mrs Martin gave me that.' He announces. 'I think she needs you to sign it. She said I can take it in with me on Monday.'

'I forgot to ask. How was school today…George Thompson?'

Catching him opening the fridge door he stops and faces me. 'You promised me you wouldn't call me that.'

'I did and I won't. Sam, people who don't know you will naturally call you George Thompson and you, have got to get use to the idea. From yesterday you became George Thompson and reacting positively to being called that, is something you must learn to take in your stride. You know as well as I do, that in a difficult situation your response should be automatic. Calling you Sam will always come first to those who know you and that will continue. Sam, please don't think I'm taking the micky by calling you George, but you are as responsible for your own safety as I am. Am I making sense?'

'I do understand, but hate being called George.'

'Isn't that the point?'

Saturday 6th September

Marcus, the manager of New Barn Farm is waiting for us by the farm shop when we arrive. First thing to take care of is unloading the drinks from the back of the taxi into his VW camper. A modern day hippie, Marcus, apart from his enthusiasm for organic farming, is a keen surfer. I should remember that, because the boys have expressed their interests in surfing and he could be useful. Marcus has agreed to drive us around to Tom's farm once we're done here and also offered to drive us home later.

Marcus first came up with the idea of a nature trail through our woodland and I've asked him to explain our plans to the guys. He is concerned about the future of farming. The lack of interest within the younger generation and what mass production is doing to the landscape. We know we must be efficient and the use of every square inch of land becomes necessary, but at what cost? The guys may not find the experience of any use or concern to them, but planting the seeds for future generations to understand will help the environment in the long term.

I'm not sure where Michaela stands, but Jack, Sam and Lucy are well taken by the farm shop. I don't think either of the boys have been to New Barn before. Most of what we sell in the shop is locally sourced or produced and that includes a wide variety of items such as bread, cakes, biscuits and sweets. Generous to a fault I set them all a ten pound limit to spend. Sam was very quick to ask, if someone doesn't spend all their money, could he have it. What can you say to someone thinking outside of the box?

The woodland we've approached the council and forestry commission over is fenced off. It is on our land and the only gated access is close to the farmhouse. In this area there are numerous bridal paths crisscrossing the landscape for walkers and hikers to enjoy and the fact it is fenced off, raised our suspicions initially. Stopping by the gate I hold back, allowing Marcus to deliver his talk.

'Right guys.' Leaning back against the gate Marcus faces us and begins. 'You've probably heard Nick talking about a nature trail recently. The deciduous woodland behind me is perfect and a wonderland of discovery for youngsters like you guys. As you can see, it's robustly protected by fencing. We initially thought the fence was erected by past farmers to keep out their livestock. It turns out, after making enquiries for the nature trail, the area behind me is listed as an ancient forest and thus protected.'

160

'How do they know it's an ancient forest?' Michaela asks.

'Good question. There are two basic methods of discerning the age of a forest. First way is by using old maps of the area. Many areas of the UK have maps dating back many centuries. Rather basic by today's standards, woodland was always one of the land marks clearly recorded. During those times of uncertainty and dispute the crude maps made it clear to all land owners, who owned what land.

'Secondly, you can determine the age of a tree without cutting it down by taking a few simple measurements. Measuring the circumference of the trunk at a certain height and multiplying the distance by a known growth rate of tree species, will give you the age. I understand the method is very accurate.'

'How old does the tree need to be?' Michaela continues.

'Over four hundred years old. My understanding is, if a tree was planted on or before the year 1600 AD, then it's listed as ancient. Back then, trees such as the Oak were highly sought after, because of ship building. The ancient woodland trust are running tests and checks for us now and will confirm their findings. While undertaking this they believe they may have found something else of interest which requires further investigation. I was informed of this about a week ago and told they were bringing in the British Wildlife Trust to confirm their findings. What they think they may have discovered is a rare species of bat, called the Greater Horseshoe Bat.'

'I don't like bats.' Lucy pipes up.

'Not many of us do. The fact is, they are harmless creatures who feed on the one pest we all hate…insects. It may sound like it but it's not all doom and gloom. Think about this, an ancient forest, rare bat species, bluebells and wild garlic in spring, who could ask for more?

'The original plan was to have a circular trail around the woodland, with a guide to talk about the points of interest. With Penrice Farm now available we'll simplify the trail to a walk down to the farm, where we plan to keep livestock the public can engage with.'

'What sort of livestock?' Michaela again asks.

'Yet to be decided upon. We need to know what we can and can't do with the space we have at Penrice Farm. Let's say for instance sheep, because lambing is a great crowd puller. Pigs, pygmy goats, chickens, those type of breeds. The list isn't endless but we feel we should keep to the breeds the public associate with British farming.'

'What about cows?' Sam asks Marcus.

'Another good question. There won't be room for cattle at Penrice farm but up here at New Barn, we have a large herd of Welsh blacks. If we can work out the best way of keeping the public safe and they can see, we may include a tour of the milking parlour and perhaps a walk through the calf pens. As you can see there is a lot to discuss and this will take time to put into place. I reckon about two years. The spring of 2005 is a reasonable target. The boss may think differently.'

'A workable business plan, Marcus, that's what I need from you.' I inform him.

'Can I help with the animals?' Sam asks Marcus'

'I will encourage you too, as long as your dad doesn't mind. I think it's a wonderful idea and you'll enjoy the experience. Let's talk nearer the time. I can teach you how to handle the animals, how to feed them and look after them. How does that sound?'

'I'd really like that, and I can tell the people all about the animals.'

'Sounds like a plan to me, Sam. I'll look forward to teaching you. Anything else guys?'

'What happens if you can't have a nature trail through the woodland?' Jack asks, which please me. Up until now he's been rather quiet.

'We have been advised, that if we avoid sensitive areas of the woodland for conservation reasons, there shouldn't be a problem. They just need to identify those areas before we make a start. The trail itself will be constructed from natural materials. Lined by sustainable logging the infill will be bark chippings, or something similar. This method is the least disruptive to the local ecosystem and user friendly. I think we have time.' Marcus continues, looking at his watch. 'Would you like to take a quick look at where the milking is done?'

162

Walking behind them on our way back across to the farm I decide to give the milking parlour a miss and go and pay my bill in the shop. It scares me thinking about how much mother spent on todays' party. I don't class her as being extravagant but where entertaining is concerned, she's always gone over the top.

Crossing the car park I notice a vehicle turning into the drive I recognise. Brad's black Range Rover is very distinctive. What does he want? Altering my direction I hurriedly walk towards him in the hope the others won't see him. Pulling up right in front of me, Brad jumps out of his car. It's obvious he's not happy.

'What the hell do you think you're doing?' He chastises me.

'Spending quality time with the boys and our guest. Not that it's any of your business.'

'This isn't a nine to five job. You don't clock out at five on a Friday and back in at nine on a Monday morning. You are required to out there looking for answers.'

Coming to a stand right in front of him I could easily lose my temper. He knows my situation better than anyone and he's out of order.

'Looking after the boys is a full time occupation. There is no clocking in and out. Doing things together as a family is very important and I have no intention of letting them down. I'm walking around with a fucked shoulder and one kidney. For your information, that was only three months ago and there are times when I struggle. So save you breath for someone who cares. I told you and the others at the time the boys came first and that my friend, is exactly what I'm going to do.'

'I, we, need you out there. It's important.'

'And why is that? Is it because I've been more productive in the hours I have worked, than the rest of you lot put together? May I remind you here that I was working on a lead but no, you told me to back off. What exactly is it you want from me? You are the one who stopped me doing my job and I can assure you, that hasn't gone down too well with me. I suggest you think again before shouting your mouth off the next time.'

163

'I had a reason for stopping you. We have a man on the inside at Marstons. He's been there for about six weeks. You going in there asking lots of questions, could have placed our operation at risk.'

'Why the fuck didn't you tell me?'

'Because, you didn't need to know.'

'There you go again! Let me do my job or forget it.' Turning my back on him I stop. I have more to say. 'Incidentally, what has your man on the inside discovered?'

'Nothing yet. It takes time to gain confidence. He has suggested, your man Alf Roberts isn't involved.'

'And I suggest differently. If you don't let me pursue this you may regret it. He's involved, take my word for it. I just need time to prove I'm right. If you really want my help then help me. Have Alf Roberts followed.'

We're the first to arrive at Tom's place. That statement is thought provoking. Technically, for the next few days or so, the farm is still Tom's. After that it will become mine. With so much history here moulding my life, it will always remain Tom's place to me. It will be interesting to see how everyone else views the situation in the future.

After unloading the beer and soft drinks from Marcus's VW camper, he disappeared off back to New Barn. I'm to phone him when we're ready to go home.

Tom has placed some rickety old chairs and a couple of benches he found in the barn outside in the courtyard. It's not a bad afternoon, weather wise, in the lengthening month of September and it's not a bad idea of his. For someone like me who smokes, it's much appreciated.

With the others in tow and Tom shuffling along behind them, Sam is once again taking the lead and giving the guided tour. He's really taken to the idea of an educational farm and hands up, his recent input has been invaluable. I would go as far as saying, without him it may not have happened. It takes something quite special for me to admit that. Watching him, with his expressive nature as he explains to the others what he knows, he comes across as being very passionate about the future. That sparks an idea. Sam would be very disappointed if his ideas were pushed to one side and forgotten. I should approach Marcus to see how he feels about including Sam once all the measurements and obstacles are recorded and we have a reasonable idea of what we can and can't do. Sam's ideas may be very different to the way Marcus sees the future and what's possible. Sam though is a very intelligent young man. He listens, he takes his time to think about things, in depth at times and if Marcus explains to him in detail the reasons for why and why not, he will understand. He will have his say, as he is now and that is a good thing, but has he got it in him to compromise.

Right from the very early days Tom said I would achieve great things. I don't see my life's work in the same light. I have been successful and I've worked long and hard to achieve that. If that is conceived as greatness, then who am I to argue. If that is true then I've had a lot of help along the way. Tom himself was and is my mentor. He has given me a lot of his time, talking to me, advising me, guiding me towards making the right decisions and choices.

Jan has always been my greatest critic. She has never held back in telling me I'm wrong. No one likes being told they're wrong and I'm no exception, but by creating doubt, challenges a person and makes them stop to think about what they're doing.

My dear friend Beth was by far the most influential. She and her weird friend Henry Sinclair claimed I possessed a seventh sense. I've never really subscribed to that claim or fully understood their reasoning, but it's fair to acknowledge things have happened right in front of me I have no explanation for. Like the vision I had out at the hostel, when I saw the name Alf on the hostel wall. No one else did because it wasn't there, but why did I? Is it subliminal? Something I may have seen before that suddenly made sense. I have also been told that I'm always in the right place at the right time. I think that's because I'm persistent and luck or a seventh sense has nothing to do with it. I liken that to standing at a road junction day in day out, because at some point you will witness an accident. It's a simplistic view point of my life and not what others think they see or know. That view has been challenged more recently and my teachers could be right after all.

Inside helping mother our conversation is light and topical. Early for the party she wasn't ready so in the absence of the others, I'm the one left to give her a hand.

'Will you be selling Penrice House?' She asks.

165

'I will. As soon as the business is transferred into my name I'm going to put it on the market. I'm told the housing market is quite strong at the moment. It's going on at £249.950.'

'Hope you don't mind me saying, isn't that a little on the high side?'

'It's a big property, Mother, with plenty of room to expand. I know what I want to achieve from the sale so let's see what happens.'

'Are you trying to recover your loses from buying the farm?'

'Put bluntly…yes. Having said that, our future plans for the farm won't come cheap.'

'I've heard all about your plans and I think it's a wonderful idea. Educating the kids of today about farming can only be a good thing. Nick, love, getting old is a terrible burden. There comes a time when you feel useless and life begins crumbling around you. Knowing the farm will be taken good care of in the future is most comforting. It distresses me when I think we nearly let you down and I'm grateful for your help, and love. How can we ever thank you?'

'You can by sitting back and enjoying your retirement. That is what you should be doing after all those years of working your fingers to the bone. I'm happy if you're happy and I'm pleased I could help.'

'Time for a beer, Boy?' Tom bellows as he enters the kitchen alone.

'Sure. Where are the kids?'

'Sam's going to show them where the nature trail will come out of the woods onto your land.'

'He's not likely to know that?'

'He seems to know. He gave a good talk over there you know. Don't miss much…does he?'

'He certainly doesn't.'

'Reminds me of you as a youngster. Got a bit more upstairs than you did.' He adds, pointing at his head.

'Can I say something?' Pausing for a moment I face them. 'Sam has quite a unique character. He never ceases to surprise me and I have become more than aware of how people around me have warmed to him. But I have another son, Jack, who is equally as important, if not more to me because he is my flesh and blood. I divide my time between them as equally as I can and I'd like you to do the same. I don't want Jack leaving here today thinking he's been left out. All I ask, is you talk with him. Ask him how he is and what he's doing. You know, is he working or going to college. Ask him about Lucy and how she and the baby are. This is all new to him too and God knows, he's been through a tough time as well.'

'We didn't realise, Nick, love.' Mother replies. 'We hardly ever see Jack to talk to him.'

'All the more reason for taking the time too now. I apologise if it sounds like I'm having a go, but it will mean a lot to me if you treat them both the same.'

I know I shouldn't do this under the circumstances, but when Tom hands me a glass of beer I take it outside into the courtyard and sit on one of the benches for a smoke. Giving myself time to think is a coping strategy for me. Lighting a cigarette I lean back against the house wall. Hoping for a few peaceful moments to myself I know Tom is on his way outside. I can hear him shuffling along in my direction. Making his way over, he plonks himself down next to me on the bench. Silence prevails while he rolls a cigarette.

'You alright, Boy?' He finally asks.

'No. I'm juggling too many balls and sooner or later, I'm going to drop one of those balls onto the ground. The consequences of that occurring could be life changing.'

'You still working? Cos that won't help matters.'

'I am working. I have no choice at the moment.'

'Course you have. No wonder you're struggling.'

'You don't understand.'

'Try me?'

167

'Tom. For the sake of others something's are best left un-said. I think the time is right to tell you. For the last ten years I have worked for the government. It works on a part time basis. When my skills are required I'm called upon to serve my country. It pays well and until three months ago, it worked well. I can't tell you too much, but what I'm involved with at this time is very important. People are relying on me to do my job. It'll be over soon, then I'll take a back seat.'

'Make sure you do. What you're planning to do here is going to occupy a lot of your time. When this other business is over, see that you do take a back seat. I may not have said this to your face, but I think what you're intending to do here is a great idea. My forefathers may turn in their graves but the old place will come alive again.'

Once everyone had arrived and settled in, mother invited us to help ourselves to the food. She has put on a wonderful spread. Something for everyone's taste. Then why am I surprise she hasn't gone over the top. I paid her bill in the farm shop. Taking a pew outside I'm joined by Jack and Lucy.

'This is a great idea, Dad.'

'Do you think so?'

'Of course it is. Sam is really excited and can't wait until the animals arrive.'

'How about you?'

'Come on. Spit it out.'

'With everything that's going on I'm worried I might let you down and I won't be there when you need me. Seeing this through to the end will take up a lot of my time. I'm not sure this is the right time for embarking on such a big project.'

'Dad, its fine. If you need my help at any time, just ask. And you're not letting me down. Remember the other day when we spoke about the letter mum sent me? What you said to me then made a lot of sense. I'd hardly call that, letting me down.'

'Can I ask you something personal?'

'Would you like me to go?' Lucy asks.

'No, Lucy. I'd like you to stay and hear this.' Taking a sip of beer I turn to face them both. 'Does the fact we have changed Sam's surname to Thompson upset you?'

'No. Not in the slightest. It was done for all the right reasons and I'm perfectly fine with it. Please don't think I'm upset with you for doing what is best for Sam.'

'You know you can do the same if you wish. I'd be made up if you did. Will you give it some thought?'

'Jack and me have talked about this. We weren't sure how to approach the subject so we decided to wait for the right moment.' Finishing, Lucy gives Jack a gentle nudge.

'Dad. I would be proud to change my surname to Thompson. It would mean a lot to me. I'm not a Morris, I'm a Thompson.'

Leaning across to give Jack a hug, Lucy grabs the glass out of my hand before I spill it everywhere.

'Let's find out how we go about this, Jack, and if it's alright with you, we'll do as soon as possible.'

'I'd like that.'

Resting my head on Jack's shoulder I look ahead at Lucy. She has a lovely smile on her face. Starring at her I address Jack's emotions.

'We should have spoken about this sooner but as always, we've had other things to worry about. I'll see what I can find out first thing on Monday.'

Chilling out after we'd eaten Tom starts reminiscing over the old days. It doesn't take him long to target me and I can only sit in silence as he recalls the embarrassing memories of my fishing exploits. The boys find it particularly funny and are quick to ask Tom if they can have a go. Leaving us to wonder where he's disappearing off to, Tom returns with three old fishing rods in his hands. Set up they're ready to go, but they've seen better days. In saying yes to the boys he tells them they should really have a day license to fish, but as the land either side of the river is mine, it shouldn't be a problem. He informs them I will show them where to find the bait they need. I not impressed by

169

that. It's a dirty job. Richard obviously sees I'm not impressed and offers to show them. He is well aware of what is required to dig up the bait because together, we've spent many an hour in the past fishing down on the river.

They all disappeared leaving myself, Jan, Tom and Mother in the peace and quiet of their absence. Stuffed after helping ourselves to the fantastic spread we sit back and relax. Nestling into the chair next to Tom in front of the range I watch as he rolls a couple of cigarettes. I'm savouring the moment. Two days ago this was never going to happen again. How quickly life and circumstances change.

Facing the door I see James walk past the side kitchen window. I had invited him but he had declined my invitation on the grounds he was busy. Coming to a stand in the doorway I notice he's clutching a rolled up piece of paper in his right hand. Knowing what I had asked him to do for me I invite him inside.

'I have something you might like to see.' James informs me. Excusing myself I step outside to talk to James in private. 'I called in a few favours to get this, so I hope it's worth my while.'

'Bribery, James?'

'Call it what you like. I have been at the office since 9am collating this information for you. I reckon it's worth a few hours overtime.'

Reaching his car James rolls out the paper on the bonnet. I'm impressed. Taking my time to study and digest the information the two family trees he's worked on, answer a number of questions I have, but not all of them.

'Talk me through this, James.'

'Fine. It's not conclusive and there appears not to be a connection between Alf Roberts and Paul Linnette. What this does tell us, Alf Roberts changed his name from Alf West shortly after his twenty-first birthday. A friend of mine is sending me a copy of the deed pole for confirmation. Why he made the change isn't known. There could be any number of reasons why he did but interestingly, his home address remained the same. Sort of suggests he wasn't in conflict with his parents.

'Paul Linnette on the other has only has one parent named on his birth certificate…his mother Alexis. I couldn't find any record of her ever marrying. A copy of his birth certificate is also being sent over to me. Call me old fashioned, but you'd only make a person a director of your company for one of two reasons. A financial investment, or they're family.'

'So you're suggesting Paul Linnette could be Alf Roberts' son?'

'It stacks up. Paul was born on the 31st May 1959, which makes him forty-four. Alf would have been seventeen at the time. Having a bastard child back them was frowned upon and it looks like someone took great care in hiding the father's name. I could be wrong with my thoughts and I will look into that.'

'Alexis Linnette. Is she still alive?'

'Yes. Alexis is sixty.'

'Do we have an address for her?'

James directs me to the bottom of the page. 'That's correct as of the 2001 census.'

'Crundale. Where's that?'

'A village north of Haverfordwest. I believe she owns and runs a B &B there. Look, if you're planning to pay her a visit I'll join you. If she is connected and involved it could be dangerous on your own.'

'On one condition, James. You let me do the talking.'

'Suits me. My eyes and ears do my job for me.'

'I'll meet you at the office at 9am Monday morning.'

'Why don't we pay her a visit tomorrow morning? She's more likely to be at home at the weekend.'

'Because Sam is playing football and if I miss that, there will be hell to pay.'

Chapter Nine

I'm shattered. Saturday wasn't a late affair but it was full on. I struggled to maintain my involvement in the proceedings after James left. I didn't disclose this to him but his diligence has given me a lot to think about. Far more than I expected and I became detached because I wasn't in a position to follow up on his news and that played on my mind. Until I know more I will keep that to myself.

Our potential meeting with Alexis Linnette this morning could reveal much more and my concern is, can I trust her? Lying awake last night well into the early hours, I went over and over in my mind what I should and shouldn't say to her…and in front of James for that matter. It all comes down to my need to know the facts without alerting her to a problem.

Sam didn't help matters yesterday. It wasn't his fault but after his game in the morning, all I wanted to do when we got home was to prepare myself both mentally and factually for today. Sam's hyper mood made that impossible. Bouncing off the walls and insisting I played football in the garden with him, really tested my tolerance levels. His team, The Bluebirds, had a comfortable 6-0 win and Sam scored three of their goals. Coupled with the news that his re-registration had been agreed, made him impossible to reason with.

Worryingly for me, Matt Wilson pointed out a couple of gentlemen from other clubs watching Sam. They didn't approach during or after the game but one of the two gentlemen was definitely making notes. That prompted me to remind Matt he should inform me if anyone made inquiries about Sam and he, or any other club official, should point them in my direction. Right from the start I was informed the football club don't like parents getting involved and in principle I accept that. This though is a delicate situation and I wasn't the one who suggested Sam should be playing at a higher level.

Ms Linnette's B&B is easy to locate in this quiet and small village. Set back off the road the U-shaped drive allows easy off road parking. The B&B looks recently painted and the garden well tendered. Rather isolated for my liking, the appearance gives a good first impression.

Noticing a cord to ring the doorbell I give it a sharp downward tug. Waiting an age for a response I repeat the cord pulling which seems to have the correct effect. When the door is finally opened we're informed the door is always open and there's a service bell on the hall table.

Ms Linnette is nothing like I had imagined her to be. Then, I'm not sure what I expected her to look like. Tall, slim with long greying hair she reminds me off Beth. Perhaps she too is a white witch.

'Ms Linnette, my name is Nick Thompson. I'm a private investigator working under secondment for the police. If you have a few minutes to spare I'd like to ask you a few questions about Alf Roberts.

'Bloody man! I haven't seen or spoken to him in over thirty years. What's he done now? You'd better come in.'

Following her through the house to the kitchen at the back I explain to her who James is and why he's here. Once we enter the room, she offers us a seat and puts the kettle on.

'We're not sure, Ms Linnette. That's why we're here. There is one thing I'd like to clarify first and it is rather personal. Your son Paul, is Alf Roberts his father? I ask you that because we've discovered that Paul is, or was, a director of Alf's company West's Garden Services.'

With that Ms Linnette joins us and sits down at the table. 'Alf West as he was then. Yes, Paul is Alf's son. We were both sixteen when it happened. When I told Alf I was pregnant he went mad. He lashed out at me, called me a slut amongst other things and said he didn't want to see me again. When I look back, I thank my lucky stars I got out of that relationship. He changed after that and became known as a bully, a thug. Not a nice person to know and when he found out I was seeing someone else, he beat the shit out of him. Alf did six months inside for GBH. To protect the family name he changed his surname to Roberts as soon as he legally could.'

'Did you tell Paul this?'

'No. Paul was a lovely child and we had some great times together as he grew up. I didn't know this at the time, but when Paul was about fourteen he started seeing Alf on a regular basis. He's turned out like his father and I have precious little to do with him these days. Sad, but I don't want anything to do with either of them. When Paul left school at sixteen he started working

173

for Alf in what I would describe as a very dodgy garden business. How they made money and spent it like throwing confetti around I'll never know…and I don't wish too. Is that why you're here?'

'Ms Linnette…'

'Please call me Alexis.'

'Alexis. What does Paul do now?'

'As a child Paul liked dogs. After working for Alf, then Marstons for five years he bought a plot of land and opened a dog kennel business. I understand he's a trainer and registered dog breeder. When he cares to phone me he goes on and on about how successful he is. Makes loads of money he claims. Trust me, after all I did for him as a child and a single parent, I don't see a penny of that.'

'What type of breeds is Paul into? Does he have a particular breed he likes?'

'Greyhounds are his main love…so I'm told. He imports them from Ireland, trains them up and sells the promising dogs on for big profits…so he says.'

'Racing dogs I assume?'

'Yes. Paul tells me he works with breeders in Ireland who have a good reputation and secures an entire litter which have pedigree and potential to be winners.'

'Do you know how many pups there are in a litter?'

'Not sure. I think it can be up to twelve.'

'What age would he start training the greyhounds?'

'Again I'm not sure. I think Paul once told me they need to be at least one year old. Paul has his own circuit and trains them himself. I haven't spoken to him in some while, but I believe he has at least five dogs of his own that he races.'

'And you say he gets these greyhounds from Ireland?'

'That's what he told me.'

'How does Paul bring them over to Wales?'

'He has a specially adapted truck he uses and collects them himself. Fishguard to Rosslare isn't that demanding from where he's based.'

'Are his son's involved in the business?'

'Sebastian is, Kristian is in his final year at school. I assume he'll follow his brother into the business.'

'Alexis?' James buts in. 'What happens to the greyhounds that don't make the grade?'

'Doesn't bare thinking about…does it? Can you tell me what this is all about?'

'I'm afraid I can't.' I reply.' 'This is an ongoing investigation and until I'm satisfied otherwise, I cannot comment. I trust you won't speak to Alf or your son Paul of our visit?'

Outside I lean against my car and light a cigarette. Exhaling I look at James. 'You're the expert. What do you think? Can we trust her?'

'She certainly wasn't giving much away. She was extremely relaxed despite her verbal distain towards Alf and her son Paul. Then you never really pushed her for answers,'

'There's a fine balance, James, between getting the answers you want or risk upsetting a potential witness. Alexis appeared to volunteer the information, so I rolled with it.'

'Was she telling us the truth though?'

'That's what I need you to find out. James, this isn't one of my personal escapades, it's official business, so you must keep anything you've heard to yourself. I'd like you to find out all you can about Paul Linnette's kennel business, from top to bottom. Who he deals with, who works for him, who he sells to and you may need to ask Graham to run a financial check on him.'

'We don't know where his alleged business is, or what it's called.'

175

'No, but Alexis stated that from where he's based, it isn't that demanding to catch a ferry over to Rosslare. That narrows the search area down and when you add in greyhound training, he won't be difficult to find.'

'What happens when I do find what you need?'

'Feed that information straight back to me and me alone. Then forget it. Right! You're not in a hurry are you?'

'Nothing that can't wait.'

'Good. I need to go via Haverfordwest on the way back. It shouldn't take long.

Calling in at my solicitors briefly, I asked him if the paperwork Jenny had left Jack is a valid document and enough to allow him to change his surname to Thompson. His conclusion led him to say it was but he advised me to check with Jenny's solicitor. I will do that in the comfort of my own home.

At James's expense I took a little detour too. I wanted to see the building and layout of Forrests. It's much larger than I expected and has two well defined business hubs. Frozen and fresh food departments. From the outside it looks to be a big concern which has already generated my interest. Not concerning Brad's initial idea of fish products but one, as a nation, we import on a large scale from Eire…potatoes. With the right contacts, how easy would that be? Tucked in the middle of a sack of potatoes and subtly marked on the outside, who would know the difference…unless you were in the know? I'm not going to discount this possibility simply because of what Alexis has told us and it's worth finding out if both avenues are being used in conjunction. Do I though, need to discuss my thoughts with Brad and Wallace at this point without obtaining hard facts?

Walking through the house I come across Jan vacuuming the lounge carpet. I know she does this from time to time, but I've never actually seen her undertaking the task.

'Coffee?' She shouts, before switching off the vacuum cleaner and heading for the kitchen…which is unusual.

'What have you done?' I ask, joining her.

'What makes you ask me that?'

176

'Because your normal response is to say something along the lines of, "put the kettle on I'll be with you as soon as I've finished this". '

'You'd better sit down.'

'I don't like the sound of this.' Pulling out one of the kitchen stools I sit and face her. She looks a little sheepish.

'Linda's back. She turned up at my front door late yesterday afternoon with all her gear. She's left home for good and asked if she could stay a while until she finds herself somewhere to live.'

'I hope you said no?'

'How could I? She's a friend, Nick, a friend in need. A couple of weeks won't do any harm.'

'Not to you…maybe. I'm telling you now, if she finds a place here in Saundersby I will go mad! And if she starts interfering in my life in any way, I will seek to have a restraining order placed on her. So make her aware of my intentions, and you will not discuss any of my business with her…particularly Tom's farm. I hope I'm making myself clear?'

'That's a little harsh…on both of us. She needs our support at a time like this. Look at what we've all done for you? We've helped you at every stage along the way and we're still doing that. She's not a bad person, just very vulnerable right now. Please don't push her away.'

'I have no intention of pushing her away because she'll not get close enough in the first place. She needs to understand that. I don't want to see her and I don't want to talk to her. Please convey my wishes to her or things around here will change.'

Standing, I walk back through the house to my office at the front. My thoughts remind me, it never rains but it pours. If I wasn't so pre-occupied I probably would have seen that coming. Stepping inside my office I'm closing the door when my mobile rings. Wallace. What does he want?

'Nick! Where are you?' He bellows.

'Why?'

'I need to talk to you, and not over the phone.'

'I'm busy. Can it wait?'

'Not really. I need you to organise something for me.'

'I'm at home working, but not for much longer.'

'Stay put. I'll be right over.'

Jan isn't talking to me. That becomes painfully obvious when she answers the front door and shows Reg into the kitchen. The scowl she gives me when I ask her to leave us in peace says it all. I'm sure Reg senses the friction between us.

'So what do you want to talk to me about?'

'I need you to talk to Sam for me.'

'About what?'

'The Avon and Somerset police have requested he looks through some mug shots they've put together in the hope he may recognise someone.'

'Why don't they send the pictures to me?'

'There's something else they'd like him to do. They've requested he shows them where he made the drops. They want to monitor these places for further activity.'

'He's never going to agree to do that and I'm not going to force him.'

'It's important, Nick. You know I wouldn't ask otherwise. Please talk to him. It will be better coming from you.'

'How do they propose doing this, because he's not going to walk the streets?'

'All taken care of. It will be in an unmarked police car with tinted windows. Three police officers and you in the car with him. Sam will sit in the back between you and one of the officers. The two non-drivers will be armed with automatic side arms. You and Sam will both wear bullet proof jackets at all times. Is there anything else you'd like to know?'

'How do we get there?'

With me, in the same set up. The intention, while this is carried out, is to follow the car you and Sam are in. As you would expect me to say at this point, this must stay between you, me and Sam.'

'When?'

'ASAP. It's that important.'

'What about his schooling?'

'Talk to him first, then we'll deal with that. I think both of us trust Fiona Martin.'

'Why is it I always get the shit end of the deal?'

'Because in this instance, you are Sam's dad and that carries with it the responsibility. We're doing all we can to make this as painless and safe for Sam as we can. Convincing and reassuring him it will be ok, is your job. Nick, I can't stress enough how important this is. If it helps, I'll organise a time and day to take Sam to our driver training school. Let him sit in the car with a trainer for a spin around the track. You too if you like, because I know how stressful this whole deal is for you both.'

'The way you drive! I think I'll give that a miss, but thanks all the same. Thank you for showing your concern. It is a very difficult time.'

'May I ask why?' Pausing to answer I stare dead ahead of myself. 'Is there a problem?'

'I'm not sure. Sam is far too eager to please me, wants me to sing his praises and I'm not sure it's genuine on his part. Yes he's publically said I've done more for him than anyone else has ever done and that's a nice thought, but Sam is a very intelligent young man and just maybe, he's using me.'

'Is that what you think?'

'I don't know right now. Can't put my finger on it, but I feel something isn't right.'

'You two do need to sit down and talk. I suggest you focus on what is right for Sam first and not allow your decision making to become clouded. He may well be taking advantage of what you are doing for him, but coming from a background like he has, wouldn't you embrace someone's generosity?

179

Giving him a safe and stable environment to grow up in is exactly what he needs and deserves. Try not to think too deeply about this and don't let your doubts cloud your mind. I know you do talk to him when a situation arises. Whatever you may think, don't stop doing that. You two have got some serious talking to do, and I suggest you do it very soon.'

From the moment Alexis Linnette told us about her son's involvement in Greyhound training I have been racking my brain, searching for the name of a gentleman I met several years ago who keeps racing dogs. Eventually I found his name and contact number in my client list on my computer. Steve Johnson lives on the outskirts of Swansea and that's where I'm heading.

When I phoned Steve he told me we met over five years ago in a public house in Laugharne. We spoke for an hour or so that day and my resistance to abstain from drinking alcohol, because I was driving, prompted an arrangement for a session a couple of weeks later. It turned out to be one of those evenings when I vaguely remember going home. Sadly, work has always got in my way and like many other instances, we lost contact. I'm driving now and won't drink, so history may repeat itself.

I'm beginning to regret expressing my views to Reg regarding Sam. Venting my thoughts and frustrations could be a misplaced comment and taken as a negative thought…that I'm giving up. I could be subconsciously aware that Sam has picked up on that recently, because after the initial intensity of doing what was right and best for him, that pressure has dwindled somewhat. Whose fault is that? Mine, his, or what people are asking of me? I want to retire and they know that. I have no desire to work full time and be a father to Jack and Sam at the same time. My issue is, I like to resolve things to the best of my ability and that does take over my life. I can't, and don't want to do both.

Steve is sat with two other people when I enter the agreed meeting place in Laugharne. It's already approaching 2pm and I'm mindful of picking Sam up from school on time. See how the simple, everyday things in life have become important.

I don't know the people in Steve's company, but I'm soon introduced. I make it very clear at the same time that I'm driving and not drinking. The atmosphere is relaxed as the conversation evolves around his greyhounds. My first question provokes a sharp intake of breath from Steve, followed by a sarcastic laugh.

'Steve. Do you know, or have you ever had any dealings with a man called Paul Linnette?'

'Once, and never again.'

'The man's a charlatan. Tricked us out of a few thousand some years ago.' Steve's partner Sandy informs me. 'We paid good money for an eighteen month old greyhound he'd trained.'

'Said it had a good pedigree,' Steve continues. 'And he told us it was more than capable of achieving top grading. Scorcher was the dogs' name. It went lame on its first trial race, pulled up on the first bend. The vet told us later that Scorcher had an underlying problem which was probably a birth defect. A lame dog, Nicholas, will never run again. On the strength of that we asked for our money back. Paul Linnette had the nerve to tell us we'd been training Scorcher wrong and wasn't going to give us our money back under any circumstances. Accidents happened he said and we should deal with it. Won't be dealing with that bastard again…that's for sure.'

'Didn't you employ a vet to check the dog over before you parted with your cash?'

'We should have done but he said it was part of the deal. His vet would check it over for us and he declared it fit. We still have the documents somewhere.' Sandy adds.

'Do you remember the vets' name?'

'Not off the top of my head but if you think it's important, I'll dig the documents out and let you know.'

'Perfect. Tell me something, do you know anyone else who has had a problem with Paul Linnette?'

'Not that we are aware of, but as you've asked I'll put a few feelers out.'

'Thank you. Steve, have you still got my mobile number?'

'Let me check, Nicholas.'

While Steve plays with his mobile phone, looking for my number, Sandy turns to face me and asks the one question I always get asked.

181

'Has he done something wrong?'

'I'm not sure yet but the more I learn about him, the more I hope he has.'

When I picked Sam up from school, on time I should add, he immediately sensed something is wrong. In return I don't know how I should handle this. In the time I have got to know him, as well as I think I have, I know he won't like this. I feel I should soften the blow because this will undoubtedly open up some bad times and experiences for him. Our short trip down to the harbour is conducted in silence. Him looking at me, waiting for me to say something, is unnerving. Now probably isn't the right time to talk about my doubts.

A late all day breakfast in the harbour café might do the trick. Sitting as far away from the counter as possible, I know it's down to me to open this difficult conversation. Sitting opposite me I can see he's agitated.

'Sam, I need you to hear me out first before reacting. I had a visit from DI Wallace this morning. The Avon and Somerset police have requested you do a couple of things for them. Firstly they'd like you to look through some mug shots, as they refer to them, in the hope you might recognise someone. Secondly, they'd like you to show them where you made the drops. We know, particularly me, how difficult you may find this but it's very, very important. Sam, you have to understand that if you really want this over and done with, we should do this for them. I have expressed my concerns to Wallace and he has reassured me everything is in place to keep you safe. Please, for our sake, do as they ask so we can move forward and enjoy life as a family together.'

'I don't want to do it, Dad!'

'Is that how you really see me?'

'What do you mean?'

I can't help myself. I'd previously made up my mind not to mention my doubts, his commitment to what I'm doing for him, but I have this undying need to know the truth. Over the years I have been used in many different guises and although in some cases that has been financially beneficial, it has become tiresome...a burden. Looking out of the window, Sam slowly turns his head to face me. He has tears rolling down his cheeks.

'Don't you want me to live with you anymore?'

'This has nothing to do with whether I want you to live with me. For your information I do but, Sam, I need you to do this for us, not just you and me, for Jack as too. So we can be free to live our lives the way we want. No gremlins, no hang ups. To be a united family. I don't want to spend the rest of my life looking over your shoulders, and mine, for potential dangers. Sam, in time, I want you to be independent. Walk to school and back with your friends without relying on me doing the school run. We both need to feel comfortable about you going out by yourself and coming home safely. Doing what is right now, like helping the Avon and Somerset police, is part of that progression. We have both made fantastic progress and done some good things for each other, like you talking to Tom for me and we shouldn't spoil that after all we've done. Life could go wrong very quickly and I don't want that to happen. Is that what you want to happen?'

'No.' He whispers while shaking his head.

'Trust, Sam, and right now I need your trust like never before.'

Sam pushed his food around for a while – I think more in defiance than anything thing – but eventually ate every last morsel on his plate. I'm of the opinion he was thinking over what I said to him. We haven't spoken more than a couple of words since. Outside he strides off in front of me and stands himself by the drivers' door, blocking my way. I believe he may want to confront me.

'You're not driving home.' I flippantly respond.

'I don't want too.' He automatically retorts. 'I want to say sorry.'

'For what?'

'Being stupid. Selfish. I've had to be like that since I remember because I had to look after myself to survive the shit they gave me. I'm sorry, Dad, but I can't help it at times.'

'It's ok, Sam. I do understand. You're talking to one of the most selfish people you'll ever meet. I too have had to be very selfish at times and like you, simply to survive. We all do it from time to time and it's not a bad thing, because looking after number one is very important. Standing up for what you think is right or believe in is a strong character trait, its knowing

183

when to compromise that's important. Sam, I am fully aware that going back to Bristol isn't something you want to do. I can assure you, I don't want to go as much as you do, but please think about the long term benefits for you, Jack and me.'

'I will go. Please come with me?'

'That has never been in doubt young man. I will be at your side the entire time, in my bullet proof jacket.'

'Do I get to wear a bullet proof jacket too?'

'You certainly do. It'll be more like a trench coat on you.'

'What's a trench coat?'

'Showing my age, aren't I? It's first-world war coat the men were issued with to wear while they fought in the trenches. Sam, I'd like to thank you for being so honest with me. That goes a long, long way in my books.'

I'm not entirely sure who will benefit from our frank discussion, or who will feel the most reassured by the outcome. We both knew his involvement with Barry Mullins and Larry Winstone wasn't over and that he is a vital witness in the conclusion of that episode but in fairness to him, we have both pushed it to one side. Taking in where we're at, I'm suggesting we should go home when my mobile rings. Bloody modern technology.

'Steve! How are we doing?'

'Sandy's found the name and address of the vet you asked about.'

'Brilliant. Steve, I'm out at the moment. If I text you my email address, can you send the details over to me? If you can, will you scan in the document and forward that at the same time?'

'I'll ask Sandy to do that. She's out at the moment walking the dogs. I'll ask her when she gets back.'

'Thanks, Steve. Oh, there's one last thing. Did you claim on your insurance policy for your losses?'

''No. We we're going too but we changed our minds. We may have had to put Scorcher down if we did, so we decided to keep him as a pet and manage our losses.'

'Thanks for that, Steve. Speak to you soon,'

Tuesday 9th September

My morning has gone from bad to worse and I've yet to see Jan after we had words yesterday. It's pouring with rain, as it does on a frequent basis in this part of the country. Jack wants a lift into work, Sam needs dropping off at school and Michaela's mini bus has broken down. She has to be at the Royal Hotel in Fenby at 9am for a group conference…as she described it and needs a lift. I should get myself a hackney cab license and a metre fitted in my car, one of those super-efficient ones that don't miss a single metre of road mileage.

Dropping Michaela off last outside the Royal, for reasons unclear to me, I decide to head for the hostel. Don't know why because my main agenda this morning is speaking to James and he's in the office.

Things have certainly moved on. The hostel is surrounded by temporary mesh fencing and out of bounds to the public. Gwyn Roberts porta cabin office is inside the exclusion zone. I wonder where she is at the moment because Wallace was asked not to interfere. Taking in all I see as I amble towards the rear of the building, where some activity is taking place, I stop for a moment and stare at the wall where I saw the name Alf. Nothing unusual happens on this occasion, other than it becomes clear that Superintendent Lewis is a man of his word. He made it quite clear this would happen and it has…a thorough search of the site. Distracted, someone calls out my name.

'Nick! You got my message then?' DS Thomas enquires. Confused, I reply "no" to his suggestion, because I didn't. 'So how come you're here?'

'I dropped my house guest at the Royal and thought I'd take a look while I was out this way. Why did you leave a message for me?'

'We were right.'

'Of course we were.'

'Want to take a look at what we've found?'

'Not really. I don't wish to seem aloof, but I'd rather not spend the rest of the day walking around smelling like a bonfire.'

'Fair point.'

'Enlighten me. What have you found?'

186

'The cause of the fire was down to a faulty deep fat fryer. When I say faulty, someone with a good knowledge of electrics tampered with the wiring.'

'In what way?'

'Well. Whoever switched off the fryer the last time it was used followed close down procedures, but the fryer had been rewired to stay on. The user may not have known that. Left on it over heated and burst into flames, making this a case of arson.'

'How come your forensic team didn't find that in the first instance? From what I saw, your new evidence was there for all to see in the first place.'

'I agree with you. I have asked for them to be suspended from duty until further notice while we conduct our investigations. We'll know more then. As yet, the reason behind this arson attack is nothing more than guess work until we've completed the search of the building. That shouldn't take more than two or three days.'

'Where is Gwyn Roberts?'

'Working from home for the time being and yes, we are monitoring her phone calls. We're in the process of interviewing all of the staff, whether on duty at the time or not and that includes Gwyn Roberts. We're also interviewing and taking statements from the guests and running preliminary checks on each individual. It all takes time to put together. I'm sure you understand that?'

'I do, perfectly. What concerns me the most, considering this is a hostel, is how someone can simply walk in, tamper with the fryer and walk out without being noticed.'

'Unless it was someone you'd expect to see, or certainly somebody not out of place.'

'You're convinced then it was an inside job?'

'Without a doubt.'

'That rules out Hanna Green.'

'How do you mean?'

'Hanna was DI Wallace's number one suspect. She didn't turn up for her court sentencing on two accounts of arson and he was convinced, this attack had her MO written all over it. We'll never know now will we. I however don't think even she was capable of something as sinister as this, but as her best friend, David Griffiths worked here, I can see why he thought that. He was found dead in his room a few hours after Hanna's body was found. I think you can rule both of them out.'

'But they could be the reason behind the arson attack?'

'They are my thoughts. It's the who and the why, that's evading me, and the very reason I doubted the original forensic findings. I have established that David Griffiths was a dealer, which means he was getting his drugs from somewhere. He worked here, most of the time unsupervised and when you take into account that nothing to prove he was dealing turned up in his room, he had to be stashing the gear somewhere.'

'You think they were murdered...don't you.'

'I think someone was covering their tracks...by destroying the evidence. When we get the pathology results back...we'll know. Tell me something. Was the chip basket in its rest above the fat?'

'I believe so. What are you suggesting? The evidence was placed in the chip basket.'

'How good is your forensic scientist?'

I phoned DI Wallace several times before I left site. He didn't answer his phone but I'll try again later because I want to know if he's had the pathology results back. Those results could be vital.

Pulling up outside my office my attention is drawn to Ed Morgan standing in the middle of the quayside looking back at his workshop. Deep in thought, I hope he hasn't changed his mind. Before going inside my curiosity gets the better of me.

'I'll be out by the end of the week.' He announces, without looking at me. 'I've sold a lot of my junk, the rest I had taken away by a scrap merchant. I know it won't cover the money I owe you, but I gave Graham a grand...in cash.' Turning to face me he continues. 'Have you found a new tenant?'

Joining him I look into the workshop. Virtually empty of his crap, the space is much larger than I remember. It'll need a lot of work doing, but it's perfect for Richard's business requirements.

'I had a new tenant lined up the day you told me you were leaving.'

'You didn't waste much time. The alarm system will need fixing. Hasn't worked for months.'

'Isn't that a condition of your tenancy? Leave as found.'

'Behave yourself. Besides, Richard can do that.'

'I guess that'll be his first task before moving in.'

'You bastard! You had this all planned.'

'You were the one who told us you were calling it a day. The rest simply fell into place. Richard's business is expanding and this space suited his requirements perfectly. Coincidence, Ed, nothing more.'

'Sad moment, Nick. Thirty years of hard graft and for what? A few spare pennies in my pocket. Shall I tell you something? My best work in that time and one I'm very proud of, lies at the bottom of the bay in hundreds of pieces.'

'My boat.'

'Yes, your boat and with that gone, Nick, there will be nothing left of my time here serving the community to remember me by.'

'I think the locals will always remember you, Ed.'

'For my drinking perhaps, nothing else.'

'You certainly kept the pubs afloat.'

'Very funny. Listen, Nick, I ain't good at goodbyes.' Ed says, holding out his hand. 'I know you're a busy man and I may not see you again before I go.' I offer my hand and we shake. 'All the best for the future and I hope everything works out for you and the boys. Good luck young man.'

'Thank you, Ed. Good luck to you too and your new life in Devon. Remember one thing, Sam and I might not be here today if you hadn't reacted so quickly that terrible morning. I will be eternally grateful for your help. You saved our lives and I will remember that act of bravery for the rest of my life.'

'I was only doing what anyone else would have done. If you're ever down Devon way, make sure you pop in and say hello.'

'Likewise, Ed, you know where we are and to put the records straight, you did a great job on the boat.'

'Just to see you blow it up.'

'Accidently, Ed, accidently.'

'I bet your insurance company don't see it that way.'

'I'm working on that.'

From the day I first held the keys to this building in my hands, Ed Morgan has been my soul tenant. We've had are disagreements over the years, mainly over his rent, or the lack of it and his belligerent attitude towards life in general, but I'll miss the old fart. His going, signals the end of another chapter in my life but I'm not of the mind to change that event. Ed's business isn't investible, nor was Tom's for that matter. Apart from the personal side there is one huge difference. Tom's land will always be worth something and if I, we, get that right, far more than I paid for it. Sad really, Ed was right when he said he was part of the fabric of this community. Today's modern society is, and will continue too, tear apart local communities. Reflecting on this, hands in my pockets, I join James in our office. Heading for my desk I notice him look at his wrist watch.

'I'm not late.' I utter in defiance.

'Heaven forbid I suggested you are!'

'You get the email I sent to you last night?'

'You seem a bit subdued, boss. Everything OK?'

'I'm fine, James.' I respond, sitting down and relaxing back in my chair. 'I found out this morning that the hostel fire was deliberate.'

'So it is a case of arson?'

190

'As I suspected it was. Someone tampered with one of the deep fat fryers. My problem is, although I have numerous pieces of the jigsaw puzzle to work with, there is nothing in between to join them together. Worse still, I'm relying on DI Wallace and his cronies for information and that is very slow forth coming.'

'Well the good news is, I have found the information you wanted and I've asked Graham to run a financial check on the kennel business. He's out today, in court I believe, so I won't have that information until tomorrow. I'll go and print off what I have got.'

By the time James returns I've hauled my weary frame out of my chair and sat myself down on the window sill, staring out of the window.

'Apart from Graham's bit, it's all there.' He states, handing me the paperwork. 'Nothing out of the ordinary as you would expect. Their websites are impressive. That doesn't come cheap...I know.'

'What am I missing, James? The two people who probably did know are now lying in the mortuary. I have no actual proof to validate Alexis Linnette's story and Mrs Parry's claim that her son worked on Fridays with someone by the name of Alf cannot be substantiated, and I can't just barge in at the wholesalers, Forrests, asking questions.' Standing, trying to pull myself together, I continue to voice my doubts. 'I need to get someone inside that kennel business.'

'You're looking at them. They don't know who I am.'

'This isn't a reflection on your abilities, James, but this needs to be someone in the know. Someone who is involved within the greyhound racing business. Someone who knows what they are looking for and what they are talking about.'

'Give me a few hours to brush up on the ins and outs of becoming an owner, question me and let's find out. You'll be surprised by what I can do when pushed.'

'It won't work.' I tell him, sitting back down at my desk.

'What have you got to lose? Surely it's worth a try?'

'There's far more to greyhound racing than reading about it. Like our business, it's about the tricks of the trade. How to gain an advantage and become a winner and believe me, they'll know the difference between an expert and novice. Thanks for the offer, but no thanks. The last thing I want, if they are involved that is, is to make them suspicious. To make this stick, we need to catch them in the act.' Looking down at the paperwork James has given me, I have a light bulb moment. 'Well done, James. You have given me an idea and it might just work.'

I have driven over to Haverfordwest to see the editor of the Weston Telegraph, Jason Foggety. Pausing outside, looking at the papers latest headlines posted in the window, I'm hesitant. I am in a hurry to conclude this investigation for a number of reasons and under the circumstances, am I doing the right thing. There is only one way to find out.

Jason is sat in the front office staring at a computer screen when I step inside. 'Nick!' He exclaims, when he sees me. 'How is the farm acquisition going?'

'It's moving along. We haven't exchanged contracts yet but I'm told it's only a formality.'

'You will give me the full story when you have. What are your plans for the place? Knock it down and start again?'

'You'll be the first to know when the deal is signed, sealed and delivered.'

'So, how can I help you today? Please, take a seat.'

Taking up his offer I get straight down to business. 'Do you still run the articles on local businesses?'

'Sounds like you've stopped reading my paper. We do occasionally but it's rare. The uptake on the promotion we ran fell dramatically so we stopped. My belief is we became too expensive. A full page spread in the paper doesn't come cheap and these days, the internet has a much wider audience than us. Are you thinking about advertising your business?'

'No, I'm sorry to say. We have a website, much the same as our competitors and it works well for us. I'm here, Jason, testing the waters. I have a job for someone like you to do, without raising suspicion.'

192

'First and foremost I'm a reporter and turning up uninvited always raises suspicions.'

'I'm sure it does. How does cold calling by phone fair? Better or worse?'

'Pretty much on par from personal experience. I share the opinion that if a business wants or needs our services, they'll make that call. It's as black and white as that.'

'Sorry to have wasted your time, Jason. It was just a thought. I'll work something out.'

Standing to leave Jason begins questioning me. 'Do you mind me asking what this is about?'

'It's fine. You're better off not knowing.'

'I'm always looking for a good story, Nick. You of all people know that. There's a slim chance I might already know something. Grabbing an exclusive out from under the noses of other tabloids, works wonders for the circulation figures.'

'Sorry to inform you, but its information I need, not a next day front cover exclusive. I'm not looking for the bull in a china shop approach here. Guess work, glorification and rumour mongering has no place in my line of work. Hard and fast facts that can wait another day to be told, that's what I need.'

'You know you've got me hooked. I'm intrigued. Tell me, is this something to do with the fire at the hostel?'

'That's a police matter. Nothing to do with me and as you're fishing for information, I should leave.'

'Well, if you change your mind, you know where to find me.'

'It's true what they say isn't it? Never trust a journalist.'

'Comes with the territory. Despite your doubts, we do our very best to make sure we print the truth. We do check the validity of the reporting but I would agree, at times that can appear ambiguous.'

'And there's the difference. I work with hard facts, and sometimes my intuition and those are confidential. Not out there for the public to read between the lines and form their own opinions with. This conversation will remain between us, Jason. If you go into print with any part of this, you will have much bigger fish to deal with than me. I suggest you be very careful with what you put into print.

'That sounds like a threat.' He counters as I reach the door.

'For you information, what I'm involve in is serious stuff. I thought I could trust you to do me a favour, but it seems I have misjudged you. You're not the man you pretend to be.'

'Come again?'

'How many times have you printed in your paper that you have the local communities' best interests at heart. Fake reporting, Jason, that's what it is. You don't give a toss about the local community and one day, that will come back and bite you in the arse. The way you're portraying yourself is a disgrace and that kind of selfish attitude could mean you'll miss out on the biggest exclusive in a long time.'

'And that's blackmail.'

'Make sure you're well insured before you go into print with that statement. I'll be watching.'

I'm annoyed with myself. Walking back towards my car I question myself over why I thought I could trust Jason Foggety. He's a journalist, a reporter, a man constantly on the lookout for the next big story and wiling to place his reputation on the line with what he prints. I made a mistake thinking I could trust him. I do need someone on the inside who can ask questions without raising concerns. A promotional business article, in my opinion, was a good angle to peruse, and still could be with the right person on-board.

Deep in thought I'm miles away working out what my next move should be. My total lack of concentration and visual awareness leads me into a situation I was keen to avoid. This isn't one of those right place, right time moments.

194

'Hi, Nick. How are you?' Linda asks as we come face to face in the middle of the busy High Street. Still seething from my heated exchange with Jason, I tell myself to keep calm. 'Fancy going for a coffee?' She adds.

'Not really.'

'Nick, I know you have a problem with me being here. You have got to understand that this is my home, where I grew up and I have every right to be here. I have spoken to Jan and I do respect your wishes, but I could end up buying the house next door to you if it suits my needs and there's nothing you can do about that.'

'I beg to differ.'

'How do you work that out?'

'I don't think the current owner would agree to that.'

'How would you know that?'

'As the owner of the property next door to me, I do know.'

'Oh very clever, but I think you get the gist. Since leaving uni my daughter, Maddy, has worked for Stena Lines ferries sailing between Fishguard and Rosslare. She's renting a room in a shared house at the moment which is very expensive, so I'm looking for property that caters for both our needs. If I find a place that suits both our requirements, I will make an offer. Regardless of what you think or say. If that happens to be in Saundersby, Fenby or the village, you are the one who has to live with that…not me. You don't own me, Nick, and you never will.'

'That's a relief! Now, if you don't mind, I'm losing money standing here listening to you. I'd like to wish you happy house hunting, but I'd be lying if I did.'

'You arsehole!'

'That's better. That's the Linda I like. The one that hates the sight of me.'

Watching Linda turn her back on me and walk away is something I have witnessed several times over the years. On previous occasions it was for the best. I admit, each time she did, I had hoped it would be the last. Today is different. She is going nowhere and perhaps, living on my doorstep, this very situation could become common place. Linda has also thrown me a curved ball. Something she is blissfully unaware of thankfully. By telling me her daughter, Maddy, works for Stena Lines ferries is music to my ears. I have yet to find out exactly what her position is within the company, but knowing when Paul Linnette travels from Rosslare back to Fishguard, in his specially adapted van, would be very useful.

'Nick! I apologise. Can we start again?' Jason offers, joining me in the middle of the street.

'Why? So you make sure you get your exclusive?'

'Partly yes. When you said this was serious stuff you're working on it took a while to sink, but in the reality of the situation it became clear to me that you genuinely needed my help. I can and will if you still want me too.'

'Are you prepared to sign an affidavit to that effect?'

'There won't be a need for something as drastic as that. I'll guaranty it.'

'Meet me at the office tomorrow at 9am.'

Going about my business I'm thinking about Jason and how much I can trust him when my mobile rings. Wallace. The very person I want to talk to.

'Nick. Are you in the office?'

'No. I'm about to head back there now. I'll be half-hour or so.'

'Can I meet you there?'

'Sure. What's this about?'

'I'll talk you through it in half an hour.'

Returning to the office my first priority was to phone Jan and ask her to pick Sam up from school. She's agreed to do that for me and stay with him until I get home. She added that she wishes to talk to me. I'm in no doubt what that is all about.

DI Wallace is sat behind my desk talking to James. Asking James to give us a few minutes of privacy, I ask him not to disappear. There is something I'd like him to do for me. My next task is to move DI Wallace out of my seat. I'm not comfortable with him sat there. Moving one of the spare chairs to the opposite side of my desk, he reluctantly vacates my chair.

'We've had the pathology results back.'

'About time.'

'There were some anomalies as a result so I had toxicology tests done on both Green and Griffiths. That's why this has taken so long. What I am hoping as I work through this, that these results might mean something to you.

'I'll start with Hanna Green. As we both thought she was an alcoholic. I'm told that was the main contributing factor in her liver failure. She was also HIV positive. Whether she knew that we don't know but we're checking her medical records. Hanna also had a significant level of heroin in her system, all of which I'm informed by the pathologist, contributed to her death.

'David Griffiths was also an alcoholic and heroin user. Large quantities of heroin were detected in his blood samples. The toxicology tests found large amounts of paracetamol in his gut which rather suggests he took an overdose.'

'Or he was in a lot of pain for some reason.'

'That could be the case. The tests however threw up something rather less convincing in both cases. Traces of something called, capnocytophaga canimorsus, were detected in their stomachs. I'm told it's commonly found in dog saliva and very dangerous to humans.'

'I'll bare that in mind next time a dog tries to lick my face.'

'That's the point. It's very unusual and as far as we know neither Hanna nor David owned a dog, or any pets for that matter, so it's unlikely to be a coincidence.'

'A lot of the street boys have dogs for company. That could have happened at any time.'

'That's possible. However, the pathologist is of the opinion that this, whatever I called it, had contaminated the heroin they were using. Any thoughts on his theory?'

'You're the one with the answers. What do you think?'

'As a matter of interest, as I'm paying you, what are you working on? I've been made aware that you have suggested to DS Thomas he has the contents of the chip fryer tested for drugs, so you know something.'

'It was a passing thought. You guys have found nothing, other than the fire was deliberate. For the reason as to why someone would set fire to the hostel, tell me a better way of destroying any evidence.'

'You're avoiding my question. As you seem hell bent on doing so I want a detailed report of your activities on my desk by the morning, or you are off the case. Am I making myself clear?'

'I'm not working on the hostel fire, so get off my back. Agent Harvey is fully up to speed with my findings and that is all you need to know…at the moment.'

'I knew you would say that. Convenient, isn't it? Let me ask you something. Do you think there is a connection between the fire at the hostel and Hanna Green's and David Griffiths' deaths?'

'Yes, but not directly. Give me forty-eight hours, I'll know more then. Is there anything else?'

'I'd like to talk to you about Sam while I'm here.'

'Go on.'

'Have you spoken to him about going to Bristol?'

'I have and as long as you keep your word over his protection, he'll do as you've asked. Happy now?'

'Friday. We'll pick you up at 8am. I have spoken to Mary Robinson about our intensions. She'd like to join us to support Sam and I have agreed. I have also spoken to Fiona Martin and she has given us permission to take Sam out of school for the day. Are you happy with those arrangements?'

'We both want this over and done with.'

'Fine. I'll confirm the arrangements tomorrow.'

'We'll be ready whatever. Reg...' I say standing up. 'I think I may have found a connection. I need time to make sure my beliefs are right before your mob go charging in. This thing about the dog saliva, you could be on to something. Please give me time to work on this.'

'Forty-eight hours is what you asked for. That's all you've got. Don't let me down, that's all I ask.'

James has seen DI Wallace leave. He returns to the office minutes later. I want to go home so I don't waste time.

'James. What is your work load like?'

'Busy, as normal. Why?'

'I would like your help for a couple of days, if it's possible. It will be mostly telephone work to start with, backed up with field work if things go to plan.'

'I'm sure I can rearrange my time to accommodate you. Is this official business?'

'It is and you will be paid for your time as long as the protocol is followed. Are you in?'

'Sure. When do we start?'

'Be here at 9am tomorrow. I'll explain everything then.'

Home, I'm greeted by a rather quiet Sam. Sat watching the TV he says very little as I pass him on my way to the kitchen. Ironing, Jan is also watching TV in the kitchen. Her mood is no better. I must address this situation. I employ her as my housekeeper and more recently, a child minder. Not my mentor and personal adviser.

'I've spoken to Linda. If that is what this wall of silence is about. I know why she's looking for a place in this area and I accept her reasoning. What I won't accept is her involving herself in my life. How you deal with that, Jan, is your business...not mine. I'm not going to insist you don't see her, that has nothing to do with me but you must take into consideration...my wishes. If that is a situation you feel you can deal with, then we'll say no more on the subject.'

199

'When did you see Linda?'

'Earlier, while I was in Haverfordwest. She told me about her daughter Maddy and why she was looking for a place in this area. I can't stop her doing that and as long as if doesn't involve me, so be it.'

'I've taken on-board what you have said so let's leave it there. All I ask is that you'll be civil towards her if and when you bump into one another.'

'Same goes for her. Look at what she said to Sam that time. It's not acceptable and I won't have it!'

'He's not right. You should go and talk to him. He hasn't said more than a couple of words to me since I picked him up. I'd say he is worried about something.'

I have learned it's not unusual for Sam to be quiet and he'll talk when he's ready too. His mood could be to do with Friday and if Fiona Martin has spoken to him on the back of DI Wallace phoning her, he has good reason to feel worried.

Sam doesn't move a muscle when I sit on the sofa with him. His gaze remains firmly fixed on the TV. I look for the controls but they're not obvious.

'Want to talk, Sam?' I ask. He says nothing. 'Is this about going to Bristol on Friday? Has Mrs Martin said something to you?'

'I know I have got to go,' he tells me, before turning to face me. 'I know I have to do the right thing but I'm not looking forward to going. I've promised you I will and I will. If I have to go back to Bristol for them, there's something I'd like them to do for me.'

'What do you have in mind, Sam?'

'I don't think they'll let me, but I'd like to see my Mum's grave. I never got to say goodbye to her, Dad. Can I do that and put some flowers on her grave?'

'I'm sure it will be fine. They'll understand. Do you know where your mother's grave is?'

'No.'

'OK. So we'll need to find out where your mum's grave is and we both know a lady who can help us.'

'Mary.'

'You do know she'll be with us on Friday?'

'No, I didn't know.'

'Well, she has asked to be with you on Friday to support you. Are you OK with her being there?'

'I don't mind.'

'Why don't we go and call her now? See what she says.'

'Can we? I really want to see my mum's grave, Dad.'

'Would you like to speak to Mary and ask her yourself?'

'Yes.'

'Let's go and make the call in the privacy of my office.'

I didn't see that coming. Sam has always blamed his mother for what happened to him. He did what he was told to do by others and with the little he gained from drug running, kept his mother's craving, her habit, her need for the next score, coming. He went without food for days at times, unless it accidently fell off the shelf into his pocket and he hated his mother for that. Wanting to lay flowers on his mother's grave, which is likely to be no more than a small wooden cross pushed into the ground to mark the spot, could be a turning point in his life. Blaming others for his previous situation and not his mother, might see him through these next few months. Directing the anger he held for his mother in a more productive way, is the right thing to do. Offering Sam my chair he sits down while I dial Mary's number. She answers my call almost straight away.

'Hello.'

'Mary, It's Nick Thompson.'

'Oh high, Nick. How are you? Everything alright?'

'We're fine, thank you, Mary. I understand you're accompanying us on Friday.'

'I think I should be there with you and to support Sam? I'd love to help.'

'It's fine with us. I have a young man sat with me who would like to ask a favour of you. I'll put him on.'

Passing Sam the receiver I crouch down beside him so I can listen to what is said. 'Hello, Mary.'

'Sam! How are you sweetheart? I hear her ask. 'What is it you would like to ask me?'

'Do you know where my mother's grave is?'

'I do, Sam. I think I should tell you here that your mother was cremated. That means there is no actual grave to see.'

'But you do know where she is?'

'I do. Am I to gather from our conversation that you'd like to go there on Friday when you're here in Bristol?'

'Yes please. I want to put some flowers on her grave.'

'I'm certain we can arrange that for you, Sam. It's a lovely thought. Bless you.'

'I'll make sure it happens, Mary. Leave it to me.' I shout so Mary can hear me.

'Tell your Dad I will.' Mary responds. 'I'll bring a vase and some water with me to put the flowers in. If that's OK with you?'

'I'd like that. Thank you.'

Passing the receiver back to me Sam sinks back into the chair. I can see he's visibly shaken by this. I think I would be in his situation. That realisation of never seeing his mother alive again has finally hit him. That's tough on anyone, no matter the age. Too soon in his case, but he has people around him who can help him through this traumatic time and help cushion this experience for him.

202

'Mary, we'll see you on Friday. Thank you for taking the time to talk too Sam.'

'My pleasure. Anytime, you know that. Take care of him, Nick.'

'I will, don't worry.'

Replacing the receiver I look at Sam. I don't speak or make any kind of gesture. I'll wait for him.

'I did love my mum.' He whispers.

'Do, Sam, do. Good or bad she will always be remembered in your thoughts.'

'I have been thinking a lot about mum ever since we decided to change my name. You said I will always be Sam Cornish and I should make my mum proud of me. I want her to be proud of me.'

'She will be, Sam. Why don't we treat Friday as the start of that process? Your mother will be proud of the fact you're standing up against the evil that surrounded you as grew up. Do it for her and you can tell her all about it when we visit her grave?'

'Will she hear me?'

'If you want her too. Yes.'

'I do want her too. Can we go out for a while?' He asks, standing up. 'I need some fresh air.'

That makes me laugh. I say that a lot, when I need some time to think. 'Of course we can. Go and change and grab a coat. It'll get cold later.'

Making a call on my mobile I return to the kitchen for my car keys. Jan is still ironing and watching TV. In an unusual happening, DI Wallace answers his phone first time.

'Reg, I need you guys to me a favour on Friday.'

'Always a hitch with you. What do you want?'

'It's not for me, it's for Sam. Sam wants to put some flowers on his mother's grave while we're in Bristol. Under the circumstances I wouldn't normally ask but this is important for Sam. I have spoken to Mary Robinson and she is OK with it.'

'Not a good idea for a number of reasons. Leave it with me.'

'No! Say yes so I can let Sam know tonight. Believe me, this could be for the benefit of all parties concerned. I'll explain when I next see you. Is that a yes then?'

'OK, yes, but we cannot hang around for too long. I'll organise it first thing in the morning.'

'Thanks. You won't regret it.'

'I sincerely hope not.'

Finishing my call I realise what I have done. Stupidly I have allowed Jan to hear every word I've said. That is a bad mistake.

'You didn't hear that conversation. It stays within these four walls. Not even Richard or Jack know about this so I beg you to keep it to yourself for Sam's sake. Sam and I are going out for a while to get some fresh air. Can you wait until we're back before you go home? And please, not a word to anyone. Can I trust you?'

'Yes. I promise.'

'I hope you're sincere, because a certain young man's life may depend upon it. Please bare that in mind before you speak.

'Jan, you may think my business with Linda is a trivial matter and you are most probably right. I have far greater issues to deal with right now and Sam is just one of them. Give me some space to deal with my problems before criticising me over my attitude towards her.'

I have driven the short distance around to the village. Coming here was Sam's idea. Despite my warning, although his jacket and rucksack are on the back seat of the car, he's rolled up his jogging bottoms, taken his shoes and socks off and is paddling in the surf. He says the water is quite warm. I'll take his word for that. In up to just below his knees, I have remained on the sandy beach. The distance between us has put paid to any serious conversation we might have held.

Soon after 6pm, with the daylight beginning to fade, I suggest to him that we should make a move. My words prompt a more meaningful exchange of dialog. The upshot of which is, he'll come out of the water if we can have a drink in the pub before we go home. I'm not going to argue with his bargaining skills.

Opening the car for him it soon becomes clear why he brought his rucksack. Sitting down on the wall he opens his rucksack and pulls out a towel to dry himself. Premeditated or what! Then what does it matter if it makes him happy. Joining him I open the conversation.

'Why here tonight, Sam?'

'Because you like coming here. You told me once that it's not always about me so I thought, if I can go for a paddle, you can have a pint.'

'I won't argue with that, and a pint after the day I've had will be very welcome. Thank you young man.'

'That's OK. It's my way of saying sorry.'

'What makes you think you need to apologise to me?'

'Because I've been a little shit latterly.'

'Fair play. I knew something was wrong with you, Sam. I couldn't put a finger on what it was and you didn't want to discuss the matter with me. I tried to talk you out of your mood but you clammed up every time. You refused to talk and that's not good. Once you did open up, see how easily it was resolved?'

'I know. I'm sorry. I'll try not to do it again.' Tying up his shoe laces he stands, throws his rucksack into the back of the car, grabs his jacket and puts it on. 'Why do you like coming here, Dad?'

'It's a long story.'

The pub is busy. Late season, the older generation take advantage of the peace and quiet the late off season affords. Sat outside with our drinks, we both sit facing the beach.

'Are you going to tell me why?' Sam enquires.

'I'll only bore you.'

205

'I won't find it boring.'

'OK. The village means a lot to me, Sam. It's where the boy in me became a man. You could say, it's where I grew up. The village has a special place in my heart for many reasons.'

'How?'

'Up there…,' I start, pointing in the direction of the sheer cliff face. '…is what I consider to be my special space. I would sit up there for hours on end working through my problems, while looking down at the sea and the village. Most of us have a special place they go to and think. Up there, the sound of the wind in the trees and roar of the ocean, has a wonderful calming effect. It's where I first met Richard, where he asked me if I'd like to have breakfast with him and his mum, Jan. That's not where the story starts, but where it really began. More recently, it was where the story nearly ended.'

'How do you mean?'

'I did something very wrong and felt there was no other way out other than jumping.'

'I don't understand.'

'I was in big trouble because I seriously injured the man who shot us. I didn't kill him, but I doubt he'll walk again. I hit out in anger, revenge, because in their wisdom, I was told by the hospital that both you and Jack had gone. Hadn't made it. That was my fault. I placed you in danger and Jack was running away from the same man who shot us, when he was hit by a car. All my fault, Sam. How was I going to live with that guilt? If it wasn't for Richard, I may not be here today sat talking to you.'

'How come?'

'Richard talked me down. He stopped me doing the most stupid thing I have ever considered doing. He did for me that day what real friends should do. He reassured me, told me they would all stand by me whatever the circumstances. That life can go on. I was in a mess both physically and mentally but I listened to what he had to say. I was distraught, full of guilt and grief, but I knew he was being sincere. That experience has taught me the value of talking, discussing my problems openly.

206

'Richard helped down to a waiting ambulance. As I was being treated a helicopter landed nearby on the beach. I thought they had been looking for me because of my boat and thought nothing of it. When they told me they were going to fly me to the hospital for treatment I refused because I hate flying. They were having none of it and insisted I did as I was told. The rest you know, but it didn't end there. I was both overwhelmed and angry when I found out you were both alive. I was angry with them because they lied to me. I did something very wrong because they didn't talk to me and tell me the truth. That, Sam, is something I'm finding very difficult to deal with. I'm not talking here about Graham, Richard and Jan, they didn't know either. I was angry with the authorities, especially DI Wallace.

'I know I go on and on to you about talking about your problems and to discuss those problems with me. I do that, Sam, because I don't want to see you suffer in the same way I did. This village has become a soul mate to me. A place I can relax and think. Like now, I doubt I would have ever told you all this, other than here. That's how much the village means to me.'

Home, Jack stands waiting at the bottom of the stairs. Starring at me his first words are "where have you been?" Closing the door Sam disappears off towards the back of the house.

'I needed some time to talk to Sam,' I reply. 'And now I need some time to talk to you.'

'I want to talk to you too. But not in front of the others.' He informs me.

'Well now you might understand why Sam and I went out? There are some things others don't need to hear. Shall we use my office for this chat, or can we go out the back so I can have a smoke?'

'I'm not bothered.'

'Give me a minute. I'll see you out in the garden.'

Closing the patio door behind me I join Jack and light a cigarette. Asking him if he'd like to go first he says he's not bothered, so I take the initiative.

'Couple of things, Jack. Firstly, I have spoken to the registrar and we do have all the necessary documents to legally change your surname to

Thompson. If you wish to go ahead, all we need to do is make an appointment.'

'Of course I do. Why wouldn't I?' He snaps at me.

'It's OK, Jack. I was just making sure you haven't changed your mind. The second matter I wish to discuss with you is a little more delicate and it must stay between us.' Starring at me, questioning my choice of words, he says nothing. 'Relax, it's nothing to worry about. I need to tell you that I'm taking Sam to Bristol on Friday. Without going into any great detail the Avon and Somerset police wish to interview him. They also have a few other things they'd like him to assist them with. In return, he has asked them to do something for him. Something that has caught us all by surprise, I can tell you. Sam has asked if he can see his mother's grave while we're in Bristol and place some flowers on her final place of resting. He has never been there, which I'm sure you will agree, is very sad. I can only assume, they considered it too dangerous for him at the time. Friday is going to be a very tough day for him and I don't know how he's going to react to the ordeal. All I ask of you, until this is all over, is that you give him some space. We all need to. On and off he's been very quiet the last few days, which you may have noticed. Don't push him. He'll talk when he's ready to. Please bare that in mind over the next couple of days.'

'Will you be late home?'

'Not sure. We're leaving here at eight in the morning and I'm not sure how long this will take. Why?'

'It puts paid to my plans.'

'Not necessarily. If it's important, we'll work something out for you.'

'It is important. Lucy asked me if I'd like to go away with her and her parents for the weekend. I'd really like to go, Dad, but I haven't said yes yet because I didn't know what you'd think.'

'I think it's a great idea. Getting to know and understand her parents is something I would recommend. You have my full blessing, Jack. Go away for the weekend and enjoy yourself.'

'Thank you. The plan is to leave here after lunch on Friday. Stay Friday and Saturday night and head for home after breakfast on Sunday. If that's alright with you?'

'Of course it is! I'm absolutely fine with it. May I ask, do you know where you're going?'

'Greyhound racing.' He informs me and think how ironic that is after speaking to Steve. Not that he hadn't had my full attention, but his statement renews my interest. 'Somewhere near Cardiff, I think. I've never been greyhound racing and it sounds like fun. That's why I want to go, and be with Lucy of course.'

'How come they all go greyhound racing?'

'They go two or three times a year. Lucy's uncle, her mum's brother I think, owns greyhounds and when he's racing them at Cardiff they go and cheer him on. We're going to have a meal at the stadium before the racing starts and Lucy's parents have booked rooms in a hotel about two miles from the stadium. And before you ask, I don't know what the sleeping arrangements are.'

'Never crossed my mind. Lucy's uncle you say?'

'Yes, on her mother's side.'

'Does this uncle of hers have a name?'

'Why?'

'Because I'd like to talk to him.'

'I can ask Lucy if you like. Are you thinking about buying a greyhound?'

'Definitely not. Let's just say, it's other business.' Pausing to put my cigarette out in the bucket placed on the patio for that very purpose, I continue. 'I guess you'll be needing some cash to go away with. Bit of spending money and to pay for the room.'

'It hasn't been mentioned yet, but I feel I should offer to pay my way.'

'It's the polite thing to do.'

209

'I'll ask Lucy if she knows how much the room costs. Thank you, Dad, and I will be careful around Sam.'

Wednesday 10th September

DI Wallace is leaning against the back of his company car when I arrive at the office. Yesterday, he gave me forty-eight hours to come up with some answers, so something has changed. Could be they've changed their minds over Sam going to see his mother's grave. I hope not.

'What is Foggerty doing here?' He quickly asks while I get out of my car. 'I have waited outside for you because I have no wish to engage in any sort of verbal communication with the man.'

'Why are you here?' I respond. 'You gave me two days to sort myself out. For your information, I have something I need him to do for me. Do you have a problem with that?'

'Damn right I do! He's not a man I would trust. In it for himself. Surely you know that?' Pausing for a moment he looks me in the eye. 'You don't trust me either…do you?'

'In a word…no. And I trust DS Thomas even less. You my friend, lost that trust several months ago and you know why.'

'That's all in the past. We've moved on, Nick.'

'Have we fuck? I relive that day every time I see Jack or Sam. How can I ever trust someone again when they were prepared to lie to me? You people will never understand what you did to me then, and what I did as a result of your lying. It's not just Jack and Sam who needs help.'

Needing a packet of cigarettes I walk away from DI Wallace in the direction of the town shops. My outburst has been on the cards for some time now. I'm more than aware that I'm not functioning as a human being because of that day and I know they can see that. I need time to sort my life out and they are not giving me that time or space. It is business as usual where they are concerned. Good old Nick will deal with this problem. Well he's not! Aware I'm being followed by DI Wallace I carry on walking, but he catches up with me.

'Sorry, Nick. I had no idea you felt this way. Can we start again?'

'Too late.' I tell him, stopping in my tracks as I do. 'Far too late to apologise to me. The damage is done. Last job for me, Reg, so let's get on with it. What do you want?'

'Fine. Forensics found some prints on the fryer. We ran them through the data base and came up with a match. Old, but they are Alf West's. A man we know today as Alf Roberts. He is the husband of Gwyn Roberts, the manager of the hostel.'

'I know.'

'I thought you might. That's why I'm here. Do you know where he is? We raided their house in the early hours of this morning. They weren't there and it looked like they left in a hurry. Work with me on this, Nick, so we get a result quickly.'

'How long have you got?'

'As long as it takes.'

'Give me ten minutes to deal with Jason Foggerty. I'll be in my office.'

'Do you need anything?' He asks sheepishly.

'A packet of cigarettes would be useful.'

With a sincere apology and the promise of being in touch tomorrow, Jason Foggerty made a hasty retreat. I sense there is bad blood between him and DI Wallace and like the latter, he has no interest in speaking to him.

Moments after I've sat down behind my desk, DI Wallace joins myself and James. His first action is to place a packet of cigarettes on my desk. As he goes to close the door the phone on my desk rings. Answering the call straight away our receptionist informs me there is a Mr Harvey downstairs and he'd like to speak to me urgently. Asking her to send him up, I replace the receiver. DI Wallace barks a sharp response in my direction.

'If that is Foggerty, I'm out of here.'

'It isn't.'

Hovering in the doorway I watch DI Wallace's reaction when he sees who our guest is. To the best of my knowledge it's a first for Brad, so it too must be urgent.

'Why are you here?' I hear Wallace ask Brad as he walks into the office. Closing the door behind him, Brad looks at James.

'We don't need you, James. I'm sure there must be something else you need to be doing.'

'James stays where he is.' I snap, standing up. 'You need to hear what I have to say and as I have involved him, I want to make quite sure I don't leave anything out.'

'He's a civilian. A private investigator. That's classified information, Nick, and you should not be involving James in these matters.'

'Too late. I already have and if you care to listen, you'll discover why.' Gathering my thoughts I lean back against the window sill and wait to continue while Brad makes himself comfortable in my chair.

'You might want to hear what I have to say first. I'm not comfortable with James being in the room, but if you say we can trust him, then I'll continue.' Waiting momentarily for a response, he continues. 'I don't think it's a good idea you guys taking Sam to Bristol on Friday.'

'It's all arranged.' DI Wallace butts in. 'It has taken us a long time to arrange this with Sam and we're not going to change our plans because you don't think it's a good idea. Would you care to expand?'

'How do you now we have arranged to take Sam to Bristol on Friday?' I ask with good reason. 'As far as I'm concerned, that's classified information.'

'Are you sure you want to hear this?'

'I'm listening.'

'I may have a requirement for armed response units on Friday. When we looked at the logistics in great detail we knew we would need at least eight units placed at strategic points to achieve our goal. I was informed only six units could be made available. When I questioned the deficit, I was confidentially informed of the reason why. I understand why this should take place, but Friday isn't good timing. Gentlemen, I need those two extra units.'

'What we are doing on Friday is totally unrelated.' DI Wallace argues. 'We have those armed units at our disposal for a very good reason, as I'm sure you are aware, and we will have them.'

'Gentlemen, gentlemen. You are making a big mistake. A week ago we received a tip off from the National Crime Agency that a shipment of coffee from Latin America is arriving at Avonmouth docks this morning. The consignment is a perfectly legal transaction by a leading coffee supplier in this country. However, a very reliable source has informed us that the consignment contains cocaine with a street value in excess of 30 million. The container is being unloaded today and will be detained by customs and excise for at least twenty-four hours. In that time scale the container will be searched to confirm our information. Resealed, the container will be released on Friday morning with a clearance certificate for onward movement. That's when we take action.'

'That doesn't make any sense!' DI Wallace offers. 'Seize the cocaine on the spot so it doesn't reach our streets. The hours we waste clearing up after it has costs the ordinary tax payer millions. What you're proposing just isn't logical.'

'I take your point, Detective Inspector. However, our own intelligence suggests the container will be high jacked soon after it leaves the docks. Certainly well before it reaches its destination. Our aim is to stop them in the act of highjack and detain them and who knows, that very ploy may lead us to Mr Big.'

'And that will bring an end to all of our problems?' I add.

'Who knows? What is does do, is reduce the amount on the streets and those who have lost money will become careless in their need. A lot of people owe a lot of money and to stay alive, they will take chances. Mark my word.'

'Well, I hope you are right. As you seem to have this all sorted, you won't be needing me again.' I suggest, standing and heading for my desk.

'Nick?' DI Wallace asks. 'We both know he's wrong. We still have work to do and that includes going to Bristol on Friday.'

Reaching my desk I open the top draw and take out two brown envelopes. Dropping one on my desk in front of Brad I offer DI Wallace the other.

'If this is what I think it is, you can tear it up and put it in the waste paper bin.' Brad scowls.

'Reg. I'm waiting on a phone call which may decide where I go from here. If you have the time, I'll tell where I'm at. That's why I insisted James stayed put. I don't want to forget a single detail and he's here to remind me.'

'You're missing the point here guys.' Brad insists.

'Really? And you have no idea of the bigger picture. We're going to Bristol on Friday, whatever you say or think.'

'Too risky, Nick. What if someone recognises Sam while you're in Bristol? They might think he has something to do with the drugs find. Think about that, Nick.'

'See! There you go again. I'm tired of being told what to do and when to do it. We're going to Bristol on Friday because it's very important. Important to the Avon and Somerset police, important to me and very important to Sam's future.

'As you have probably guessed, these are my letters of resignation from both authorities. The originals of which have been posted. I'm finally calling it a day at the end of the month because I can't cope. In the interim, I'm going on the sick.'

'It's not as simple as that! You know that.' Brad continues, raising his voice.

'It's going to happen, Brad, so sit still and listen.' Returning to the window I resume my relaxed position, leaning against the sill. 'Over the past few weeks I have found myself arguing with just about everyone. I'm sure you both will testify to that. I have had arguments with Jan, Linda, Ed the boat builder and Jason Foggerty. More seriously, with Tom Morgan and mother and if it hadn't have been for a certain young man, they would have sold their farm cheaply to a developer. I have even had my doubts about what I'm doing for Sam, which regretfully, in a moment of weakness, I express to you, Reg. The reason for this unforgivable behaviour and I should say here that I haven't told anyone, not even the boys because I don't want them to worry, I am facing further major surgery on my shoulder. I am in constant pain. I'm not sleeping that well at night and I've had to stop taking the prescribed painkillers because they have caused a kidney infection. My doctor is looking into that but the only option open to me at the moment is paracetamol. Thankfully, my kidney infection is on the mend, but my shoulder isn't. If it gets any worse I may have to stop driving. Not being able to drive is a huge problem for me, so the less I do may extend that time. I don't have a date yet for the surgery and I have been told, because it's classed as non-urgent, that could be at least six months from now. Even if I do go under the knife again early next year, I will face months of physio afterwards and even then, full recovery depends on the success of the surgery.

'I want to tell you, this has affected me mentally. Coupled with events four months ago, I'm not coping. I'm tired, my decision making is poor and I can't concentrate. I'm a disaster waiting to happen. Right or wrong, that willingness I had to jump in feet first and ask questions later has gone…deserted me. There is something else to consider here too…my responsibility to the boys.

'You need to know, Brad, that Friday is more important than anything else at this time. Sam needs to open up. Tell us what he knows and has seen to release himself from the mental burden he carries with him. I have sat down and spoken to him on a number of occasions about the importance and he's in a place now where he wants to help. One of those concerns is his freedom. He's growing up, finding his way. He needs to feel safe and free to do what he wants. Not worrying about who might see him. Going to Bristol on Friday is the start of the process. I told him the other day that it won't be long before he doesn't want me, or Jan on occasions, to drop him off and pick him up from school. He cannot go on hesitating by the front door just in case. I want him to feel comfortable about walking to school with his friends, or meeting them down in town to go fishing or a swim. He is not the only one who needs that reassurance. Yes it would be easy to criticise me, saying things like I shouldn't have taken on the responsibility, but I have and I will see it through. To achieve that I need your help, and Sam needs mine. Please accept my apology if you believe I'm letting you down at a critical time, but I do need to step back and deal with my personal problems.'

'Why didn't you say something?' Reg asks me. 'We would have understood and speaking for myself, I do understand. All I ask from you, is to bring me up to date with your findings.'

'Naturally. Of course I will. I am caught between a rock and a hard place. This has been my world for thirty odd years and it will be difficult to walk away from but I must. I will tell you where I'm at with this and continue to help in any way, from behind my desk.'

Brad is unusually quiet. Sat staring directly ahead he's fiddling with my desk blotter, running his thumb up and down on of the corners like a deck of cards. I want him to challenge me, to get his feelings off his chest out into the open so I know where he's at. I have made my own feelings very clear and this time, I mean it.

'Reg. Before I start spouting off about the ridiculous tasks I have been given and the brick walls I encountered along the way, there's something I'd like to clear up first. The murder of Owain Parry, are you any closer to solving that?'

'It's an ongoing investigation and unless you have some new information regarding that case, I'd rather not discuss it in public.'

'I'll take that as a no then. Is it true then, that you suspect he was dealing drugs?'

'Like I said, it's not up for discussion.'

'Have you based your suspicions on the fact that traces of heroin were found in his jacket pocket?'

'You have been talking to Mrs Parry…haven't you? Let me tell you something about Mrs Parry. She lied to us to protect her precious son. I'll say again, this is an ongoing investigation and you should not be talking to a suspect unless we ask you to.'

'But after searching the house, isn't it true you found nothing to substantiate your theory?'

'That is correct. We believe he wasn't working alone.'

'What if it was the other way around?'

217

'How do you mean?'

'What if Owain was buying, not selling? It easily explains away why you found traces of heroin in his jacket pocket.'

'I'm listening.'

'Why are you bothering us with this crap, Nick?' Brad finally asks. 'There are far more important issues to deal with here. Why don't you clock out and go home?'

'I'm telling you this because you both need to hear what I have to say, so please let me finish. By the way, Brad, has you man on the inside made any progress?'

'Inside where?' Reg offers, as Brad diverts his glare down at the desk once more. His reaction speaks volumes.

'I must assume here, Reg, that you know Owain Parry worked as a deliverer driver for Marstons wholesalers?'

'We explored all leads at the time. It seems Owain was regarded as the model employee.' While Reg continues I become aware of Brad looking at me. 'They told us he was a good timekeeper and worked hard without complaining. They were unaware of his drug dealing.'

'Owain wasn't dealing, he was buying.'

'If you have proof of that, I'd like to know about it?'

'Forrests, Nick?' Brad mumbles.

'I thought that would get your interest. One of the first tasks you spoke to me about was looking into local suppliers, with particular interest in fish products supplied from Eire. Finding out David Griffiths worked at the hostel, under the circumstances presented at the time, I decided to start there.'

'Wait a second!' A rather animated Reg says. 'This person on the inside, is that at Forrests?'

'Yes Detective Inspector. But you haven't got that from me. Would you care to continue, Nick?'

'Yes please! Set up in her temporary office, Gwyn Roberts, wife of Alf Roberts, although totally disorganised was very accommodating. However, she also lied through her teeth when I spoke to her.'

'In what way?' Reg interrupts.

'I'll come to that in a moment.' I snap and let out a sigh of frustration. I think they get the message. 'I asked her about here suppliers, as instructed to do. When she initially ran through who they were, she mentioned Forrests. At that point I asked her if I could look over her latest invoices. There were a lot. Too many to digest all the information in one go so, with a promise of bringing them back in the morning, I asked her if I could take them with me and look over them in my own time. She didn't object.

'I was in a hurry myself because I had personal things to do and wanted to pick Sam up from home on my way past. The first thing I did once I'd returned to the office was to photocopy all the invoices. To be honest, Sam did that for me and did a fantastic job. He's a very methodical young man.'

'Get to the point!' Brad scowls. 'You have told me this already. Why are you still interested in Forrests when I told you to forget about them?'

'Because I found out that Alf Roberts works or worked part-time for Forrests. When I spoke to Gwyn Roberts she told me her husband had a very successful garden business when in fact, he went bust in March 2002 owing the tax office a lot of money. Gwyn must have known that because she was a director of the company. She also told me Alf's forte was erecting summerhouses and garden sheds, that type of construction and his basic knowledge of electrics came in very handy.'

'Interesting? That suggests he could be responsible for the kitchen fire at the hostel.' Reg offers. At least someone is listening.

'You found his prints on the fryer. It makes sense to me. Alf also had access to keys and if he used the side door, no one would have seen him coming or going.

'Which reminds me. David Griffiths was the pot wash at the hostel. According to Gwyn Roberts, apart from her denying all knowledge of his drug habit, told me he often went in early to see in the deliveries and put the stock away. Deliveries I might add, that on occasions Alf Roberts helped with. He helped a young driver called Owain Parry on the busiest days of the week. Mrs Parry told James and I that her son hated a man called Alf because, instead of speeding up the delivery round, he slowed it down by making unscheduled drops.'

'Are you suggesting Alf Roberts murdered Owain Parry?' Reg asks.

'Maybe. Maybe not. I think Owain knew what was in those extra drops and had to be silenced because he threatened to spill the beans. What I am fairly certain of, he caused the fire at the hostel to destroy any evidence linking himself to David Griffiths. To get in and out early in the morning David Griffiths had to have had keys to the kitchen area. Gwyn admitted petty theft was common place in the hostel and for that reason, when not in use the kitchen area was kept under lock and key. You, Reg, told me that when you searched David's bedsit, it was clean. Nothing was found to substantiate he was dealing. By your own admission you said that was unusual, simply because people like David are known to keep records of who owed what and how much. As a matter of interest, did you find any keys in his bedsit?'

'No.'

'May I be as bold to suggest that Alf, or someone he knows, searched David's bedsit and removed all incriminating evidence before you got there.'

'How? We reacted very quickly to the call.'

'It was something you said that raised my suspicions, but before I tell you I'd like to roll this back a little. Brad, I was given the unenviable task of monitoring and recording all shipping movements in the county. You expressed the importance of that task because there was a bad batch of cocaine on our shores and we needed to pull out all the stops to find the source before further deaths are recorded. To the best of my knowledge there have only been two deaths recorded so far, David Griffiths and Hanna Green. Don't you find that odd? Doesn't that suggest to you they were targeted?

'Brad, you had or have a particular interest in an Irish connection and Forrests have that in an abundance. Take one basic product like potatoes. They import tons and tons of spuds every year by the lorry load directly to their depot. It's an area I wanted to look into and as a point of interest, the hostel receives potato deliveries from Forrests on a regular basis. As a result of being stopped by you, Brad, I'm none the wiser and I'm disappointed your man on the inside has nothing to report. That's all down to you now. I do however think I may have an answer to your conundrum, Reg. Tell me something. Are you aware that Alf Roberts has an illegitimate son?'

'Not before you suggested it. Remember, our investigation into Alf Roberts is still in the early stages.'

'Let me help you out here. Alf Roberts spent time inside as a teenager for ABH. He beat the shit out of a lad because he was seeing his ex-girlfriend who was pregnant at the time with his illegitimate son. Her name is Alexis Linnette. Paul Lynnette, Alf's son was also a director of his failed garden business. Paul has two sons. Sebastian and Tristian. Tristian is in his last year at school while Sebastian works for his father, Paul.'

'Wait! You mention someone called Seb supplying drugs to the guys on the streets. Is he one of the same?' Reg asks.

'It's not a common name in these parts. I'm inclined to believe it is but I've yet to prove that. James, would you like to take over?'

'Sure. We went to see Mrs Linnette once I'd done some research and she confirmed our thoughts. Paul Linnette is her son and she told us that she raised him alone until he was about fourteen. Out of the blue Alf appeared on the scene and Alexis claimed that's when her son changed. He became a horrible child. When Paul left school he went to work with his father and was made a director of Alf's gardening company. Alexis actually told us that she didn't understand how they threw money around like confetti when the business was failing, and she didn't want to know or have anything to do with them.'

'So the gardening business could have been a front?' Reg adds.

'It looks that way. I'm struggling to find any evidence at all to suggest they were actually trading. I have found some invoices but they were false. Paul though, does run a legitimate, profitable business.'

'Doing what?' When Reg asks that James turns to look at me.

'Dog kennels with training facilities. That's where I'm at. I can't just walk in there to see for myself, so I was looking for someone who could…without suspicion.'

'Jason Foggerty isn't your man.' Reg snaps.

'You'll be surprised what the offer of an exclusive can do, with a free half page advert on offer to boot.'

'What sort of training facilities?' Reg continues.

'Paul Linnette is a registered dog breeder too. However, his main love is racing dogs...greyhounds. Our understanding is, that is why he has the training facilities. We're led to believe he buys a litter of greyhounds from breeders in Ireland as yearlings, which can be as many as twelve at a time, and does the initial training himself. Alexis informed us Paul travels over there on a regular basis with a custom built trailer to collect the greyhounds himself. Reg, when you told me about the post mortem results and the bacteria found in the stomachs of both David and Hanna, the alarm bells started to ring. My gut feeling tells me they are using the dogs to import the drugs.'

'I have come across incidences of this.' Brad offers, deciding to join in. 'Cocaine and most powered drugs are placed inside a sealed container, usually something along the lines of a durex, given to a hungry dog who will swallow it whole and they wait for nature to take its course. Not perfect and accidents happen, like the bag splitting inside the animal but the dogs are replaceable. If the dog should puke the container up and damage occurs, the contents could become contaminated. Dog saliva is very dangerous to humans. If you know that and knowingly give the contents to someone, that would be classed as murder. All supersession on your behalf, Nick, but unusual enough to follow up. Do you know when his next sortie to Ireland is?'

'No. I'm waiting on a phone call from someone who owns and races greyhounds. They don't know Paul Linette. I have asked them to say they are looking for a good greyhound, one which has the potential of becoming a winner. I'm hoping they will be given a date, or at least invited to the kennels to take a look at the dogs.

'There is another avenue. One I really don't wish to get involved in. Linda has resurfaced and she is looking for a place in this area for herself and her daughter, Maddy, to live in. Maddy works for Stena Lines on the Fishguard to Rosslare crossing. I have no idea what she does for Stena and after my recent argument with Linda, I very much doubt she'll want to talk to me. It is worth looking into though. Maddy might just be the person we need to find out for us, or she might know the person who can.

'I'm done gentlemen, in both senses of the word. I feel sure James will help you if you need any further information. My personal feeling on all this, as they have been very careful thus far, is we need to catch them in the act. There is one last thing, Reg. I spoke to a young lady by the name of Ellie Simpson the other day. She was Owain's girlfriend. I spoke to her because Owain's mum told us, the last time she saw him he said he was on the way to see Ellie and wouldn't be late. I questioned his movements because if he was on his way to see Ellie, why was he going in totally the wrong direction? Ellie eventually confessed to me that he was buying her some weed to smoke on his way over. Owain also bought her brother some heroin on occasions. I think that might explain why you found traces of heroin in his jacket pocket. I don't know this, but if you are looking for Owain's murderer, I suggest you start with Alf or Sebastian. They had cause and reason. He posed a risk to their operation.'

'Let me ask you something, Nick.' Brad asks. 'From what you are suggesting, you think we're wasting our time inside Forrests?'

'On the contrary. I think we have two problems. If I am right and I'm not saying I am, I think Alf and Paul wanted a bigger slice of the action and to achieve that, they had to make changes.'

Chapter Ten

Thursday 11th September

I'm in a strange mood this morning. I don't think I'm the only one. Sam has been very quiet and I do understand that. Tomorrow is going to be a difficult day for him and it must be playing on his mind. I'm not comfortable with the idea of him being dragged around the streets of Bristol but that is not the root cause of my mood.

For many months now I have openly said I want to retire. Physically, and perhaps mentally, I see it as the right decision. Oddly, this morning, I'm having second thoughts. Am I making the right decision? Yesterday, after our unscheduled meeting at the office, call it what you wish, I took myself away from everything for a few hours to be alone with my thoughts. Driving my car with no particular direction, I stopped a number of times in places that mean something personal to me. One of those places was Henry Sinclair's old cottage. I don't know why.

From there, a couple of miles inland from New Quay, the view of the Preseli Mountains is spectacular. A place of historical interest. The inner circle of blue stones at Stonehenge originate from there. Mystery and mythical stories surround the mountains and as a self-proclaimed druid, there's no doubting why Henry chose to live there. Through Beth Rhys, I understood Henry was convinced we still have a lot to learn about this area and its unwritten history. I too have a lot to learn about Henry and his beliefs.

What happened there a week or so ago bothers me. The second, identical envelope found on my doorstep, even more so. I didn't over stay my welcome there yesterday. I half expected something to happen, like before, but it didn't. I have always hated and dismissed Henry's belief that I was his chosen one, his prodigy, at every opportunity I had. Perhaps I went there yesterday to test his theory. My belief is, if Henry is desperate and wants to contact me, he would have done so yesterday.

I have a lot to think about. My own direction being the main protagonist. I do need time out for sure. That's not up for discussion, but where will I be at in six months to a year from now? My pending operation, my attitude to work may finally dictate that outcome. If though, in a year from now I'm fit enough to work, I know I will become bored but of course, there is the farm to keep me occupied. Yesterday was an important start. Today, finding where my priorities lie ranks high on my list. My health is top of my list because that will affect everything. Following that, my list of things to do and in what order, is longer and more complicated than I'd wished.

There's New Barn farm for instance. Marcus is a great manager and his progressive thinking is refreshing but on occasions, he needs to be reminded of who the boss is. The farm doesn't demand my full attention. I do though need to keep an eye on the expenditure and profit margins. As the owner, that is my job. In conjunction with New Barn there's the recent acquisition of Penrice farm. I understand the contracts are being exchanged tomorrow, when Penrice becomes my farm. When that is confirmed, the work to make the place profitable and successful begins in earnest.

Out of the goodness of my heart I told Tom and Mother they could stay on in the house, but I wasn't going to spend a penny on the place at this stage...inside or out. On reflection, the latter is a mistake. Sitting no more than fifty metres away from the barns, where our future plans lay, it is in a terrible state. Having made a promise to them and saying I wasn't investing in the house, how do I wriggle out of that one? It's fair to say that until the visitor centre is up and running, earning money, I have no desire to spend money unnecessarily. The challenge there for me is, I may be forced too. The exterior at least. I like the idea of the nature trail and education centre and if it should come to fruition, we must manage our budgets. However, we should approach this idea from a realistic point of view. Keep it basic and allow the public to engage safely. Nothing exotic or dangerous.

There's also the mansion to consider. I rarely go there but Brad uses the place on a regular basis for his work. He fought long and hard to have the monitoring and data system installed by the agency and makes good use of what it offers. All of which is the property of the agency we work for. I own half of the mansion but when I use the computer equipment, even I must ask permission to sign onto the network and login under strict procedures. Something I omitted to do four or five months ago and reprimanded for my personal use. The set up has a huge value and not just in monitory terms. After my misuse, onsite security has become 24/7. If I leave the agency the computer room will be out of bounds to me and I'm hearing on the grape vine, I may need permission to stay at my own house. Brad has already hinted that if I resign or retire, they will decommission the installation and remove the equipment...at our expense.

My view is, they installed the kit, they can take it all out again…at their expense. It's only the hardware and software that has any real value. They can leave the rest to gather dust for all I care.

A couple of weeks ago I took the boys and Lucy with me when Brad arranged to meet me there. When we arrived Jack asked me how much I thought the mansion was worth. I plucked a figure of 3-3.5 million out of the air. Sat in over a thousand acres of land, some of which is rented out to local farmers, I may have underestimated the combine figure. Five million is closer. Half of that is a lot of money to forfeit and I may need that money to fund my latest venture.

I'm in no doubt that the likes of Reg and Brad are talking about me behind my back. That is their prerogative. It does bother me when I think about the topic of their conversations. The boys are part of my decision making and why shouldn't they be? They are not the main reason for why. Both of my associates have known for a long time I want to retire, long before I found myself in the current situation with the boys. I feel now is as good a time as any.

Sam is a quandary. I see my task, although for the right reasons he changed his surname to mine, is to manage his progress. In reality, isn't that the duty of every parent, managing the child's challenging route through to adulthood? What I do know about his life is disturbing and yet, apart from the occasional relapse, he's coping remarkably well with the massive changes. In my mind that raises a very important question. Who "is" managing who? More importantly, who is managing Sam's life? Mary Robinson appears to have more than a passing interest in his welfare and Sam's adoption was no more than a formality. That's not how it works but under the guise of security and safety, very few questions were asked. Sam has repeatedly refused to open up and talk. Now he has agreed to, under pressure to do so it must be said, Mary wants to be present. I think she's hiding something. She is his social worker but I think she needs to be there to advise him to be economic with the truth. I have no proof to think that way, other than everything has been made to easy for Sam and myself. I opened up to Reg and expressed the way I felt about the situation to him. I told him I felt something wasn't right. I believed at the time it may have been my problem, my perception of the situation. I know I have an over active mind at times and think too deeply about certain issues. In this instance, I think I have good reason to question it. When Mary has visited us at home she has always insisted on talking to Sam alone first before involving me. In a way I have understood that, but they have never discussed their private conversation with me, unless others were present.

Reg didn't have the time to see me when I phoned. He claimed he was too busy and hadn't prepared himself for tomorrow. When I told him this was about tomorrow he agreed to meet me on Castle Hill in Fenby later. Like always he keeps me waiting, in conditions more convivial for winter.

'This had better be good.' He informs me. 'My time is of premium, so let's make this brief.'

'It's good alright. Shall we take a walk?'

'Why the secrecy?'

'Last Monday I expressed my doubts to you about Sam. How he went out of his way to please me and do what I asked without question. I told you I felt something wasn't right but I couldn't put my finger on why. Well now I think I know.'

'How does this involve tomorrow? He's doing what we're asking him to do and that can only be a good thing.'

'Reg. I don't want Mary Robinson sat with him or in the room while he's being interviewed.'

'Why ever not? As his social worker she has every right to be in attendance. Can't change that, Nick.'

'Then he's not going.'

'Wow! Hold on here. Mary is behind everything good for that young man. She should be present.'

'My point exactly. That's what bothers me.'

'Care to give me reason for this change of heart?'

'I think she may be involved.'

'Oh come on! Mary has her odd ways for sure, but she is dedicated to her job and held in great regard. You really will be digging a large whole for yourself if you continue with this.'

227

'Am I? If I'm so very wrong, tell me why Mary didn't know where Sam and the other boy were being taken? And why, when he ran away, did he phone Mary and not the police. Let's face it, it's a much easier number to remember.'

'Because he was scared and didn't know who he could trust. He knew Mary could help him, so he phoned her.'

'Or Sam knew he couldn't talk to anyone else. When I first met him he had nothing to his name except the clothes on his back. I later learnt he left his bag behind when he made a run for it. Why, when running for his life in a blind panic, so we are led to believe, did he remember to take Mary's phone number with him?'

'He'd memorised it. What else?'

'A ten or eleven digit phone number. I don't think so. Not in the state he was supposed to be in. I believe he kept the number about his person in case of an emergency. Why would Sam want to do that if he didn't know he was going to that house?'

'This is not enough, Nick, unless you have proof. Sorry, I'm not buying into this.'

'Wait!' I ask, raising my voice to stop him walking away. 'We both know Porterhouse fucked up. He failed to complete the job Sir Richard was paying him to do. You were right to isolate both Sam and Jack after the shooting because they were in a place they couldn't get to. Days after we returned home, Barry Mullins turned up to finish what Porterhouse failed to do. Why? And why Mullins? As far as we know the two men didn't know each other. So ask yourself, why did both men want Sam dead? And who told Mullins how and where to find him?'

'So you think Mary had a hand in this?

'I don't understand why Mary, or someone else in the social services for that matter, didn't remove Sam from what has been described as a dangerous situation until his mother Jessica passed away. She was a prostitute, a drug addict with previous health problems who was incapable of taking care of him. Reg, I was shocked when he told me he didn't go to his mother's funeral. Why didn't he? Was someone frightened he would say something out of place while in an emotional state saying goodbye to his mother?'

228

'Let me get this straight. You have reason to believe there's a connection between Mary Robinson, Barry Mullins and Sam? Is that what you're saying?'

'That is exactly what I'm suggesting. Look at the mind games she played with us? One minute he's going to live with foster parents, then, before we know it, he's changed his surname to mine and I've adopted him. We both know it's not as simple as that. Adoption can take months, years even and only then when checks are made. It's all been handed to us on a plate.

'Look at the facts as we know them. Sam basically lived on the streets. He's had to fight for everything he wanted or needed. I don't see that in him. Not one bit. It's almost as if he's lived in my house all his life. That's what I have been questioning, because they are very, very different life styles. If this is genuine, I would have seen traits of his previous existence in his behaviour, and I haven't in any shape or form. I'd like to know what he was promised. You must have questioned why Mary contacted me and not the police?'

'Where do you want to take this?'

'Does this mean you believe me?'

'You're asking me questions I can't answer and yes, you are casting doubt in my mind.'

'Thank God. I thought I was going mad. My suggestion is, we let Mary turn up. Once we're ready to start, separate them. Use an excuse like, you want Sam to talk to the child physiatrist on his own before you start the interview. I want to see their reactions because if they are hiding something, one of them will break. Sad thing about this situation is, Reg, I have adopted a lovely young man who just might not be the real deal.'

Chapter Eleven

Friday 12th September

Reg phoned me late last night with an update. He tasked one of his colleagues to undertake some background work on Mary Robinson and they came up with some interesting information. After going around the houses, explaining in great depth how they found this news, he finally gave me the information I was waiting for. Mary Robinson and Barry Mullins are blood related. Second, or more likely third cousins. Knowing I was right doesn't necessarily make me feel good about myself, but it proves I was right to question her role in all this. Today could be a defining day for us and somehow, I have to keep this revelation to myself.

Our journey to Bristol was uneventful. Reg and I did hold a short conversation over the current issue locally and even that was low key. Delicate information of that nature should not be discussed openly. Other than that it was a sombre trip, apart from the incessant chatter of the coms in the unmarked police car.

Arriving at our destination we are most definitely in the middle of the countryside, not the city as believed. I'm quickly told that the new looking modern building is their training and wellbeing centre. Their judgement on this being a safer environment for Sam is met in total agreement.

Stretching my aching limbs after a two hour plus car journey, I'm hesitant. My thoughts suggest this could go horribly wrong. God only knows what is going through Sam's mind. At the moment he is blissfully unaware of my agenda and if I'm allowed to speak, I'm sure he'll end up hating me. Watching Sam being helped out of his bullet proof Jacket Reg takes advantage of the distraction.

'Play it cool and do not jump in with both feet.' He whispers in my ear. I know he's right, but my anger currently aimed at Mary Robinson will be difficult to contain.

Entering the building through the main entrance we're greeted by three people, one of whom is Mary Robinson. Informally, the other two introduce themselves as DS Read and Paula Collins. Paula is the child psychiatrist who we're told, works with the police, not for them. At a guess, I would say she's in the age bracket of 40-50. As we're asked to sign in at the desk for security reasons, I notice Mary has an A4 folder tucked under her arm. When we're all signed in at the desk, Paula takes the rains.

'Sam.' Paula starts. 'Before we start this formal interview I'd like to talk to you and assess whether you're fine to do this. It's important that you understand what the process of having an interview involves. Get you settled in, if that makes more sense? It shouldn't take too long. Is that ok with you?'

'I'll be right beside you, Sam.' Mary adds. 'So don't worry.'

'I'm afraid that won't be possible Mss Robinson.' Paula counters Mary's words, and I like her approach. 'I understand, Mr Thompson, you are Sam's legal guardian.'

'I am.'

Not giving in easily, Mary tries to put her point across. 'I must insist Mrs Collins. I am Sam's social worker and can give you a good insight into his past.'

'Mss Robinson. This is a police matter, not a cosy social services chat over a cup of tea. I will assess Sam's wellbeing for myself. I understand too that DI Wallace and DS Read would like to talk to you while Sam and I have a little chat. Isn't that right Sir?'

'Yes. That is correct.' DI Wallace confirms.

'Mr Thompson. Would you like to join us?'

Nodding at Paula I see Sam take a quick glance in Mary's direction. DI Wallace sees him too. Encouraged to follow her, Paula opens the door behind her and gestures to us. Doing as we're asked, Mary continues with her argument. She is definitely not happy with the situation and tries to tell us that what we're doing isn't legal. Reg is having none of her arguing and politely asks her to calm down. He reminds her of where she is and then insists she follows him.

Passing through the doorway we enter a short corridor. As we walk Sam takes hold of my hand and asks me why Mary isn't coming with us. Before I have the chance to reply, Paula does.

'Sam. Mary isn't sitting in with us at the moment because I want to know what the real Sam thinks.'

'But she always comes with me.'

'Why do think that is? Does Mary feel she has a duty to answer the questions for you? If she does, I won't get to know you and that is important for me. More importantly right now, how you see your future.'

Stopping, Paula opens a door. Inside the small room are a table, four chairs and a tape recording machine on the table. Asking us to take a seat she closes the door and joins us. Sitting myself next to Sam and I sense he is very nervous.

'I hope you don't mind, but I'd like to record our conversation to assist me with my research into childhood behaviour.'

'It's fine by me.' I offer.

'I don't want to do this.' Sam retorts.

Turning on the recorder Paula responds. 'Why not Sam? We are here to help you. Your dad and I want to get to know and understand the real Sam. Can I ask you something, Sam? Would you prefer to have Mary sat next to you, rather than your Dad?'

'Can we go, Dad?'

I look at Paula. I know I'm not supposed to get involved but I'm desperate to hear his response. To my relief, Paula nods her head.

'Sam. We are being given the chance to end this once and for all time. I want you to know that you're not the one in trouble here. So please, tell us the truth.'

'I can't.'

'Why not?' I answer.

'Because Mary is my friend.'

'Is she, Sam? Or are you frightened of what could happen to you if you do tell us the truth?'

'I don't want to get into trouble.'

'You are not going to get into trouble. Sam, if Mary has been bullying or threatening you, we can put a stop to that here and now. But to help yourself, you need to help us.'

'I didn't want to do it! They made me.' He responds angrily.

'Made you do what, Sam? Paula calmly asks.

'Mary promised me that if I did one more job for them and kept my mouth shut, she would find me somewhere nice to live.'

His confession has me sitting back in my chair. I knew something was amiss, but that hurts. Mary has bribed him and they appear to have used me. His statement suggests Mary has been controlling him all along and to get what he wanted, he went along with her promise.

'Are you all right, Mr Thompson?' Paula inquires.

I don't respond. My personal feelings, my reaction to what he just said, says more than enough. If I were to open my mouth and voice my opinions at this point, I will say the wrong thing. Realising the difficult situation Paula continues. 'Who are they, Sam?'

'Mary and Barry Mullins.' He offers. 'Please don't tell her I told you.'

Paula sees me shaking my head in disgust. 'Mr Thompson. Why don't you go and get some fresh air, or a glass of water? I'll continue with this.' I shake my head again. I'm going nowhere. I want to hear this first hand.

'I'm sorry, Dad.' Sam tells me, turning to face me. 'I had to do what they said or they would hurt me. Please forgive me!'

Seeing I'm struggling Paula carries on. 'Did you do this one last job for them?'

'We went there but the other boy fell down the stairs and broke his neck, so I legged it.'

'So you didn't get to do what they sent you there to do?'

'No. I was scarred they'd hurt me too.'

'Why did you phone Mary and not the police?' Paula doesn't know this story, I think, so now I will get involved.

'She told me to.'

'Why?'

'Because we weren't supposed to be there. She said if anything went wrong I should phone her and no one else.'

'Did you memorise her number?'

'Didn't need to.' Pulling out his jean pocket to show me he continues. 'Mary had a label sewn on the bottom of my pocket and put her number on it. She also put the code number on it.'

'Code number? Code for what, Sam?'

'The safe.'

'You had the combination for Sir Richards safe. Why?'

'Barry said it was full of expensive jewellery and if I took it, they could retire and leave me alone.'

'Why you? Why didn't Barry do it himself?'

'He said I was the sneaky one and if anyone could pull it of...I could. The other boys at the home called me tiptoe, because I could sneak in and out without anyone seeing me. I use to raid the kitchen at night for crisps and things for the older boys. They would leave me alone if I did.'

'Did Mary know it was you?'

'I think so but she never said anything.'

'Where did you go, Sam, when you sneaked out of the home?'

'Larry's.'

'Why? To pick up your deliveries?'

'Yes.'

'Let's go back a little here. Where exactly was the safe?'

'In the games room behind a picture of Sir Richard.'

'What would you have done if the games room door was locked?'

'I'd pick the lock. Larry taught me how to do it. He said it was useful to know how if I got into trouble anytime. I could pick the lock on a bike and get away.'

'But you'd need a set of special keys for that.'

'I've got some, or had some. Don't know where they are now.'

'Nothing like that was found in the house.'

'They were in the van on the inside of the petrol flap. Pushed into a piece of blue tack to stop them falling out. All I had to do was to take a pillow from the bedroom, collect the keys and when I was finished, give everything to Bob.'

'Who is Bob?'

'The minibus driver. I don't know what he was going to do with the stuff, I promise.'

Slamming both of my hands on the table in anger, I stand. Time to have this out with Mary. 'This is unbelievable.' I mutter.

'Please don't go, Dad!' Sam begs, but it's too late.

'All I ever wanted was honesty. Instead I got a pack of fucking lies.'

Slamming closed the door behind me I pause for a second in the corridor. Sam was balling his eyes out when I left him and if I really care, I should stay with him. This is Mary's doing...not his. Blinded by my anger I go in search of Mary. They are not difficult find. Through a window in the first door we passed along the corridor, she is sat talking to DI Wallace and DS Read. I invite myself in. Reg reacts quickly and tries to stop me. I close the door behind me and lean against it.

'This is not a good time, Nick!' Reg shouts. Blocking my way I respond angrily.

'She is involved in all this shit. Ask her who tiptoe is?' As Reg turns to face Mary I push past him. Mary tries to defend herself.

'Detective Inspector Wallace. I have no idea what he is talking about. If this is some sort of game you're playing with me, then I should leave. And believe me, I will report this.'

By now I have reached the table. Placing my hands on the table I lean across and put my face in Mary's space. 'You know exactly who tiptoe is. Don't you?'

Placing his hand on my shoulder Reg tries to pull me away, saying as he does, "This isn't the time or place". I'm not finished and until I'm done, I'm going nowhere.

'Why don't you tell these kind officers what you and your partner in crime asked tiptoe to do for you? I'm sure they'd like to know.'

'Whatever he said to you is all lies.' Mary stupidly says. Not that I needed too, but I haven't mentioned Sam.

'So you do know who tiptoe is? Why am I not surprised? Reg, I want you to arrest her.'

'All in good time, Nick.'

'Well at least bloody caution her before she walks out on you.'

'Who is tiptoe, Nick?'

'Who do you think? Sam, and we have recorded his confession. You need to listen to that but do us all a favour first, lock her up. You bloody cow, Mary!'

Venting my anger and frustrations I kick out at a chair, sending it across the room into the far wall. Reg quickly grabs my arm and marches me to the door.

'That's enough.' He shouts. 'Go and wait outside for me. Smoke a few cigarettes to calm yourself down. I'll come and get you when we're finished.'

Finding myself a quiet place to sit, well out of the way, my mind is racing. Lighting a cigarette I settle myself on a low brick wall bordering a raised flower bed to think. This is a mess. Mary has been so deceitful I'm inclined not to believe a word she has ever said to me. For a start, the paperwork regarding Sam's adoption. That's probably not worth the paper it's written on. I have mixed feelings there too, because if Mary has consistently lied to me...so has Sam. I could balance that by believing he lived in total fear of what she might do. It appears he was compliant because he wanted to stay with me. Why oh

236

why, didn't he confide in me? He didn't trust someone…that's for sure. My thoughts worry me. Do I really want to continue looking after Sam when there is no trust?

Nearly an hour has passed. On the ground in front of me lay six cigarette butt ends. I'd best do something with those before they write me a ticket for littering. Out of the corner of my eye I see Reg approaching. About time crosses my mind as I scatter the butts with my foot.

'Go on, say it. I told you so,' I offer. Sitting down next to me he answers.

'That has never been on my mind. Nick, while DS Read and I listened to Sam's tape one of his colleagues checked Mary's paperwork. I have to inform you, whether you want to hear this or not, that everything is in order. I have sensed this could create a problem for you but, you have legally adopted Sam.

'We spoke again to Mary, on the grounds of Sam's confession and she confessed to her involvement with Barry Mullins and his criminal activities. For your ears only, we have charged her on two counts. Perverting the course of justice and aiding and abetting criminal activity. I'm certain there's more to come. She's going nowhere, until the van arrives to take her away.

'We are required by law to contact the social services and inform them of our findings but I wanted to talk to you first. I need to know what you want to happen where Sam is concerned.' Shaking my head as if to say I don't know, Reg continues. 'I understand you may want time to think this through but, Nick, if we don't give the social services' some positive news, they will take him back into care. You know he doesn't want that to happen. He's in bits in there and he needs the only friend he has right now, to help him. That person is you, Nick. So stop feeling sorry for yourself and get back in there to see him. Sam is sitting with Paula in the canteen area. Come on, I'll go with you.'

Walking slowly back along the access road towards the entrance my pace is slow. 'You're quiet.' Reg suggests. I am. I have a lot to think about in a very short space of time. 'You were right to voice your concerns last night and I appreciate that. You have given us a massive lead on this case. So much so that DS Read and I have agreed to leave this where we are for the time being with Sam. We would however like you and him take a look at the mug shots we've prepared before we go. If that is alright with you?' I'm not sure it is and stop walking. Reg stops and faces me. 'For God's sake. That young man needs your help. You heard what he said in there and you know how they treated him when he got things wrong. Do you really want him going back on the streets to live a life of crime? You were right, I didn't agree with what you were doing for him in the beginning. In your own words, he's blossomed under your supervision and done some good things for you. Doesn't that count for anything? I got the impression you didn't think we listened to what you were saying, but we were. Just give him a chance to prove your doubts wrong. Let him say sorry to you a hundred times. Let him cry on your shoulder when he needs too. He's young. He can change and will…with your help. You, Nick, need to open your eyes and clear your mind to see that.'

Opening the canteen door for me Reg lets me step inside first. The canteen is a large area and I guess if they're running courses here it would need to be. I don't see Sam and Paula immediately. She has sat him down in a corner over to my left. He is staring at me when I look in their direction. Sam is a good looking young man but his blood shot heavy eyes and frowning face distort his features disproportionally. Pausing momentarily, Paula suggests I join them at the small table. Joining them I pull out one of the spare chairs, sitting myself down opposite Sam.

'Sam and I have been having a nice chat, off the record I will add. He has something he wishes to say but I would like to say a few words first. If that is ok with you, Mr Thompson?' Nodding my head in agreement, I let Paula continue. 'Good. I'm sure you are aware of this but to make this very clear to you both so we all know where we are, Sam is the victim here. He has suffered both mentally and physically from his experiences and those wounds will take a long time to heal. Helping him through these tough times will take time and a lot of care. Sam will need understanding, encouragement and careful management along the way. I would like to follow his progress and his wellbeing while we work together to achieve his goal. Sam and I briefly spoke about his time with you and from what he tells me, he's doing very well. I do however believe you may have doubts over why that is. He believes it may have something to do with Marry Robinson, that she was dictating his every move. That in fact, she was telling him what to do and when to do it. There is another side to this Mr Thompson. Sam tells me you've done a lot of talking, discussing things together and he now knows the importance of that. He also told me you have always asked him to tell the truth but Sam, as you are now aware, had a problem with that. He thought he would get into serious trouble if he did and worse still, they would hurt him if he spoke out of turn. We all know Sam isn't in trouble. So before Sam speaks, I'd like to know if you are prepared to continue helping him with his progression? For what it's worth, from what I have read and heard, you have demonstrated to us you do care and I believe you are capable of helping Sam to achieve great things. I'd like to hear your personal thoughts.'

'My thoughts? I'm not going to prolong this for Sam. I don't want to hear him plead his case. I'd like him to give me a big huge.'

Sam doesn't need a second invitation. He's out of his chair and sat on lap with his arms around my shoulders in seconds. He crying and I'm pretty close.

'I'm sorry, Dad,' he snivels.

'So am I sorry, Sam. This shouldn't be happening. We both know what we need to do, so let's make it happen.'

'I will. I promise.'

'No more lies. No more secrets.'

'I promise. I like living with you and Jack. You take me out to some nice places. You watch me play football. Jack is like a brother to me and I can't wait until Lucy has her baby. Lucy promised me I can be a page boy at their wedding.'

'Wedding! That's news to me.'

'They were talking about getting married the other day, so I asked Lucy if I could go. She said I could be her page boy then.'

'You'll be a bit old to be a page boy when they get married.'

'Lucy said they were thinking of getting married next summer.' His words send shivers down my back. Jack and Lucy are only sixteen. Where on earth do they plan to live? Pulling Sam off of me I look him in the eyes.

'You're winding me up...aren't you?'

'No, Dad. You asked me to tell you the truth...so I am!'

239

'This is wonderful.' Paula utters. 'Look at the way you're interacting with each other. It's so natural, perfect. Fantastic to see. I'd say the future is very bright.'

Settling Sam on my knee I turn to address Paula. 'I do have one problem. We are due to put to some flowers on Sam's, Mother's grave this afternoon while we're in the Bristol area. Sam doesn't know where that is. Mary Robinson said she did and would take us there. I don't want her having anything more to do with us so we need a little help here. Is there any way we can delay informing the social services of this until we have been to her grave, because quite frankly, I don't trust anyone in her office right now. I'm done with surprises and anyone from her office could turn up uninvited.'

'Good point, Nick.' Reg agrees. 'I'll ask DS Read if he can help us. In the meantime, get yourself something to eat and drink and when I return, I'll bring the mugs shots for you to look through.'

Sam was hungry. Despite my persistent nagging this morning he didn't have any breakfast. Considering the circumstances I do understand why he didn't. Before we left home he told me he felt sick. Quite naturally, worry has that effect on a person. Now, with everything out in the open, I sincerely hope so anyway, he told me he was starving.

After exchanging contact details Paula bode us farewell, promising, as long as Sam was happy with the situation, she will be in touch early next week. He agreed to her wishes, telling us that he was happy for Paula to monitor his progress. Sam is of course the one person most affected by Mary's behaviour and acknowledging he needs help is a big thing for him. I can only do so much for him and he does need professional help and guidance along the way. Something that has become painfully obvious, Mary Robinson didn't give him.

Reg Wallace came clean in the end. He had doubted my wisdom in taking Sam on full time from the outset. Outside, in a long unscripted speech, he said a few things which really bought home my reasoning behind taking on the responsibility. In one of those thought provoking moments, he said I was the only friend Sam had and the only person right now who can help him. Knowing what I now know, he was right. Then, when he asked me if I wanted to see Sam back on the streets living a life of crime...I knew he was right. I realised then I had every right to be angry with Mary...but not Sam. Like Paula said, Sam is the victim in this. I truly see that now.

240

Sam polished off a full English breakfast. I'm sure the lady behind the servery over-heard our conversation or saw our situation unfold and generously piled extra helpings onto his plate. He got through it all. He most certainly was a hungry young man. Me, I settled for a cheese and onion sandwich and a bag of crisps.

Not long after Sam had devoured a large bowl of vanilla ice cream smothered in chocolate source, DS Read re-appeared. Joining us at the table he and DI Wallace take a seat. Placing a folder on the table DS Read speaks first.

'Good news,' he says. 'We have spoken to the vicar of St Judes and he carried out the short funeral service for your mother, Sam. He has agreed to meet us at the crematorium in an hour from now. He knows where you mother's ashes are and would like to say a few prayers in her memory for you. Would you like that, Sam?'

'Yes please,' Sam responds quietly.

'Great. We'll do this as quickly as we can,' DS Read continues, opening the folder. 'And make our way to the crematorium.' Pausing for a moment DS Read turns the folder so both Sam and I can see the photographs easily. DI Wallace stands and hovers at my left shoulder. 'Take your time, Sam, have a good look at each mug shot and let me know if you recognise anyone. Is that ok?' Once again Sam responds by saying yes quietly.

While Sam slowly and carefully starts to work his way through the photos I become aware of DS Read watching us for a reaction. When Sam turns to the sixth image I automatically lean forward. Its picture of a lady I've seen somewhere recently.

'Something wrong, Nick? Wallace asks.

'I'm not sure. When was this picture taken?'

'About three months ago. Not good quality I know. It's a still from a security camera in a local bank. On that particular day £45,000 was paid into a Jersey account by three different individuals at the same time.' DS Read replies. 'Do you know her?'

'I'm really not sure, but there is a strong likeness. It's not a woman I have met. When I spoke to a lady by the name of Alexis Linnette recently on a similar investigation, she informed me she had little contact with her son Paul

241

because of his alleged drug dealing. While we chatted I noticed a photograph on her Welsh dresser taken on her son's wedding day some twenty years ago. The woman in this picture looks very much like her, only a lot older.'

'Do you know her name, Nick?' Wallace asks.

'No, but I know where to find her…if I'm right. And so do you.'

'Take a look at the next photo, Nick, please. What do you think?' DS Read adds. Turning the page I'm in no doubt.'

'That is definitely Paul Linnette. Older and balder, but it's him alright.'

'Do you know either of these two people, Sam?' DS Read continues.

'I think I've seen the lady before, with Barry Mullins.'

'Thank you, Sam. Would you like to continue?'

Sam obliges. I watch as he continues this task. On his way through the file he identifies one other person…who I don't know. Concluding the task DS Read thanks us both, closes the folder and asks me to write down the address of Paul Linnette. When DI Wallace sees what I have jotted down he asks me if I'm quite sure.

'Perfectly sure. You know I've had my suspicions about their activities for some time now and I'm not the only one. There's something else you should know. It's my belief that the drug dealer in Fenby, a lad by the name of Seb, is their eldest son. I also believe he could be involved in the murder of Owain Parry last year.'

What makes you believe that?' DI Wallace prompts.

'Ellie Simpson, Owain's girlfriend, stated that he was on his way to buy drugs the night he was stabbed. To the best of my knowledge, that end of Saundersby wasn't an area frequented by David Griffiths. He was purely a Fenby dealer. It all makes sense to me, but I'm known to be wrong from time to time.'

'You said you're not the only one, Nick.' DS Read interrupts. 'Is someone else involved in this case?'

'I'm not at liberty to answer that.'

'What Nick is saying, DS Read, that this case is a multi-agency investigation.'

Reaching the crematorium we're greeted by the vicar of St Judes. An unassuming man, dressed in his regalia, he is softly spoken. On the way here we undertook a tour of the area where Sam grew up. Not a particularly enchanting place to live. He did however manage to point five places he remembered running and selling drugs at. Two of which were entrances to a local, council run park. Another two were car parks of local superstores and the final one, which came as quite a shock, was a local private school. I gathered the local public park is well known to DS Read and regularly monitored but it appears from his comments, not as well as he'd been led to believe.

Without Sam's knowledge, DI Wallace removed the items required for this particular part of today's itinerary from the boot of Mary's car. Something he is completely unaware of. For my part, to make this special for him, I have a surprise for him. In my man bag is a small plaque of remembrance for his mother, Jessica. I hope I have the birth and death details correct.

Walking slowly through the grounds I fear the worst. There is something I'm sure Sam will ask and it's a question none of us present today can answer. A question any inquisitive mind would ask and Sam most certainly falls into that category. My fingers are crossed he doesn't stop and wonder, because doing so could drive a wedge between us. What with everything else going on at this time and what we have both gone through to get this far, him asking and needing to know, could do irreversible damage.

Somehow Sam has failed to pick up on the extra baggage our police escorts are lugging around. He may have assumed that that was par for the course and part of our protection. Flippantly, I hope they picked up the right bags for the moment ahead.

Deep into the grounds, in a lonely isolated place, the vicar comes to stand close to a huge oak tree. Barely noticeable a small, thin plain wooden cross marks a place on the ground close to where the vicar is stood. Stopping some metre or so behind the vicar Sam looks at me without uttering a word. In a strange way I can imagine what maybe going through his mind. Something probably along the lines of, is this where my mum was buried? If that is true I can empathise with him, because without the vicar's knowledge and the short service he conducted at the time, no one would ever know. It is a pauper's grave. She came into this world with nothing and certainly left with nothing.

Then again that's not strictly true. She left behind Sam and he of all people deserves better. Turning to face Sam the vicar offers a few words of condolence.

'Sam. This is where your mothers ashes where committed to Gods earth. I said a few prayers for her then and gave her God's blessings of eternal life. Would you care to join me in offering her your blessing?'

Sam is still looking at me. I have no idea what is really going through his mind but just maybe, I can make this a little easier for him. Turning to face the officer standing behind us I gesture to him to pass me the holdall he's holding. Taking it from him I sit it down on the ground in front of Sam to open. Inside the large holdall is an earthenware vase with the name Jessica etched on the front and a large bunch of flowers, for him to place inside vase once it's placed onto the right spot. Sam becomes very tearful when he sees these items and assisted by the vicar, they kneel down on the ground beside the small wooden cross together, where Jessica's ashes were infirmed. In total silence they place the vase on the ground and arrange the flowers.

'Shall we say a few words in remembrance, Sam?' The vicar asks. Stepping forward I kneel down beside Sam and give him the small inscribed plaque on which his mother's name, and birth and death details are etched on. It has an attachment fixed to the back so he can push it into the ground in front of the vase.

'Jessica Cornish. A much loved Mother who is greatly missed,' he reads. Pausing for a moment he looks at me. 'Thank you, Dad.' He tearfully adds.

'My pleasure, Sam. When we're ready, we'll have a proper headstone made.'

Once Sam has placed the plaque where he wants it, the vicar stands and encourages us to join him. Bowing his head he begins to recite a few prayers of remembrance. Mindful of Sam's state of mind I place my arm around his shoulders in support. Ending with the Lord's Prayer, a very solemn moment of silence follows.

Thanking the vicar for his time I suggest to Sam that it has been a long day and we should head for home. Pulling a bottle of water from the bag, Sam pours it into the vase of beautiful flowers and although hesitant, he tells me he's ready.

'We'll come back.' I reassure him. 'In the meantime, we'll design a proper headstone for your Mother together.'

'I'd like that. Thank you, Dad. For everything. Do you think my real dad will ever want to find me?'

My heart sinks. This is exactly the moment I dreaded, the question I didn't want to confront, but I must be realistic. 'Do you want him too?' After a few moments thought he answers my question.

'No. Not really.' He answers to my relief and continues. 'It could be someone like Larry or Barry and they weren't nice. None of my mum's friends were very nice. I love you, Dad, and Jack and Lucy…and sometimes Jan.'

'Why only sometimes?'

'She's bossy, but she can be nice…too!'

'She has her moments, that's for sure.' Taking hold of his hand I suggest we should catch the others up. Left behind out in the open here we are vulnerable but, they may have thought we needed a little private time together to talk.

Chapter twelve

Saturday 13th September

When I finally turned my mobile on yesterday I had a million missed calls, most of which were from Brad. A slight exaggeration, but there might just well have been. One of the missed calls stood out…Michaela. In the confusion yesterday I had forgotten all about her. I didn't tell her that. As a guest in my house that's not good. She was working in Narberth and needed picking up once she had finished. Sam and I arrived home about four o'clock in the afternoon and raced over to pick her up. Very apologetic for my oversight I treated them both to a pleasant meal out. I had thought about inviting Jan. With all that has happened recently she has always been there to support us. Not without controversy it must be said, but whether she believed I was right or wrong, she was always ready to help out. Close to making that call I remembered Linda had moved in with her and that changed the dynamics. It had already been a testing day…without her asking lots of questions. My mobile was quickly placed safely back in my pocket.

I'm first up. Mentally exhausted, the serenity of my own home is just what I need this morning…relaxing. I did check if Sam was all right before I came downstairs and hearing him snoring his head off was comforting. The young man has more days like yesterday ahead of him and on the surface, he appears to have coped very well. That will be better gauged when he decides to get up. He can sleep all day if he likes because God knows, he's earned the right. I'm not going to disturb him.

I should phone Brad. Six missed calls there were from him, not the million I suggested. That suggests though, that he has something important to discuss with me and I'm also curious to learn if DI Wallace has acted on the information both Sam and I had given him and DS Read yesterday.

Although not early, gone 9am, I'm not surprised when Brad appears in the house. By arrangement he has his own set of keys to my place but only lets himself in if he knows I'm at home. I'm out on the patio having a smoke when he joins me.

'I tried numerous times to get hold of you yesterday.' He begins without any sort of greeting. 'Why didn't answer my calls?' Turning to face him I'm annoyed by his attitude.

'Time you listened to what I say my friend. I told you I was going to Bristol with Sam so the police could interview him. For you information it was a worthwhile trip and a productive day.'

'In what way?'

'This is the point where I say it's out of my hands now. I suggest you talk to DI Wallace. What Sam disclosed and what I saw has given them a positive lead which I would think they are following up as we speak. How did your day go?'

'That's for me to know and you to wonder.'

'I see, that's how it works? Would you like me to arrange an appointment with DI Wallace for you so the multi-agency investigation can progress this?'

'That's enough, Nick. I am your boss, don't you forget that. What Sam disclosed and what you saw is my business and I want to know. Actually my friend, I want to talk to Sam…this minute!'

'I think you should go and leave me your set of keys. Sam is not going through that again and if you try, I will make life very difficult for you. Now please leave and go speak to DI Wallace.'

'That's not happening.'

'Yes it will and while you're insulting my intelligence, DI Wallace is probably way ahead of you and possibly out there making arrests while you're wasting our time. Something you obviously haven't achieved.'

I can see by the look on his face that I have touched a raw nerve. He had a bad day yesterday and needs rescuing. Rubbing his chin he's staring at me, clearly pondering whether I'm telling him the truth and if I am, what his next move is. I should help him out, just to get rid of him.

'All bar one issue, my job is done. It's over for me and my intention from this day on, is to dedicate my time to my family. Talk to DI Wallace because he's not about to include me any further, never has done and never will.

247

He likes the glory, you know that. For you Sam is out of bounds, but if DI Wallace feels the need to include you, then that is his choice, not Sam's. I will make this very clear to you. He, we, had a very tough day yesterday and we're not going through that again and as you're not about to share your information, this conversation is over.'

'You're lying to me.'

'Really! Go speak to DI Wallace and then tell me I'm lying. Goodbye!'

Three cups of coffee and countless cigarettes later, Michaela appears in the kitchen with a handful of washing in her arms. A very tired looking Sam appears soon after.

'Thank you for a lovely meal last night.' Michaela says. 'I didn't mean to put you under any more pressure.'

'My pleasure, Michaela. It was my fault. I simply forgot you had asked me to pick you up.'

'That's ok. Can I use the washing machine?'

'Of course. Help yourself.' As I reply to Michaela, Sam puts his arms around me and I respond. 'Good morning, Sam. How are you feeling this morning?'

'Ok.' He responds.

'Just ok? How about we have some breakfast first and then we can decide what we'd like to do today?'

'Can I talk to you first?'

'Always, Sam. You know that.'

'I go.' Michaela offers. 'I'll just do this and go back up to my room.'

'No!' Sam replies positively. 'I don't mind saying this in front of you, Michaela.'

'Are you sure, Sam? I don't want you to think I'm being nosy by listening into your private conversation.' She responds.

'It's ok.'

'I'll put the kettle on.' She informs us.

Sitting down at the breakfast bar facing each other I wait for Sam to speak while Michaela goes about her business. It takes Sam a little time to compose himself before he speaks. 'Are you still cross with me?' He asks.

'Not in the slightest, Sam. I was angry for being lied too but that wasn't your fault, it was Mary's and she will pay for what she put you through. I'm not sure if you totally understand the whole situation because there are a number of other things she's done but young man, you shouldn't worry about what happens to her. She brought it all upon herself.'

'I thought they'd believe her and you were going to leave me there. Let them take me back to the home. I don't want that to happen.'

'And it won't, Sam, ever. I want to help you grow up, become a professional footballer if you wish but like I've always said to you, it has to work both ways. We help each other and always be truthful to one another.'

'I will. I promise. Would you be disappointed with me if I said I have changed my mind and I don't want to be a professional footballer?'

'That's a very sudden change of heart. You love you're football. How come you have had such a massive change of mind?'

'Everyone keeps saying I am an intelligent boy and I don't know if I am. If I am intelligent I could do more...couldn't I?'

'If you put your mind to it...yes, but becoming a footballer has always been your dream and you know I would never stand in your way if that is what you wanted to do. Likewise, Sam, any career choice you make in the future.'

'I want to help you with the farm. I could go to college and learn all about the animals. How to feed them, look after them and help them when they are sick. I'd really like to do that.'

'That is a lovely idea but what about your football? Oddly, I was going to ask you this morning if you felt up to playing tomorrow.'

'I still want to play football, it's good fun and I know I could make lots of money, but I really, really want to help you.'

'Sam, that is fantastic for you to say so and I'd like it very much if you were involved with the farm. We can do a good job together and we shouldn't change your thoughts, but I think we should hold this conversation in a few years from now. See where you are then. In the meantime we have work to do, like drawing up the plans. I have already spoken to Maddison on that very subject. Remember one thing, this project isn't going to happen overnight and we may face some difficult situations along the way. Do you think you're ready for that?'

'Yes. And yes, I do want to play football tomorrow.'

Looking up, Michaela is looking at me. 'I guess here, you're about to ask me the same thing?' I suggest. 'I was going to talk to you about the farm before I went home. It really interests me too.'

'Well, well. I'm sat talking to potentially my first two employees. Michaela, we'll talk again. In the meantime, perhaps you'd like to give some thought to what you can bring to the new business.'

As I finish my last sentence my mobile rings. It's James. What on earth does he want on a Saturday morning? Before I have the chance to say anything, he is off and running.

'Sorry to bother you, boss, but you need to hear this.' He rants.

'Hear what, James?'

'Forgive me for saying this, but you need to get yourself to Fishguard before midday. There is something arriving on the midday ferry I feel sure you'll want to see.'

'Can't you deal with it? I have Sam and Michaela with me and I can't simply abandon them.'

'No! You need to be here to witness this. I have just spoken to a lovely young lady by the name of Maddy Jefferies and she has given me the information you have been waiting for.'

'Maddy Jefferies. "The Maddy Jefferies". Linda's daughter? Good luck with that one, James.'

'You're not listening to me…are you?'

250

'In a word…no.'

'Paul Linnette is booked to arrive on the midday sailing from Ireland. I'm told he is transporting livestock. Greyhounds to be more accurate. That's not all. There are two shipments of potatoes arriving on the same ferry bound for Forrests. Listening now?'

'Have you seen or spoken to DI Wallace on your travels?'

'No,' he informs me.

'Stay put. I'll be in touch. Keep me up to date if anything changes.' Ending the call I look at both Sam and Michaela in turn. 'I guess you got the gist of that? I, we, may need to go out.' Standing I continue. 'Let me make a phone call first.'

Heading outside onto the patio away from their tender ears – the least they know the better – I light a cigarette and take a couple of long draws before phoning DI Wallace. When he answers my third attempt it quickly becomes evident he isn't that pleased to hear from me.

'Not now, Nick!' He says rather bluntly.

'Yes. Now, Reg.'

'Don't tell me what to do and when to do it! We are about to raid Paul Linnette's place so back off.'

'Don't is my advice.'

'I don't take advice from you, Nick.'

'You need to this time because he's not there. Paul Linnette is currently on a ferry due to dock at Fishguard around midday with a shipment of greyhounds in tow. Apparently, on the same ferry, there are two shipments of spuds on their way to the wholesalers…Forrests. I'm not about to tell you what to do, but I think you should be there to welcome them home. Do you want me to inform Brad?' His phone suddenly goes dead. I'll take that as a no then.

Three attempts to contact Brad are met with the same response. "The number you have dialled is not available. Please try again later." At this point my personal thoughts are…sod him. Phoning James he answers immediately.

251

'James I want you to stay put. I think DI Wallace is on his way but I can't be sure. He wasn't very forthcoming but I passed on the information you gave me and he hung up on me. Don't interfere if he turns up but if he wants anything, tell him what you know. Having said that, if he chooses to stop them at customs, make him aware that he should also have people at Forrests and the Linnette's place. Have you got that?'

'I won't be interfering, that's for sure. Are you going to meet me here?'

'This is a police matter now, so there's no need for me to be there. Stay safe, James. Keep your head down and keep me up to date with any developments. In the meantime, I'm going to try and get hold of Brad.' Ending the call I put out my cigarette and go back inside. Sometimes it's nice to see the conclusion. I would like to be there but I must put Sam and Michaela first. That is how much my life is changing and truthfully, this is down to DI Wallace now and not the time to let Sam down.

Sitting back down facing Sam I place my mobile safely on the breakfast bar. No sooner have I taken my hand away my phone begins ringing again. Looking to see who the caller is, I notice the incoming call is from Richard and verbally express my feelings out loud in front of Sam and Michaela. 'What's the matter with people this morning? Don't they know its bloody Saturday?' Answering Richard's call I sarcastically respond to the intrusion. 'Richard! What can I do for you this Saturday morning?'

'Good morning to you too.' He returns. 'I'm in the office and taken a call for you from a guy by the name of Roger Butler. He asked to speak to you personally. Says he may have some information regarding Owain Parry. I have taken his number and told him you'd give him a call.'

'Sorry Richard. I'm having a bad morning. Text me his number and I'll phone him when I have a minute. Thank you.' Ending the call my mobile soon bleeps indicating I have a message. 'Bloody technology. There was a time when we couldn't wait to own our first mobile phone. Now we all have one they're an intrusion to our life. A 24/7 pain in the arse.'

'I wouldn't know.' Sam mumbles.

'Watch this space young man. For a number of reasons I actually think you should have a mobile phone.'

'Do you mean that?' He asks excitedly.

'I do. For your safety and my peace of mind more than anything. But, Sam, so you know, it will be a basic model with restricted number calling and a limited monthly outlay…to start with.'

'Can we go out this morning and get me one?'

'Sadly, as you have of heard, I have a lot to take care of this morning. Maybe we'll go and take a look after football tomorrow morning. If that's ok with you?'

'But we will go?

Wishing to continue with this conversation my mobile ringing yet again interrupts any progress. Noting its Brad I give my apologies and head outside. This could be important so I'd better take this.

'Brad?'

'Are you at home?' He asks.

'You know I am.'

'Stay there, Nick. I want to say first that you were right about DI Wallace. He is the most obstructive person I have ever had dealings with. Having said that, based on what you have told us, we have come to an arrangement. He's going to deal with the Paul Linnette side of this and as we have a man on the inside at Forrests, I'll deal with that. There is one thing I'd like you to do for me and that is to get your man away from the docks. If he's seen snooping around it could change our plans.'

'What are your plans?'

'Not sure I should divulge those but you are part of this, I will. Customs have been briefed and agreed to let both parties through unchallenged.'

'I get that. That's what I would do. Catch them in the act.'

'Exactly. Get hold of your man soon as.'

'I'll phone him straight away.' Ending the call my thoughts turn to James. He's done a good job and I'm confident he can take over my job role within the firm.

'Yes boss?' James answers.

253

'James, Brad has requested you get yourself away from there. He and DI Wallace are on the case so we'll leave them to it.'

'No problem. Have I got time to get Maddy's phone number?'

'It's your life, James, just don't involve me.'

'Are you really that anti?'

'I'll answer that once you've met her mother. Now get going.'

While I'm at it I dial the number Richard sent me. My curiosity regarding Owain Parry's murder remains a priority, so it's worth a call. My call is soon answered.

'Is that Mr Butler?' I ask.

'It is. Who's calling please?'

'Nick Thompson. I gather from one of my colleagues you may have some information for me?'

'It's possible I might have. I'm not sure it will be of use to you but I thought you should know.'

'And this information is in regards of Owain Parry?'

'It is, well I think it is.'

'Would it be convenient to meet you this morning?'

'Absolutely. Where would you prefer?'

'Where's best for you?' I prompt, sitting back down at the breakfast bar where Sam as it happens is helping himself to a second bowl of coco pops. No wonder my weekly shopping bill is horrendous.

'My partner and I are living and working in Narberth now. We're in town at the moment having a coffee in Millie's café.'

'Can you wait there for me? I'll be about half an hour.'

'No problem. See you then.'

Ending the call I turn to face Michaela. 'Millies. Isn't that where you work?'

'It is.' Michaela informs me. 'Why?'

'We're meeting someone there in half an hour. I was wondering if we'll get a staff discount.'

'You'll be lucky.'

'Is there a phone shop in Narberth?' Sam inquires, spraying his coco pops in every direction.

We're a good twenty minutes late arriving at Millies. I'd like to blame our late arrival on parking issues in town, but it was Sam's fault. He insisted on showering before we left home, which is a good discipline to have, but he then couldn't find his county football shirt to wear. He eventually found that in the lining basket. Just as well it wasn't dirty or muddy. I understand his passion to wear a rivals' football shirt in town but it does bring into question his sincerity over not wanting to play football at a higher level in the future.

The café is busy. With Sam and Michaela in tow they follow me inside. Pausing to close the door I take a good look around. Close to the servery I see two gentlemen sat facing us, one of whom gestures to me to join them. I immediately take that as being Mr Butler and head in their direction. As I weave my way through the café I glance over to see where Michaela is. She has made her way to the counter and already deep in conversation with an older lady.

'Mr Butler?' I ask.

'I am. Please call me Roger.' He responds and stands offering his hand. Shaking hands Roger introduces the man sat with him. 'This is my partner Will. Oh, my, gosh!' He continues, looking in Sam's direction. 'You must be, Sam. We've heard and read a lot about you. It's a pleasure to meet you. Please, take a seat and join us.'

Making sure Sam is ok and seated I park myself down next to him. First thing I do is hand Sam a menu. He's bound to be hungry, despite eating us out of house and home.

'I apologise for being late. We had a small domestic issue to overcome.'

'Nothing serious I hope?' Roger enquires.

'I couldn't find my county football shirt. Dad said it didn't matter but I wanted to wear it this morning because we beat Narberth six nil last week and I scored three goals.'

'The young lady who came in with you, do you know her.' Roger asks.

'We do. That's Michaela. She's staying with us at the moment.'

'She works here…doesn't she?'

'Long story, but yes she does work here. Michaela is Austrian and here on an educational and vocational exchange trip. The hostel the students were due to stay at had a serious kitchen fire and I was approached to help them out. As I had a spare room I said I would. It's only until the end of the month and she's no problem.'

'Sounds like you've got your hands full.' Will offers.

'Dad does too much.' Sam decides to tell them. 'We're always driving around doing something or the other. We went to Bristol yesterday.'

'I don't think we should be discussing that, Sam?' I add, staring at him.

'No,' he says quietly. 'I forgot.'

'People will know soon enough but until then, for many, many reasons, as you well know, what happened yesterday is only for us to know.'

'Sorry, Dad.'

'Its ok, Sam. Just remember that. I imagine you guys are probably curious but for legal reasons I cannot discuss Sam's business in public. Nor should Sam. I will say to you though, it's far from being over and Sam has some difficult days ahead of him. The least we say now, the better it will be for Sam in the long term.'

'We do understand…don't we Will?'

'We certainly do.'

'May I say,' Roger continues. 'It lovely to hear Sam calling you Dad. I sense you have a good understanding.'

'We're getting there, Sam, aren't we?'

'Dad's good to me. He's giving me a second chance and I love him for that. In a minute he's going to buy me a bacon sandwich and a cup of tea.'

'What a good idea.' I respond.

Asking Roger and Will if they'd like something I send Sam off to ask Michaela if she wants anything and could she order for us. While Sam is otherwise occupied I get down to business. Roger quickly replies to my first question.

'Will does hair dressing part time and one of his regular customers is Beca. Sorry, Beca Parry, Owain's mother.'

'While I was cutting her hair on Thursday,' Will continues. 'Beca told me you paid her a visit recently and asked her about Owain's murder. She told me she found it very difficult talking about that awful day because what happened then has changed their lives forever and who ever committed the crime, is still out their walking our streets. Beca is worried by the fact you haven't got back to her, like you promised, and she would like to know if you have any news.'

'Moving on,' Roger butts in. 'The noise we had to tolerate from the youths riding their mopeds and motor bikes in the woods near where we lived nearly every night was bad enough, but Owain being stabbed close to our house was the tipping point. That was scary and we felt unsafe in our own home, so we decided to move. We live here in Narberth now because of Owain's death.'

'We have two small dogs and often walked them past the place where Owain's body was found. When Will told me about you visiting Beca it triggered a long conversation between us. We went out on the evening Owain was murdered to meet friends in The Royal Oak. The odd thing about that evening, was the lack of noise. Most nights the youths are in the woods racing their bikes until all hours. It was deathly silent that evening. Gosh! That wasn't the correct terminology. I apologise. Anyway, when we arrived home that evening there were blue flashing lights everywhere. Probably as many as three of four police cars blocking the road ahead of us, so we knew something serious had happened. We didn't know what until the following morning when it was all over the local news.

'Will and me were off the following day so we took the dogs out in the morning and decided to take a look at where the youths were riding their motor bikes. Don't know why but I decided to take my camera with me. I think I wanted to record the damage and destruction the yobs had caused so I could report it to the council. While we were there I took this.'

Taking a digital camera out of his shoulder bag, Roger turns it on, scrolls through his pictures and shows me a photograph of an old, beaten up moped which has a damaged front wheel.

'It didn't have any number plates so I found the chassis number and took this picture,' Roger continues. 'It could, I hope, help you with your enquiries. We think one of those youths might know what happened.'

'It's possible. I'll grab a pen and piece of paper and right it down. I know someone who might be able to trace the number for me.'

'Already done.' Roger says, handing me a slip of paper. Taking it I place it on the table in front of me and pull my mobile out of my pocket and speed dial James.

'It's alright, Boss. I'm out of there and nearly back at the office.' James answers.

'I never doubted you, James. I need you to do me a favour though. Does your friend at the DVLA work on Saturdays?'

'Sometimes. I can check for you. Why?'

'I want a chassis number from a moped traced. If that is possible. I want to know who the last registered owner is.'

'Text me the complete number and I'll call him. Anything else you need while I'm out?'

'Not that I can think of but stay by your phone and let me know ASAP.'

'Will do.'

Sam sits down next to me as I'm typing in the chassis number and sending it over to James. He places the cafe bill in front of me and asks what I'm doing.

'This is important, Sam. You know that.'

258

'So is buying me a phone.' Is his reply. His reaction is rather frustrating. I know he wants this phone and I have made that promise to him, but he must learn to be patient. I choose not to respond. I feel sure he's playing up in front of Roger and Will to gain maximum affect.

Another round of teas and coffees, coupled with a jumble of idle chat, Sam isn't the only one becoming fidgety. It has been half an hour since I phoned James. They say no news is good news but if I don't hear from him soon it might be too late. If he doesn't return my call, what I do next is up for debate, and difficult with Sam and Michaela in tow. Informing Roger and Will we're off I bid them farewell. Back out in the street I'm agitated by the situation. Heading in the direction of where I parked the car, Sam and Michaela walk on ahead of me. Sam though is very quiet. My understanding of his moods tells me his silence is because he's annoyed or upset with me. On occasions, his silence is pure tiredness as a result of nightmares and lack of sleep but today, I fancy it's this phone business.

Today it's not particularly warm and the threatening clouds above suggest rain is expected so reaching the car before the heavens open, is a welcome relief. Before setting off I attempt to call James but his mobile is engaged. It's possible he could be phoning me. I hope that is the case. Sam takes exception to the delay. Sat directly behind me, he begins pushing his feet into the back of my seat. Enduring this for as long as I can I snap at him, demanding he sits with me in the front. Without a word he does as I ask to avoid a more severe telling off. While he belts himself in my mobile rings. It's James.

'What have you got for me, James?'

'We're in luck. My mate, Buddy, is working today. It's a blue and white Honda 50. Last registered owner was Owain Parry.'

'When was that?'

'Registered to him in April 2000. I have the plate number too. Is that helpful?'

'Yes. Text it to me please, James.'

'Straight away, Boss. Is it who you expected it to be?'

'No. I'm going to go via the Parry's place on the way back to the office. Stay put, James, I may need your help.'

Pulling up outside the Parry residence I tell Sam and Michaela to stay put. No arguments. Conducting a couple of sharp raps on the front door Mr Parry cautiously opens the door and peers through the gap at me.

'Mr Parry? Is your wife at home?

'Who wants to know?'

'Nick Thompson.'

'Just a minute.' He informs me, disappearing, leaving me standing on the doorstep. When she finally comes to the door she has a look of worry about her.

'Mrs Parry? I'll be as brief as I can. Did Owain own a Honda 50?

'He had a blue and white one. Why?'

'Have you still got the Honda?'

'No. Owain sold it about eighteen months ago to one of his mates to help fund his driving lessons.'

'Does this mate of his have a name?'

'Owain never said. I'm sorry.'

'I'm going to ask you one more time, Mrs Parry. Was Owain in debt, and I mean to anyone other than the bank or financial institution?'

'No! Certainly not. I have already told you that. As far as we're concerned he took great care of his money.'

'So if I told you I know he was buying drugs for his girlfriend Ellie and her heroin addict brother, what would you say?'

'You're lying. That's what I'd say. Mother's instinct, Mr Thompson.'

'Well I'm not. Logically, that's why the police found traces of heroin in Owain's jacket pocket. Ok, Mrs Parry. You know I'll find out the truth so if you change your mind, you know where to find me.'

It's nearly 12-30 when we arrive back at the office. I have decided, if James is in agreement, to leave Sam and Michaela in his care. I'll bung him a few quid to buy them lunch to keep him sweet. I need to be at the Linnette's place when DI Wallace starts his investigation, and if I'm right, makes arrests.

Entering the reception area I'm confronted by James sat talking to a young man I have never seen before. Not wishing to involve Sam or Michaela I send them upstairs to wait my office. I think the tone of my voice suggests I'm not messing around. Once they disappear I look questioningly at James and wait for him to explain.

'This is, Kai, Nick. He has something to tell you I think you'll want to hear.' Sitting down next to Kai I ask him if he has a surname. He refuses to tell me. Accepting his reluctance, for whatever his reason, I continue by asking him why he's here.

'You've gotta promise me you won't tell anyone?' He mumbles.

'I sort of understand your reason, Kai, but you know if it's serious I'm obliged by law to do so. If that is because you are worried about your personal safety, then I will be discrete. Do you understand that?' Kai is hesitant. I sense he's very uncomfortable sat here with myself and James. 'Take your time, Kai.'

'I was there the night Owain was stabbed. I didn't see it happen, but I know who did it.'

'Sebastion?'

'No. It wasn't Seb. It was seb's grandfather.'

Sitting back, taking in his confession, I reply. 'Are you sure it was his grandfather, Alf Roberts?'

'Definitely. I was with Seb when he appeared in the woods screaming at everyone to get out of there. He had a fucking knife in his hand. He told all of us to say we hadn't seen him and if anyone asked, we weren't there either.'

To say the least I'm a little surprised by Kai's confession, but not shocked. Owain knew and worked with Alf and according to Mrs Parry, there was bad blood between them. Just maybe, Alf knew Owain was about to spill the beans and had to silence him. Possibly too, Alf could have set fire to the

261

hostel in an effort to destroy any evidence. Not that DI Wallace has found any evidence to back that up.

'Ok, Kai. I can see why you're worried. They are dangerous people to know. Is there somewhere you can go while we sort this out?'

'I could fly out to my dad's place in Spain but I haven't the cash to buy a ticket.'

'I'm thinking more over the next 24 – 48 hours.'

'I'll live rough if need be.'

'No young man. Like it or not you are a key witness and you may in the near future be required to give evidence in court. I need to keep you safe. Are you ok with that?' Kai nods his head in response. 'James, take Kai home to collect his stuff and I'll meet you back here in a couple of hours. Get him something to eat while I'm gone. Is that alright with you, Kai?'

'I think so.'

'You'll be fine. I have a place in mind where you'll be safe, so please don't worry. One last thing, Kai, why now? Why have you waited until now to come forward with this information?'

'Ellie told me you'd been asking questions about Owain.'

'Ellie Simpson?'

'Yes. I didn't tell her what I know but I knew you'd find out sooner or later. I don't want to get into trouble, Mr Thompson, so I came to see you.'

'Make you feel better does it?'

'Not really. Scared about what might happen next if anything.'

'Ok. Get Kai organised, James, and out of sight until I get back.'

Chapter Thirteen

Later

Ellie Simpson can wait. I feel sure that between her and Kai, they know what really happened that fateful day and who took the Honda 50 from Owain. After dropping Sam and Michaela at Tom and mothers, who promised to feed them, I drove at speed over to the Linnette's place. Taking a detour via Forrests, slowing right down as a pass, Brad appears to have things under control. Then he's always been a control freak. The two lorry loads of potatoes have been impounded and sit away from the main warehouse. I hope my hunch is right. There has got to be tons and tons of potatoes to sift through and that very exercise will be an extremely time consuming.

The Linnette's place is awash with police vehicles. Forensics, dog handlers, four meat wagons, numerous patrol cars and several unmarked cars. This has definitely stretched their resources. Reassuring never the less, even more so when I spot Paul Linnette's converted lorry sitting on the driveway at the edge of their property.

Finding a space to park some quarter of a mile away along the road I hurriedly make my way back to the house where I'm confronted by two police officers. This provokes an action I have not yet had the pleasure of doing. Waving my MI5 Id under their noses they reluctantly allow me to proceed. I can imagine these provincial forces don't come across one of those Id's very often and probably unsure what the correct procedure is. But I'm in and where I need to be. As I amble up the driveway little appears to be happening and little or no order to what is occurring. Ahead of me I see a familiar face. DS Thomas who clocks me roughly at the same time as I he. He's appears to be surprised by my being here and strides purposefully towards me. This could be twice in one day I think while I fish my Id out of my pocket again.

'This is a crime scene, Thompson. What are you doing here?'

'Working.' I answer, flashing my Id in front of his eyes. 'Is DI Wallace here?'

'Yes, sir. Please follow me.' Now that is satisfying.

Following in his footsteps, in the direction of a large open fronted barn housing industrial machinery, my sight is drawn to the contents. This is an ideal

263

place to store a Honda 50, so I deviate and decide to take a look inside. It doesn't take me long to spot what appears to be a motor bike, tucked away behind a small tractor and covered by a tarpaulin. Lifting the tarpaulin gently up a blue and white Honda 50 reveals itself. Bingo! The damaged to the front wheel is a dead giveaway. As I start looking for the chassis number plate, DS Thomas has crept up on me.

'I hope you're not tampering with vital evidence?' He suggests.

'I'm not. What I am doing for you is, your job.'

'I doubt that. I'm told you do everything for your own benefit. Not on my watch, Sir.'

'That won't be for too long.'

'What won't?'

'Your watch. Now give me a hand to pull this heap of shit out into the daylight.' Before I have the chance to grab the bike DS Thomas stops me and hands me a pair of blue latex gloves.

'We can't be too careful. I was only joking with you, Nick.'

'Not your first mistake, DS Thomas.'

It's a bit of a struggle but once out in the daylight I locate the chassis number plate, wipe the crap off the surface and check the number with the one Roger wrote down for me. As I expected, it is a perfect match.

'This Honda 50 puts Sebastion Linnette at the scene the night Owain Parry was murdered.'

'Are you certain of that?'

'I need to talk to him.'

'Not sure we can let you do that.'

'Yes he can.' DI Wallace adds, joining us. 'We've got him locked up in the back of one of the meat wagons.'

'On his own I hope.'

'We're not stupid, Nick. We have kept them well separated so they can't collaborate their stories.'

'Where are the Dogs?' I enquire.

'Still in the van. We're checking over the kennels first while we wait for the vet to arrive. He's going to administer something to make them shit and wait to see what surprises we have.'

'I won't wait with him.'

'Nor me. That's what we pay him for. Before I take you down there, what do you plan to say to Sebastion?'

'Why don't we see if he's in a talkative mood?'

'As a matter of interest, why are you looking at the moped?'

'On good information received, it places Sebastion at the scene the night Owain Parry was stabbed.'

'How do you know that?'

'Why don't we go and talk to him?'

Delayed in my wish to talk to Sebastion by the vet arriving and being given quite specific instructions by DI Wallace on what he wants, I find myself waiting at the back of the meat wagon alone. When Reg appears from around the front of the vehicle with a colleague, who opens the rear doors, I pause for a moment before saying anything.

'Sebastion. We meet at last.'

'Who the fuck are you. Piss off will you.' He says in a raised voice. 'Friend or foe. Your choice.'

'You're no friend of mine, so fuck off and leave me alone.'

'Fine. As long as I make you aware before I go that you are going to be charged with the murder of Owain Parry, its cool with me.'

'I have no idea what you're talking about. I was nowhere near the place.'

265

'Your moped says differently and I do have photographic evidence to prove it.'

'Have you fuck?'

'For your information, yes I have. Did Owain owe you money?'

'No!'

'So he wasn't buying heroin from you that night? Did he get into debt with you?'

'Don't know what you're talking about. Never met anyone called Owain.'

'I beg to differ because I know otherwise. The Honda 50 we've just found in your barn was registered to Owain, so how come you have the moped?'

Reg pulls me to one side to have a quiet word in my ear. 'Are you making this up because if you are, you're fucking up my investigation?'

'Let me continue, Reg. You'll see.' Turning back to face Sebastion, I continue. 'DI Wallace, I'd like you to charge Sebastion Linnette with the murder of Owain Parry.'

Again he pulls me away. This time with intent. 'You don't have any proof. Stop this.'

'Haven't I? I have a witness under my protection who knows who stabbed Owain Parry that night.'

'Who?'

'I need to hear it from the horse's mouth.'

'Sebastion Linnette. I'm arresting you for the murder of Owain Parry. You don't have to say anything…'

'I didn't do it! Please believe me?' Seb shouts in a desperate tone.

'Then who did?' I ask.

'Alf.'

'Alf who?' I question.

'Alf Roberts.'

'Your grandfather.'

'Yes.'

'Why, Sebastion?'

'Because Owain was going to drop Alf in the shit.'

'Was that because Owain knew what Alf was delivering while out on the rounds with him?'

'Yes.'

'How do you live with yourself, Sebastion? Knowing your grandfather is a murderer? Satisfied, Reg?' I ask, walking away. 'I'm done with Sebastion for now. You my friend need to find Alf Roberts.'

'We know where he is but the Spanish police couldn't arrest him. We had no solid evidence to give them. They are watching him so I'll get some of our guys to go and pick him up. I was going to tell you this before but I've been busy. We found traces of cocaine at the hostel two days ago in the remains of a walk in fridge. We suspect David Griffiths was hiding the stuff for him and it's possible they fell out. I'm on it, Nick.'

'You bastard! Thanks for letting me know…Constable Wallace.'

'Fuck off. Nick.'

'I will if you wish. Just remember what you've said when I speak to Superintendent Lewis and justify my bill.'

'Not now, Nick.'

'Don't ever say that to me again. In fact, as I am retiring you won't have the pleasure.'

As he storms off, for some unknown reason, I decide to take a look at what the vet is up too. Not that I really want to, but the results of his endeavours could have serious ramifications for one young man.'

'How long does this take?' I ask the vet.

'Who are you sir?'

'Nick Thompson…MI5.' I respond, holding my ID card out in front of him. A bloody hat trick in one day. I may have second thoughts about retiring, now they all know.

'About half an hour, sir.'

Needing a coffee I make my out to the road where they have parked a mobile canteen. Someone shouting for DS Thomas draws my attention. The shouting is coming from the converted lorry Paul Linnette brought the greyhounds over in from Ireland. I'm standing at the back doors looking inside before DS Thomas gets there. At the back of one of the dog gages a police officer has pulled the rear panel off and neatly stacked inside, are a number of clear bags full of a white powder. Cocaine or heroin I'd guess.

'Out of here, Thompson!' DS Thomas growls. 'MI5 or not, this is my bag.' Pushing me aside he clambers inside and screams for forensics before anyone touches the bags. His mannerism appals me. Another DI Wallace in the making. Yes they have a job to do, but I feel sorry for the officer who made the discovery. He won't receive any credit for his diligence. From my experience, it's always going to be, look what I found from DS Thomas. I'm no expert but I reckon there is anything between 5 and 10 kgs of drugs stashed in that compartment. I have no idea what the street value is but once cut, that's a lot of hits. I've seen and heard enough to know my call was right…with James's help of course. To complete a successful day and make me happy, is knowing my theory over the dogs correct. If I am right, it could explain Hanna Green's and David Griffiths untimely deaths. I will wait for the dogs to do their business, but I do need a coffee now.

Standing in the middle of the road, sipping at a cup of something they described as coffee and drawing on a cigarette, I watch with interest the unfolding investigation. Suddenly I hear an urgent call over their personal radios of officer down. Just about everyone I can see reacts to the call. Running in the direction of the dog track I drop my hot drink and follow. I am cautious. I have no desire to become the next man down, so I remain a safe distance behind the charge. Once beyond the race track I come across officers restraining a number of men. It's quite a scuffle but my real attention is drawn to a building beyond the melee. Desperate to know for sure I slow down to a gentle pace and

take a wide berth. My initial thoughts tell me they may have found a cannabis farm. The closer I get to the building, the more distinct the smell becomes. Its cannabis alright. No doubt. This has become a good day for me and decide to leave them to it.

The vet is a very patient man, then on his hourly rate I don't blame him. Looking in, no news is good news…so they say and continue down to the road for a coffee. Maybe I should take a look in the Linnette's kitchen on the way past for a more decent brand of coffee granules. I hope I'm right where the dogs are concerned because I'll claim for James's hours on my bill. If he's lucky, he might be paid enough to buy Maddy a coffee sometime. Passing Pauls van and with the greyhounds safely kennelled, the officer are ripping the vehicle apart. Shame, then he won't be needing it for some time to come. Without a doubt, I have an air of pride in myself for doing a good job. That thought leads me into hoping Brad and his crew are also having a good day. That would be the icing on the cake. If today does prove to be my swan song, there is one downside to my involvement. I have let both Sam and Michaela down. They both said they didn't mind, but I can't stop feeling guilty for leaving them at the farm with Tom and Mother. Particularly Sam. He is going through a tough time and his unprovoked comments earlier are probably because his needs are greater than mine. I accept that and know I should be there supporting him.

The moment I see the vet go into business mode, I'm there, waiting and watching. It's vile. Some poor bastard will have to clean that shit up, and sift through it for evidence. That evidence though is clear to see. I count three, no four durex shaped bags excreted from the first dog to react. One of which has split in the process. I need to find DI Wallace and leave the vet to do his job. He needs to see what I have witnessed, proof really of my first thoughts. DI Wallace proves difficult to find. Far too much going on, even for a clever mind like his. Close to where the cannabis was found I hear him before I see him. He's an angry man, that's for sure. Probably frustrated more than angry, barking out his orders to those poor souls trying to make sense of all this in the confusion.

'Not now, Nick. Can't you see I'm busy?' Clutching my ID card I reply.

'Follow me.' I add sternly.

'What is it now?'

'The dogs have produced and you need to see this.'

'I'll be ten minutes.' He informs his sergeant. 'This had better be good.'

'Oh, it will be.'

Reg is unusually quiet. Standing with him looking at the mess the dogs have made, the stench becomes overwhelming.

'Heroin I'd guess.' The vet offers, though it's difficult to understand him while he's wearing a filtered mask. 'This one here,' he continues, pointing at the split bag. 'Would cause serious issues to anyone who ingested it.'

'In what way?' Reg asks.

'I won't go into all the details or try to pronounce the scientific names, but certain dog fluids can be highly poisonous to someone who has ingested or come into contact with the contaminated drug.'

'Why would you want too?'

'If you were desperate for a fix, would you know or care?' I suggest. 'Dealers don't care. That bag is worth maybe a grand to them. They aren't going to throw it away. I think, Reg, you need to arrest Sebastion Linnette for knowingly dealing contaminated drugs to Hanna Green and David Griffiths because that is how they died.' Before he walks away, his look says it all.

In a strange way, walking away from a job I've enjoyed doing over the past thirty years will in no doubt leave a big hole in my life. Parking my car at the front of my farmhouse, seeing Sam and Michaela crossing the yard, surveying the dilapidated farm buildings, a new era of surprise and hard work is just beginning. Hopefully the project will keep me busy.

They are unaware of my arrival, so I sit and watch them for a few moments. There are a few years between them, but they appear comfortable in each other's company. There is a possibility Sam sees her as a mother figure. Heaven knows, his own mother wasn't a good role model.

'Hi guys.' I shout, as they head back towards the farmhouse. Sam reacts immediately, running across the yard to greet me.

'I've had some good ideas about what we can do.' He tells me, coming to a stop in front of me. 'There's a strange man in the kitchen talking to Tom and mother. James dropped him off a while ago.'

Shit I think. In the midst of everything I had forgotten about Kia. Why James saw fit to drop him off without telling me I don't know. I have some explaining to do. Following Sam into the kitchen, Kia is sat on one of the dining table chairs by the fire next to Tom, smoking a role up.

'Well, well, well. Look who it is? I thought you had retired, boy?' Tom growls.

'I can explain.'

'Is this another one of your long lost offspring?'

'Leave him alone, Tom.' Mother says, coming to my rescue.

'Nick should know me by now, and know that isn't going to happen?'
'That's enough, Tom. You're only sat there now through Nick's generosity.'

'It's fine. I should and do need to explain myself. Kia needs our help for a few days. He's not in trouble, but Kia needs to keep his head down and stay away from trouble until things settle down. I thought he could use my room until this blows over.'

'We understand.' Mother tells me. 'You are staying for diner…aren't you? Its nearly ready.'

'Sure, but I need to talk to Kia in private first.' Kia follows me outside into the yard where I light a smoke before speaking. 'I can't say too much at this stage, other than say we've had a successful day. What I need to from you is, where do we go from here? By that I mean, is there anything you should tell me like, who else is involved? Who else do we need to know about? Is there anyone else involved you're frightened of who is involved with the Linnette's? I can't help you if you refuse to tell me and you only have a couple of days to come clean. Then you are on your own. Think seriously about what I'm saying here for your own sake. We all know here that someone else will quickly step into the Linnette's shoes, selling drugs on our streets. So now is a good time to speak up and put these people away before that happens. If you need time to think it over, Tom or mother have my number. For the sake of my adopted son, Sam, I have lots to do for him tomorrow, so contact me early on Monday. I will put things right with Tom and Mother and as I own this farm, they will do as I ask. Don't let me down, Kia. Are you alright with this arrangement?'

'I don't know what to say. I'm finding it difficult to take this all in'.

'Don't say anything right now. Give yourself a little time. In the meantime, shall we go and eat?'

Chapter Fourteen

Sunday 14th September

We're late, which doesn't explain why the car park is so busy this morning. Sam's game is at home against one of the less fancied and least known teams and my BMW isn't so conspicuous alongside numerous 4x4's and other top of the range cars. Something is going on which might explain Sam's sudden change of mood. The fact he doesn't question it speaks volumes. Leaving him the car keys and insisting he locks the doors from the inside, I storm off to find the answers.

Surrounded by a group of men, eight or nine I'd guess, wearing their club jackets, Matt Wilson isn't difficult find. Without uttering a single word I grab Matt by the arm and drag him to one side.

'What did I say to you?' I shout at Matt. 'It's clear to see who they are and I told you what I would do if this happened.'

'Believe me, Nick. I have no idea how this got out. I will find out, trust me.'

'Bit late for that…don't you think? Tell them all to take a hike otherwise Sam is out of here and you won't see him again. We can't make them leave but if Sam wants to play, they will not speak to him, or me. Is that clear?'

'I think this may have something to do with Sam's registration. If I'm right, it's clear they rate him.'

'For your information, Sam isn't interested. He wants to play football but not on their terms. He may change his mind at some point but he's told me he doesn't want to become a professional player and he's nowhere near ready to commit the rest of his childhood to playing football. I cannot go into details for legal reasons, but he's missed a lot of that already in his short life. What Sam needs is trust and understanding. I hope you understand that?'

'I do understand. It is his choice. Sam is a rare talent, Nick. If he isn't ready, he isn't, but the older he gets, the less chance he has of making the top grade.'

'Just tell them what I've told you and I mean it, or there will be consequences.'

Walking away I know I'm being watched. What Sam wants is the priority here and in my anger I have left him alone in the car. On reflection, not sure that was such a good idea, so I hurry my way back to the car. If he's seen what is going on he could be in a terrible state. I can't see him as I reach the car and knock gently on the driver's side window. Seeing his head pop up from the back seat behind the driving seat, he has tucked himself down in the well out of sight. He quickly clambers into the front, presses the door unlock button on the dash and opens the door to get out. I believe this is my fault and I feel very guilty for leaving him but it's fair to say, he is the talented commodity here…not me.

'That car.' Sam utters as he points at a red range rover. 'It belongs to the youth team scout for Bristol City. He's ok, but I don't want to go back there.'

'Sam, I've had words with Matt and in no uncertain terms, I've told him what I thought. Would you like to go and buy a phone, instead of playing this morning?'

'No! I want to play.'

'Are you sure? There are at least eight men there waiting to watch you play.'

'Why should they tell me what to do? I want to play football here. Not where they think is best for me.'

'That's some answer young man and you're right. It is your choice, not theirs. I told Matt to tell them to sling their hooks and if they stay, they are not to talk to you or me under any circumstances…at any time. If you think you can deal with them watching and you're sure you want to play, let's get a move on. I ask one thing of you, be yourself. Enjoy your game and do what comes naturally you. By all means play to impress, but don't overdo it. I want you to be successful, confident in life. That doesn't necessarily have to be on the football pitch. Remember what you said to me earlier regarding the farm. If you have it in you, Sam, you have the ability to make a success of your life in anything you turn you hand to.'

274

Sam looks straight at me. He's clearly taking on board what I have said to him. Right now I have no wish to stop him doing the things he wants to do and when he makes those decisions, I will be right beside him. When he picks up his football bag from inside the car, the message becomes very clear. Sam has made his own mind up.

Without being accused of being disrespectful, the game was so one sided it was embarrassing. Sam, Liam and Brodie are slowly forming a partnership in mid-field. The opposition barely got out of their own half throughout the game. The trio were, in my opinion, outstanding. The final score of eleven nil to Sam's team really didn't do them the justice to the way they played. With so many uncoordinated players behind the ball, crowding them out, made playing the beautiful game difficult at times. Finding space, was the one negative. One thing I noticed as the game progressed and dependant on the area of play, was how one of the three lads sat a little deeper. With time and space to work with, some terrific balls were played forward and opportunities to score came thick and fast. I am biased but Sam saw that first and Liam and Brodie soon caught on. They were superb. Sam only scored once from a free kick on the edge of the box. How he knocked the ball up and over the five man wall into the top of the goal is for him to explain. I'm sure he'll try.

We don't dwell after the game. It's time to buy Sam a mobile phone and get home before Jack does. He does have a key for the front door but I'd like to be there when he returns. Before we left I made time to shake Liam's and Brodie's hands for a job well done this morning, which they appreciated.

Sam is now the proud owner of a Nokia 3310. To say he's pleased is an understatement. He has his own number but he's on my contract and I have limited his usage to twenty pound a month…to start with. While we were in Haverfordwest I checked in with Michaela, who is working, to make sure she was ok for lift home. Making sure she was, Sam and I headed for home.

Jack isn't home, which is a relief. I felt I should be at home when he arrived back from his weekend away with Lucy and her parents. Preoccupied with his new phone, Sam dumps his kit bag at the bottom of the stairs and disappears off up to his room with the phone in his hand. That should keep him quiet for a while.

I'm gasping for a coffee. Making my way to the kitchen I switch on the kettle and sit on a breakfast stool waiting for it to boil. I find myself reliving and reflecting over the past 48 hours. It's been tough. From witnessing Sam going through hell, and he did, to worrying that my hunches were right, the last two days have been traumatic and draining. My moments of deep thought are disturbed when I hear the front door open. Out of my seat in the blink of an eye, expecting to see Jack, I'm confronted by a very tired looking Brad. Tucked under his arm is what looks to be a brown A4 envelope. Not another one crosses my mind.

'Make me a coffee, Nick,' he asks. 'It has been a long night.' Walking past me into the kitchen he keeps the envelope to himself. Hopefully it's not from Henry Sinclair. That would be a relief.

'How did you get on yesterday?' I enquire, getting out another coffee mug.

'Over six hours, Nick, to unload two lorries. As we unloaded each pallet we set the sniffer dogs to work and came up with absolutely nothing. Not a single positive Id.'

'We can't all have been wrong?'

'You weren't at the Linnettes. From what I've heard over the grapevine, it's been a huge success. We knew something was amiss so we started to look deeper. Like you, because of what took place at the hostel and what DI Wallace has subsequently discovered there, we picked our way through every single bag. In desperation we cut open each bag and set the dogs to work again. Still nothing. As you can imagine, it was frustrating and we began to think we'd been set up. Then, as luck would have it, one of our operatives noticed a minute difference in the package markings on some of the bags. In the word potatoes on these bags, the horizontal line of the capital "A" was incomplete. At a glance it looked like a printing error and honestly, to a naked eye and you weren't looking for something different, you wouldn't have given it a second thought. We concentrated on these particular bags and although the dogs didn't pick anything up, we found this.' Watching him open the brown envelope and pull out a clear, sealed evidence bag, Brad sets it down in front of me. 'Looks real enough, doesn't it? However, watch this. So you know, this has been logged, forensically tested and I have been given permission to show you.' Taking the potato out of the clear evidence bag, with some effort, Brad separates the look alike into two halves by twisting it apart. It's hollow inside. Although there is nothing to see, it is clear as to what the intention is. 'Clever, hey? We have found in excess of fifty of these beauties so far and still counting. Each one of these contains a half a Kilo of

Heroin. The seal on this is well engineered and once washed and mixed with the real macoy, very difficult to detect…even for the sniffer dogs. I have never seen anything quite like this, Nick. These guys are smart which keeps them one step ahead of us. We must make ourselves smarter, be one step ahead of them at ground level to stop this.'

Brad didn't stay long. He drank his coffee while we had a quick smoke outside on the patio. He has a lot of work to do to put this case to bed…so does DI Wallace. I won't miss helping them. Before he left he shook my hand, said thank you and wished me luck for the future. His meaningful words came across as a goodbye. We will meet again because we have business to finalise…the mansion. My view is to sell the place, or make me a good offer. Its size lends itself to becoming a plush hotel for a large holiday company to convert. I'm certainly not of the mind to be involved at any level in the future. The reality of Brad's words, for some reason, hit home. Being involved in something, anything thing for a protracted length of time is difficult to turn your back on, but I must and move on. I still have my own business to worry about and my intention is to remain involved, in an advisory capacity…as and when I choose. Top of my list to do, as it stands, is to talk Jack out of getting married. Sam may not like that because he wants to be a page boy, but in my own mind they are way too young. I do understand their reasoning. They have a baby on the way and on the surface, marriage appears to be the correct direction for them to follow for the child's sake, but is it really at their age?

When Jack finally arrives home I'm not so quick to react. Hands up, I had fallen asleep on the sofa in front of the TV. I have vague recollections of Sam talking to me at some point but otherwise I was dead to the world. Now I'm not a prude but stepping into the hallway and seeing Jack saying goodbye to Lucy in a romantic fashion, I look away. I don't look again until I hear him say, "see you tomorrow" and close the front door.

'I expected you home earlier.' I manage to say, hoping not to appear too embarrassed.

'Lucy's dad wanted to drive home via the Brecon Beacons. We stopped a few times so he could take in the views.' He informs me, parking his holdall alongside Sam's at the bottom of the stairs. 'Actually, Dad, the views were spectacular.'

277

'So you've had a good time? Come here'. I add, holding out my arms. 'Give me a hug.' As we hug I speak again. 'It's good to have you home.'

'It was nice to get away somewhere different but it's good to be home, Dad.' He responds. 'What's for dinner?' He then adds. I haven't given dinner a single thought and neither Jan nor Michaela are here to help us out.

'I'll get us a takeaway.'

'On a Sunday!'

'Fish and chips then from the chippy down near the harbour.'

Following Jack through the lounge to the kitchen I watch as he automatically heads for the refrigerator and helps himself to a can of coke.

'So? How was your weekend?' I enquire.

'It was great, Dad. I had a really lovely time. Lucy's parents were fantastic and good fun. Before you ask, me and Lucy had separate rooms. So you needn't have worried. I didn't fully understand how the betting worked on the greyhound racing. Lucy's dad did try to explain how the system worked and what to look for but it went straight over my head. When I chose a dog, I closed my eyes and stabbed the page with my finger.'

'I do hope you weren't betting. You're not old enough.'

'Lucy's mum placed the bets for me. It's far more exciting when you have money on a dog, screaming out at the top of your voice for it to run faster. We had a great night.'

'I'm pleased for you, Jack. It's probably done you the world of good.'

'Do you know something? I doubt they would have invited me had it not been for you.'

'What do you mean, Jack?'

'Lucy's parents would not invited the so called son of Tony Morris away for the weekend. I know what Tony is and they wouldn't have trusted me either. I want to thank you Dad for never giving up on me, and what you are doing for me. I have never experienced anything as good as that and I was never likely too, living with that man. It means a lot to me.'

278

'Thank you for saying that, Jack. It means a lot to me too. Seeing you happy, enjoying life, in a steady job means everything to me. By not telling us the truth your mother put us through hell but we're past that now and we both know that by working things out together, we can and will make it work.'

'What did happen between you and mum?'

'That's for another time, Jack.'

'Changing the subject before we get too emotional, how did you get on while I was away? You know, with Linnettes and Owain Parry.'

'It's still ongoing but very successful so far…so I'm told. Everything went to plan and several arrests were made. Because of that I have stepped away from all that shit, Jack. Finished with it.'

'Completely?'

'Well, I will stay involved with my business. Purely form a management point of view, but that's it. I'm done, Jack, that's a promise.'

'You've earned the right Dad, but no going back on your word.'

'I'm sure you'll remind me of that.'

'Where's Sam?'

'He's up in his room playing with his new phone. I took him into Haverfordwest after football and bought him a Nokia 3310. I thought it was time he should have one and seeing as you have a company phone, it seemed the right thing to do.'

'I totally agree. Now we can both keep an eye on him…for his own safety that is. Are you going to celebrate your retirement?'

'Funny you should ask me that. I have pondered over the idea of doing something but what, and who to invite. Do I keep it personal, like close friends and family, or do I invite every Tom, Dick and Harry along?'

'You've got me there, Dad. Depending on what you decide you would like to do, it could cost you an absolute fortune to invite everyone you know.'

'True enough, but where do I draw the line, Jack?'

'Your retirement party, Dad, do what you think is best for you.'

Monday 15th September

With Jack back at work and Sam safely dropped off at school I have one thing left to sort out. Arriving at the farm unannounced, Kia is standing outside the yard door smoking. Probably a bit of weed. On Saturday when we spoke at the office I could smell it on him. It's his choice, so I won't say anything and as I approach, he makes no effort to hide the fact.

'Morning, Kai.' My words make him jump. He's either out of it or miles away in thought. I'll give him the benefit of doubt. 'We need to get you sorted out.'

'I'm going to stay at a mates in Swansea.'

'Is that a safe environment for you to be in?'

'Yeah.'

'How are you getting there? Is your mate picking you up?'

'No. He's banned from driving at the moment.'

'How do you plan to get there?'

'Hitch.'

'I'm not sure that's such a good idea. If you give me your mates address and your mobile number. I'll make you a deal.'

'What sort of deal?'

'Address and phone number first, and a guaranty you'll stay put in Swansea. Like it or not, you are a key witness in all this and you may need to give evidence in court sometime in the future. Please don't make this any more difficult for yourself than it already is.'

'Fine.'

'Write it all down for me. Shall we go back inside to find a pen and piece of paper for you?'

Doing as I've requested Kai hands me the slip of paper. Checking the details and the fact it's legible he prompts me for the deal.

'So what's the score?'

'I'll drive you into Whitland, buy you a one way ticket to Swansea and make sure you get on the train. Do we have a deal?'

'Sure.'

'Why don't you go and pack.'

I stood a short distance away from Kia as we waited on the platform, so not to embarrass him. Seeing the train arriving I phoned the number he gave me. Answering what was an unknown number to him I wished him luck and reminded him that I will check out the address he gave me. I also warned him of what could happen if he simply disappeared. I think he took it all in, but there's always a level of uncertainty attached. Watching the train depart I'm done with all this and head for home. On my way home my mind soon turns to my retirement do and potential guests to invite. Mentally I arrive at the number of twelve, which includes myself, Jack, Sam and Michaela.

I have two issues. I must invite Jan, but do I included Linda? She has been hostile towards Sam in the past and that cannot happen again. Living temporarily with Jan her exclusion could be deemed as hateful, revengeful and cause huge friction. I need to be very careful. DI Wallace is also a problem. He's undoubtedly very busy but not inviting him and his wife would be like snubbing him and he may think I'm rubbing him up the wrong way. Sarcastically, he'll miss my input once I've officially retired. Privately, I would described him in one single word...leach. Close to home I decide to head for the office. Add a personal touch to the invite. Plus, I need to clear out my desk for James. Always kept locked, some of my cabinets contain personal and private documents of which are for my eyes only. They will go home with me and locked away in my own office.

My first task is to get hold of an old mate of mine...Barry. He manages The Prince of Wales public house in Narberth and a good place to eat and celebrate.

'Prince of Wales. This is Barry speaking. How can I help?'

'Hi Barry. It's Nick Thompson.'

'Hi mate! How's it going?'

'Good mate. What about you?'

'Pleased the peak holiday season is coming to an end, but otherwise good.'

'Barry, I have a few phone calls to make first this morning but I'm phoning to find out what your availabilities are this week. I'm looking at either tomorrow evening about 7pm or Wednesday at the same time. How are you fixed?'

'How many for, Nick?'

'Twelve, possibly fourteen.'

'Let me take a look.' Moments later he comes back to me. 'All good for either night.'

'Fantastic. I'll confirm the day with you by lunchtime.'

'I'll pencil both days in for the moment. So that's up too fourteen people at 7pm, tomorrow or Wednesday.'

'Yes mate. Thanks for your help.'

'No problem. Speak to you later.'

Waiting at the school gate for Sam I notice, as he ambles across the playground that he is clutching his phone as if his life depends on it. That concerns me. Not wishing to pressurise him for answers we walk back to the car in silence and although it is drizzling, I suggest we stop at the harbour for an ice cream. He tentatively responds with a simple yes. Something is definitely wrong, but there are the odd occasions when I feel it is best not question him. Close to the harbour Sam eventually opens up.

'My teacher took my phone away me.'

'She what?'

'She said it was the schools rule. No pupils are allowed phones in the classroom. It was on silent, Dad, so what did it matter, and I wasn't playing with it.'

'Right! We're going back to sort this out.'

'Please don't, Dad, it will be ok. Can you write her a letter tonight for me to give to her in the morning?'

'If you think that is best, then of course I'll write a letter for you.' We're late arriving home. With everything sorted as far as it can be it is time for me to really relax and start enjoying life. Walking through the house to the kitchen I find Jack home and sat drinking a cup of tea talking to Jan. Why is she still here crosses my mind as I pick up the days mail to sift through?

'Something else arrived for you today.' Jan informs, handing me another brown A4 envelope with "Words of Wisdom" neatly written on the front. My heart sinks. How can this be?

'Do you want me to go?' Jack asks.

'No, Jack. There are no secrets in this house.'

'It was leaning against the front door when I arrived to let Michaela in. The main gate was closed, Nick, so God knows how it got there.'

'Words of Wisdom.' Jack says quietly. 'Isn't that the same as the last one? And what was written on the note you asked me to pick up?' He continues while stand speechless glaring at the envelope. 'What does it mean?'

Slowly I become aware they are waiting for me to say something. I could dismiss this one like I did the previous but Jack has already made the connection. Where do I start trying to explain this when I know it isn't possible?

'Is it about me?' Sam asks with an air of concern in his voice.

Jan has fixed her gaze upon me. She knows a little about this but I have never been entirely open over these envelopes. I shake my head at Sam and positively reply "no" to his question. I hope I reassured him, but with continued doubts over what he may have seen out at Henry's old place, I'm not so sure. I can't have this hanging over my head for ever so I decide to tell them about Henry Sinclair. I will make it as brief as I can and try not to scare them. Picking up the envelope and checking it is still tightly sealed, I ask them all to join me in the lounge. Asking them to take a seat I know this is going to be complicated.

'I think you all know a little bit about Henry Sinclair. We stopped outside his old place not all that long ago. I can't remember if I told you that I wasn't interested in his beliefs, or ever engaged in any conversations with him on that subject. I didn't believe in him or his beliefs then, and I still don't

'I like you all just to listen. Please don't make any sort of comment as I try my best to explain. You may not believe me but in my hand I have what I would describe as, impossible evidence. If what I'm about to I say frightens you or you feel uncomfortable at any point, please feel free to get up and walk away. Now! This may come across as fantasy, something you might see on TV and to date, I have no logical explanation for what I have seen and witnessed, but here goes.

'Henry Sinclair died thirty years ago. He had terminal cancer and knew he didn't have long to live. Before he died, he dedicated the time he had left on finding his successor. Henry claimed at the time, I was that person. He was desperate to pass on his beliefs to me.' Slightly dramatic, I drop the envelope onto the coffee table. 'Henry was a Druid, and ancient religious group who worshipped, and still do, everything worldly and he if didn't pass on his words of wisdom, his teachings, they would be lost forever and a day.' Looking down at the envelope I continue. 'His life's work would be lost. I have to assume, because I wasn't interested, that that brown envelope contains all his knowledge and understandings of his druid world. If I we're to open the envelope, as I was encouraged to do at the time by a white witch by the name of Beth, I would become responsible for the continuation of his life's work and passing on his teachings. I have no intention of doing that, and no one in this room will ever, ever open one of these envelopes.

'The cottage we stopped at the other day is where Henry died. It's where I found him hanging by the neck from a branch of an old apple tree in his orchard. He'd been dead for some six days. The police recorded his death as suicide, but I have always found that difficult to believe. Henry was a frail and weak old man riddled with cancer and suggesting he climbed that tree before falling to his death, didn't make sense. There were no other aids in the same vicinity. Ladders, chairs, nothing

'After a two long hours of waiting and being interviewed, I was allowed to go and told to take Beth with me, who had arrived with DI Wallace about half an hour after I found Henry's body. She was making a nuisance of herself and Wallace wanted her out of his way. My first home here in Saundersby was Beth's old flat and it suited my needs. Incidentally, I brought it from her because she had inherited a cottage near Threeman Bridge which had a huge garden where she could grow her own herbs, and dare I say it, drugs.

'Four days before I found Henry's body, he turned up at my place looking for Beth. It was strange. He was strange and I sent him on his way to Beth's place and thought little more of it. I was right in the end to call it strange, because according to DI Wallace, Henry Sinclair had been dead for two days when he knock on my door.

'Something else, which I have no explanation for, happened the day I found Henry's body, but as sure as I'm sat here with you now… it did. Walking Beth to my car, which was parked in the exact same spot the day we went there, someone was sitting on the bonnet of my car. I knew who it was immediately…Henry. I was hesitant, as you can well imagine, simply because it could not have been Henry. I didn't say anything to Beth for two reasons. I didn't want to raise her hopes, let her believe it was all a dream and Henry was still alive. I also wanted to know if she could see what I was witnessing. Beth didn't see Henry, even after I had sat her in the front passenger seat of my car. Henry was still sat there as I walked around the front of my car to the driver's side and I ignored him, simply because he wasn't there and couldn't possibly have been. I was on a case at the time which involved driving to and from Cornwall. As I passed where Henry was sat, he spoke to me. I shit myself, in a literal sense. He said, "You are on the right track. Go to Burrowhole. If you are smart, you will find the answers there." I knew this couldn't be happening, and looked away. When I looked back…Henry had gone.

'That same day, I had sat on the grass verge waiting for DI Wallace or someone to come and speak to me. While I waited I destroyed the grass verge around me, ripping the grass out of the ground and throwing the remnants into the road. Walking back to the car the other day with you guys, I relived that same scene. It appeared real enough to me, but none of you guys saw what I saw. That note I asked you to pick up and read, Jack, wasn't there when we first passed the spot along the road, that was until Sam said something and I looked back towards the cottage. I had to ask you to pick it up to make sure I wasn't dreaming the whole revisit, and your earlier observation is correct. What was written on that piece of paper matches exactly to the words on that envelope?

'Like back then, I can't begin to understand what and why this is happening again after all these years. Curious at the time, Henry's words took me to Cornwall on a case that had come to a dead end, which is where Burrowhole is. DI Wallace was there. I saw him in the village one morning. Oddly, quite independently, we had made our own way there. We didn't speak and I found absolutely nothing connecting me to what I was investigating. I was about to throw in the towel when something quite extraordinary happened. Returning to my hotel for a bite to eat and a couple of pints, I was feeling isolated and vulnerable away from my own turf. Heading into the hotel bar to get a drink, I froze. Sat at the bar, chatting up the barman…was Beth. Knowing I had been so careful in not discussing my business in public to anyone, this meeting was far more than luck. In the time I had known Beth, she had never taken a holiday. So why now and why there? After a lot of banter and slagging each other off, she finally divulged her reason for being there. She claimed Henry had paid her a visit. He had a message for me but couldn't deliver it because a greater force was stopping him. She informed me Henry told her where I was and asked her to deliver the message for him because it was important. As you can imagine, it freaked me out. Not only was Henry trying to help me, he supposedly knew where I was. I don't believe in the spiritual world, or the afterlife but applying logic to the situation, things didn't stack up. Until then it was easy to dismiss events like that by calling them luck, a chance, a premonition perhaps, but Beth turning up in Cornwall, some two hundred miles away, changed everything.

'The message was very simple, but meant nothing too me. "Beware of Rays". That was all it was. When I finally got home a couple of days later my distain for Beth and Henry was tearing me apart. I hated them because my belief then was that they were using me for personal gain. I felt I was their puppet. Not only did I need to stop that, I felt they were forcing me to open the envelope to embrace Henry's wish. How I would achieve that was beyond me. In the end I figured that I should force the issue and pay Henry's old cottage a visit to search for clues. It was the day before his funeral and I thought that, not only was it a long shot, his funeral could draw this to close before I discovered the truth.

'I was very apprehensive going alone into the unknown. I did what I had done the last time. I walked around to the back of the cottage. If I had to break in there was less chance of being seen. I needn't have worried, the back garden door was wide open. My first thoughts were to congratulate DI Wallace on his security measures, but that soon changed. Was the open door an invitation, a welcome home gesture from Henry? I fought with myself to put that thought aside. I had to go inside to challenge Henry and given the chance, that was what I wanted to do. Cautiously I entered the cottage and slowly made my way around the downstairs rooms. I felt nothing while I nosed around but took in everything I saw. Henry certainly was an untidy man. The rooms were cluttered with his books and paperwork which I assumed were references to his work as a druid. Beth had told me he was an Archdruid at one time. In his circles, that was a privileged and prominent position. I chose not to look too closely at anything in detail. His life meant nothing to me.

'Walking up the stairs I stopped halfway. I had the most bizarre thought, telling me I would find Henry lying in state on his bed. Much to my relief he wasn't, but my current state of mind told me Henry was capable of anything. What I did find in the smallest bedroom made me feel sick. The room was empty other than the fact, all the walls were covered from floor to ceiling with photographs and newspaper cuttings of me. All of it was about me. My life and what and what I had achieved since I had lived in South Wales. It was sick. Henry had been stalking me. I cannot put into words how it made me feel. I just stood there in a void, not knowing what to do. If Beth knew about this, why didn't she tell me? If Wallace had conducted a thorough search of the cottage, why hadn't he told me? I wanted answers to those questions.

'Standing there, wanting to rip everything down off the walls, I heard the floor boards creaking behind me. I shit myself. Turning to face the doorway there was nobody there or nothing different to be seen, except now, there was a brown A4 envelope lying on the floor in the doorway. On it were the words... Words of Wisdom.'

Mentally exhausted I collapse onto the chair in a trance like state. In the background I hear Jan tell the guys to leave me alone for a while. Suddenly I'm all alone. I thought this nonsense had long stopped. Clearly it hasn't, what with the experience at Henry's old cottage and the vision at the hostel. How can you not believe when things like that happen? I don't want to simply accept my reasons for why they are, which are vague at best. Thirty years ago I believed Henry was trying to control my life. I think he still is, only this time…the envelopes are not for me.

Printed in Poland
by Amazon Fulfillment
Poland Sp. z o.o., Wrocław

25351527R00163